FUGITIVES OF LOVE

BY
HOFJAM

CHAPTER 1

Lola gave a big sigh of relief as the bus finally neared the stop to her home. Today's journey had seemed exceptionally long for a lot of reasons and had been worsened by a drunken, clinically obese man that slumped himself next to her despite sitting on the last row to avoid sharing with anyone. She believed he had deliberately denied her the only luxury she could derive from public transport by ignoring a handful of empty seats. Just when she began to doubt if he was really drunk, he moved closer to her and fell asleep snoring his head off shortly afterwards. The more she moved away the more she was crushed, in the end she gave up, hoping and praying he got off before her. The strong, repulsive body odour mixed with alcoholic and cigarette smell emanating from the man made her extremely nauseous.

As she battled against her willpower not to throw up she wondered if this was just an isolated incident or the man had a personal grudge against her, but she still empathised with innocent commuters with no alternative but to be subjected to similar discomfort in public transport. Her employer, A.B.C. & D. (Alfra Brava Computer & Digital Ltd) have just relocated to Birmingham city centre, with a new modern, sophisticated and spacious building but no privilege of enough parking spaces. Such was many companies headache in Birmingham city centre and its manufacturing heritage now been heavily superseded by service industries! At least she was lucky to drive to work thrice a week and could be five days if she topped up the twenty pounds shortfalls of her employer's subsidy.

A fortnight ago, when filling the parking slot for the month, she had left today and the next two days out because she had booked them as annual leave. Her line manager unfortunately okayed one day despite filling in the leave request form five weeks ago as opposed to the company's policy of four weeks. The most painful part of it was her finding out yesterday.

She prided herself for living in one of the affluent part of the region and the outskirts of the city centre but was most importantly twenty minutes walking distance to work compared to driving that had increased from fifteen to thirty minutes because of the twelve weeks road works in her area. Strangely enough Lola preferred walking as an effective way to exercise but was always scared of the corners and alleyways leading to her house. She looked forward to summer so she could enjoy her walk home no matter how late she left the office.

Suddenly the man next to her jerked and belched out loudly giving her a fresh whiff of his colossal odour of alcohol, cigarettes and garlic; she repulsively wondered why his breath smelled like stagnant sewage when he opened his eyes, looked at her and got on his feet. Heaving a big sigh of relief, she hoped the rest of the day turned out better than it'd been so far.

Not again! The drunken man was not only blocking her way with his size but had made the driver stop at the two previous without getting off. As the driver approached her stop she pressed the bell to alert the bus driver and tried stepping in front of the man but unsuccessful, finally the bus stopped and Lola was forced to push past him. She inhaled some more fresh air to rid herself of the nasty smell she'd left behind, but when she turned round, there he was right behind her. She stepped aside for him to move on whilst she tried to reduce any visible crease on her favourite steely blue trouser suit with her palm. She went further by sniffing herself for any unpleasant smell, but gave up when she realised there wasn't much she could do for now no matter how revolting. She looked up to see the man stroking a dog that had just being handed to him at the bus stop, whilst toying with the dog lead. He bent over and whispered something into the dog's ear and the dog reared up aggressively and started raging with its teeth exposed at no one in particular. Whilst the dog was raging, the owner's fixated gaze made her look away in trepidation, but she was more mesmerized at how quickly he'd recovered from his drunkenness.

As she headed home she wondered how many more tricks the man had under his sleeve, but this was quickly eroded by her gratitude that the dog didn't get any closer and finally the thought of the busy programme ahead. She couldn't wait to be home and finish packing for her Wolverhampton trip; it was going to be a phenomenal reunion with her relatives from all over the world! The dog's frantic and ferocious bark suddenly prompted her to make increasing the gap between herself and the dog an utmost priority. Damp your fear with nice thoughts! Thank God it's Friday! She became excited when she remembered the fun she was going to have with this long weekend, Monday was bank holiday and Tuesday had been booked off as her annual leave. All things being equal, she might call in sick on Wednesday if Akin supports them staying longer with her relatives in Wolverhampton. After all, it's not everyday her cousin gets engaged or married. Yes, a lot of memorable things had happened this week especially the number of her aunts, uncles and cousins she'd spoken to that were looking forward to meeting her in a matter of hours.

What an adventurous week! The thought slipped to her mind as she waited for the traffic light to change at the busy wide road. Whilst wondering why the office had been nothing but terrible and busy this week she was just relieved it had all ended! But today had been full of challenges; first alarm didn't work in the morning so she was nearly an hour late in waking up but was saved from being late for work by the taxi driver turning up on time. Something she would never have done if Akin, her fiancé hadn't borrowed her car and failed to return as promised. She hoped he made it on time to pick her up this time and not his usual style of last-minute-rush.

Apparently, one of the reasons she wasn't granted leave today was because of the two meetings scheduled for today. The first meeting was just before midday which would have been very brief and straight forward if the company smoke alarm hadn't gone off falsely. After everyone had rushed out of the building to the fire assembly point, it was now discovered it was a hoax alarm which made getting on with the meeting difficult especially with two of the managers already late for their next appointments. The second meeting was the monthly finance team which was fast forwarded by the M.D. for reasons best known to him alone. With the meeting nearly over, Amy the new receptionist brought in a recorded delivery document addressed to the Finance Director. Amy, who thrived on the attention she was receiving cat-walked from one end of the big conference room to the other and twirled before placing the document in front of Scott, the Finance Director. She stopped in front of Lola as she cat-walked back, smirked at her before finally moving on to shut the door. She'd never been able to place her because of sneaky, evasive nature that soon backfired after falsely accusing her.

This must be really important to go through this trouble! Meanwhile, Lola felt she was trying too hard because of the men and might just snap into two if she wasn't careful and judging by the look on everyone's face she was not alone.

Amy joined the company five weeks ago and had already dated and dumped three men; the last straw that broke the camel's back was accusing her of trying to snatch her latest conquest.

'Snatch who? How preposterous! You two could never ever fancy or date the same man!' April took the words out of her mouth. Her close friend's and colleague's swift interception and honest remark still echoed in her head as the deafening silence in the room reminded her of where she was.

Scott had just finished reading the document, put them all together and looked straight at her with contempt as he passed the document over to Lynne, the Purchasing Manager. For the first time Lola saw him take his thick glasses off to reveal nothing but scorn and disdain in his once amazing blue eyes. She'd never been able to place him and had never needed a reason to worry until now. He was always polite when dealing with her but she could tell it was all a charade, but fixing his gaze on her confirmed her innermost fear as the real Scott became evident. Lynne finished with the documents, passed it to her assistant before joining Scott in fixing her with a brief cold accusing gaze. Lola retaliated by concentrating on Lynne who frowned and started twitching her nose; something everyone knew she would do when under pressure or if trouble was brewing.

'No! Can they really do that?' Roxanne, who had just finished reading the document asked in bewilderment before she passed it on to the next person.

Befuddled Lola tried to stare back but there were too many feisty and scornful eyes.

The more her colleagues read the document, the more the concerned looks but none of them thought it right to explain further and worse still she would be the last to get hold of the document, and no one would want to swap seat with her under the circumstance.

The dog's persistent bark made her realise they were closing in on her when it finally penetrated her thoughts again, which was confirmed when she looked back.

Rather than fretting, she instantly decided to be proactive by taking the first available turning on her right, an unending, narrow alleyway sometimes used by teenage lovers for their ungodly acts. She'd never enjoyed walking alleyways on her own especially this one simply because of the exposure to danger amongst other things.

Her mind suddenly went blank when she saw the man and the dog coming towards her with the dog's nozzle off! With his quick pace he seemed taller, fatter, meaner and determined. The dog not being nuzzled not only unsettled her already troubled mind, but made her more panic and anxious to be inside her safe and sound house. Still, she wanted to be brave and not let the fat man sense her dog phobia this time! But her panic reached a higher level when she remembered being attacked by a stray dog around fifteen years ago. She knew she had to act fast when the memory before and after the attack became too vivid as the gap closed up between them. Her desperation and determination to be home quickly was sparked by her renewed phobia for dogs big or small. If only they would let her be! Her happiness at seeing the dog stop for a wee was short lived when her eyes met the man's evil ones and she saw that gratifying smirk again as he perused her figure flirtatiously. She quickly shied away, but not for long because she could still feel his eyes burning through her skin. Whilst trying to look ahead, their eyes met. She cringed when she saw him slowly running his tongue over his bottom lip and nearly threw up when she remembered his revolting breath.

He bent over to give his dog a stroke and whisper into its right ear as he did earlier. This was all too familiar to her, this time the dog did not only rage but nearly broke off the leach. The smirk on his face became more evident as she neared them but she didn't want to give anything away, she couldn't afford to!

She instinctively took the first available turning without bothering if the turning took her further from home or not.

As the sky's face darkened, she became frightened especially when she felt a gentle wind sweep past her. Quickly, she tucked her handbag underneath her armpit and started jogging to increase the gap should in case they followed her. Jogging leisurely, she remembered meeting a lanky man being dragged by this huge dog last week, the stress on his face still amused and made her realise the dog had overpowered his owner. As far as she was concerned, there were too many species of dogs for her to contemplate understanding them. Moreover, most dog owner's hardly ever scooped their poops yet they enjoy taking them walking and leaving the mess behind. How irresponsible! But the man she was running away from was the worst experience she's had so far.

She increased her speed as she approached the end of the alleyway and gasped with fear when she collided into a big blue Great Dane running in opposite direction. Her heart instantly jumped into her mouth. Thankfully, she was relieved to notice that the dog was nuzzled. The collision threw them both off balance, but the pair struggled to steady themselves as the dog whimpered loudly before turning back sharply. The dog was still whimpering when she heard a man yell Bravo desperately, which made the dog whine painfully afterwards. Weakened, confused and frightened by the shock she'd just experienced she leaned her back and weight completely on the wall for support whilst wishing fervently that the wall or the ground would open up and swallow her up till the man and his dog disappeared. She became convinced that it was the only way she could avoid further meeting with another dog ever and wondered if squealing like the dog would take this terrible strange feeling away. The shock was so severe that her lips began to tremble violently whilst her eyes became deeply shut fearing that opening and seeing the dog would probably give her a heart attack and definitely kill her. With her back painfully pinned against the wall she swore, never again!

She'd never in her life been so scared of dogs until now. The thought of running out of the alleyway seemed right, but her legs wouldn't move neither would her eyes open. She heard movement and voices in and out of the alleyway, wanted to open her eyes, run or speak but she seemed to have been deserted by her senses, there was absolutely no will power.

Finally, the shock began to recede as she gradually regained her strength and was able to open her eyes, the voices of a man and woman became clearer. She decided to move out as soon as she could and had taken only a few steps when the Great Dane strolled past her again. Lola's nervousness returned with a vengeance but did not affect her legs thankfully; her heart was pounding so hard she thought it was going to explode. The urgent need to increase the gap became a priority over her heart, she looked only to realise that the nozzle was off. She kept on her pace but was constantly checking on the dog, and almost froze when their eyes met and the Great Dane stayed put still staring back at her. Her first instinct was to run but she couldn't because the dog might chase her so she began to walk ahead but totally focusing backward at the dog.

Suddenly, she screamed out loudly and nearly jumped out of her skin when she hit something solid before being steadied by two firm hands. A strong cocktail of fear, anger and relief overtook her as she quickly noticed the broad shoulders and the two powerful hands of a strong, tall man. Lola was obliged to gaze up at him despite her five foot eight inches height with flat heeled shoes.

'Sorry.' They both said simultaneously with embarrassment.

Lola staggered backwards to break free of his gentle but firm grip when she realised it was the same voice calling out the Great Dane earlier.

'Are you okay?'

She smiled because the comfort in his deep voice subdued and calmed her fear and anger, before wriggling out of his grasp. He got the message and placed his hands on his side.

His gaze was transfixed on her long and thick eyelashes that looked all spiky because she was scared and nervous. He noticed she had no make up on, though she was a bit skinny for his taste but he knew many men would find her attractive.

'You and your stupid dog nearly gave me a heart attack.'

His eyes appraised Lola's nicely styled braids for a while, then a smile curved around his wide full mouth. She felt his eyes burn through her skin as she walked away whilst he called for his dog.

'I'm sorry, he's in a playful mood, and the colour of your outfit kicks him off too.' He shouted after her in the deepest voice she's ever heard.

Within seconds the dog moved ahead of her and stopped in the centre of the alleyway forcing Lola to stay rooted. She suppressed her anger and strutted on, frustrated that the dog still wasn't moving and she hissed out loudly.

Like a prompt, blue Great Dane ran backwards to Lola and started to circumambulate her. For a while she was amazed at not being scared, and wondered whether she was convinced this man would handle the situation or she was emotionally drained of the day's turbulence. Still confident in the situation, she took the first step to walk away and was shocked by what followed! The dog growled before gripping and pulling the lower part of her trouser. In a state of paroxysm and confusion she found herself momentarily rooted to the spot. She instinctively grabbed the dog's owner out stretched hands and clung to him whilst the Great Dane circumambulate the two of them intensely. She was left with no choice but to tightly wind her arms around his neck and her legs around his waist to avoid further physical contact with the dog. The owner's height made it impossible for the dog to reach her trouser or legs pointing horizontally ahead.

The unexplainable effect of this stranger's nearness to her was so severe that she could feel his body heat steaming off, and his heart beating in harmony with hers. Ironically, she felt so comfortable and secure that she momentarily forgot about the dog and his palaver. Weird, wild fire rolled through her body that made some strange alarm bells ring in her head.

She stiffened and loosened her grip as Akin's disapproving look flashed through her mind, and quickly consoled herself that she wouldn't have been in this situation if he'd picked her up as they'd initially planned. This was immediately followed by Mama's voice rebuking her that a dignified woman does not crumple either because she was petrified of dogs or because an attractive man invaded her space.

Despite the dog owner's body showing no sign of tiredness or stress, his eyes showed his frustration at the situation, which made her wonder if it was because of the Great Dane's behaviour, effect of her weight on him or he was bothered by their closeness.

'He's getting tired,' he interrupted her thought.

Rebelliously, she dropped her foot on the ground, loosened her grip before kissing her teeth long and hard again. The dog immediately resumed its growling, barking and began to circumambulate them again. This time she clung tighter with her attention fully focused on the dog growling harder, and jumping desperately higher to reach the dangling bit of her torn trouser.

With her arms around his neck, frustrated, she looked at the stranger and shivered when their eyes met, she couldn't understand why, but was sure he noticed. As she quickly looked away she felt him raise his hands to her back but quickly changed his mind by putting them in his pockets, his thoughts were impossible to read as his facial expression became hard and grim.

'I see, he thought you were encouraging him to continue.'

His new discovery of the dog's behaviour gave him an idea of how to handle the situation better. Without warning he blew a long and loud whistle which made Lola's ears screech and equally made the dog stop and heed his owner's command.

She instantly realised that he would not only make a formidable opponent but finding his vulnerable spot would be difficult, which made his control over the situation an added sign of his strength. This was a big relief for everyone. She noticed he was more attractive when his nicely shaped eyes widened beyond belief just before sealing it with an adorable smile!

Lola set one foot down, loosened her grip, and couldn't believe the total calmness and the obedience of the dog that was now seated and busy wagging his tail.

'I am ever so sorry,' he broke the silence gently as his gaze locked hers up.

She suddenly felt light headed, but was immediately relieved as soon as he released his grip and set her foot down. She staggered backwards as her knees went weak but one strong hand immediately reinforced her support. Her eye caught sight of the damage done to her trouser, but was too weak to mention it for now. Instead, she'd kissed her teeth before she remembered its effect on the Great Dane who was growling and at alert.

His owner repeated his long whistle and the dog instantly became seated.

She couldn't bear another whistle. 'Can you refrain from whistling for now please?'

The harshness in her tone annoyed him but he decided to ignore it. 'That darned dog needs taming!'

Lola noticed the anger on his face disappear as quickly as it appeared. 'He thought you wanted to have some fun with him.'

'Fun with a dog?' She huffed. 'Over my dead body!'

'Well that could be arranged.' Her remark and reaction provoked him. 'A bit drastic I'd say?' He quickly added to calm the situation.

'I'd take it the way I deem fit and you could **do** the same.' Lola eyed him repulsively.

'I'm sure Bravo meant no harm.' He met her gaze with a light-hearted chuckle.

'A bit too late for that now,' she tried stretching her creases and nearly kissed her teeth in frustration again.

Ignoring her comment, he remarked; 'I deeply regret this incident, whatever it takes.'

She considered his statement insulting and conceited. 'Tame your darned dog! It's ripped and ruined my trouser!'

'My sincere apologies for that, hold me responsible for whatever the cost.'

The authority underlining his voice and his control over the situation upset her even more. 'Are you winding me up? Of course you are responsible for it all!'

He opened his mouth to speak but changed his mind.

Her anger grew when she remembered this was the only suit Akin had ever bought her, and was more furious when she saw the extent of the damage. 'You and your dog ... I wonder where your dog gets this madness from.' She stopped to assess the impact of her words and was surprised to see his face darken ominously.

'I cannot reiterate enough how sorry I am and my willingness to refund you your expenses no matter the price.'

She looked scornfully at this man in total control of the situation and became more desperate to rattle him.

But instead of a reply he humoured her with a smirk.

She's had enough to last her a lifetime!

She found the smirk on his face and his arrogance deeply offensive and wanted to penetrate through. 'What if it's not refundable? That stupid dog should be put down!'

The man's face suddenly felt like a shutter had just come down on it with his eyes dangerously darker. His hands were clenched at his sides and when he finally spoke it was through his teeth clenched. 'Then you have my deepest regret.' He whistled softly at his dog and was about to leave when she spoke.

'Are you telling me that your darned dog ...'

His facial expression remained cold and his voice was calm when he spoke. 'Like I'd said, he meant no harm, and that "darned dog" is named Bravo.' The dog heard his name and started barking and jumping again. 'Stop it, Bravo!' He commanded strongly. In no time, the dog became subdued, sitting right on the spot whilst wagging its tail.

'If you don't want any compensation, the least we could do is walk you home,' he took a leach out of his pocket and beckoned the dog to come over.

She so desperately wanted to stop being at any dog owner's mercy. She was sure he was mocking her! Consumed with fury, she met his angry gaze. 'I'm not one of your dogs!'

'Thank God for that!' Without waiting for her reply he walked past her. He chuckled whilst his arm gently brushed against hers, but was more amused by how her brown irises could be dilated and equally dazzling especially when furious.

'Damn you two!' Still fuming, she shifted her upper body to avoid further body contact but her limbs unfortunately stayed put and tilted her off balance. Whilst attempting to steady herself she lost her balance completely and was still struggling not to make a fool of herself when she felt a sharp pain in her ankle which inevitably made her right leg go weak and unable to support her weight. As her weight collapsed she screamed! He was in no time beside her grabbing and preventing her from falling flat completely.

She heaved a big sigh of relief that she wasn't flat on her face. 'I've hurt my ankle'. She snivelled when the pain became sharper.

With only a breathing distance between them again, his eyes inadvertently dropped on her chest when he asked her to lean against the wall, which made Lola more uncomfortable than she could admit.

He went on his knees to examine her ankle. 'You've probably sprained it'. He deliberately delayed rising to avoid any eye contact or further embarrassment for both of them. Oh boy! How could such a lustful thought come to mind under this circumstance!

She tried to ignore the excruciating pain and hold back the tears but realised it was too late when she felt them rolling down her cheeks, with some eventually dropping onto his hand and bringing him back to reality.

'That darned do ...' she stopped when she realised how much his support meant to her right now, which diabolically made her cry even more.

He finally stood up to face her but the grim look on his face did not give her any clue as to what he was thinking or feeling. Suspecting she was embarrassed from the way she flustered her lashes, he shied away to make it easier for both of them.

Despite his looking away, she was still mortified and angry for loosing her composure in the presence of a stranger. But she quickly blamed it on the pressure she was under and the hectic day she had in the office today. Right now she was convinced the whole world was out to get her, things had been going wrong since she got that stupid text from Akin in the middle of the night that he couldn't pick her from work despite having her car but promised he would be home on time to make it to Wolverhampton with her.

Last night she went to bed with high expectations for today, the plan was to leave work early enough and finish packing for her trip. But Akin had vanished at the last minute again. She understood he had his hands full at the moment but dropping her in a situation like this must stop!

'What do you mean you can't make it?' Lola had called him immediately after the message, but somehow the line was so bad that she couldn't understand him. 'How am I supposed to run all my errands tomorrow without a car?' But she still couldn't hear him.

Finally he promised to call her back, which still left more questions unanswered than before. 'I'm very sorry sweetheart; I'll make it up to you. I have an issue that can't be postponed for another minute; in fact my life depends on it. But I promise to be home on time for Wolverhampton.' The sincerity and desperation in his voice convinced and equally bothered her. But his line went dead before she could probe further, she'd immediately tried his mobiles and tracing the call, but the result still brought her no joy. Sleep finally overtook her in the early hours of this morning after she was tired of worrying her head about him.

She'd met Akin severally two years ago but only became friends after attending a job interview in her office and only started dating him five months ago, after another meeting at her colleague's wedding party despite previous, countless turndowns. She hated to describe him still as a "boyfriend" which to her trivialised their relationship especially when she spoke about him to adults within her family. The biggest culprit was her grandma who couldn't wait for her to tie the knot and give her some great grand children. As Mama always stressed, it was the next thing in her life and should not be taken lightly. But she'd always told Mama that things were different in her time compared to now and she didn't want a man just for marriage sake. But she always told her she'd understand as she grew older and she truthfully was. She would admit to anyone her intrinsic warmth of feeling complete and whole despite her uncertainty that he really loved her as she did him. Overtime, her doubt of his love had been channeled into trusting him completely. Especially after Akin had explained the complications in his life and had begged her for time to sort a few things out, but what she didn't know or expect was how his numerous last minute ditch would leave her to pick up the pieces. Mama advised her to be seen as supportive as possible, to follow her heart and not to be seen as a fool or a nagger.

The deepness in the man's voice swiftly reminded her where she was when he asked her to try and walk without support. She put her foot down and realised it could not sustain her weight, which forced the tears through with a vengeance.

Seeing the pain in her eyes made him more determined to help and ease her burden. They were both in their own little worlds when he asked her to put her arm across his shoulder and lean on him.

'No thanks, I'll manage.'

'How?'

'By leaning on these fences.'

He stepped aside and prompted her to lead the way. Lola wanted to argue again but changed her mind immediately.

'Can I at least have that?'

She removed her purse and put it in her breast pocket before thrusting her handbag into his outstretched hands.

He toddled after her with the dog, a few occasions she tripped and he was ready to steady her. At a point, she gasped painfully when she was stung by an ivy bush on one of the fences she leaned on. Their eyes met when she stopped to look back at him and the feeling for both of them was familiarly captivating.

He lagged patiently behind until she got to a house with no fence and watched her hop for a while. He quickly offered her more support when he noticed that the excruciating pain made her breathing heavy. Swiftly, his two firm hands lifted her by the upper arms as his long fingers were tightly pressed around her arm muscles.

He spoke firmly when he noticed she was about to object. 'Let's get you home and call the doctor.' He waited for a reply but was surprised when none came. 'It will be silly of you to refuse my support this time'; he felt her stiffness against him. 'If you can't relax then I would have to pick you up, your choice.'

The seriousness underlining his tone told her this was not an ordinary threat. As the pressure of his firm grip began to cause her pain, she asked for a break, but what she really needed was a close friend to lean on instead of a stranger like the man beside her. She realised she would have been home if she'd allowed him to pick her up but then what would Akin say if he saw her so up and close with another man? But she wouldn't be in this situation if he had picked her up in the first instance! As she got weaker and eager to be home, the urge to slide her arm across his shoulder for support became stronger but then her courage failed her again.

'Are we still far?'

She replied with a shake of her head. 'Just a couple of houses more', as she expected, he didn't seem the least surprised. 'I take it you don't need direction?'

'I'm sure you won't leave me wanton.'

'Definitely not under this circumstance.'

'I sincerely hope not,' he replied before he whistled at Bravo who immediately kept up the pace.

They were quiet for the rest of the short journey.

Finally, she told him she was home when they got to an end terraced house. He set her down and quickly reached to push the white metal gate open for her. Hip to hip, with her arms across his shoulder they were both able to squeeze past the driveway side by side like partners in a tango dance.

She was disappointed not to see her convertible Audi in the drive which means Akin was still not back yet.

What the hell is Akin playing at? She would need to get a serious grip if she wants to make it to Wolverhampton tonight with or without him! But her greatest worry was what would happen if she became allergic to her encounters with the dogs today.

He beckoned upon the dog who had now stooped by Akin's new car. In no time they were at the front door waiting for different things; Lola was waiting for him to turn his back with his dog and leave her to her own device, whilst he lingered for her house keys so he could escort her in.

She locked his gaze for a while before she bade him goodbye but was sure the words didn't come out. If this man knew her intentions he did a perfectly good job by pretending otherwise, and tightening his grip on her just as she tried to break off and support herself.

'Adam Salvador,' he finally broke the silence with a stretch of his hand for the keys to her apartment.

Lola was searching, measuring, deciding but kept her eyes on his, as she had when she first set eyes on him and Bravo. She managed a smile again, a hesitant sly, smile that touched his heart when he noticed how her dimples glow charmingly.

Finally, she decided to level her gaze with his and match the name to his rectangular forehead and a well defined face and a lean jaw. 'Lola …' she ignored his hand and rolled her key ring around one of her fingers.

There was a cynical smile around his mouth that quickly disappeared as soon as he composed himself

'I know it's rude to invite oneself into other people's house, but I'm sure this is an exception. But if it makes you better not to let me in, so be it.' Without pushing further, he gently settled her on her door step and asked her to lean on the wall. Adam took his jacket off and spread it on the floor before beckoning her to sit on the concrete step. 'Stretch your leg gently.' He supported her hind leg by placing her handbag at the back of her knee.

She reluctantly did as instructed but wondered how he would react if she told him to excuse her.

'Bravo come here.'

They were both amused watching the dog racing from one end of the garden to the other before coming back to its owner with its tail bristled. Adam whistled twice, and the dog went as quiet as a corpse.

'Sit Bravo.' He commanded firmly and the dog quickly obeyed.

She decided to cooperate with Adam so he could leave with his dog as soon as possible and eventually expose her to lesser risk.

Whilst Adam was dealing with Bravo she decided to put her keys back into her pocket and zipped it up. He turned round only for their eyes to meet but Lola recovered quicker than him.

'May be the dog wants to go home,' She felt a sharp pain in her ankle but ignored it completely.

'So do you and I.' He stooped to level his face with hers.

'I'm home and I'm okay now.'

He looked pensively at her. His mocking expression made it apparent to Lola that he knew she was lying. But he deeply fought the urge to ask if her long eye lashes were false and ask a more relevant question instead. 'Have you an ice pack or any pre-packed frozen food?'

'I said I am fine.'

'I heard but you still haven't answered my question.' Without wasting any more time he knelt in front of her and gently placed her foot on his thigh for support.

The tickling sensation she'd been mistaking for anxiety forced her to withdraw her foot instantly. The mocking look appeared again, but she couldn't work out its exact meaning. 'We could be here all night if it's okay with you.'

He didn't look like a criminal but then again, it was never written on foreheads! Even though it was safer they were outside, she was eager to see their backs and start packing. Retrospectively, Akin's absence meant more time for her, it also dawned on her that nothing she said or did would change his mind so she decided to compromise by reluctantly sliding her foot back onto his thigh.

Meeting no objection and without further eye contact, he reached to undo her boot's lace for proper examination.

'Do you mind?' Lola sneered and withdrew her foot once again, but was met by a sharp pain that made her groan out loudly.

He stopped, and waited for her to push her foot back in voluntarily. When she didn't, he raised his hands up and spoke, 'Sorry that was too presumptuous of me, surely you can't expect me to examine your ankle with your boots on.'

Instead of a reply he was met by a cold stare.

'Perhaps I should let you do that yourself.' He rubbed his hand off his trouser and gently stood up to tower over her.

Her eyes met his but the blank expression on his face made her more determined to stick to her guns. 'Then I'll do it myself.' She eyed him intensely as she reached for her shoelace.

After three unsuccessful attempts, she looked up at Adam and wasn't surprised to see him entertaining himself at her expense. She couldn't bear the pain but pleading for his help wasn't an option either, and neither was giving up. As she summoned more courage, she agreed with him, moreover she was in so much pain that she couldn't pinpoint the exact source of the pain let alone confirm whether this was a serious injury or not.

With a final determination, she reached for her shoelace again and vowed to bear the pain no matter what! After undoing it, she looked up triumphantly and they both smiled, but she shied away first whilst Adam's smile lingered around his mouth longer.

He brought his face closer to her foot before he finally spoke. 'I think I can see where the tenderness is.'

Without asking her, he gently placed her foot on his thighs and looked up to her face for objection but there seemed to be none. Without asking her Adam could easily see she was fatigued but removed the boot and her sock instead. He stopped and read the yellow inscription of "single not desperate" on the black socks before handing it over to her with a full smile.

She felt violated by having her foot resting on a complete stranger's firm and yet tender thigh. His long, strong fingers brushing past her skin evoked a feeling she could no longer ignore. As she remained baffled that her own body was betraying her, she concluded the acknowledged fact that she'd missed Akin more than she'd realised. But she finally concluded it was not everyday you sprain your ankle or find your foot on a stranger's lap for examination.

No word was said from either party for what seemed for ever, Adam seemed consumed with examining her ankle and foot with an intensity that could not be imagined. Her calf was beautiful, the ankle was slim and interesting, with a proportionally nice and well-groomed toe nails. He reckoned her narrow foot would be either size five or six. He gently turned her foot, with no response he progressed to turning it anticlockwise until the sharpness of the pain made her scream. As she became increasingly embarrassed for being at the mercy of a complete stranger she was equally happy for not having smelly feet, a total contrast to the smell from her body. That she diabolically thanked all the dogs that came across her today!

He pressed a part that hurt her and she tried to wriggle her foot out of his grasp but instead caused herself more pain.

'That is probably inflamed,' he remarked by pretending he was not aware of her agony. 'It's nothing serious but could be quite painful.'

'Thanks for letting me know,' she caught herself rubbing her hands on her laps wondering about life and the precarious circumstances she found herself. Bizarre how one mishap of being car-less could end up in a fatal injury? The mixture of emotions, admission and realisation overwhelmed her to tears she struggled to hold back. She shook her head in disbelief at her inability to distinguish fear from gratitude and fatigue.

Adam's icy look began to melt with time. 'You would need medical attention, but a first aid treatment would not cause any harm.'

Adam's statement was interrupted by some music from his jacket. Quickly, he reached for his breast pocket and took out a mobile phone. He asked the caller to hold on whilst he gently put her foot down and getting himself up.

'Sorry I have to go soon, something urgent has come up.' He then asked the caller to continue before gesturing to her he would be back. A soft whistle got the dog on his feet.

Lola decided to sneak in whilst Adam was engrossed with his conversation. She singlehandedly got on her feet and painstakingly opened her front door. The last she saw of him was when she caught him watching her as she hopped inside and had barely finished locking the door when the bell went.

'Its me Adam,' he replied.

'Yes,' she said as she peeped from the letter box.

Amused by her reaction, he chuckled loudly and put the phone away from his mouth before he said, 'I will try and see you tomorrow but please seek medical help if possible tonight.'

She replied okay through the door.

'Promise?' He moved his face close to hers from the other side.

'Promise,' she retreated when she discovered what he'd done.

He for once threw her a genuine smile exposing a set of brilliant white teeth. 'That's more like it,' She heard him say before he turned round and left her to secure her door.

CHAPTER 2

Lola choked and coughed uncontrollably after sniffing herself to confirm the source of the abhorrent pong engulfing her, but was diabolically thankful for Adam's strong aftershave which slightly defused the smelly atmosphere. Whilst hoping Akin understood the importance of this trip to Wolverhampton, she scanned her surroundings for any sign of his last minute note as usual and was relieved not to find any. Avoiding being the cause of their late departure, she quickly dashed to the bathroom with her throbbing ankle whilst anticipating his return any moment. Moreover, she knew how much he hated to be kept waiting coupled with the fact that she had not finished packing and with many gifts still unwrapped she thought it best to prioritize everything. Whilst her whole body felt itchy as a result of her allergic reaction to dogs, she commended herself for getting her priorities right but became equally nervous with the nasty setback. Her foot was already on the stairs when she realised that climbing up and down the stairs would be extremely difficult under the circumstances especially with the packing that couldn't be delayed. Without further deliberation she changed her mind to settle for the guest en suite bathroom downstairs and was smiling with appreciation for having two bathrooms in her three bedroom house when she saw a white envelope addressed to her in an all too familiar handwriting.

Inside it was a letter from Akin explaining that he would not be coming home this weekend and most importantly he wouldn't be able to take her to Wolverhampton, blaming the pressure of work as usual. She staggered and would have fallen if she hadn't hung onto the balustrade.

For the first time she understood the gravity of Mama's warning and shuddered as she stripped off her clothes with a full knowledge she would never wear any of them again, not even with the strongest bleach or a metal sponge.

She struggled to relegate the frustration that was eating her up as she washed the shampoo off her newly braided hair style. Not leaving much to chances she scrubbed her scalp, and sadly remembered the time, money and effort she'd recently put in the hair purposely for this trip. Failing to accept defeat, she thought of other means of getting to Wolverhampton and had considered Roxanne as the best option when she realised Billy needed her more at this critical moment. Her second option was to get a taxi from home to Wolverhampton with her only reservation being the uncertainty of how expensive it might be. Despite her financial commitment in the past two months her cousin deserves it all. She was tempted to opt for the train and worry about the only problem of boarding once she got there, but the unexpected outcome of how badly she would react to this dog got her worried sick. Two absurd thoughts crossed her mind; to ask one of her cousins to come for her all the way from Wolverhampton on a busy day for all concerned or beg Adam for a lift, after all it was his stupid dog that had caused all this! But then again her fear of her allergic reaction stood in the way once more.

As she sat on the edge of the bathtub dampening her hair with the towel, she was amazed at how quickly the compelling odour had improved and was prompted to jump up and open the window wider for some more fresh air like the rest of windows downstairs.

Dogs … big or small! She loathed and despised their aura and odour especially because of what they do to her. Apart from being allergic to them they always made her edgy and tense, principally for always freezing and hyperventilating her whenever they walked up to her for a sniff. And most importantly for being vindicated by dog owner's for reacting negatively to their dogs, without any care or understanding as to whether she had a phobia or not. She still could not recollect any creature on earth evoking so much negative vibes from her. Whoever said dogs are men's best friend definitely meant Guide Dogs alone!

Whilst still hoping to travel, she examined her ankle for the umpteenth time and prayed that her allergic reaction was minimal despite the intense itching. Her family knew she inherited her allergic reaction to dogs and her strong smell from her paternal granddad, which had always been an added disadvantage whenever she came across any dog.

With her ankle throbbing so badly, she finally decided to take some strong painkillers and hopefully take a taxi to Wolverhampton tomorrow no matter the cost. She admitted to herself that she'd rather be out there with her relatives instead of being stuck at home and feeling sorry for herself. Realising that the situation was out of her hands, she deliberately avoided pondering too much over her pitiful situation by empowering and channelling her thoughts to positive thinking.

Her mind wandered to the man and his Great Dane whilst she scrubbed herself with a traditional sponge. Unable to answer any of her questions she wondered what it was with her and dogs today or on the other hand, what was it with people and dogs generally? Is it a fashion statement, or for companionship or for any other reasons known to them? The more she tried to avoid dogs the worse the situation became, was it fate, coincidence, carelessness or perhaps they could sense her fear and phobia? All said and done, she would always remember today's doggy encounter as a tragedy. It would be a miracle if she only had rashes from this breed of dog because their physical contact was too close and personal.

Lola reminisced the up and close encounter with Adam Salvador. He would undoubtedly be over six feet in height with the physique to compliment his firm upper body secured by broad shoulders and strong muscular arms. When she clung to him, she noticed there was no superfluous flesh. Contrastingly his face was chiselled, hard and lean which was at odds with the lush sensual curve of his mouth. His jet black neatly cut hair personified a much lighter, naturally tanned skin reminding her of an Arab Sheikh that had just freshened up after a stormy desert trip. Judging by his last name, he must be a British of a Portuguese descendant especially with his unblemished accent. In a nutshell, Adam Salvador had the looks and a smile any woman would die for. Something strange about his hazel eyes told her he wouldn't forgive easily. And the soft Musk from his aftershave was so sensational that she nearly asked him for the brand so she could buy the same for Akin.

She tried snapping herself out of the incident by convincing herself that a man of such composure and look would have been used to ladies throwing themselves at him. She felt embarrassed when she tried to convince herself that feeling helpless, being reduced to tears, clinging to another man who was a complete stranger without reticence was not a big deal but proved much harder than she expected. To further her point she vividly remembered feeling his heart beating as fast as hers and the strange effect it had on both of them. How could she forget his facial expression when he saw her in tears and his strange reaction when he felt his heart beating in complete harmony with that of a stranger? And she for once agreed with her inner voice that seeking an answer would for now be too presumptuous and premature.

Delightfully, the long bath did wonders to her spirit and body, but simply wished she could say the same about her ankle and the rashes for once and for all. Getting settled was more of a challenge than she anticipated but was equally relieved she got there in the end, ensuring she gathered everything she needed close to her favourite recliner pleased her immensely. With the table lamp focused on her ankle, she was amazed to note that the swell had gone down but the pain was still as excruciating as ever. Realising the discomfort involved in seeking medical help; she decided to apply Mama's traditional method by massaging it with a balm and wrapping it afterwards with crepe bandage. She was halfway to her meal when the phone rang.

'Hi Roxanne,'

'I've left messages on your phone.' She went further without waiting for her reply. 'When are you leaving for Wolverhampton?'

'Change of plan.'

'I didn't think you would still want to go considering what happened today.'

'A lot of things happened today.'

'I know my dear; I would have come down if I knew for certain you were home.'

'I didn't plan to.'

'Okay.' Roxanne wanted to mention what happened at the office earlier today but found herself struggling. 'Lola, what happened in the meeting today-.'

'I hurt my ankle on my way home.' She deliberately interrupted her to avoid discussing the subject. 'Nothing serious though.'

'True.' She knew her well enough. 'But serious enough to make you miss a family gathering you've been so much looking forward to.'

The silence dragged on longer than usual with both unsure of how to approach the most prioritized subjects on their minds. Lola was not ready to discuss the subject that was eating her up, but toyed with the remote control button instead.

'Is there anything I can do for you tonight?'

'Like what?'

'I don't know; maybe drop you a takeaway or something.'

'Sounds tempting but you are fifteen minutes late. I'd rather be on my own tonight.'

'Sure, I understand.' Roxanne quickly changed the conversation to something safer. 'What's Akin saying about it all?'

'We haven't had the time to discuss it in details.' Lola faked a yawn to avoid further questions about him. Yet, another taboo subject for now! How could she explain what she didn't understand? Roxanne had not approved of Akin from day one and saying anything negative about him would not help her relationship with either of them.

'I'll see you elevenish tomorrow then.'

'Sure, maybe you can hear all about it if you drive me to Wolverhampton.' Lola quickly placed the phone down to avoid giving her the opportunity to reply, whilst waiting for the pain killers to work and put her to sleep. Already relaxed, she decided to shut her eyes instead of straining them by reading and worsening her thumping headache. Realising her body was tired in contrast to her brain she chose to put the phone beside her pillow hoping Akin would call, she wanted to reach for her mobile phone but suddenly became too lazy to get up for her bag.

She rebuked herself for not giving Roxanne the chance to finish her sentence and wondered whether she'd missed any valuable advice or warning? To her Roxanne was a matured, intelligent, shrewd and professionally astute colleague and friend who was always honest no matter the circumstances. Her valuable advice had shed a lot of insight into a lot of incidents happening around her working life lately. Lola simply wished she'd listened more to her ex landlady and line manager!

Her office had been like a war zone since last month when a small section of the building was gutted by fire with her cosy office being one of the worst affected. She was moved to another temporary section with little or no privacy to carry out her payroll duties. With no one listening to her complaint of inadequate resources in her new environment, she carried on regardless. Her new frustrating situation fuelled by those who held her responsible for the Bonus crisis gave rise to the biggest and the worst payroll blunder she could ever imagine. She overstated a handful of salary including hers, Roxanne's and some of her closest colleagues and understated five sales staff's figures on the BACS form she faxed to the bank. The template normally sent by post in advance by the bank for the following month had been gutted by fire so she's had to create a substitute manually after waiting endlessly for another duplicate promised by the bank. With no single mistake on the payslips she became convinced the mistake was not her own doing but a deliberate and calculating effort to discredit and smear her reputation.

She could have been well equipped for the situation if she'd listened to Roxanne's warning that the fire was incident was not an accident.

'Why would anyone want to set the building on fire?' She remembered asking after swallowing a mouthful of vegetable salad.

'Don't get me wrong, I was just warning you to watch your back in your new crowded environment.'

Lola eyed her suspiciously as she chewed another mouthful and would have probed further if they weren't joined by another colleague. For the next couple of days, she forgot to continue the conversation and now the payroll blunder. She would never ever get her own salary wrong even if she was drugged! But then what better way to tarnish her reputation but by such a blatant controversy!

Situation became critical when three of the salesmen concerned came charging at her open office raining abuses and calling her unpleasant names without any regards to company's policy. Bob then added more salt to her injury when he later called her into his office and verbally warned her for distressing five sales staff and accused her of trying to defraud the company. Not only was he aggressive, belligerent, overbearing and condescending but he coerced her into admitting that she was under some kind of pressure and couldn't cope. She gulped and glanced desperately around his office for any form of distraction but his insulting words kept piercing through. She was still waiting for her opportunity to apologise for whatever distress the mistake might have caused when she felt the tears trickle on her arm.

Even though she berated herself for crying uncontrollably he stopped, but not because of his compassion or remorse but for his triumph towards achieving his goal to present her to his brother and colleagues as incompetent and emotionally unstable. After that he would urge his approval to transfer her to a department he considered less threatening but where more bullying could be actually perpetrated. To avoid being described with one or more of his usual slogans such as having a chip on the shoulders, or lacking proper attitude, being negative, not committed, not a team player she let him do all the talking whilst she only listened. Her only regret was not listening to Roxanne's accusation that the fire incident was deliberate and her advice to secretly record their conversation whilst in the meeting.

It was morning when she was woken by vibration from underneath her pillow only to discover it was her phone. She was awfully disappointed to hear her cousin's voice, Sade, who said everyone was wondering why she never turned up yesterday and had not bothered to phone either. She had concluded that either Lola was dead or something close to that, but concluded that the latter was more appealing and she only wanted to confirm. She felt terribly guilty letting her and her senior brother getting married tomorrow down. Her reputation for being chatty and hilarious didn't pay off when she instantly noticed Lola was not in the mood for her dry jokes. Sade's next question was asking if she'd seek medical help to which she joked back that she would have done it eventually if she had not been awoken by her. She rounded up by stressing her wish for her to attend tomorrow's wedding ceremony before finally bidding her goodbye.

Lola paused briefly to contain her emotions before expressing her profound disappointment at the situation and a further promise to update her later in the day when her stomach grumbled loudly for food just as the conversation ended.

The pain instantly resumed on her ankle with full force when she went to the kitchen for a meal, and was still there having her meal when the door bell went twice consecutively and then again before the door finally opened. She looked at the clock and was not surprised it was eleven fifteen as Roxanne promised yesterday. Akin had insisted she took her spare keys from Roxanne but was sure glad she hadn't simply because of days like this. His argument was the angle of his personal threat of their closeness when he actually hid behind the excuse of her invading their privacy. He could not understand the bond between two people of disparaging cultural backgrounds and such age gap. And he failed to accept that the concept of the two women's bond was not only in what they'd been through together but the fact that one always knew when the other wa in need. He eventually conceded the day he lost his keys and got to her for her keys only to remember she'd already told him she was travelling to Coventry for training. It was Roxanne who saved the day by giving him the duplicate keys.

I could do with a bit of cheering up now! Akin where are you and how could you do this to me right now? She tried to recollect whether there was a row between them the last time they were together but was quickly interrupted by Roxanne's voice.

'I'd left messages on your phone.' She explained after exchanging greetings. Her gaze was fully focused at Lola's bandaged ankle. 'I was already turning the key when it occurred to me that he might be back and I didn't want to bother you, is he?'

'That's okay; you saved me a trip to the door.'

Roxanne put her handbag on the floor and went on her knees for a closer look. 'How did you say this happened?' She looked up to her for the first time she'd been in.

'I clashed into a mini donkey.'

'A what? You never said you were going to a farm.'

'It was a Great Dane but it looked like a baby donkey to me.'

Roxanne stood up with her petite frame, her small mouth, face and sharp eyes all widened with surprise. 'You mean a dog did this to you?'

She nodded whilst waiting for her to overcome her shock. 'It's not as bad as it looks,' she lied to reassure the older woman from thinking the worst.

Instead of a reply she looked at her face and smiled nervously.

Lola on the other hand eased her worries by explaining the funny side of yesterday's incident and was finally glad when the older woman changed the subject.

'Jade resigned.'

'Voluntarily or was she pushed?'

Roxanne snorted. 'She would never volunteer for a thing like that; remember she just got divorced … and a disabled son.'

'Yes and … four-year-old twin sons.'

'And in the process of buying a new house.'

'She's bought it, mortgage came through last month. She was chuffed to be close to her family at last.'

'Yes so they could all help her with the kids, she said.'

'Poor soul! It's not official yet, Billy is thinking of returning to work.'

Lola clipped her tongue on the roof of her mouth to make the "told you so sound". 'Has he finally agreed with everyone that his brother was going to ruin the company?'

She was trying to be careful with her choice of words. 'Slowly ... very slowly.'

She eyed her guest skeptically. 'What did his doctor have to say about that?'

'He advised him not to risk it.'

'Meaning what?'

Roxanne giggled before she replied. 'In the end, he said nothing stressful and not more than ten hours a week.'

'And Billy?'

'You know what he's like, just glad that he was okayed to return to work.' Roxanne was pensive for a while.

'Does that mean more power to you both inside and outside the boardroom?'

She smiled with a shrug of her shoulders.

'How could you say getting married to the big boss of A.B.C. & D. wouldn't change anything?' Lola watched her think deeply before smiling reservedly. 'But you wish you two had been married before this don't you?'

'Dead right my dear.' She accepted the cup of tea Lola offered with thanks and wrapped her hands round it before she sat on the kitchen stool that was pulled out for her to sit on. 'It breaks his heart with what Bob had turned the Company into; he said not doing anything might kill him first.'

'That I can understand. What's Bob got to say?'

'About?'

'About his big brother's return.'

'He doesn't need to know and no one's going to tell him because it's still a top secret.'

Lola studied her friend's face and wondered why she was panicking. With the two women both looking grim and quiet, it was obvious they wanted the same thing. She personally couldn't wait for Billy to return to work.

'Are you Okay?'

Lola nodded her head. 'The timing is lousy.'

'Why?'

'We've just lost an expensive legal battle to a rival company, rumours are already flying that bonuses would be affected especially those staff that are less than two years in the company.' She stopped to sniff into a disposable tissue. 'I wish he could return now that the Bonus crisis is boiling.' Her expression was masked with concern but she didn't look away. 'I'm sure everyone at work will blame me if they don't get their bonus this year as Scott and Bob said.' Whilst her voice remained shaky her eyes searched for truth as well as comfort.

'Don't forget you said "if".' Roxanne closed the gap to embrace her friend.

'But it looks imminent.' She broke free to scan her face. 'In fact very imminent.'

'But they can't blame you.'

'Yes they will.'

'Only the nincompoops.'

'We must be working with a lot of them.'

'I'm afraid so.' She added passionately.

'Because bad news travels faster than smelly fart, and it's much easier for everyone to blame me than anyone else.' Lola broke free to blow her nose. 'I'm sure someone somewhere is out to get me and I think they already have.' She admitted openly before she broke down uncontrollably. 'It's like someone wants to dump a Pandora box that's not mine on me.'

Roxanne tip toed on her five foot two frame to reach and wipe away her tears. 'Don't be daft! Maybe you need to take some time off.' She hoped her voice didn't sound as shaky as she felt.

'I'd rather not. That will only postpone the problem.' She dropped the tissue in the bin and reached for another one.

'Agreed, but it will also buy you time to be strong.'

'All I care about is for my name to be cleared of this controversial sleaze.'

'And that as well.' Roxanne's voice was now steady because her friend had stopped crying.

'But taking time off work will only conclude people's suspicion.'

Roxanne knew she couldn't assure her in the way that she wanted and didn't want to make a bad situation worse either. 'Let's get you seated; we don't want you exerting unnecessary pressure on the bad ankle.'

Lola was glad of the suggestion because of the sharp pain already spreading beyond her ankle and also decided to enjoy the rest of their time together by leading the way. 'Are you packed for the holiday yet?'

'Yes almost finished with Billy's too.'

'I bet you can't wait.' As they sat comfortably in the living room she surveyed the petite woman with a big heart and mouth who had for nearly three years grown to be a valued friend and colleague. She'd really been blessed to have known her and might not have been with her current employer if not for her. It goes without saying that the icing of the cake was her engagement to Billy the semi retired A.B.C. & D. Managing Director. Roxanne was already on her way to the kitchen when the door bell rang.

'I'm not expecting anyone so don't bother yourself with it.' She shouted with a big sigh of frustration.

But Roxanne was keen to get the door. 'Maybe Akin had lost his keys again.'

The voices she heard made her strain her ears to hear what was being discussed and with whom but without success. 'I'm not interested in any sales pitch today,' Lola shouted after her whilst she adjusted the reclining chair to her desired comfort.

'You have a guest,' she smiled weakly at the unpleasant look she'd seen on Lola's face many times before. 'He says he has something for you.'

'He?' Lola's brows arched in surprise and gestured to her to make a u turn and send the guest away. Roxanne suspecting what her reaction would be had instinctively invited the mystery guest in, and was hinting this to Lola with her hand but without any success.

After so many unsuccessful hinting, she stepped aside for her to see. The shock and surprise on Lola' face was unbelievable when she saw Adam in the entrance busy studying her family portrait. Roxanne noticed Lola's reservation but spread her arms helplessly and shrugged her shoulders that she could not justify why she let a stranger in. The two women exchanged looks in mutual silence as they focused on Adam who had became more engrossed with the portrait.

'Hello,' the two women eventually chorused together.

Adam smiled before he replied politely, but found it hard to take his gaze away from the picture completely.

Lola enclosed her hand around her ankle hoping to minimize the pain whilst watching him intensely.

'How is your ankle fairing?' Adam finally asked as he sat facing the two women.

'Too early to tell what is damaged but I'm sure I'll live.'

'Have you sought medical opinion?'

Lola smiled slightly before she replied; 'where is the time? All I'd been able to do so far was have a good sleep.'

Roxanne wanted to speak but suddenly decided against it.

'I think I'll leave it till Monday.'

'No you won't!' Her guests chorused their disagreement spontaneously.

She looked from one to the other and wanted to disagree but decided against it. She also attempted to accuse the pair of conspiracy but realised they were only meeting for the first time.

'Why haven't you phoned your G.P. yet?' Adam asked with an underlined authoritative tone.

'It's Saturday,' Roxanne who wanted to be supportive defended lamely.

'Then go to the A. & E.'

The two women exchanged looks before they both giggled.

'She hates hospitals.'

'Who doesn't?'

'She doesn't have a G.P.'

Lola stared at Roxanne with disbelief.

'You don't need to have a G.P. to go to hospitals.' He was surprised at the irritation in his voice.

'No I've never needed one.' She tried to play it down with a smile but didn't succeed.

'Well you do now,' Adam reached for his phone and started scrolling. 'Do you want to go to A. & E. or you want me to arrange a home visit?' Lola was yet to answer when the phone was picked from the other end, missing out a perfect opportunity to come up with an escape plan.

'Can you speak to Dr Mason?' The two women had hardly said anything when he interrupted them, and pushed the phone into her hands without giving her chance to decline.

She explained what happened and where she was hurting to the man on the other end. She was relieved at how easy it went and was equally glad he didn't ask her any personal question except her address. The doctor praised her for her first aid treatment and said he was relieved that the swell had gone down from yesterday, after which he asked to be transferred to Adam. On receiving the phone he thanked the doctor who said he would call back in five minutes before hanging up.

'Right ladies,' he clasped his hands together triumphantly. 'Dr Mason is the head of the local surgery and he is the second generation. We can either go to his surgery, arrange for home visit or we go to A. & E.' Adam deliberately stopped to watch their reaction and wasn't surprised when Lola asked for the older woman's opinion, but she only shrugged her shoulders.

'I thought home visits had now been cancelled.'

He eyed Roxanne before shrugging his shoulder modestly at Lola who responded immediately. 'I think I'll have the home visit please.'

'Good, in that case get ready to answer some tough questions.' He had started dialling his number before finishing his sentence.

'Tough questions?' the women asked in unison.

'Show me a woman who doesn't find answering her age tough,' he was again interrupted by Dr Mason's voice on the other end.

Adam voluntarily excused himself from the living room whilst she answered the doctor's question to the best of her ability and only beckoned on Adam at the doctor's request.

He strolled in with a sombre expression as he took the phone from Lola and ended the conversation with a smile before he replied with; 'Yes, I'll try.'

'He says he will be here in fifteen minutes time but I've got to go now; tell Dr Mason to call me if necessary.' He advised Lola to take things easy before he excused himself from the room. The two women were still debating about who should see him off when he spoke from the hallway. 'I forgot to give you this.' He gently placed her mobile phone on the coffee table before pushing it towards her. 'Judging by the names on it I suspected it was yours.'

At first, she wondered what was going on but reality quickly dawned on her that she'd neither set eyes on her phone nor answered any calls from it since yesterday; she inadvertently thanked him and agreed it was hers. This was then followed by some secret questions of how her phone got into his hands followed by what if he had read all her text messages.

'I'm sure it's yours,' he interrupted her thoughts with assurance.

Roxanne knew that look well enough. 'I bet you didn't realise your phone was missing.'

She turned the phone on but it died immediately and was about to try again when he ruined it!

'Bravo found it in the alleyway later last night.' Adam had barely finished his statement when she dropped the phone like a hot cake.

His surprised gaze shifted from the younger one to the older woman's.

Since waking up, the roller coaster of events had pushed her allergic reaction away from her mind until now.

Roxanne reached for the phone, removed the cover, and wiped it thoroughly before connecting it to a charger beside her. 'Did she tell you she is allergic to dogs?'

So gobsmacked was he that when he finally replied his voice sounded strange and far away. 'No, she didn't.' He not only felt ashamed and guilty for being harsh with her yesterday but upset with himself for just realising it. The concern on his face became more evident when he moved closer to examine her. With his eyes fully focused on her he asked the first question that came to him. 'Tell me she was joking.'

'Honestly, she comes out in rashes; I've seen it too many times.'

For a while, total silence consumed the room which confirmed that Roxanne's admission bothered him immensely. They both watched him fully focused assessing the visible part of Lola's body for any sign of rashes before finally shifting his gaze back to Roxanne and desperately expecting her to say she was teasing him. With the silence stretching longer than he could bear he continued. 'How many days does it take for the rashes to come out?'

'In a matter of hours and sometimes two to three days.'

'Do they come out everywhere or …' Adam let the rest of the sentence drift as the guilt he tried to hide reflected in his voice and all over his face.

Lola shrugged her shoulders nonchalantly. 'Some are already on my upper arms and shoulders.'

'What do you use for the rashes?'

Her reply was another shrug of her shoulders.

'Palm oil.'

'He wouldn't know what it is, would he?' Lola criticized her guest.

Palm oil? The door bell went whilst the women were waiting for him to ask what palm oil was. Meanwhile, he pondered over it for a second before he concentrated on his next question. 'Do you work?'

'Afraid so.'

'We work for the same company, A.B.C. & D.' She deliberately ignored Lola's irritation at her unnecessary disclosure.

Adam quickly suppressed the anger that name evoked in him. 'A.B.C. & D. eh?' His vast knowledge on commercial legal matters coming handy but he still wanted to know more. 'Wasn't there an article in the new business journal about a new contract bid from the City Council?'

She soon realised how quickly Roxanne had fallen for his charm. 'Yes still ongoing.'

'And a smear campaign from your main rival?'

'Spot on again.'

Lola murmured between clenched teeth to prevent her guest from saying too much to Adam. Their eyes met and she immediately recoiled, but would have ideally liked to shudder her to eternal silence if possible.

The deafening silence in the room was interrupted by the persistent door bell. Her irritation subsided as she watched Roxanne leave to get the door but was surprised to find Adam's face closer when she looked back. Despite wondering why such proximity, she wanted to tell him his nearness was bothering her but reckoned he would misunderstand her. As she became more unsettled with his intense gaze deeply scrutinising every fibre on her face she decided to lean back on her sofa and stare at the ceiling. She was constantly changing position to try and avert his piercing eyes burning through her skin. Whilst he gave no indication that he noticed her discomfort he didn't show any sign that he was perturbed by it either. After running out of option, she glanced back and it took all the strength she had to keep her eyes focused. For what seemed like twenty four hours his hazel eyes challenged her brown eyes in mute comprehension with one secretly commending the other's efforts. Lola finally shied away when her stomach muscles clenched and wouldn't stop churning.

He acknowledged her discomfort and his victory with a slant of his right eyebrow and a smile before he leaned back on his seat only to resume with an unimaginable intensity. She is not the most beautiful black woman he had known or met but she was much prettier than he originally thought. A bewitching little face that one could never be bored of, long natural curling lashes protecting large brown eyes that glowed of innocence and virility. If anything fascinated him in her it was those eyes! He noticed her nose was neither pointed nor flat but was in harmony with her face, her mouth was moderately beautified by soft, full nicely curved lips. The deep dimples on her cheeks highlighted her cheekbones and accentuated the shape of her eyes more. Adam loved women, period! Black, white or dual heritage as long as they are pretty and feminine and he could connect with them especially through their eyes. Despite his belief that eyes had a mind of their own he wondered if what hers were telling him were what he wanted to hear?

Suddenly his mind went blank when the intensity of his piercing eyes attempted to overpower hers which she coincidentally found greatly disturbing than she'd like to imagine.

Not wanting to concur to defeat she came up with a perfect plan. 'Roxanne!' She shouted desperately and was about to go for her when she walked in with another man.

'Dr Mason is here for you.' Roxanne stepped aside and made a theatrical bow.

Adam looked like he'd just come off a spell. He stood up to shake the doctor's hands after suddenly remembering his surroundings.

'I haven't faced so much interrogation in ages.' The doctor remarked jokingly as he quickly tried to connect with the situation whilst exchanging greetings with Adam.

The doctor's admiration and affection for Adam became instantly obvious as Lola watched the two men hold tightly onto each other's hands. The doctor let go first but followed it up by a pat on Adam's back.

The doctor's surprised expression that confirmed the two women were not blood related only lingered on long enough for them all to notice.

Adam was still on his feet when he urged Lola to mention her rashes and allergy to dogs.

'What are the rashes like?' The doctor asked.

Lola pulled up her sleeve to show him some of the rashes she'd recently noticed. The doctor moved closer to examine them.

'Do you remember what you once told me about palm tree?' Adam asked the doctor after his examination. He chuckled loudly. 'Have you got an alternative prescription to palm oil?'

'Palm oil from palm tree?' The doctor took his glasses off and continued to nibble its frame. 'A West African product good for cooking as an alternative to vegetable oil and used for first aid treatment.' He looked from one surprised face to the other. 'Remember?'

'Was it the folklore that says nothing on a palm tree waste?'

'Yes!' Lola couldn't hide her amazement and disbelief as the two men analysed an original African product accurately and impressively.

'I must have told you that many years ago then.'

'Yes, on your last return from Lagos.'

The two men locked gaze in silence before Adam nodded his head in some kind of a silent agreement. 'Palm wine is tapped from the tree as a drink, the leaves are used as broom, and the outer skin of the palm seeds makes the palm oil leaving the palm kernels.'

'Amazing how you still remember.' The doctor now opened his briefcase and took a piece of paper out and scribbled on it.

Adam was already by the door before he spoke again. 'I'd better let you get on.' Roxanne seized a perfect opportunity to excuse the doctor and the patient by seeing him off.

'Does palm oil work for your rashes then?' They both heard the doctor ask as they left the room.

She wanted to add that the residue from palm kernels was used to make fire but nodded her head instead and bade them goodbye before watching them leave.

Dr Mason was a very pleasant middle-aged man, completely bald of his red hair and lanky but still attractive. Lola was of the impression that he must be close to Adam and his family especially his mother. He agreed that she'd sprained her ankle, but referred her to the Hospital for an X-ray to eliminate the possibility of a fracture. He prescribed a strong painkiller, a balm for her ankle and a cream to be applied on the affected area with rashes up to three times a day. After which he advised her to temporarily wrap her ankle with a compressed bandage and to rest her foot in a raised position with the ice pack on it till the pain and swelling subsided. She was also given a week's sick leave. He handed her the sick note, closed his briefcase and wished her full recovery before making his way to the door.

'Please phone the surgery straight away if the rashes or allergy deteriorates and be very careful with your ankle.' He reiterated just before he disappeared from her view which was shortly followed by noise from the door being closed.

CHAPTER 3

This morning, Lola woke up to a text from the acting M.D.'s office still wanting to know if she required a lift to enable her attend the meeting. She decided not to respond and take the matter in its own stride but wondered why she was feeling very queasy. Her soul searching mission concluded with two main concerns; Akin and work. With her head feeling heavier than necessary she decided not to plan anything but lie in and let things take their natural course.

She rebuked herself for letting her employer's pressure get to her on her third day of a week's sick leave, she examined her ankle and fervently hoped she had not become one of those boring disillusioned employee that couldn't keep off the office even whilst on leave. A sharp pain from her ankle consoled her that she wouldn't go far even if she tried.

Her employer was in deep crisis with no hope of it fading away. A.B.C. & D. as it was often called was an I.T. company that offered technical support, repaired and maintained computers and printers of all makes to small, medium and large companies all over the country. The company also had five big regional workshops opened to the public who wanted a walk in advice or service their equipments.

She'd enjoyed her job and mutually respected most of her colleagues except the ever greedy, money grabbing sales staff or the B.D.U. (the

Business Destruction Unit) as Billy often called them. They couldn't wait to blame her for the uncertainty surrounding their bonus payouts.

As at last Friday, she was still hopeful that Billy would kindly authorise her to pay the bonus to every other department except the B.D.U. who according to him were already well remunerated with full expenses, Company cars, pension and commission on top of their fantastic salaries. He had asked for employee's attendance records and sick leave reports the last time he called and had also hinted that he would also use them as a yardstick for bonus payout. Then there was an email from the Credit Control Manager stating that she received a fax informing her that one of our biggest customers had gone into receivership, so she urged the concerned department to withdraw technical support immediately. Apart from a major setback to the Company and its hundreds of employee, it would also cast more doubt over the already uncertain bonus payout, but Lola was equally relieved that it had absolutely nothing to do with her and it might just exonerate her if bonus was not eventually paid out.

Whilst in the Credit Control Department, she made uncountable enemies in the B.D.U. when she insisted that credit checks should be carried out on new customers. Her line manager agreed with her in principle only but wasn't bold enough to take, Bob, the acting M.D. who was then the Finance Director on. And the manager that successfully stipulated that credit checks should be carried out on orders exceeding one thousand pounds was eventually sacked by Bob for insubordination.

As if one bad news wasn't enough for one day! Whilst in the Finance team meeting, a recorded delivery document arrived from one of their major suppliers. M.A.D. Peripherals who also sub contracted their end users technical support contracts to A.B.C. & D. in return for some percentage. The two companies had both come a long way in the industry. Much to her astonishment she was still haunted not only by Friday incident but also by their threatening words!

Since the attached invoices were long overdue for payment; you are hereby strongly advised to settle them within the next seven days or face legal action.

We also have strong reasons to believe that one of your female staff members had connived and colluded with some of ours to defraud us and engage in unauthorised purchases and discounts. As a result of this we shall be suspending all future transactions and no further payments will be made to your company until this matter has been thoroughly investigated and resolved.

Meanwhile we would like all our outstanding invoices to be settled according to our credit agreements.

Yours
Finance Director
M.A.D. Peripherals

The next four pages were the copies of the invoices in question and the subsequent ones being the copies of Purchase Orders she allegedly faxed over, not only directly linked to her but happened before her transfer to Personnel Department!

Her initials at the end of the Purchase Orders meant that she not only raised them but she was also one of the supervisors in the Bought Ledger Department then! How could she forget such big amounts?

She spread the four invoices out evenly for a closer scrutiny as her eyes danced desperately from one page to the other hoping to find a clue to discredit all the documents but the longer she looked the more convinced she was! The number of eyes piercing through her seriously hampered her concentration. Finally, she lifted her head to stare back when the intense look was stabbing and burning through her brown skin. She was already unpopular with her controversial reports which triggered the uncertainty surrounding the bonus payout and now this! She found herself at a momentary loss with chills crawling from her head to toe followed by a dread of what would come next. In her desperate attempt to be brave and remain comfortably seated, a delicate shudder ran through her whole body. 'These invoices are over a year old! And I can't remember any of it!'

'Obviously Lola! That makes it okay then.' Such was Scott, the new Finance Director's sarcastic reply.

How would you know? You weren't even here then! Her mouth quirked up on one side and a soft sigh escaped her instead. An uncontrollable urge wanted her to round the saga up by quickly owning up and agreeing that she'd made a big blunder but was suddenly restrained by the big burden that would come afterwards. 'I find this really hard to believe.' She quickly glanced at Lynne, her ex line manager for some kind of support that this was truly a mistake from their supplier's.

Unfortunately she was still battling with her own demon as her nose twitched consistently, something Lynne only did if under pressure.

Scott, who was now Lynne's line manager sat back looking across the room to assess the impact of the news on every one's face. 'And once again, it makes it acceptable.' He studied Lola's reaction before he continued. 'We obviously won't be able to afford any bonus with these outstanding invoices.'

Lola fortunately saw through his charade that he was gloating at her misery. 'That won't be entirely my fault.'

The confidence in her tone thinned Scott's lips with frustration and anger.

'I'm sure there is a mistake somewhere.' Roxanne who sat some chairs away from her quickly interrupted to diffuse the tension about to emanate between them. 'What do they take us for? A bunch of fools?'

'Can I point out that these invoices were dated about the same time I was transferred to Personnel Department!'

'And the same time the new in house software was launched.' Roxanne added.

'What a coincidence!'

Despite eying Scott for his last comment, she was more concerned with the motives behind this strong accusation and what would become of the mutual concessions and friendship that had coexisted between the two companies for decades.

Before the live networking system, Lola spent a combination of seven months in both Bought and Sales Ledger Department. The manual system always ensured that the Company's Purchase Order forms were properly filled with a valid P.R.O.N. (or otherwise known as Purchase Requisition Order Number) and appropriately authorised by a manager before ordering from suppliers. Although procedures were not strictly adhered to by many managers who would rather exhaust their petty cash before phoning the Bought Ledger for a P.R.O.N but it worked. This problem was further compounded by Company's operating style with most Field Engineers phoning the Call Control or their supervisors to order and deliver parts to them on site, making a very large proportion of delivery outside the office.

With the live network not only easing the bottle neck on Bought Ledger, but call controllers as well as managers were free to order parts quoting a uniquely generated call out reference number that would be quoted on the sales invoice which will be forwarded to Bought Ledger for a corresponding P.R.O.N.

The new network system had linked the entire department to live P.R.O.N.S. (Purchase Requisition Order Numbering System) for more accurate management report and proper accountability, easy and quick financial monitoring by the Finance Director and his team. Above all the network system had immensely improved everyone's performance and professionalism by reducing unnecessary duplication of pedantic roles. So far, no major mistakes had been detected, which made Lola and many others believe strongly in the new system. At the early stage, a handful of old managers took early retirement because they felt out of place with the new technology, to save cost the management merged the Bought Ledger and the logistics into one department.

At the end of every week, Bought Ledger staff would reconcile the P.R.O.N.s and send purchase reports to every department to authorise purchase listed against their department.

'There is only one way to find out.' Reece the young Sales Manager of five months interrupted her thoughts. Good at his new role and job but couldn't stop boasting about his record performances, coupled with the reputation of being too light hearted and constantly putting his foot in his mouth. He quickly grabbed the phone and started to dial, more worried about the implication of suspended sales on his personal and department's sales target and commission for the months to come.

'Who do you want to speak to?' The panic in Roxanne's voice instantly unsettled her melodious voice.

Lola watched her brush a strand of blonde hair away from her face as her electric blue eyes remained fully focused on Reece for a miracle.

'My mate Dan, one of their newly appointed directors.' His cockney accent suddenly seemed sharper.

'Yes! At least he should know.' Everyone echoed hopefully. With everyone in suspense time went slower, the deafening silence in the room made Lola's heartbeat uncontrollably faster and louder.

The smile on Reece's face was immediately wiped off after he exchanged greetings with Dan on the other end. 'No, it can't be that serious!' With his freckled-face squeezed up, he put the phone back on the rest and informed everyone that Dan said he couldn't talk much about it for now. The sound of the phone on the rest not only ended everyone's suspense but almost made Lola's heart explode.

'Why?' Roxanne was unable to hide her disappointment.

'Because he was in a meeting with the other directors but he strongly emphasized the seven days deadline three times.'

Lola looked from one face to the other, lingered a bit on Cathy who was busy taking notes for Bob before finally resting on Roxanne's who had every reason to be worried sick. Underneath the bright and funny personality displayed to colleagues, she knew the real Roxanne and right now all that concerned her was for her wedding to go as planned. Lola had always teased her of taking work too far when she knew about her past with the company's boss, Billy, and long before they agreed to tie the knot secretly to avoid Bob, the younger brother sabotaging their plan. Any more financial mishap in the company would definitely jeopardize the wedding arrangement especially the expensive honeymoon.

'They have the best legal representative in the industry.'

Not only did she refuse to let her emotion get the best of her despite Scott's cold and hostile gaze burning on and off her skin, but she almost told him to put his glasses back on. She finally pulled herself together against all the odds around her. 'These purchases relate to the network project and servers we abandoned over a year ago.'

'Sixteen months ago to be precise.'

Lynne's helpful remark finally empowered her to probe deeply. 'True indeed, why now and what took them so long?' For the first time in a while all looks were shifted from her to their immediate partners for possible answers.

'Let us not forget we are a service company and some of our end users pay more than well enough for these comforts we've always taken for granted. Isn't there a possibility that we made a mistake by missing these purchases out?'

She could have throttled Reece for the unnecessary menacing remark.

'You mean an oversight?' Roxanne elaborated. 'But isn't it bizarre that the two companies could have made such a mistake simultaneously?'

'The P.R.O.N.S. won't allow us to make such a mistake without one of the director's intervention.'

'Because Bought Ledger's P.R.O.N.S. was not only linked to individual supplier's credit limit but had been defaulted not to issue any number if our outstanding value with any supplier reaches fifty grand at any given time. And it very rarely happens.' She once again supported her ex manager.

'But we sometimes do.'

'Yes, as Lola said very rarely and the system would request for a pass from one or two directors to authorise such a purchase.'

'To me that explanation fully support why such a big transaction would not be recorded in the first place.' Scott's contemptuous gaze wandered to everyone in the room before finally resting on Lola.

She'd already replied before she realised she was playing into Scott's hands. 'Yes and tell the department concerned to burn the paperwork too.' She looked back at him without blinking.

Scott pretended to ignore her for a while and deliberately directed his question to Lynne. 'Why don't we do it anymore then?'

'I suppose it's because you now authorise such large purchases.' She shifted from her seat before she continued. 'And every Manager now has the freedom to access the live P.R.O.N.S. as long as we have a signed delivery note by their director, and authorisation in our weekly report.'

At first, Scott's lips thinned with frustration but his face suddenly relaxed before he spoke. 'Were you not on maternity leave around sixteen months ago?'

Attentive Lola became paralysed with fear as she suddenly realised how vulnerable she was and getting an insight into his strategy nearly made her heart drop into her guts.

Lynne not only twitched her nose again but was quiet for a while. 'Oh yes, I'd forgotten.' She laughed her silliness off, leaned back on her seat to relax and stopped twitching her nose immediately.

'Leaving you in charge.'

Lola looked at him solemnly for the first time and saw a sardonic smile cross his face as he triumphantly put his glasses back on.

Frantic, confused and desperate she resolutely faced him and cringed with fear for what she saw in his eyes.

'Also, these Purchase Orders had your unique number and were ordered during the developing stage of the in house software.' Scott's triumphant voice was now filled with a newly charged authority and condescension.

Realising that she not only has more at stake than anyone else in the boardroom but also that Lynne didn't have to help if she didn't want to. 'So it seems,' she hoped her reply sounded resolute enough.

'And these are debts that had to be paid whether we like it or not.'

Her spine became stiffened again in desperation to compose herself. 'Agreed, but I would remember any authorisation be it by mail or memo for such large purchases especially when I allegedly generated the P.R.O.N.S.'

'Allegedly?' He tried to trivialize her point by mimicking her accent.

'And would have ideally made allowance for it in the cash flow forecast and the cashbook the following month or upon the receipt of the invoices.' Lynne candidly boosted her confidence again.

'Assuming we never received the invoices?' He looked across the room to assess member's moods.

'Why?' Lynne challenged.

'Okay let us agree with him even though I seriously wonder why. But why have we never received the delivery notes too?' Lola exhaled all the breath she'd been saving inside all at once when she saw Scott's lips thinned venomously again. His disappointing expression could be compared to that of someone who'd been shot by a close friend at a close range.

'Maybe we should phone and ask for the delivery notes.'

'Later Reece!'

'Invoice was late and no delivery note was attached with the copies I say this supports my claim that they're up to something.' Roxanne's stern warning vibrated across the room.

Cathy who all along had her head buried taking notes looked up and was surprised to see all the women nod their heads in agreement with her. 'For the record how much does all these invoices come to?'

Yes! Make sure you write that in your report! 'Seven hundred and fifty grand.' Lola's voice sounded so faint that she doubted if anyone heard her.

'Three quarters of a million pounds?' All attention was directed at Roxanne for a change as her voice shrilled through the boardroom. Whilst their eyes met, the panic in her eyes made Lola wish she had not convinced her to delay her wedding at all, but smiled nervously at her instead. Roxanne smiled back warmly as she tapped on her wrist watch to inform her of her next appointment. 'Why now?' She whispered followed by a big sigh of frustration.

'That's a million dollar question Roxanne. He giggled before he continued. 'They possibly need it to cure Neil senior cancer.'

'Reece!' All the women in the boardroom rebuked him sharply whilst Scott's expression remained grim.

'Sorry ladies.'

'Don't we have a credit limit in place?' Roxanne asked to put the meeting back on track.

'No we don't.'

'Why?'

'We replaced it with a contra agreement.'

'*Contra?*' Roxanne's lack of accounting knowledge finally became obvious.

'Yes, they owe us as we do them so we both agree to net it out at the end of the month.'

'Did Billy not terminate all contra agreements before he retired?' Reece who joined the Company after Billy retired had been obviously gathering his own facts about the semi retired director.

'Yes with the exception of two other companies and M.A.D. Peripherals.'

'Because they're all Billy's good friends?' Reece's mouth preceded his brain as usual.

'But he set a contra limit.' Lola noticed the sparkle in Roxanne's eyes at the mere mention of her future husband.

'What's the amount for M.A.D. Peripherals?'

'Up to fifty thousand every month.'

'If there was a contra agreement between the two companies why have they not tried to clear any of these old invoices before now? They of all companies should understand the essence of prompt invoicing especially with these sizeable amounts.'

'Exactly and why haven't they ever reflected these invoices in the past statements?' Lynne asked to support Roxanne's statement.

'But there is no smoke without fire.' Scott remarked impliedly as he rested his look on Lola. 'Neither would M.A.D. Peripherals go through this trouble for nothing.'

'Out of curiosity, how much do we owe them really?'

Quickly, Lynne rose and placed a piece of paper on the projector but did not reflect, after several unsuccessful attempts Lola came to her rescue. 'All in all there is an outstanding balance of £200k.' She concluded after explaining the breakdown of the last three month's transactions including Contras and disputed invoices.

'How much do they owe us?'

Everyone exchanged looks because the Credit Control Manager had been recently suspended by Bob the acting M.D. because of personality clash and her assistant had just gone on maternity leave. The next in line was Janice who had been quiet all along because of laryngitis but was forced by Bob to attend the meeting regardless. She approached the projector nervously.

After several failed attempts to place the document on the projector properly, someone called Lola's name to assist. She scanned their faces and was still surprised to be met by a frosty look from Scott. Quickly she sprang on her feet and placed the document properly on the projector and went back to her seat leaving Janice with her presentation.

Total amount of invoices M.A.D. Peripherals owed us was £950k. She'd boldly written at the bottom of the page.

'Before or after contra?'

Before. Janice quickly scribbled.

'They owe us nine hundred and fifty thousand pounds whilst we owe them two hundred thousand pounds.'

'And the difference is the £750K.' Reece interrupted anxiously with a loud bang on the desk.

'And that is supposed to be a bizarre coincidence!'

'Pure speculation, Roxanne.' Scott remarked crisply as he struggled to quiet everyone else down.

And for the umpteenth time since Friday, the puzzle of who could be so vindictive to set her up needled her as badly as the implications behind Scott's insinuations, comments and demeanour throughout the meeting. Someone had obviously gone through a well-orchestrated plan to discredit her reputation and competence. She was so deep in thought wondering what more could have been done to worsen her situation when she heard her phone ring. She'd already replied the caller before blaming herself and felt worse when she heard who was on the other end.

The man introduced himself as Romeo Redford the acting M.D.'s new P.A. and was summoning her for an emergency meeting scheduled for the following day. All her explanations to him that her mobility had been greatly impaired fell into deaf ears nor did her excuse that she couldn't drive nor catch a bus help her in anyway. He eventually acknowledged the receipt of her sick note when she consistently asked the same question but promised to speak to his boss and get back to her. When he did she didn't pick his calls hoping he would give up but the persistent Romeo kept leaving strong messages on all her known contact numbers.

Finally, she got tired of his unrelenting calls and picked up the phone. With a big sigh of relief he explained that the boss insisted she either got a taxi and be refunded if receipts were provided or agree for someone in Logistics Department to pick her up.

'I'm I going to be driven from inside my house into the office or what?' Lola eventually vented her frustration at the P.A. who refused to take no for an answer.

With total disregard to her question he went straight to the point that a letter signed by the acting M.D. himself requesting her to attend a meeting in person the following day was to be delivered by hand any time from now. "I do apologise if I'd caused you any grief or if my tone was too abrupt or authoritative but I'm only following orders." He ended his conversation and cut the phone before she could reply.

She had barely made sense of his statement when she heard the doorbell chime and was surprised to see one of her colleagues from the logistics department on her door step. Her first reaction was to ignore him but she instantly changed her mind for two good reasons; firstly, he'd seen her through the window and secondly she'd done nothing wrong. But the ultimate decision maker was when her mobile phone rang and it was Romeo again telling her there was someone at her doorstep.

'Okay …'

'Could you collect the letter from him please?'

'Hell No!'

'Miss … Anif, it's imperative that …'

'No, you listen Mr. Redford, it's not imperative that he comes to my door to harass and intimidate me especially when I'm on sick leave. It's not imperative that you bully me because you have access to my personal details or impose your uncompromising and insensitive orders on me. Why don't you do us all a favour by phoning and telling him to drop the letter through the letter box the same way you did me?' She was still shivering uncontrollably as she replaced her phone when she instantly decided against attending the meeting tomorrow.

As her nerves calmed she realised she needed to attend to defend herself but was coming round to it mentally when the door bell chimed with persistent loudness; angrily she yanked the blind to give him a piece of her mind but he'd coincidentally answered a new incoming call on his mobile. Whilst hanging on to the blind and hoping he pressed her bell again he instead saved everyone the hassle by waving at her and turning away with his mobile still stuck to his ears.

Before Billy's early retirement, she never dreaded going to work even when she was ill. To her, a meeting with his younger brother was like being stuck between a hard stone and a rock. She wasn't particularly afraid of having a meeting with him but more of herself being too expressive, moreover he had a reputation of bringing out the worst in her when she was calm and focused unlike now that every aspect of her life had got the best of her.

To her, Billy was a people's man, a thinker and a cerebral in comparison to Bob who had been mostly described by many of her colleagues as the M.D. without people or management skill but a lazy, patronising, social bulldozer with a gruffly voice that wouldn't mind selling his own mother for some profit. She believed the genesis of their problem was their fundamental difference in business values, ethics and ethos. Neither did the monthly report she regularly presented to Billy help her situation, she'd been reliably informed that Bob had strenuously requested that her report went through him but his brother vigorously refused. Billy had, before his compulsory retirement requested for autonomy over Lola, Roxanne and three other employees with the vested power to hire, fire or even transfer them to any department he deemed fit.

She'd often wondered why Billy offered his younger brother such a crucial position if he didn't trust him, but Roxanne explained that Bob was a nasty insurgent better controlled inside rather than outside. Lola had always found the sticky situation disenchanting and unappealing since she'd been solely in charge of every staffs and employee's salary, wages, commissions and bonuses. The last straw was the removal of B.D.U.'s commission from Bob and his cronies when he was accused of reckless commission payout and recruitment. She'd often thought of resigning and had attended a few successful interviews, but was always hindered by either the crappy salary or the mundane roles. She'd often consoled herself with Sade's advice that she should be thankful for being black, young with a high flying job and a Post graduate qualification. Having expressed her concern about the increasing numbers of enemies at work, she was assured that the brothers wanted an independent staff to present an unbiased and realistic report from someone they trust.

To buttress Billy's point, his younger brother employed ten new Sales staff in addition to the existing seven. And for some bizarre reasons placed seven out of the ten newly employed Sales staff on the same fantastic salary scale and remuneration as their existing colleagues, whether they performed or not whilst the rest earned higher than everyone else in the department.

'We don't have the resources for seventeen sales staff.' Roxanne had complained after Bob called to tell them both about the news.

'Not to worry, they will be on the field most of the days.'

'Good, which means they don't get paid if they don't perform.' Her gaze shifted from Bob's to Lola's for confirmation but she was doubly disappointed. 'They are on salary aren't they?' She whispered.

He nodded his head as a sad remorseful look quickly appeared and disappeared from his face.

Her mouth was wide open in disbelief. 'Who gave you such authority?' Her question echoed throughout the quiet office. She sighed in exasperation as she towered her five foot two inches height over him

'Why would you triple the department within such a short period?'

Lola was impressed by her friend's challenging question, because the two women should have been ideally involved with the selection, interview and recruitment process. Neither of them was aware of the need for more Sales staff and neither had any provision been made in the budget for such. With Roxanne's question left to linger and no forthcoming answer, she as usual let her emotions get the best of her by calling her brother-in-law all the forsaken names under the sun. Whilst Lola nearly capsized with shame and embarrassment she realised only Roxanne could get away with mouthing Bob off, and still wouldn't have cared if her emotions were not involved.

Roxanne stood upright and exhaled deeply. 'I'd better leave before I loose total control and possibly do something I'd regret.' She turned the door handle and looked at him scornfully. 'May God help us!'

Lola watched Bob did what he always did best, tapping his expensive pen on his desk with one hand and squeezing his stress ball with the other to gradually rid him of the destructive anger. With no word from him, she stood up to leave but was called back to her seat; she slowly sat back as she waited anxiously for what was to happen next.

After tapping for a while longer he looked straight into her eyes as he spoke, his eyes cold and detached. 'Just wanted to remind you of your sensitive department and where your loyalty should lie no matter what.' His tone was stern and firm.

She could only remember nodding her head like a string-puppet and couldn't imagine the situation getting stickier.

Just then, she heard her letter box rattle and looked through the window to see the post man leaving for her neighbour's door. With her nerves fully settled she hopped to the door and picked all her letters. She swore silently after reading the official four paragraphed letter signed by Romeo Redford. He told her the meeting was scheduled for tomorrow whilst the letter stated two day's time at noon. She was already calling him for his blatant blunder but she restrained herself and decided to play the waiting game. For once, she agreed that not knowing might be good, who knows whether she'd been called in to get sacked!

CHAPTER 4

Lola woke up feeling grumpy and miserable, but was glad and relieved to hear Akin's voice on the phone downstairs still talking about his aunt who was just recovering from stroke and how her craving for pepper soup was finally granted yesterday.

She quickly decided to get up and freshen up before facing him.

'Aunty finished it all and asked for more!' She heard his excited voice over the phone just as she shut the bathroom door.

Despite the missing days between them, she was befuddled that their main conversation yesterday was about his aunty and his work, never mind her health. She was honestly delighted about his aunt's progress because she believed the quicker she fully recovered the more time they could spend together as a couple. Trying to give him the space and time he so much begged for didn't mean she should be treated like a seasonal overcoat, the thought upset her but she cautioned herself to thread carefully and find the perfect opportunity to express her concern. She was nearly finished when he knocked on the door to say he had to pop out making her inflict more damage to her ankle as she unsuccessfully tried to rush out of the bathroom for a chat and snug.

He promised to be here first thing in the morning after telling her about his little accident yesterday.

'So how's Aunty?' She finally asked.

'She's responding to treatment and was able to eat yesterday and I couldn't leave her.'

'Glad to hear it,' she thinned her lips to avoid saying anything offensive since she'd upset him once for asking if she'd been diagnosed with attention craving and mental illness.

She settled in front of the mirror to examine her face closely whilst wondering whether to phone Dr Mason's surgery now or later. Thankfully the medication did wonders for the rashes except for one side of her face which as usual proved stubborn. As she stroked the inflamed side she wondered if it was better Akin didn't see her in this state, but wasn't convinced she would have actually chosen that. Grottier than she'd ever remembered, she took her time to get dressed and occupy her present time with what was meant for later.

She followed her scent and glanced sideways to see a bouquet of roses on top of her special album and a note explaining that he ran away to avoid being infected with her rashes because of his susceptibility.

As usually expected, Lola's stomach was taut with mixed expectation as she reached for the blue album she'd labelled "Mum". This particular album had until now been deliberately placed out of reach because of the strong emotions it always evoked in her, but also sporadically drew her like a magnet because she believed it held the keys and answers to some of the riddles in her life. In it were many pictures of her mother which she had skillfully and hierarchically arranged to her personal taste and strengths. This was her usual and effective way to meditate and mourn!

Today's urge to look at it was irresistible, possibly because it commemorates the twentieth anniversary of her mother's death or the other challenges in her life. She had devoted extra time to pray for her soul and vowed not to cry but instead gave more alms to charity. Judging by her past reactions, she'd mostly felt more invigoration than sadness after looking through it except the last time, when she fell out with her dad for asking some deep, uncomfortable questions he was not ready to face himself.

Her heart somersaulted as her mother's angelic smile welcomed her on the first page with her as a toddler in her arms, both dressed in green floral African prints. Her mother's naturally shiny hair was parted into two in the middle and bounded by matching hair bands whilst hers was woven into four with ribbons tied at each end of her hair in bow followed by other hair accessories. Their closeness to the camera brought out more of their facial features. Lola looked meekly at the camera whilst her young mother looked happy, radiant, and beautiful. Her dad only informed her during one of her recent inquisitions that the picture was snapped the day they were leaving England for Nigeria which made it her last picture with her mother.

Lola was born in Birmingham exactly eleven months after her mother joined her father, an Engineering student on scholarship at Birmingham University. This became her driving force and determination to settle back in Birmingham regardless of her aunt's and cousin's effort to prevent her from leaving North London. Her four months stay with Sade and her mum did not only open her eyes to the challenges ahead but was also the longest time she'd ever recollected spending with any relatives apart from her grandma and father. Despite the void left by her mother's death and the growing desire to fill it, she'd always considered herself lucky to have been showered with twenty years of love and support second to none from her grandmother and her biological dad. Leaving her safe cradle of Lagos for Birmingham at the tender age of twenty one had dealt her with challenges beyond her imagination but her crowning glory was the attainment of her Post Graduate qualification in the same University as her father. She didn't realise how fulfilled she was until her father admitted it on her graduation day.

With Birmingham filling most of the void in her life simply because of the pride of reliving her dad's educational experience and the frequent buzz that she'd either crossed or walked her mother's path, stood on the same stop or shopped in the same place as when she was alive. This to many people might be trivial but it mattered a great deal to her and her well being. But her only makeover area was love life which incidentally was a major role in returning to Birmingham in the first place.

She was approaching her third birthday when she travelled to Lagos with her mother and was over eight years old when she realised her dad would be arriving soon from England. What Lola didn't know for almost a decade of her innocent life was that the woman she thought to be her mother was actually her paternal grandmother and that her biological mum died shortly after arriving in her motherland and never made it to join Lola's father back in Birmingham. Looking back now explained why she'd often wondered why Mama not only looked older than any of her classmate's mums but was always treated with reverence. So for eight years she was under the illusion that Mama was her biological mother until her older schoolmates informed her that she was actually her paternal grandmother.

She could remember arriving from school to find Mama lying sick in bed and sat next to the older woman who began massaging her head as she praised her ancestral lineage. 'Mama is it true that my daddy is your son?' She slipped it in when the older woman was coughing to clear her throat.

Her hand stopped moving before she replied with a question. 'Who told you that?'

Lola was determined not to let the objection in her voice deter her. 'Some older students ma.'

There was no reply but a deeply drawn slow breath as she slowly got up.

'Is it true you are not my Mama?'

She scanned Lola's face for a while before she shook her head negatively with remorse. She tried to speak but the shocking expression on her face was so severe that her voice betrayed her.

'So you are not my biological mother?' Knowing what the answer was pushed the tears through uncontrollably.

Contritely, Mama's bitter reply was not only weak but sounded cautious and distant.

Tears began to roll down her little face as her mind and head became overfilled with questions. She spoke a few words but they were all muddled up.

Finally, she reached for the picture frame by her bedside and looked at it for a while as the warmth sparkled in her. 'Mama you said that was you.' Her tears were now under control but her voice was still very shaky.

'No I said that was Mama.' Still holding onto the other side of the picture frame with the silence dragging on, she pulled her closer and hoped to encourage her to speak her mind. She was a bundle of delight but her sensitive nature sometimes indicated how to approach matters around her. 'Lola, I could never be as pretty as that woman in the picture.' She paused for her reaction and smiled when their eyes met. Mama bent her aching head to peep into her eyes and tried to encourage more smile but unsuccessful. 'My Jewel,' she tickled her chin and was disappointed she only responded with a weak smile.

She looked at the picture with a renewed determination, speaking quietly and thoughtfully. 'That means what they said was true.'

The older woman puffed out loudly. 'Which is?'

She sucked in her snort and toyed with her fingers. 'They said my mummy was dead.'

The sadness in her granddaughter's voice and eyes paralysed and froze her whole body. With her heart feeling like it had been violently jagged into pieces with the sharpest object imaginable, she struggled to remain seated but was too weak. Almighty God, please ease our burden! Mama suddenly realised her lack of preparation for the mighty pang her fragile body was currently experiencing.

Lola's grip tightened on the picture frame whilst her eyes remained focused on the couple smiling at her. Yes, Mama was right her mum was a beauty! Unable to explain the warmth that overcame her she smiled at the picture. She looked up only to frown at her grandma who was just relieved she was coming back to her old self. She realised her granddaughter was struggling to relinquish the anger she felt towards herself and everyone close to her for being a fool all these years. How could she have been so gullible not to have seen it? Culturally, anyone old enough to be your mother would be addressed as mummy. Her intense look at the photograph was beginning to worry Mama when she noticed the warmth gradually spreading all over her face. That's the meaning behind "it takes a whole community to raise a child".

'My daddy?' She asked pointing at the man in the photograph.

Mama nodded her head with a warm and affectionate smile.

She heaved heavily as she hugged the picture close to her chest and shut her eyes. Mama's frail heart constricted as she not only felt shut out but also utterly powerless. Her helplessness peaked when more tears rolled down her cheeks despite her eyes being shut. Suddenly, she rushed to the other room and locked herself in the little closet she'd made for herself and her fairy friends. At least they don't lie to her! Mama was too weak to chase after her.

Lola recollected waking up and jumping out of the bed she shared with Mama in the middle of the night. She was still wondering how she got there when her curiosity was aroused by the voice of a man coming from the living room, she jumped out of bed to find out but was surprised to meet Mama at the entrance. Quickly, she went on her knees to greet her whilst the older woman started praising her ancestral lineage again and carried on until her voice began to shake with emotion whilst Lola responded by whimpering.

Mama suddenly stalled leaving the man to fill in until she joined him to continue the chorus shortly afterwards. Lola who has heard her lineage praises too often soon joined the chorus silently to the very end that was only meant for special occasion. She lifted her head up to check if his face was regular, but he seemed busy with something he was holding.

She was finally able to observe him closely when he stood next to Mama, she quickly looked away when their eyes met and he grinned at her. He had on a pair of brown designer slipper with the front opening exposing a set of recently cut toe nails, a light brown linen trouser and a stripy coloured short-sleeved shirt. She lifted her head to look further when her eyes hit the bull's eye! The dimple on his chin looked very familiar like the man holding her in the picture before she arrived in Nigeria. Lola now turned her head to fully look at him. Yes! This was the man holding her in the picture she'd shown Mama earlier and he didn't look anything like herself or Mama! How could he be her dad then? It was easier and safer to believe she had a dad when he was in the picture with mummy but not like this! He is nothing but a stranger to her! She'd just found out this morning that she'd been playing her grandma for mother and …

'Lolade!'

A light tap on her shoulder brought her back to reality.

'What's wrong? Why do you look dreadfully worried?'

Still on her knees, she wanted to reply her but was unable to speak.

'Please get up,' Mama stretched her hands towards her, helped her up and pulled her close to her side. 'Did you sleep well my beauty?' She asked in her pampering voice.

Lola nodded in reply, glad that was easy. The stranger now towered over them with his hands in his pockets, his eyes fully focused on her and still grinning.

Mama dragged her to the nearest dining chairs and gently sat her on her lap. 'Are you ready to tell me what's wrong?' After a few minutes of waiting she pushed a carrier bag towards her and implored her to look inside it. 'Here.'

Lola peeped inside the carrier bag to discover it was full of sweet. Her first reaction was to dig into the bag but she instantly withdrew her hands to her sides when she looked up to find four anxious eyeballs fully focused on her.

'Go on and dig deep.'

She protested by shaking her head negatively.

'They were brought especially for you all the way from Birmingham in England.' Mama explained and waited for her reaction. With no response she moved closer to her ears and whispered. 'Come on let's show some appreciation.'

The desperate plea in her voice pushed Lola to try harder as she looked at the bag for a while before finally taking the bag with a smile. With the contents emptied on the dining table for all to see, she decided to look at the man facing her with his hands in his pockets and still grinning.

She was still looking at him when she heard Mama's heavy sigh of frustration after exchanging look with the man. The stranger took one giant step forward, opened one of the sweets and offered it to Mama who accepted it with thanks and asked to be excused shortly afterwards. Lola suspected she was going to spit the sweet out and smiled to herself.

The stranger knelt in front of her with his palms filled with sweets wide opened towards her. Still ignoring him, he poured the sweets back onto the table and turned it into a game by clenching sweets in one hand and asking her to guess which hand was empty. Their eyes met and he smiled but she retreated back to the sweets before crossing her arms over her chest. Desperate for new invention he unwrapped one sweet with his mouth, and pretended to savour every moment despite his dislike for sweets and delicacies. His comical act intensified when he noticed her tension and grimness melting away. In his frantic effort to amuse her he choked on the sweet and was rushing into the bathroom when she burst into continuous laughter thinking he was still entertaining her, until he returned with Mama closely behind.

Whilst Mama and the stranger were busy whispering she reached for her portrait with her parents, and kept looking at it fondly.

'You are beginning to look like her.'

Her first reaction was a frown. 'You mean like my-?' She stopped to look back at the picture.

The stranger closed the gap before taking a similar picture without a frame out of his pocket. The surprise on her face amused him immensely. 'Who is this?' He asked pointing to her as a baby.

She surprised them both by stomping off to the man and snatching the picture off him. 'That's my mummy!' She replied jealously and placed them side by side on the window closest to her. 'Mama says don't touch my mummy's picture.' She scolded and returned to her original position only for the stranger to bring out another picture of the three of them which the two females had never seen before.

In it the stranger knelt down with Lola comfortably sitting on his shoulders whilst holding onto her wrists, right beside them was her mummy's smiling face levelled with hers. The most appealing was the big framed sunshade Lola had on her face and the way she beamed at the camera. 'Who's this beautiful baby?' He interrupted her thought.

'Me!' She cheered loudly raising her hand like in the classroom.

The two adult laughed before they both echoed; 'Good girl.'

'Clap for yourself,' the stranger said.

Reluctantly she did but only after looking at Mama for approval. 'Lola show him how brilliant you are.'

'That's mummy and that's daddy.'

'You are the most brilliant girl I've ever met … well apart from your mother of course.' He dipped his hands into his pocket and sprayed multiples of ten and twenty pound notes on her forehead.

She took all the money to Mama who asked her to say thank you.

'I have one question for you and if you get it right I will surprise you with the biggest, best and most expensive present on earth.' The stranger gestured the huge size by spreading his hands out far and wide. 'What present do you want, Lola?'

'I want a big, nice singing doll with long hair and lots of clothes with shoes.' She replied shyly.

He gave a big sigh of relief before he spoke. 'Okay let's shake on it.' He stretched out his hand for her to slip her little one into it before wrapping it up with utter joy and delight! His first contact with his daughter in nearly six years! Still holding onto her hand he asked; 'Who am I?' Afraid of being rejected he held his breath in dreadful anticipation.

Lola thought of nothing but the toys she'd been promised even though she doubted toys of that size really existed. 'You are daddy!'

Another sigh of relief but he wanted more. 'Your daddy?' He asked as he switched his index finger from himself to her.

She nodded cautiously before she spoke. 'Yes!' Then she nodded with her eyes focused on their interlocked hands.

Elated and feeling like his favourite football club had just scored a decisive goal he seated her onto his shoulders and started to circumbulate with her till they were both dizzy.

For some minutes Lola forgot about shyness and hostility towards the stranger, neither was she bothered when Mama left the room and returned shortly with a big bag.

He carefully set her down by the bag and asked her to open it herself.

Lola opened the bag and screamed joyfully when she saw dolls of different sizes – white and brown in colour but all with long and glossy hair. As her eyes twinkled with exhilaration and delight she was instantly drawn to the biggest doll of all which was coincidentally brown like her skin colour. Daddy knelt beside her and helped her sort the toys out, she looked back at him adoringly and returned his smile for the first time.

With so many toys from this stranger who called himself her dad all in one day, she began to wonder whether there was really any need for her apprehension especially with Mama solidly behind her. All her remaining walls of barrier shattered when three of the toys started singing and dancing.

'Which one do you like best?' He interrupted her thought.

Lola genuinely smiled at him for the first time, stroked the big brown doll's dark long hair with a toy comb and pointed at it.

'Me too.'

'What are you going to call it?'

Surprised and impressed with his question she amazingly glanced from one adult face to the other whilst they were enthralled by her swift bond to the doll.

'What's the dolly's name?'

'Shhh,' she gestured to him as she rocked and patted the doll before laying it on its back. She glanced from Mama to daddy and finally decided it wasn't a bad idea to have a dad after all. 'I'm going to call her Brownie.'

Bayo Anifolase resisted every urge to hold his daughter by standing at the door and watching her in bewilderment. Young, pretty, intelligent, and already growing into a spitting image of her mother. With a soft groan he realised coping with his wife's death was going to be tougher than he had originally thought. He already dreaded the day she was going to ask him about how her mother died. 'Do you like your toys then?' He asked to quickly change his thinking pattern.

She replied with a nod of her head before continuing to use Mama's scarf as a blanket for Brownie.

'Are you going to say thank you to daddy then?'

'Thank you.'

'Now go and say thank you properly,' she insisted firmly but gently.

Lola slowly took a few steps closer to her dad and shyly swayed from one side to the other with her thumb in her mouth.

'Doll's shoe is on the floor,'

He seized the opportunity to close the gaps between them by picking the doll's shoe by her feet and stretching it to her.

'Mama, her name is Brownie and not Doll.' She corrected before finally summoning the courage to close the gap and collect the shoe.

'Now say thank you to daddy properly.'

Still apprehensive and remaining rooted with her head bowed she timidly knelt in front of her daddy with a louder thank you.

'Good girl!' he reached out, picked her up and gave her a big hug. To calm her further, he gently put her down and stooped so his face could be levelled with hers. 'Oh my God who is a big girl? What has Mama been feeding you?' Judging by her subsequent responses and reaction he was finally relieved to know he was making progress.

'Tell dad what you like eating the best.'

Lola looked back at her with a wide smile across her face. 'I like rice, eba, bread, black-eyed beans, yam, and Dodo.'

'That's my girl!'

Having forgotten her recent acrimony she went for the sweet and could never remember any other time she ate that much sweets.

Bayo Anifolase had never missed a day in visiting his mother and daughter since they reunited six months ago by coming round for supper after work and leaving for his home after putting her to bed. He'd permanently taken over the task of helping her with her school assignments and reading her bedtime stories, and had been surprised at how much he looked forward to their daily meeting despite his initial reluctance and reservation.

To Lola, learning had never been more exciting! Being taught by her dad put her ahead of the class and her contemporaries, head above shoulders amongst her peers and an automatic exemption from getting smacked by the teachers for her exceptional abilities and best behaviour. Before, she was on top of the class but now she was one of the best students in the school. With everyone in her school commending her positive frame of mind and teasing her that everything now evolved around what her dad or Mama said, did or bought. Being young and innocent, her ability to adapt to her new circumstances not only felt so natural but placed her at a peculiarly fascinating stage of her life where it was no more herself and Mama but with daddy as well. This to her not only made her family complete, but perfect. She had inadvertently not only grown fond of her dad but always looked forward to his arrival every evening and would sometimes refuse to take her meal in his absence. She took this too far one fateful day when her dad was overly late beyond his usual half six by refusing to eat and take her Malaria medication she was just recuperating from. At exactly half six she remained transfixed to the living room window and got excited over any vehicle that passed by and crying afterwards for being disappointed. Mama was left to bear the brunt of her agitation for three hours before she became lethargic and eventually passed out. They both realised how strongly attached she was to her dad unlike when her love was solely showered at her alone. This unconsciously bothered her as she finally put her fragile body to bed after a doctor's visit..

She woke up the following morning to find herself comfortably tucked up in her bed and only remembered yesterday's incident when her legs wobbled and her stomach rumbled desperately for food. She suddenly trembled and clutched Brownie tighter when it crossed her mind that something terrible might have happened to him like her mother,

her nightmare was short lived when she heard his voice in the lounge and luckily it was a Saturday.

His excuse was that the delivery he was expecting from England arrived late and there were lots of people around to help him move into his new house. She didn't realise that hearing and understanding were entirely two different things until Mama later explained to her that she would be moving in with her father! Does that explain mama's mood lately? She could remember the question prick her little mind then, but was soon eroded by her own immediate concern of feeling a dagger pierce her young, innocent heart, a feeling that had not completely healed with time!

'Where would you be?' She asked Mama in a weepy voice after it was reiterated and further broken down to her.

'Here,' they both replied her simultaneously.

Then the tears started flowing uncontrollably.

The two adults stood still watching, each expecting the other to act first.

'You need to go to a better school which is nearer to your daddy's house. Then you won't have to see your classmates you don't like again.' Mama spoke first.

'What of my friends?' She began to blubber.

'That boy called Sunday won't have to worry you again.' Mama struggled to control her emotion.

'Yes, they would never have the opportunity to bully you anymore.' Daddy added desperately.

If Mama thought that would make her feel any better she was erroneous, in fact they were not only mistaken but flabbergasted by her response when she started rolling from one end of the floor to the other and screaming from the top of her voice. Her dad remained especially speechless and perplexed whilst watching her with his arms akimbo. She later on gathered his reaction was the realisation and resonance of whose temper his little angel had!

Mama who'd known her so well had learnt long time ago not to converse with her, but to sit back and watch her exhaust herself to sleep.

'You will be going to one of the best schools as your cousin, Sade, and your dad's house is within a close proximity to theirs.' As usual, when their eyes met she saw remorse in Lola's. 'Brownie would not be pleased and may be ill like you if you keep flinging her against the wall because you are angry.'

Her response was just as she expected! Lola immediately sat up to receive Brownie with her arms wide open.

Mama saw the perfect opportunity and grabbed it with both hands. 'Brownie wants you to clean your nose and wipe your face before you touch her.'

She instantly did as she was told by wiping her snort and her tears with the back of her hands which made it even worse. She stretched out her hands eagerly again for Brownie.

But Mama was not ready to hand it over just yet because of her own agenda.

'Daddy's house is nicer and bigger.' She sat next to her granddaughter who now had her hands covering her wet face in protest. 'You'll have your own room, big bed,' she gestured with her hands wide open and up in the sky. 'You can put your toys on your bed and sleep together.' Mama who noticed she was peeping through the gaps in her finger, changed to the persuasive tone she always adopted when telling her African tales and folklores. Not only did she sense her granddaughter's apprehension diffusing, but she was also beginning to listen attentively. 'Lolade, do you want a room to yourself or you want to share a room with daddy.'

She instantly looked up at Mama who would only call her name in full when she wanted her alliance or cooperation; it'd been part of their personal and secret sign language. She quickly grasped the hidden connotation that she already had her own bedroom but would rather sleep with Mama and compromise to sharing her bed. Imagining a bigger bedroom to what she had now was totally unacceptable and very frightening.

'Imagine all the dolls having a room to themselves!' Mama's voice became more persuasive. She realised she had hit the nail on the head when Lola took her hands completely off her face and was still trying to imagine it all when Mama catapulted her back into the dark ages. 'Dad can take you to look at the house now if you want.'

'Yes, if you want to,' he echoed in agreement from behind the door with his hands now in his pockets.

'No!' She protested with a loud scream that shocked them both.

Bayo asked his mother if he should excuse them but she asked him not to worry.

'But I want to be with you and daddy!' She protested.

'Yes, Lolade you can still be with both of us, you'll be with me at the weekends.'

'No! I want you to come with us, I don't want to go without you.' She expressed desperately between bawls.

'I know!'

'And I want to live with daddy too.'

'Daddy wants to live with you too and shrugging your shoulders or nodding your head will not help you or the situation.' Mama insisted firmly and loudly.

But her granddaughter shrugged her shoulders again which was no surprise to her again.

Annoyed, she exhaled loudly to calm her nerves. She was frustrated and equally delighted that her plan was going accordingly. 'Lolade, if you don't stop it, dad will come and take all the toys away. Do you want daddy to take all those toys away?' She hinted indirectly to her son that he should pretend to do so.

'No!'

'How about you spend some time with daddy first then you spend some time with me later?'

'No!' Her fierce reply made her young voice echo all around the room.

With her back facing her son, a conspiratorial smile curved her lips when Lola shook her head vigorously from side to side in disagreement. 'Lolade I want answers and not No.'

'What if I take you to school and daddy picks you up or vice versa?'

Lola became calmer whilst she assimilated her grandma's last statement that actually sounded really nice.

Mama started to panic as her silence dragged on. Pretending to be upset, she stood up and moved away from her granddaughter before speaking. 'Lola says come and take Brownie away; she has stopped answering all our questions.' Lola saw a conspiratorial smile across her face when she turned away from her dad and back to her.

She continued crying and shaking her head vigorously from side to side in disagreement. 'Okay Ma, I will go and get the bag to put it in.' He turned to leave for one of the rooms.

'No! I want to live with you, Brownie and daddy!' She replied tearfully as she clutched Brownie closer to her chest.

'Myself, you, Brownie and daddy under the same roof?' Mama pretended to be surprised.

'Yes!'

She smiled victoriously at Lola. 'That's absolutely impossible.' She turned to her son pretending to be gravely confounded.

'Yes, I want Mama and daddy!'

My mummy and daddy! Not Mama and daddy. Bayo pondered over his daughter's last statement with mixed feeling and came to a decision swiftly. 'Yes it is possible; you will live with me, mama and Brownie.' He opened his arms to embrace his daughter who ran to him without hesitation.

Mama gave her son a prompt look as if he had lost his senses despite her inner delight. Right now she wanted this more than anything else.

Still embracing his daughter, he replied his mother with the same stern look before he spoke. 'We'll all just try harder to make it work for Lola's sake.' Deep down he wondered how the new arrangement would work. How on earth could I possibly live under the same roof with my mother at this stage of my life? It then dawned on him that he had gravely underestimated his daughter and had bitten more than he could chew.

'Yeaaaaah' Her young voice vibrated jubilantly across the flat as she sprang out of her daddy's grasp, gave Mama a big hug, then back to her father and ran outside singing one of her favourite cartoon's theme tune. She quickly ran back inside and stood for a while to get their attention. 'I will be calling you Ma'mi again from now on.'

The two adults exchange looks before switching to her.

'I like it better than Mama.' She shrugged her shoulders to convey that she'd made her mind up already.

The two adults looked at each other with Bayo exasperating, his expression still impassive, but was deep down afraid of letting his daughter down, but he immediately consoled himself that he owed his daughter much more. He concluded that if it made Lola so happy, to hell with his own uncertainty no matter what.

Mama was relieved that the whole episode was over with everyone getting what they wanted except for … maybe her son. She had done nothing but driven herself insane with worry since she heard her son was moving to his house. Delighted of course that he was making a progress with his life and was equally certain that Lola would be well taken care of despite her inhibitions about her happiness. But what was to become of her?

Her granddaughter was not only God sent, but perfectly timed and would have returned to England with Tolani, her mother if she hadn't suddenly died. But then again if Tolani was alive she wouldn't have been opportuned to care for Lola at the crucial time she was mourning and struggling to cope with her husband's death. Apart from keeping her company for over five years, she had absolutely enjoyed every bit of caring for the child that had kept her active, young, alive, excited and occupied. Her son was suddenly going to take all those away without a care of the devastation of his action. Anyway, she was neither going to accept it nor let him know how much it bothered and rattled her!

She marvelled herself for succeeding with her little plan and commended Lola as an understanding and a legitimate granddaughter which in essence made every participant a winner. Her only son might not be feeling as happy as the other two but with time everything would be in proper perspective. She proudly and confidently assured herself.

'At least you won't have to worry about paying my rent here anymore.' She reminded her son who had been reading the same page of the newspaper for over half an hour.

Shortly afterwards Lola happily ran inside to give the two adults a big bear hug and ran back out. A mummy and daddy in her life at the same time and under the same roof! She could now join her friends in talking about mums and dads, she'd never felt so complete and whole!

Despite feeling like a newly crowned princess on her first night in her daddy's new house she still begged Mama to sleep with her because of the overwhelming size of her room and her bed, even after he proudly informed her that the bed was specially made for her. She felt utterly out of place on her first week in her new school that it still sent shivers down her spine. The ambience spoke of nothing but excellence with the teachers all looking stern and professional in their over-ironed outfits. The school children were dropped off by drivers in their neat, extra crisp uniforms with English being the only official language allowed in the school compound unlike her old school where it was only encouraged and not enforced. Lola's lack of confidence in rising to the challenge pushed her to beg her dad for a transfer back to her old school and blame her grandma for her second language inadequacy. But Mama advised her that she had youth on her side and encouraged her to tap into her subliminal mind to regain what had been suppressed in her memory before she arrived in Lagos. With no other choice, she eventually began to settle and not only made academic progress but made friends, her parents were immensely pleased when she eventually crowned it by admitting to liking her class teacher and school better than the old ones.

She flipped to the next picture of herself posing with her parents all dressed in traditional outfits and smiling at the camera. As usual, her heart fluttered when she recollected her dad giving her the picture as a peace offering and particularly the ice-breaker of their reunion many years ago. He had started by strongly arguing that she wasn't the one in the picture and had gullibly fallen for his trick by hotly refuting his claim and eventually crying out of frustration. Her dad instantly backed down with apology and tried to console her by picking her up but ended up with a fierce kick in his sheen which made him scream and diabolically amused her. After they were both calm he offered it to her with a request of her promise to cherish it and she nodded her head eagerly.

The next one portrayed the deep love and harmony that transpired between her parents, a constant feeling of togetherness as her dad always described it. Judging by the picture Lola had no reason to doubt him, it was written all over their faces and deeply set in their eyes from the way they looked at each other. She seriously wished she could have half the love they both had for one another.

In the fourth picture, her parents held her on each side with her feet touching the ground and her baby walker right behind her. As always, looking at it brought smile to her face, warming through her heart as she simultaneously stroke through her mum's inscription of "Lolade's first giant step in the park" at the bottom of the picture. For the first time, she peeled off a bit of the transparent tape to feel her mum's handwriting and was still doting on it when she finally saw that beyond the beautiful picture was a contented, loving mother and wife who was prettier than her young daughter then despite their strong resemblance. It also clicked that her feet touching the ground not only signified her freedom of movement but also symbolised her own unique seal and bond with Land as another entity entirely. The back of the picture stated her mother's sheer delight on her daughter's fortitude and free spirit in the park and concluded on how she cried herself to sleep for leaving the park hours later. It made her wonder the kind of nightmare she put her mother through when her dad frankly stated that she was always miserable indoors as a kid and would sometimes cry for hours just to get her tiny feet outdoors. Sorry mum if I gave you too much grief!!!

As Lola wondered what always drew her to this particular picture she realised it always gave her insight about her mother's life in general and might ease the pain she'd never had the confidence to voice to any living soul including Mama.

Still deep in thought she flipped onto the next page of the album and realised she hadn't gone this far in ages. Whilst wondering if it was a good idea or not, her glance caught sight of the most important figure in her life. Her pose with her grandmother and her dad some days before she left Nigeria for England with everyone looking cheerful except her, which was understandable considering the circumstances she left Lagos. She quickly switched her mind off the controversial tragedy that made her migrate thousands of miles away from her comfort zone to Mama's constant advice that she should enjoy her youth and never be in haste to grow up. Here she was growing up alright and facing the challenges all by herself, which might have been different if her mother was alive. Would it really? She would love to believe so despite Mama's effort to convince her otherwise with another question. 'Why do you worry yourself with such things?'

The irritation in the older woman's voice still vividly baffled her.

Her first reaction was to apologise but her tongue refused to cooperate with her instinct.

'Which means you didn't believe me when I told you the last time that her reply would have been the same as your father?'

'No Ma, you once told me that my mother had gone to rest.'

Mama answered yes wearily.

'Was she tired of me or did I stress her too much?'

The older woman shook her head sideways repeatedly despite being uncertain of where the conversation was leading to.

'If she wasn't tired of me why did she bring me to you in the first place?'

'She brought you home to pay her last respect to your deceased grandfather because she loved you dearly and didn't want to leave you with a nanny and your dad was to join both of you some weeks later.'

'Where is she resting now?'

'I would love to believe she's in heaven.'

'Is she with God?'

'I don't know.'

'Is it a good thing to rest with God?'

Mama had already replied yes before regretting it.

'Why didn't she take me with her?'

'That would be terribly devastating; a tragedy moreover, you are younger than she was.'

'Why didn't you go since you were older?'

The older woman looked at her granddaughter with shock and horror before uttering God forbid in Yoruba and snapping her fingers over her head to rebuke the bad omen.

'Do you think your mother chose to leave you behind?'

'I don't think so but I terribly feel so Ma,' her voice began to shake as usual.

'I know you miss your mother terribly,' she paused to suppress choking herself with emotion. 'So do I and your daddy but as long as you remember, "Death conquers all!" '

Lola looked at her solemn expression and became more bamboozled.

Mama smiled to reassure her before moving her closer for a hug. 'My beauty, it was written that your mother would die when she did.'

Lola spontaneously moved away before speaking with a shaky voice. 'Written? By whom?'

'By Almighty God of course.'

'That's a wicked god.'

'No! Never you say that again!' Lola wasn't convinced by the swiftness and passion in her grandma's voice, but waving her index finger before her face indicated that she'd crossed the line.

When she spoke to continue her voice was calm and quiet. 'The sixth and last pillar of Faith is for every Muslim to believe in destiny be it good or bad. She remained inert knowing fully well that Mama would continue regardless. 'Allah the almighty created good and bad in the world and what makes everyone in this world unique is our experience in life. Death does not know the difference between a man and woman, rich and poor, nor old and young.'

'What of a mother and her baby?' Lola interrupted.

'No difference.'

'You mean death will kill mother and baby?'

She looked at her granddaughter's eyes; she saw fear and gratitude, fear of her mother's death and gratitude to be alive. She nodded her head in cordiality and continued. 'Yes death can kill mother and baby if it was destined.' Her voice was solemn and surreal for it had happened to a close member of her family.

'Then death is wicked.' She sobbed silently as the unimaginable was confirmed to her.

Mama not only realised that nothing she said could bring her mother back but was struggling to understand why her mother was dead. She must be obviously missing her than imagined. Their eyes met whilst hugging her and she caught a glimpse of Lola's face full of pain and sadness too intense for tears.

Mama's voice trembled as she spoke. 'My precious jewel, let us thank God that we are still alive.'

Surprised she was crying now as she did nearly two decades ago, but was more shocked of vividly recollecting one of the saddest phase in her life that she'd not only thought she'd forgotten but was now desperate to overcome. As she wiped the tears off, she decided to just learn to live with it and not expect too much!

CHAPTER 5

As any reasonable human being would expect, Roxanne relayed the astonishing news of the newly recruits to her fiancé, not long afterwards Billy requested for the salary breakdown figure which she had no choice but to grant. After all, he gave her the opportunity because he expected her to be impartial and she definitely intended to keep it that way regardless of Bob's warning. She'd rather be seen as Billy's spy and Roxanne's closest friend than Bob's friend because the two were honourable people who appreciated her loyalty and friendship. She was well aware of the numerous favours the company had done to her and was only obliged to repay kindness with something even better. The likes of Bob believed someone like her should either be working in the kitchen or cleaning the office or toilet. He'd often remarked that employers should treat people with accent as a disability, unfortunately for him April whose mum was a teacher with a strong Scottish accent challenged him and he quickly claimed he meant people with foreign accent.

A dramatic improvement in Billy's health after three months of uncertainty had coincided with the Company's and tax year end which every member of staff had always linked to bonus payout. A copy of the email sent to his brother expressing his deepest concern was copied to Lola. In it he openly admitted that his confidence in his directorial ability had been seriously diminished since he discovered that the millions of pounds in the Company's reserve had been halved. He fully understood that money would have to be spent on the newly purchased building to get it to a satisfied standard especially with the ever increasing cost of building materials but he could never understand the seventy percent rise in bad debt nor could he accept the unnecessary increase in the workforce. He probably wouldn't have complained i sales had equally increased in the same proportion and had incidentally informed his brother that this year's bonus payout would be rationed according to performance and not automatic. Billy spoiled the show when he requested she reported directly to him henceforth, and this to Lola was the beginning of her problem at work.

He started by asking Lola for an in-depth report or the salary breakdown for current and the past three years, and re-examined the expenses, commissions and over time paid out over the same period. With her loyalty on trial once again, her report showed a few changes with the most extraordinary being the B.D.U. which not only showed a staggering seventy percent increase but accounted for forty percent of the whole Company's operating cost and total sales figure for the year. She now went further by comparing the Sales Department target to their actual performance and confirmed that the sales department only met fifty percent of their target which was just twenty percent better than previous year considering the sales staff had been tripled. The ratio analysis of individual salary, commission and expenses to their sales accounted for up to nearly sixty percent of individual sales made.

Her report not only highlighted how expensive the B.D.U. was, but also stirred controversy and division between the Management with Billy and another director pushing for compulsory redundancy on the LIFO (last in first out) basis of staff employed and had threatened to hold back bonus if his request was not met. According to him bonus should only be an appreciation and incentive to hardworking and committed employees only. A handful of the board wanted bonuses held back till next year, whilst Bob and half of the board were not willing to compromise on anything but pay out the bonuses even if the reserve had to be used for it. Supporting Bob were Scott, Rex and Roy the Finance, Operational and Technical Directors all of whom she worked closely with and reported directly to. Billy who not only appreciated her report but commended her for it could not defend her from the claws of his brother and his cronies. His brother's argument was that the new team should be given ample time and opportunity. Lola on the other hand was worried about the implication of disappointing the hardworking and committed employees that had eagerly awaited the bonus with her worst fear being portrayed as the one who stood in their way of getting bonus. In fact, she'd overheard Roy, the Technical Director, and Bob explaining to some of the staffs that they would not be getting bonus this year because Lola, our Payroll Manager, thinks you've all been overpaid!

'Stuff it all!' As she got dressed, she exasperated at the realisation that Bob and his cronies would not even give her respite for her broken ankle. They probably thought she'd used her ankle as a cover-up to stretch her annual leave. As a silent and peaceful way to protest she decided to break the company's strict dress code and go for greyish black designer track suit top and bottom with a face cap and a black pair of trainers. She covered the visible spots and blisters with her special foundation and wished for once that the allergic rashes were still visibly fresh!

She was ready ten minutes ago, and had just looked at her wristwatch again when her door bell went. By her doorstep was one of her colleagues who'd come to pick her for the meeting in one of the Company's van. She initially refused to go anywhere with the driver because she'd never met him before and was glad when Romeo call to confirm his identity.

As they drove on, she wondered what was so important that her employment rights had to be violated and concluded that she stood no chance against them whatsoever but smiled nervously at all the negative odds against her. Conclusively, she agreed with being considered guilty and waited to be proven innocent! Bob's hatred for her had skyrocketed since her report singled him out as the biggest culprit in the expenses and overtime overpayment with half of his expenses been duplicated. In the first month, he would present the receipt and would present the credit card receipt for the same expenses three months later. Her review showed that Bob was overpaid by thirty thousand pounds in two years and closely behind him were his old cronies Rex and Roy with fifteen and ten thousand pounds overpayment respectively. She'd recently received request from C.S.A. (Child Support Agency) about his salary details with rumours that three women have applied for child support maintenance from him.

She couldn't pinpoint it, all her instincts warned her not to trust Bob, so far all his actions supported her suspicions all the way through. She could in her early months with the Company mysteriously remember smelling his creepy aura lurking around her in the thin air. She would eventually turn round only to find him in a corner pretending to be engaged in one thing or the other, but desperately waiting for their eyes to meet so he could smirk at her which she found absolutely repulsive. Lola had never believed in the strong accusations that he liked having flings with married women until she caught him in a compromising situation with Kim, one of the newly married Payroll Assistant, and witnessed the new bridegroom punching him in the staff car park three days later. She was beginning to feel cramps and strained with one of her legs when she saw the office in sight.

Her apprehension had skyrocketed by the time she walked through the revolving door aided by a stick she'd borrowed from her next door neighbour and a bandaged ankle. She was met by a skinny looking, microphone head man with an overbearing set of teeth that introduced himself as Romeo Redford and afterwards informed her that Bob wanted a meeting with her straight away.

'Okay.'

'I shall let him know you are on your way immediately.' He stated matter-of-factly.

'Can't I at least have a chance to prepare myself?'

'Sorry, you should have made extra time for that.'

'Like you would if you were in my shoes.'

'I can only apologise.'

'And I'm expected to say no problem because you are only following orders right?'

'Yes.'

She'd walked past him heading for Bob's office when he shouted after her that he was in the boardroom.

She turned round and flashed him a plastic smile when she levelled with him again and wished she'd never bothered to come! A cocktail of fear, panic and anger made her resent herself for honouring this meeting as she headed to the boardroom situated at the other end of the building.

The boardroom was one of the single largest rooms on the floor with two entrances on each side, making four doors altogether that could boast of all the latest gadgets and most sophisticated equipments any corporation could have. Her employer spent a lot of money on this face lift with the hope that it would be open for hire to the public in the near future. She was glad to make it to the first entrance with little or no pain, and was about to open the door when she heard another man's voice. She deliberately lingered to overhear what was being discussed but the only audible sound was their soft laughter which steadily got louder and deeper. She tapped lightly on the door when she got tired of leaning on the walking stick and was surprised at Bob's prompt reply asking her to enter. Exhaling deeply she limped in to find Roy, the Operations Director, straightening from his seat as they both looked in her direction.

Bob spread his hands across the comfortable leather chairs he sat on with his eyes stuck on her every step for any incoherencies in her movement. 'Please take a seat.'

As Lola sat stiffly on Roy's right hand side with her walking stick on the empty seat between them, he straightened up further from his seat whilst wiping tears off the corners of his eyes.

With all traces of laughter gone, Bob cleared his throat before he asked the unexpected. 'How many years experience of Payroll management do you have?'

If she was surprised at his question she didn't show it. 'Nearly two years here.'

'Any qualification?'

What do you think arse wipe? 'M.A. in Business Finance & Marketing'.

'We are all aware of that.' He interrupted curtly. ' mean in Payroll management.'

'May I ask why?'

The two men exchanged looks before Bob shrugged his shoulders.

'AAT NVQ in Payroll Administration.'

'How many mistakes would you say you've made since then?'

'Sorry.' Lola felt four pairs of blue eyes piercing through her skin deeper, but deliberately locked Bob's gaze to avoid further conspiracy.

Roy interrupted her. 'Do you make a habit of muddling up staff's wages?'

The seriousness in his voice made the room suddenly too hot as balls of sweat gathered and danced on her forehead. Muddling up wages would be the last thing she'll ever do! 'In what way?' She asked instead.

The two men looked at each other followed by a nod of Bob's head, after which Roy spread out a P45 in front of her. 'How do you explain this?'

She took the form in front of her to peruse it. 'Explain what?'

'Big Tom complained that you cocked up his P45.'

'He said you insulted his professionalism with this.' Roy added before snatching the P45 off her.

She was about to complain about Roy's attitude, but quickly changed her mind against it when she noticed it was exactly what they expected. Yes, a confrontational black girl that's rude, incompetent and really aggressive! Well she decided not to give them that satisfaction today.

Instead of a verbal reply, she stretched her upper body from her seat thereby elongating her neck to assert herself with her arms folded across her chest. If looks could kill, her detached haughty stare definitely would! Leaning back on her chair, she decided to thread carefully especially knowing she was outnumbered by two conniving, greedy directors who could be recording everything happening in the boardroom right now!

'He complained that the tax code was wrong, the taxes were all too high.'

She didn't say a word but her expression said it all. Who the hell is Big Tom?

Roy must have misunderstood her expression for an admission of defeat but then she didn't care. 'I'm sure you too can agree with me that you've made a big blunder. He was a high-flying and hard-working guy who felt betrayed by his employer. He says, It's bad enough when you deduct too much Tax and National Insurance contributions from our salary but to completely mock up his P45 belittles the image and reputation of this company especially its commitments to its employees.'

'And that's where I come in Layla.'

How can this imbecile still continue to mistake Lola for Layla!

With her arms still folded across her chest and staring ahead of the two men whilst she rocked her chair gently. "Remember the daughter of whom you are" Mama's constant catchphrase became the instant and perfect companion.

'Honestly Lola, I personally don't have faith in your ability as our payroll manager, and I'm not alone on this. I've got the names of those who share the same sentiments with me here.'

She was surprised that Roy didn't hand the list he waved in her face over. She stretched towards him to get a closer look at the piece of paper but was surprised he moved it further away from her. Baffled she glanced at Bob for some unknown reasons but caught him cheering Roy with a nod.

Suddenly, Roy became more critical as his voice got louder. 'I'd already complained to her about my rising taxes.'

With an idea of where the conversation might lead, her instinct told her to rise to the challenge now. 'And I already explained that you should phone or visit the Inland Revenue and ask them to calculate your salary for you.'

'That won't be necessary, I already asked the Inland Revenue for help on that.' Bob interrupted her. 'They are coming tomorrow.'

'Tomorrow?'

'Yes, at noon tomorrow.'

'And nobody thought it wise to inform me.'

'You just have.'

'But I'm on sick leave.'

'The more reason and need for more staff.'

'We already have two more staffs with payroll experience and knowledge. Did Roxanne and Kim know about this?'

'As you know Roxanne is busy nursing my sick brother and Kim is on holiday.'

'How convenient! But that didn't stop you from dragging me down here.'

His gaze dropped to the file in front of him. 'Well …'

As she expected, Roy chose a convenient time to interrupt. 'I told you I don't have the Company car anymore and you still refuse to change my tax code.'

Lola wanted to shout at him to stop whining, but she chose to compose her reply politely and explicitly. It was very imperative he understood the situation and realised that it was out of her hands! 'Sorry I can only go by the tax code from the Inland Revenue.' She scanned his sad face with his lazy, tired eyelids and quickly looked away. 'Have you phoned the I.R. and explained to them that your circumstances have changed?'

Whilst scratching his bushy beard he looked for assistance from Bob and was surprised to see him pretending to be taking note.

'Anyway, tomorrow is everyone's big chance to find out the truth about their payslips once and for all.'

'Indeed,' both men echoed victoriously.

She decided to ignore their comment and move to the next one. 'What was Big Tom's complaint exactly?'

He looked up from his desk and looked straight at Roy. 'Over to you.' He commanded.

His frown gave her so much satisfaction. 'Basically, what he said was that the P45 you gave him belonged to someone else.'

'Can I have a look at the P45?'

Roy exchanged another glance with his ally but soon realised he was on his own again. 'Must you?'

'Of course.'

'Bob has it.'

She saw the angry colour gradually creeping onto Bob's face before he reluctantly reached for the piece of paper.

'Thomas Jackson!' She called the name as she remembered why he was called Big Tom, under different circumstances she would have burst out laughing. He was just over five foot tall and had always dated big tall women. So, he was called Big Tom because of his taste in large women. 'Tom, the short Engineer, living in Wolverhampton ...- Did you say he complained?'

The men suddenly became tongue tied as they both starred fixedly at each other.

'I would love to know who the bearer of this P45 actually complained to.'

Bob tapped his pen on his desk whilst Roy continued scratching his beard but none of them was still brave enough to look at her in the eyes.

The two men realised that picking one of the best black employee in the Company was a big mistake; they'd picked the wrong one! They had hoped their choice would make her panic, but little did they know that he was one of her closest friend in the Company! 'I didn't think so because I vividly remember that his leaving salary was £30 Grand plus 10% commission right. He specifically requested for his P45 immediately after he left and I'd explained to him that he was better off getting it after that month's pay run to avoid too much tax. I also told him that his commissions would still be coming through in the next three months but he said he didn't mind that he was desperate.'

'Did you send him his P45?' The anxiety in Bob's voice gave more of his vulnerable position away.

'Yes!' What she didn't tell them was that he personally collected it from her at the car park.

'We are all aware that we cease paying commissions for sales staff four months after leaving the Company.'

'No after five months.' Roy corrected him angrily.

She didn't bother to argue but nodded her head instead.

Waving the P45 in their faces, she added. 'This was just a summary of all his subsequent commissions after the first P45 had been sent out.'

'He complained the tax and National Insurance was about a third of his total commission. Why is that?'

She decided to play hard balls and folded her arms across her chest again defiantly. 'I'm sorry I can't discuss someone else's pay details with you, especially without his expressed authority.' The silence that ensued was deafening except for her grin and giggles. For the first time her warm smile boosted her confidence.

'Why B.R.?' Roy pleaded softly.

'I would only explain this to you in general to enlighten and avoid such meeting in the future. It should be Basic Rate (B.R.) because that employee would supposedly be enjoying Tax allowance from the P45 with their new employer till the end of the tax year or whenever his or her circumstances changes. Not coding it B.R. meant duplication of Tax allowance which is an offence.'

'Expensive!' They both echoed simultaneously with relief.

'Yes, this could cost the employer a big fine.'

'Ouch!' Roy's droopy eyelids looked frighteningly glued together.

She suddenly felt the weight off her shoulders as the balance of power had now shifted to her side. 'Gentlemen, I put it to you both that Mr. Jackson did not complain about this matter …' She looked from one guilty face to the other. 'This P45 was taken- no stolen from my tray for one purpose only.' She waited for their defense, but they both remained meek. 'I'll leave you to judge yourselves on this.' Her conviction was unmistakable. 'I personally would never have handed this to anyone.' Her brown eyes stabbed strong accusation at the two greedy, manipulative conspirators.

The bitter regret and nervousness in Roy's voice was unmistakable. 'How do you mean?'

Bob on the other hand dragged a deep breath and expelled it slowly as he thumped his special pen in frustration, disappointment and disgrace.

'The top copy goes back to Inland Revenue whilst the rest belongs to the employee.'

With defeat plastered over both faces, her outrage evaporated but not without leaving a thick black cloud of despair on her mind as to where and when these controversies would end.

Luckily, she had been warned by her retired predecessor about some of her colleague's hostility towards higher taxes, especially these two. She confessed to her that the pair literarily bullied and blackmailed her to overlook a lot of things, but she didn't believe it until now.

'Have we got any more stolen P45 in or out of the closet?' She decided to confront them directly.

'No,' Roy swiftly replied whilst his ally continued toying with his pen.

'Does this meeting have anything to do with Louise your girlfriend's complaint about me not paying her over time last month?' Lola knew she'd touched a raw nerve because the lady in question only recently dumped him for a younger and junior member of staff.

'Of course not.' He interrupted her before swiftly pushing his chair back and dashing for the door. He opened the door before thanking them both for their time and concocting an excuse that he was expected in another meeting immediately.

Whilst she sat still waiting for Bob's instruction, her heart and soul were dancing and rejoicing for this victory but she knew more was yet to come. Meanwhile, Bob's gaze danced mischievously across the room except in her direction, suddenly their eyes met and she saw a determined hostility and revenge. Then she realised that she'd won this hurdle only and vowed never to forget that one woman's victory was two men's defeat. Whilst watching him, he frowned in deep thought whilst simultaneously thumping his designer pen with increasing loudness. He turned sharply when he realised he wasn't alone only to find her gaze fixated on him, ready and eager.

As his eyes thinned, she could have sworn they were not only angry but were as cold as ice, without lifting his head he thumped the pen monotonously and spoke. 'You can go now.'

She could feel his eyes burning the back of her neck as she walked towards the door; she reached for the doorknob and turned round only to meet his cold, determined stare again. When their eyes met, she not only saw an emotional psychopath but the most petrifying, unpredictable boss ever imagined.

This lass is too bloody squeaky clean and smart for her own good, luckily for him plan B has already taken effect; he would love to see how she would escape his well-orchestrated plan.

With his mind miles away she stood still watching a cynical and gratifying smile cross his ugly lips in gladness that his puzzle was all finally coming together. It would make her indebted to him eternally. And it's all in an effort to prevent the bubbles bursting!

CHAPTER 6

It was Friday evening, Lola's two closest colleagues and friends had brought the girls night out to her, she had just come out of her kitchen with their drinks, some homemade chicken and pastries into the living room. They were all going to watch a movie right after the quiz programme on the T.V.

'How was the gym today?' She asked her guests as they settled on each of her sides.

'It wasn't much fun today.'

She looked at them before she frowned. 'Just say it was simply because you missed me.'

'The whole place is being refurbished.' Roxanne scanned her bandaged foot and sipped her drink before she continued. 'They are planning to separate the men from the women.'

'I see.'

'Did I not tell you she would be pleased by the news?'

'Oh shame.' Lola pretended to sound disappointed but her mocking expression gave her away again.

'Which means you might not have met Akin in the same gym if the policy had been enforced before now.'

'Agreed, but it was only one of the many places we met. '

'Some of the members have already left.'

'Only the perverts who missed seeing women's boobs jiggle and joggle.'

'And many more still would especially with their prices going up too.' April who had been busy stuffing her mouth with the snack called "chin-chin" finally spoke. She scooped another mouthful with two missing her mouth and looked around to find the other two ladies laughing at her. 'It's so soft and yet crunchy; like a tiny form of shortbread.' She remarked after laughing at herself.

'Yes and without all the fat of shortbread.'

'You have to give me this recipe,' she reached for another handful.

'Again!'

'Yeah, I admit loosing it again.'

'Lola the solution is simple, don't give her anymore.'

'The truth is my family liked it and I'm scared of getting it wrong.'

'You will never have the opportunity to get it right if you keep loosing the recipe.'

'No, it's Lola's fault.'

'In what way?' She looked from one guest to the other.

'For making it so tasty in the first place.'

'Roxanne, I can't believe you sided with her on this. You asked me to make it for you too remember?'

She moved closer to get some more but was surprised to find the plate empty. 'Of course I did and we all enjoyed it but I don't keep coming back for more and then loosing the recipe!'

'That's still not an excuse though.' Lola shuffled to the kitchen without waiting for them to reply and returned with a smaller dish with a transparent cover. 'I was saving the rest for Akin.'

'If only he deserved your …' Roxanne quickly covered her mouth with her palm.

'What now?' Lola asked with anger and irritation.

'Honestly nothing,' deliberately giggling to weaken her previous comment before she continued. 'I don't know, I just get this strange feeling about him.'

'Common that was a feeble excuse.' Lola's trembling voice made her realise something was amiss. 'Can't you keep your feeble excuses to yourself?' She eyed her guest insultingly.

She nervously ran her index finger around her cup rim. 'I'm sorry, I shouldn't have said it.'

But she knew Roxanne so well not to doubt her sincerity especially her very strong intuition. She suddenly witnessed some kind of silent communication between her guests. 'What the hell is going on?' She sat upright to ease her pain.

'You haven't told her about the boy then?' April half stated and asked at the same time whilst she watched her shake her head slowly from one side to the other.

Lola immediately edged forward from her seat. 'What boy?' Her tone of voice was dangerously heavy with acidic edge.

'April!'

'But she has a right to know.'

'With what boy?' She repeated and rose to face them squarely but instead moaned in agony when she felt a sharp pain her ankle.

'Sorry Lola I thought she'd told you the last time we saw them.'

Roxanne didn't look at the other women but rested her head on her palm.

'Last time you saw who?'

'The last time we saw them together we heard a boy call Akin dad.' April looked at her friend for some support but none was forthcoming.

'Are you two sure?'

The two women exchanged gazes before echoing a simultaneous 'Yes,' as firmly as they possibly could.

'What was the boy like?' She asked morosely.

'Like my colour, about five or six years old and good looking like most of us …'

'April!'

'Sorry, but if it's any help the boy's mum looked like a retard who'd just absconded from a rehabilitation centre.'

Lola measured their expression before relaxing her voice. 'I hope you too have got your facts really right.'

'Why wouldn't I?' April shrugged her shoulders before checking the pair's reaction. 'You both know me better than that.'

'Roxanne, have you seen her too?'

'Yes.'

'And?'

'Honestly, I think she's melted before or …'

'Melted?'

'Yes possibly had a mental breakdown or a druggie or …'

'I see.' Without another word she slumped back to her seat as her heart rate beat faster than usual. 'Any other surprises or addition?' Her totally deflated mood was sadly matched by her voice.

'Yes, we saw them again today.' April was interrupted by her mobile phone's bleep. 'Jamie asked me to confirm whether you are coming.' She continued after reading the text message. 'The football fund raising match.'

'Yes,' what time does it start?'

'Elevenish.' She quickly replied her son's text and placed it back on the coffee table beside her.

'Is Roxanne coming?'

'She's not sure yet, it's going to be fun with tens of activities to choose from.'

'On the conditions that you pick and drop me and I get to sit because of my ankle.'

'You've got yourself a deal.' The two women clapped their hands in the air jubilantly.

Hours later, Lola and her guests were busy watching a film on the movies channel but her mind was preoccupied with the information furnished to her earlier. Apart from the Pizza they ordered tasting like cardboards in her mouth she had to pretend to enjoy the film by mimicking her friends' reactions and responses until she was caught out by Roxanne just as the film ended.

'What would you advise her to do?'

'Advise who?'

'I could tell you weren't watching the film judging by the way you've been twisting your hair and rolling your eyes.'

Lola gasped and spread her arms in the air with defeat.

'Would you rather we didn't tell you?'

She pondered over the question for a while before shrugging her shoulders regrettably.

'We really meant no harm.' They gathered round her for a cuddle and all hugged for a while until April's phone rang again.

She only said okay before switching her phone off. 'Ladies, love you to leave you.' She got on her feet immediately. 'Trevor is waiting outside. We'll pick you up tomorrow at half eleven.' She pecked her friends on the cheeks and left.

Lola who wanted to be left alone but didn't want to offend her guests faked a yawn and pretended to feel drowsy.

'I think I should leave now.' She finally offered.

'Sorry I dozed off, it must be my medication.'

'Are you sure you don't mind me leaving?'

'Yes positive. Did you enjoy the movie though?'

Roxanne nodded her head before picking her car keys and handbag. She wished her a fun day tomorrow. 'I'll try but it's a shame you can't make it.'

'I know.'

They hugged before she left for the door. 'Call me when you get home.' She waited to hear her car engine roar before heaving a big sigh of relief and was still pondering over what to do about the news when sleep truly invaded her.

She woke up in the middle of the night still without any sign of Akin or his whereabouts and stayed awake for another while hoping he turned up. A slight improvement in her ankle made climbing the stairs a bit easier so she decided to go upstairs and enjoy her sleep. But getting to bed renewed her concern. Are all financial advisers this busy? What if the man her friends saw wasn't Akin? What if he was with his sick aunty? Only if he'd let her help with his aunty sometimes but he had repeatedly turned her offer down. She'd earlier checked his diary to confirm he would be working in Scotland for the next three weeks and had promised to be home at every five day's interval. She concluded that not hearing from him meant he was on his way home and it wasn't him they saw in Birmingham today.

She would have doubted him if he hadn't driven her down and introduced her to his colleagues in Glasgow office, most of his colleagues were nice except his line manager who was worse than Bob with his no personal phone calls policy. His argument was it saved the company's unnecessary resources that could be better used as bonus. But how could a company survive without land phones? She had barely finished with the question when she dozed off.

The first thing Lola did when she finally woke up was to call his numbers and his excuse was the so called surprise he'd been working on.

'How long is this going to go on for?' She'd questioned him impatiently.

'Not long, just a couple of more weeks.' He laughed to neutralise her anger.

She would have cancelled her outing if he promised to be home on time but the only assurance she got from him was his promise to see her later in the day.

Lola tucked the note of her whereabouts underneath the flower vase in the hall way for Akin if he ever returned home before her just before the door bell went. She wasn't surprised to find April behind the door, full of smiles and eagerly waiting. The two women burst into laughter after appraising each other's similar dressing.

April who was slightly taller and older was dressed in green denim jeans and a matching lighter green blouse with frills, whilst Lola was in a brown pair with a complimenting cream blouse adorned with bigger frills. 'Great minds do think alike.'

'Great minds don't often think alike.' Lola corrected smiling as she stepped outside to lock the door and follow her.

She was quiet during most of the journey with April and Trevor doing most of the talking having already gathered that Jamie had been dropped earlier to help with setting the activities up. Lola was not only surprised at the crowd but at the large number of activities that had already started in earnest. Trevor led them straight to the coordinator named Pam. She was a fat, baggy-eyed woman who didn't need to smile before her serious overbite gets noticed. After introduction, her fat, chubby hand enveloped Lola's out stretched hand with a warm affectionate smile as she informed her that she would need to be seated because of her bad ankle.

'Then come with me please,' Pam led the three of them away and stopped on the other side of the hall with many stalls already in place but right between two stalls with two large rectangular tables joined together on either side. Tables on one side were covered with a cream lace filled with porcelain, vases, beads, various crystals and fashion jewelleries from chains to bangles and earrings. She was about to have a closer look at a ring that caught her attention when Pam spoke.

'Most of the items have got no prices on so we expect you to use your discretion to sell them from as little as fifty pence to maybe five Pounds or more, depending on how fast they move.' She appraised Lola with her grey eyes and smiled genuinely.

'Have you got a spare money bag please?'

'I'll try and get one for you shortly.' Pam moved slightly to the other side and slapped her hand on the table. 'Items here have all been individually priced, but you can give a half price discount on the cheapest price if two or more items are bought.' She pulled out a high stool for Lola to sit on. 'Is that okay for you?'

She sat on it and nodded her head.

'Okay then, good luck.' She stopped halfway in front of the tables. 'I'll send one of our young volunteers to bring the money bag and stay with you in case you need anything.'

Lola thanked her and finally had a good look around her. On the other tables were dried flowers in bunches, fresh flowers and various household plants. She hoped there won't be too many crowds blocking the beautiful view ahead, two of which was the main road and the football pitch.

After an hour, Lola had just sold the last item on the plants and flowers stalls whilst the other stall was selling considerably well when people of all sorts and sizes swarmed past her ornaments table. Then she saw someone that looked like Akin and wanted to be sure when a scrawny woman with a veiny forehead was struggling with her naughty toddler who took one of the vases and immediately smashed it on the floor. The boy started crying immediately whilst his mother began to create a scene and insisted that her son should be consoled immediately before he had a fit.

'With what?' The panic in Lola's voice was unmistakable as she watched the little boy lick his snort with high expectation.

'With what?' A croaky smile escaped her skinny throat. 'My son is bleeding from an injury sustained in your stall and you want to know what to compensate us with!' She deliberately shouted to invite more people that were already gathering round them as the toddler and his mum voices clamoured her ears. The boy quietened down when the woman in the next stall offered him a pie, but his mum knocked it off after he'd eaten it to a few crumbs.

'Sorry an accident I'm sure he would like another one, won't you son?' The boy swiftly took screaming to another level. 'How many more do you want son?'

'What's the problem Mrs Foote?' Despite the authoritative tone behind the voice, Lola unlike the rest of the crowd didn't need to look around to find out whose voice it was. She was so certain of who that distinctive voice belonged to that she secretly vowed to pull her teeth out with pliers if she was wrong.

With every one paving the way Adam stopped right in front of her as they stared at each other in mutual silence for a while.

'Sorry Mr Salvador Sean hurt himself and he was bleeding.'

The veiny woman's voice cracked through the pair as Adam's eyes narrowed slightly with suspicion before he whispered at her. 'I asked you if there was anything else.'

Mrs Foote bit her lower lip apologetically before she replied. 'I'm sorry, I didn't realise he was hungry then.'

'How many pies do you want for Sean?' Adam was still whispering to the scrawny woman. 'Five, ten or more?' He walked over to the stall and gave the woman ten pounds. 'Let Mrs Foote have ten pounds worth of pies please.'

She looked around in embarrassment with tears in her eyes whilst waiting for the rest of her pies.

Adam leaned forward to Lola and asked her if Sean had pointed at any item in her stall, she shook her head and informed him that the broken flower vase was five pounds.

Mrs Foote flashed a nervous smile when she noticed the cordiality between her and Adam who now gestured her to choose whatever she wanted. Lola noticed the same hostility she first displayed but it immediately faded when she saw Adam's reassuring nudge. They both watched her pick and fill her big handbag with porcelain, beads sets, ornaments and crystals.

'Are you counting?' Adam asked whilst clearing the broken vase.

'Yes thirty pounds so far.'

She looked at them again and squeezed a little crystal ash tray into her already full bag. 'I'd better stop now. Thank you so much the pair of ya.' She stated in a proper brummie accent and a full smile that exposed big gaps of teeth on the sides of her mouth. Still smiling she turned to her son who had now diverted his attention to a lollipop and a pound coin he received from Adam.

He thrust forty pounds in Lola's hand. 'I'll come back for my change.' He winked at her.

She impulsively flinched and tried to withdraw her hand, but he still didn't let go for a while and was only able to respond with a nod of her head.

'You two will make a lovely couple.' Mrs Foote commented croakily before she was distracted by her son. 'Don't forget to invite me to the wedding the pair of ya.' She added seriously after unwrapping Sean's sweet.

Filled with awe Lola gawped at the woman and wondered if she passed those remarks to disguise her shameful behaviour or she wanted something else. Whilst she was busy admiring Adam and Sean getting on like house on a fire he looked back at her with an inquiring lift of one eyebrow and smiled at her. She immediately concluded that this man was single.

'I can see you two are busy.' Akin's voice popped out of nowhere to interrupt her rendezvous.

'What time did you get here?' She quickly asked to cover her shocking expression.

Instead of answering her question, he eyed her and looked around suspiciously. 'Not long ago but long enough to hear her foul remarks. He tapped his wrist watch as if someone's life depended on it. 'I'm here with some friends.'

She could have sworn that the two men locked gazes ominously. Akin looked cruelly contemptuous but it immediately disappeared when Adam concentrated fully on him with his arms akimbo.

'Are you manning the stall with him?' He sneered.

'No, he'd just come to my rescue. Why?' She gazed away to look at her stall instead and noticed most of her smaller items gone, Mrs Foote had made sure of that finally.

Lola saw his nose flared and began bracing herself for the storm to follow. 'I bet he sure did.' Akin eyed him despicably just before his attention was caught by a wooden horse. 'How much is that?'

'Fifteen pounds, can't say I know who will pay that much for such a thing though.' She whispered.

'Is it new?' He eyed her with disapproval for her comment.

'I suppose so, you are not thinking of …' She didn't need to complete her sentence when she saw the same excitement she'd seen too many times on his face. Moreover, anything to divert his attention was highly embraced. Her next question was why the sudden excitement but changed her mind so as not to spoil his momentum again.

'Can I have it please?'

Lola's mouth was wide open with shock as she wondered what other surprises he had for her but complaining in Adam's presence would only make things worse.

'You don't sell wrapping papers here do you?' He asked the woman in the stall beside her.

'About five stalls to the right.' An old woman delving through the rest of jewellery pile left in Lola's stall replied. By the time she looked around, Adam's frame was about to disappear from her sight with Mrs Foote and her son.

About thirty minutes later, Akin reappeared to spend another forty minutes or so with her whilst trying to explain what happened yesterday before he disappeared again with a promise to return shortly afterwards. An hour later she was tired and wanted to go home but decided against it.

After handing over her takings with the inventory list she was asked if her stall could be filled with books.

She checked her watch and her phone for any messages but was disappointed there was none. 'What kind of books?' She managed to ask with as much enthusiasm as possible.

'All sorts, you name it, the only thing they have in common is they are all old and cheap.'

'And you think people are going to buy them?'

'We've sold quite a lot on the other side, there are just too many books, a library nearby closed down and gave us many of their books for free.'

'I suppose it's worth a try.' They both smiled before she whistled and three young men quickly appeared with boxes full of books on wheels. She asked them to put the boxes on the table so she could assemble them. By a mere chance she stumbled across a crime fiction novel once given to her by a loved one and she began selecting her personal collection.

By the time Pam came around to ask how she was doing she had twenty novels set aside for herself and finally rounded her collection up to thirty at the end of the event. She paid Pam ten pounds and asked her to add her two pounds change towards the money raised.

There was a sense of relief from April and her family as she drove out of the school compound whilst her husband sat in the passenger seat for a change. Lola was busy looking around for Akin but eventually gave up and glanced at the young man who was fast asleep beside her. Jamie had earlier described today as the best excitement of his lifetime to her. With April engrossed in conversation with her husband, Lola felt empty and apprehensive about going home and wondered if Akin came back because he saw Adam as a threat or it was a sheer coincidence. She was sadly, more frustrated because whichever conclusion she reached led her to more questions than answers. Apart from being disappointed he did not introduce her to his so-called friends and wondered if he was ashamed of her or his friends, but she would have preferred not to speculate. It suddenly bothered her to have only recently met just one of his many cousins and one of his friends. She expelled a gulp of fresh air and decided it was time to express her disappointment at Akin for his selfishness and lack of consideration. In fact she wondered if he was worth all her effort and devotion after all.

'I'm glad it's over and done with.'

'Yes, me too.' April agreeing with her husband interrupted her thoughts. 'Did you enjoy yourself Lola?'

'Yes, did you two watch the football match?'

'We did better than that, we saw Jamie score the decisive goal.'

'And we will never hear the last of it.' April stole a glance at her son still fast asleep in the back seat.

'Good, at least he's proving to you two that your money has not been wasted on all those training sessions.'

'Did you see any member of staff?'

'No.'

'I saw three and met some old friends.'

'Remember I was stuck on the same stall all the time.'

'One of them was Mr James who asked after you and I told him where you were.'

'The same old security man working for us?'

'Yes, he introduced a boy of about Jamie's age to us as his God son.'

'Interesting.'

'You mean you never saw him.'

'Not even his shadow. Glad none of them saw me though.' Lola replied thoughtfully.

'Why?'

'Because they might start accusing me of lying about my bad ankle.'

'Absolute rubbish!' The couple echoed simultaneously.

'I'm sure that's why Bob asked you to attend a meeting last week.'

'And I'm sure he wasn't disappointed.'

'Did he really?' Trevor asked surprisingly.

'Yes, he got one of his assistants to harass me till I couldn't say no.'

'You shouldn't have attended.'

'I told her the same but she wouldn't listen.'

'You know what your problem is?' Trevor asked with his head turned towards her and didn't wait for her to reply before he continued. 'You are too conscientious.'

Lola couldn't agree with him more. But what Trevor chose to ignore or didn't realise was he as a British from Afro Caribbean descendant only needed to work twice as hard to prove himself and she would need to work five times harder to prove herself despite being born in England. She considered herself lucky for getting a skilled job in her relevant field despite her obtaining her first degree overseas. She thought of Nigerians and other Africans with professional qualifications beyond their first degree all stuck in a menial or semiskilled jobs that did not pertain to their expertise all in the name of surviving!

After applying for numerous jobs and no offers, she tried the agencies but they wanted two years working experience with no one willing to start her off. She desperately applied for a voluntary position with a scrap yard and finally got a call six weeks after she was initially refused to start immediately. Six months later, the Company proprietor referred her to his sister, Dawn, who offered her the position of a paid trainee accounts assistant and it felt good to be finally earning some money. She despite this, continued to apply for more suitable jobs with challenging roles but kept receiving rejection letters until she decided to take a payroll management course as she realised her post graduation course was nearly over. Shortly afterwards she was having accommodation problems and Dawn was planning to introduce her to Roxanne who wanted someone to occupy her house for three months whilst she was abroad. On the day they were meant to meet, Lola was approaching the bus stop when a man being chased by the police ran past her and quickly hid something underneath the bus stop seat. She was still waiting on the bus when she witnessed the man being led away by another officer. She quickly pointed the purse out to the police officer sniffing around her, she took her details for record purposes or so she thought until she received a thank you card from one Roxanne Green.

It was another week later when Dawn incidentally explained to her that Roxanne was mugged but was lucky to only have her purse back because of a police chase and an honest bystander. When Lola informed her that she was the honest bystander she quickly called Roxanne to explain it all. She later that day found the time to visit her and express her gratitude in person, by design of fate Dawn enquired about job vacancies on her behalf and was instantly told to apply in writing and mark it strictly for her attention. Lola explained that she'd responded to so many of their vacancies advertised but had never received a response, Roxanne assured her this would be different because of a newly created graduate trainee scheme for few ethnic minorities. Her exact words were "They wanted to send a clear message to the workforce and outsiders that A.B.C. & D. was an equal opportunity employer." Lola then suspected there was more to it than meet the eye but she now realised who and why- Bob and his underhand, evil tactics.

She was remarkably the first post graduate and the first black woman to work for the company, something she often prided herself in. Roxanne still remained one of her best friends and colleagues that had gone through a lot with her in those few years especially when they lived together.

Lola inadvertently wondered why April stopped the car but quickly noticed they were in front of her house when she had a proper look around. She stepped inside to find the note she left behind still in the same sealed envelope. She took the letter and examined it closely in case she missed a vital clue but the more she looked the more she realised Akin never entered her home whilst she was away. Their accidental meeting possibly explained his strange behaviour and why he was in a rush! The realisation paved way to more serious questions than ever before. If her meeting him earlier was an accident should he still react so rudely? Which means he either panicked because he was avoiding her or someone else?

As time went by, Lola realised she was getting more upset with no conclusive answer except to agree on what steps were needed to solve the problem and ensure it never happened again.

CHAPTER 7

On Adam's first visit to her house, he asked Roxanne what kind of gift to get Lola when she was seeing him off.

'She is besotted with flowers!' She replied with a tone he could never forget.

Anyone with the opportunity to visit her would notice it; with colourful flowers and plants in every centre piece of the house.

'Any particular preference?' He tried to hide his amusement and delight.

'All roses and lavender.' She bade him goodbye and shut the door afterwards.

Some days later, he went to his usual flower company to select on Roxanne's advice.

The heavy bang on the door forced Lola to her feet without giving her enough time to wrap her house coat around herself and was inadvertently reminded about her ankle by a sharp pain that instantly slowed her down. She opened the front door only to be met by an angry looking delivery man and was embraced by the smell of lavender. Without giving the delivery man the opportunity to speak she instantly stretched her hands to appreciate Akin's lovely gesture.

'I have an item for number five please.' The man threw her an indignant look that forced her to smile as she received the bundle of lavender roses. She tightened her house coat around her waist before signing the delivery note and was still in the hallway when she anxiously took the little slip to read the message, "Sorry the flowers are a bit late but it's better late than never!" Adam xxx.

Her first reaction was a mixture of disbelief and disappointment, her heart was shortly afterwards warmed by the next line of Adam's words, "Bravo said sorry too". She smiled as she went into the kitchen to place it in a vase.

Wondering how Akin would react if he found out about the source of the flowers, she decided to take her chance and place the other bouquet in the living room with the hope that he never remember to ask about it. As the smell of the flower gradually engulfed her entire house, a delightful smile and a heart warm thank you went out to Adam, he already knew the best way to make her smile!

After her brief encounter with Akin at the event, there was a feeling of consternation every time she remembered him with this morning being the worst because he had finally contacted her, very briefly though. She'd spent the past couple of days worrying about his behaviour but the feeling had now being replaced by anger and misery for missing him dearly. She was not only desperate to hear his explanation but would also like to explain all the events that had happened since his absence. As usual the line got disconnected and all her efforts to reach him on his three numbers were unsuccessful. This left a brewing anger in her guts as she began to wonder if she'd derived any joy whatsoever from their little conversation today. She had just finished reading a lovely text message from Akin apologising for his lack of consideration and a promise to make it up to her when she heard a startling knock on her door. With a beaming smile she opened the door and was surprised when she saw Adam standing face to face with her.

'How is your ankle?'

'Morning.'

'Sorry good morning. Now how is your ankle?'

'Getting better thanks.' She couldn't help smiling.

'You were advised to keep the bandage on.'

'I would have if you hadn't banged the door ferociously.'

He lifted his brows. 'I've got some magazines for you to while away your time with.' He handed the pile to her but never took his eyes off her for once. 'I've got some novels in the car if you prefer them.'

Despite being touched by his kind gesture she still wondered why. 'You wouldn't know my taste if I paid you.'

'Try me.'

'Okay bring your novels out first.'

'You are on.' He'd already headed for his car before he doubled back. 'What if you like them?'

'What if I don't?'

'Name your price.' He gestured by spreading out his hands that sky was the limit. 'Now what if you do like them?'

She paused and thought for a while before shrugging her shoulders in the end. And was still thinking of the right answer when he returned with six novels.

'You cheated! You've seen some other books by the same authors in my house.'

'No I swear to God that I didn't.' What he meant to say was he had help from Pam. 'Do you need help in getting them inside?'

'No,' she replied sharply and was later embarrassed by her reaction.

'Any way you go and put your feet up and I'll see you soon for my price.' Adam didn't wait for her to probe further before he made his way to his car.

She remained rooted on the same spot in trepidation until she heard him zoom off.

She had nearly finished cooking the fried rice she desperately craved for when she heard the doorbell.

Lola was quickly reminded about her ankle by a sharp pain that slowed her down. She opened the front door only to be met by Adam's grinning face and were both instantly lost for words but he recovered quickly.

'Hello, I thought you might fancy going out.'

'One, it's not summer. Secondly I've got a bad ankle, remember.'

'Summer is officially few weeks away. The weather is gorgeous, the sky is blue, the sun is shining and everyone is out enjoying it.'

'Fine, I have a bad ankle.'

'How about down the oval …?'

'No.'

'How about here then?' He indicated the shaded area created by the tree near her patio.

'Here?'

'Yes, why not? You still don't know me well enough to invite me inside, I perfectly understand.' He sat on a stone in the garden. 'As they say if Mohammed doesn't go to mountain …'

'Only the fools say that?' She looked at him and saw how relaxed he was despite their surroundings.

He perched himself with his legs crossed and plucked a leaf off the plant behind him to hide his discomfort.

She watched his resilience for a while before she spoke. 'I'll get us chairs.' She hurried off limping before turning around. 'Are you into exotic food?'

He smiled. 'I was born exotic.'

'So I take it you'll eat fried rice?'

'What a rhetorical question.' He tried kissing his teeth to amuse her but eventually succeeded after she was inside. 'I've been having fun with Bravo with that.' He continued when he heard her approaching and quickly met her halfway to collect the foldable stool and a garden bench she was dragging along.

'How's Bravo?' She shouted from the kitchen.

'Fine as at the last time I saw him.'

'That was not long ago right?'

Adam didn't answer immediately, as if unsure whether to answer or not. 'He's with my aunt.'

'I see.'

She returned with the pot of fried rice and two trays when they both felt a few drizzle of rain on her stool. She looked up at the sky with disbelief before casting a doubtful look at Adam's smiling face.

He suggested holding the pot but she refused because she hoped the drizzle to stop soon. 'I can smell more rain coming so we'd better get inside.'

His eyes danced mischievously followed by a victorious smile on his lips. 'How could you smell rain?' Without another word he folded the two stools and placed them back inside before following her to the dining room.

As expected he was taking note of the style and design of the room whilst she set the table. 'What would you like to drink?'

'What have you got?'

She opened the cupboard beside her, placed a bottle of water, Orange, Apple, Cranberry juice in front of him. 'Take your pick.' She smiled just before placing two glass cups on the table and sat facing him. .

He had his cutlery and watched her take the lid off the dish. 'I heard African women serve their men.'

'As you said, their men.'

'And go extra miles to satisfy their guests.'

'You were well informed.'

'How has the rashes been?'

'The cream did wonders by drying it all up within two days.'

'Can I see them?'

She looked at him to check his expression before stretching her right arm towards him.

His eyes glanced from the tip of her natural well-manicured fingernails then halfway to her elbow that was exposed. Unable to resist the urge, he touched the inside of her hand and felt her flesh against his hand. 'The blemishes are gone already.'

She stared up at him, and when he reciprocated, she saw the pleasant narrowing of his eyes. Whilst each wondered what the other was going to do they both remain trapped in a time bubble where nothing else but the two of them mattered. She withdrew her arm when she could no longer bear the ripple of his touch on her arm.

He frowned and resumed with his meal, and they completed their meals afterwards in total silence. His portion of rice was less than she expected but she believed it was compensated with three large pieces of grilled lamb followed by a glass of apple juice on ice.

'I haven't enjoyed any meal so much in a long time; you are going to one day win a man's heart through this.' He got on his feet and didn't notice the sadness his remark caused her.

Lola who was beginning to enjoy his company had almost begged him to stay a bit longer when the sky opened up. 'Through what?' She asked instead.

He reached for her jar of water and filled her glass with it. 'I was going by the African saying that the best way to a man's heart is through his stomach.'

'I see.' Suddenly she missed Akin when she realised that so much had happened in the past one week.

'I'm going to be here longer than expected if this rain doesn't stop.'

'Sorry, I didn't realise.'

'No I'm worried about you,' Adam saw sadness crossed her face and wondered whether it had anything to do with what he'd said. 'You are such a slow eater.'

She suspended the meat she was about to put in her mouth. 'And you are such a fast eater.'

Their eyes met and they burst into laughter simultaneously.

Some minutes later, disregarding the downpour he bade her goodbye and headed for the door. Lola stood by the dinning room entrance and watched him close the door behind him without another word.

Days later, Adam had just arrived from a successful business trip a day before and had been fighting this irresistible urge to see Lola again especially after her name slipped out of his conversation with Dr Mason. He'd tried speaking to her since yesterday but her phone was switched off and it was just dawning on him that he wouldn't rest until he saw her. Their last meeting had ended shabbily, but he'd rather have it so and even get soaked than making a fool of himself. It was the best way to resist further temptation after touching her arm. He commended himself for not buying her any gift whilst on trip despite the strong temptation, especially when he was buying for his family. His arguments were mainly because he wasn't sure of what to get her and secondly he was afraid she might throw it back at him.

Dr Mason had informed him that she had come back for a second sick leave extension. 'Isn't she a delightful young lady?' He had concluded to test his reaction.

Adam only studied him carefully before he nodded his head and would have probed further if there hadn't been an interruption.

He looked at his watch to confirm he'd parked his Jaguar in front of her house twenty minutes ago in his desperate attempt to enquire about her ankle or anything else that came to his mind. He could come up with a request that he wanted more of her fried rice, he wondered why he enjoyed the rice so much; was it because she cooked it or the ambience or was it Lola herself or a bit of everything he'd mentioned. His conscience had been prickling him since Dr Mason mentioned her name coupled with the six days gap in their last meeting. He felt he owed it to her till she was free to move out and about and had been trying to drop a few notes but the appropriate words evaded him. He tore another page off his note pad and squeezed it up for the umpteenth time before he finally decided to write nothing and park it all in when he remembered the flower.

He was in the restaurant with his mum when a man walked in with a bucket of her favourite red roses flowers, his mind uncannily implored him to buy for Lola too as he imagined the contrast of the red rose on her jet black hair. He was imagining her reaction at such a bizarre thought and had bought a handful when it crossed his mind that she might dislike it or react to it like she did with dogs. To play it safe, he went to the nearest shop, bought the exact replica he once saw in her house and mixed the red roses with it.

He had already knocked on the door when it crossed his mind that her partner might not be too pleased about it. But then again, it was too late to change his mind because she was already at the door with a radiant smile. She was more than delighted when he presented her the bouquets by burying her face in it without inviting him in as her tiny frame guarded the door entrance. 'These are so lovely. You shouldn't have bothered.'

Adam was more than relieved that she appreciated his nice gesture. He ordered a combination of the withering lavender rose he saw in her hallway but the lady chose to be creative with his order. 'I decided to do the honours myself.'

'This smells so strong and fresh!'

'Lola! Who is it?' Akin joined them in one quick stride. Without giving her the opportunity to reply he forced his way through to the entrance. 'You again!' Not taking his eyes off him he asked. 'Did he bring those flowers?'

'Yes ...'

He eyed him abhorrently from head to toe before yanking the bouquet off her hands and dumping them on Adam's chest. 'Take your flowers and stick it where sun doesn't shine.' Without giving him the opportunity to speak he walked up to him and tried turning him around but gave up after three unsuccessful attempts. 'Take note of this house and make sure you don't make the mistake of ever knocking on this door again.'

The anger in his voice was unmistakable but the rage on Adam's unambiguous face was quickly suppressed despite his obstinacy not to move an inch. Akin close the gap between them with their faces inches apart when he realised his threat achieved nothing.

Lola's heart froze in fear of the worst as the two men sparred and psyched each other up in what seemed to be the final showdown. She thought of standing between them but noticed they were too close, and wanted to pull them apart but became doubtful of who to pull first. Finally frustrated with her helplessness, she stomped up to them and pushed her face literarily between theirs. For once they both looked at her face surprisingly, but Adam pulled back slightly and decided to leave by saving himself and Lola further embarrassment.

'Take care of yourself Lola.' He had taken a few steps away. 'See you around.'

Akin seethed after him. *Olosi, Olori buruku!*

He instantly stopped on his track to turn and face him, his hardened jaw put the terror back on Lola's face. The anger brewing in him only began to subside when his eyes met her pleading ones and it was then he intentionally put his hands in his pocket as a precautionary measure.

Glad that the little *Yoruba language* he understood hasn't deserted him completely. *No, Akin you are the wretched and the ill-fated fellow!* He was still stuck to the root when Akin walked up to him with one pair of brown eyes desperately assessing and challenging the hazel pair. Adam remained calm regardless of his sharp reflex ready and waiting whilst Akin's oblong face expanded as his nose flared. His jealous and possessive nature had excessively clouded his logical thinking that he didn't expect his formidable counterpart to rise to his hasty and ludicrous challenge. He now had to deal with the consequence and not loose face either. So he continued psyching him up with bravado whilst equally trying to create an impressive diversion. *'Were!'* He shouted to his face and was surprised his opponent didn't flinch but only raised his right eyebrow to acknowledge his disappointment.

Many retaliatory names came to his mind but opening his mouth would definitely lead to other things and would definitely affect Lola. Yes _mad_ to be standing here but not the kind of madness you'll understand!

Lola's chest tightened fearfully as the tension between the pair escalated. Just when she thought Armageddon was here, Akin's fury started subsiding whilst his counterpart's eyes had been narrowed and darkened by anger. If there was a fight, she could easily predict how it would go judging by Adam's much taller, fitter and bigger frame.

With their faces just inches apart Adam suddenly remembered where he'd seen his face before. 'We shall see who will have the last laugh, you crook,' he whispered at him.

Akin's expression suddenly became clouded but he recovered very quickly. He was initially befuddled by his demeanour and was now disturbed by his threat, he eyed him scornfully before looking back at Lola to establish whether she heard him or not. He instead saw a woman close to death from shock and apprehension. He quickly turned back to his opponent, shook his head forlornly and kissed his teeth. '*Worthless teddy bear!*' Without giving him the opportunity to reply he went inside.

Adam watched him till he was in and only turned to face Lola when he heard her release a gulp of air that had piled up inside her. She followed closely, only stood by the entrance to stare at him silently, with their gazes locked he saw her fears and weaknesses evaporate whilst his eyes seemed to be carved of granite. Without taking her eyes off his mean, hard muscular face she stepped inside and shut the door gently behind her. Remaining transfixed he kept studying the blue door that never meant anything to him until recently and was crushing the flower when he heard their voices arguing followed by some glass object crashing. Resisting the urge to investigate, he turned and headed for the front gate when he sadly realised that he only needed to think of his aunt and paradoxically remember Lola and her blue magical door. Wishing Bravo was with him, a sadistic smile crossed his face as he imagined what would have happened if he heard Akin kiss his teeth. He took one last look at the door to try and imagine Bravo's excitement whenever they passed by Lola's house.

Akin was still going completely berserk after the door was shut and could never understand why she was so drawn to flowers, but felt like killing all flowers on earth. She wasn't surprised to see his nose flaring up, nor his oblong face bloating and quadrupling in size; this were bizarrely connected with Akin's rage but was astonished when he smashed every bunch of flower and vases around him. She leaned on the door for support to wait for him to move out of the way and to recover from the shattering noises freezing her bones with fright and making her recoil. With the face like an angry sumo wrestler he locked her gaze as he calculatingly walked back to her shouting, ranting and calling her the filthiest names that were not only damaging her ear drums but also her self-worthiness. On getting no reaction, he closed the gap and tore up her blouse, exposing her lacy heart shaped bra that only covered her nipples. She was still trying to regain her strength quickly from the shock of his methodology than why and what he actually did when he gripped her upper arm and crushed her violently against his chest. She was still reeling in pain when he lowered his head to claim her mouth, eventually overpowering her numerous resistance with his strength, desires and anger. He lifted his head up when she resisted his kisses and progressed to her neck briefly before she felt his warm mouth on her exposed nipple. Soft moans of pleasure escaped his lips as a rush of sweet sensations danced all over her body to replace her earlier anxiety.

Never mind the circumstances, he was finally making a woman of her!

He raised his head to examine her reaction and wasn't too pleased with what he saw. 'I see, so you've been doing it with that teddy bear! We shall see!' Pushing her harder against the door, he went roughly for the second nipple and bit at it.

The sharpness of the pain brought tears to her eyes and quickly made her realise the difference between angry possessions and angry passion, but also prompted her to act and be strong. After several unsuccessful attempts to push him off gently she suffered more pain by eventually yanking him off her already sore and burning nipple with her remaining strength and willpower. Without looking she felt as if her nipple had been dismembered from her breast.

He looked at her with his eyes half opened and wanted to continue from where he stopped.

'No!'

'No?'

'Yes-No.'

He bowed his head to continue again but she resisted by pushing him away.

'What's the matter? Are you frigid or you prefer teddy bear to me or what?'

She'd successfully pulled her torn blouse together and was waiting for the right opportunity to move when he grabbed her wrists and held them up to perch up her breasts so he could continue. His mouth was able to capture the other nipple, she waited for him to start enjoying himself when she swiftly broke off and clinched his jaw on both sides with her knuckles. He jerked his head up swiftly, tightened his grip on her wrists and thumped her chest with it before forcing her hands behind her.

He yanked her hair so her head could tilt backwards and watched her helplessness. He moved his face closer to hers before he spoke. 'I think I've been more than patient, don't you?'

Lola shook her head negatively and pleaded with her eyes.

'Do you take me for a fool?'

She hurt her neck as she shook her head again and moaned in pain.

She tried to plead but his mouth claimed hers aggressively whilst his tongue entwined hers, the more his tongue probed the more vile she felt, and every time she tried to resist he tightened his grip on her hair and sharpened her pain all over. With Lola beginning to feel sick he finally lifted his head only for her to see his red eyes filled with rage, passion and jealousy. With her hands still cupped behind her back, but less tight as he began to enjoy himself again with his head lowered but was more brutal and painful. Lola's paroxysmal fit increased and transformed her into a different human being whilst all her instincts pushed her to defend herself with any means necessary. Unable to explain how, she yanked her head away from his grasp and kicked him violently between his legs; making him instantly crouch and growl continuously in pain. As she shuffled past him to move away she wiped her lips with the back of her hand only to discover she was bleeding, then her furious eyes met his red painful pairs. Coincidentally, his growl began to recede as their gazes locked in total silence and repugnance. Still without a word she hobbled to the stairs, with her ankle tenderer than ever she tried to be as fast and far away from him as possible.

She looked in the mirror and saw no physical pain apart from the tears lurking in the corners of her eyes, but she realised her heart would need more fixing than the aching and burning nipple. The image reflecting back was her bare chest, her beautifully moulded breasts and her aching nipples still pulsating because of the excessive force she used to yank it away from him. This made her wonder how far he would have gone if she hadn't stopped him. As her anger and disappointment pinnacled she wondered what price she would need to pay for passion over desire and vice versa. She had not been in any serious relationship since her return to England despite numerous offers especially at work.

Just when she thought she knew Akin so well! She had never seen him behave so ruthlessly or condescending since she'd known him, but concluded that jealousy and insanity not only walked hand in hand but are siblings. As much as she shied away from the thought of ending the relationship it kept cropping up.

A similarly tragic fate in Lagos pushed her family to succumb to her desire to return to her place of birth. What gave men these rights? She noticed tears rolling down her cheeks as she stripped herself of the little clothing left on her. Knowing she couldn't stop it if she wanted to, began to run the bath with the hope of soothing some of the physical pain.

She slowly stepped into the bath tub and started trembling as one of her nasty memories she had successfully suppressed over the years finally erupted.

She had received her final year result and like most of her peers was delighted that it was all over for now and was looking forward to her National Youth Service, a compulsory scheme by the Nigerian government for all graduates under certain age to partake in a community project for the nation for one year. She had been posted to the Northern Part of Nigeria and was looking forward to the challenge ahead. With less than a week to leave Lagos for the North, it would be an understatement to describe the situation as hectic. Considering the uncertainty of the challenges ahead was not only dawning on her but also petrifying, and the fuss her family was making over it caused additional pressure.

Mama's response to dealing with the situation was equally baffling, but Lola understood that all underneath the shroud, she was as nervous about the journey as her, if not more. In nearly twenty years and despite the generation differences they had only been separated for a total of three months or less altogether, with the single longest period being Mama's two weeks hospitalisation after a car accident. She opted to be a day student whilst at the University to spend more time with her because she felt she owed it to the old woman.

She was for once glad and appreciative of Mama's zealous humanitarian gesture of helping her clear her wardrobe by giving most of her belongings out.

'I gave two pairs of your old shoes to the twins today; you know how much I love twins.'

Despite her inability to fully grasp why, she understood the full concept and it's positive impact on the numerous benefactors. She was particularly surprised as the number of children depending on her grandmother for meals or of young girls that came begging for money or other things constantly increased weekly. She could imagine them taking advantage of Mama because they knew she was going away. She took a deep breath to prevent herself from saying anything unpleasant. 'I know, you've told me this a million times.'

'Just to remind you in case you forgot. I already told them to come tomorrow afternoon.'

'Mama, there is no one in this neighbourhood that needs my clothes and the likely ones are either too big or too young to fit into them.' she protested.

'What about the other twins down the road?'

'I don't like them, they don't talk to me and you gave them my shoes already.'

Mama pulled a chicken feather from Lola's bedroom window and started picking her ear with it. 'That's the more reason.'

She watched her grandma enjoy herself as the feather tickled her ear. 'I know you are a natural when it comes to alms giving and I don't want to disobey you but it's embarrassing to approach strangers and volunteer my belongings to them.'

'Your fiancé would buy you an entirely new wardrobe.'

'That is six months away.'

'I still don't see why wedding arrangements should take up to six months and I'm surprised your father agreed to it.' She huffed.

'Because then I would have been twenty one years old and some people think twenty is such a young age to think of marriage.'

'Maybe they need to be reminded that this twenty year old is already a graduate, so marriage ultimately comes next.'

Lola ignored the pride in her voice. 'Dad thinks we should get to know each other more.'

'Listen my precious; you can only get to know more of each other after marriage.'

'I know my Yusuf already, Mama.'

Mama watched the doting expression on her face, clapped her hands in astonishment and was about to tease her when about a dozen young kids all under ten walked in for their regular weekly feast.

Lola felt the gladness in Mama's heart as she led the anxious kids into their kitchen with each of them taking their usual position on the floor mat forming a circle whilst one of them started dishing out plates and spoons. In as much as she often found her grandma too overbearing, overprotective and sometimes overzealous, the kids not only loved and enjoyed every minute of it but looked forward to it too. Both mothers and their kids could not thank her enough, a gratitude that was often extended personally to her by their parents.

Just then, there was a knock on the door and Lola fetched it. Standing before her was the newly married woman selling roasted plantains and peanuts three doors away carrying her toddler baby.

Lola who reckoned they would be about the same age returned her warm smile and was thinking of what to say when Mama came to the door.

'Here you are!' She said and stretched her hands out to the toddler who quickly jumped at it. 'Just for one hour you said?' Mama added as she tickled the toddler's chubby cheek.

'Yes Ma,' she replied almost on her knees with appreciation.

Lola excused the pair and went inside.

Later, she was busy admiring the bravery of one particular child that refused Mama's help in slicing her chicken wing but would rather battle it out herself when her best friend's cousin barged in to inform her that her attention was needed in their house. The ever trusting Lola didn't even think of asking what and why until her grandma asked her after bidding her goodbye.

'I don't know ma but I promise not to be long.'
She replied anxiously.

Mama asked further questions but was politely
told there was no time to explain. Still concerned,
she looked at her friend's cousin and was about to
ask her some questions when Lola gently pushed the
girl towards the door and assured her grandmother
once again that she wouldn't be long.

She grew up in the same neighbourhood with Bisi
but they only became good friends at the University
and got closer when she and her brother lost their
mother two years ago. The two women had become
inseparable lately and had been shopping together
for their trips daily for two weeks now. Lola believed
she had been summoned for one of their last minute
list comparisons again since she was leaving
tomorrow. She was teasing Lola this morning that
she would pay her a surprise visit soon, they both
laughed before they went their separate ways.
Luckily Bisi would be doing her national youth
service in the nearby Ogun State, a couple of hours
drive from Lagos.

She knew Bisi's senior brother worked outside
Lagos and hardly ever came home, but she
nonetheless wanted to be sure. 'Is Kunle at home?'
Lola asked as they covered the few yards separating
the two houses.

The young girl did not answer but shrugged her
shoulders as they walked on.

'Is she ill?'

'Yes, headache and stomach ache.'

'Now she tells me, common let's hurry.'

Lola was often jealous of the bond between Bisi and her brother despite the three years gap, growing up together was fun and loving because he was always around to protect her. The three of them went to the same university, but Kunle was in his final year when they were in their first year. It was then he first asked Lola out but she declined and he continued to pester her until his pressure eventually began taking its toll on their friendship but Bisi was blinded by brotherly love to see what the problem was. Finally, she fell out with Lola after discovering that Tunde, her brother's best friend that she fancied was only using her to gain Lola's interest.

At the University, Tunde was every girl's dream, good looking, descent, and suave with the only problem being Lola's unpreparedness for relationship. To everyone, the mystery was how the two men could be close friends for Kunle was condescending and unlucky in the looks department but his loud mouth and his prankish nature was Lola's biggest turn off!

It was during one of the two ladies frank discussion that Mama overheard them arguing and she intervened as far as imploring Kunle's parents to warn their son to let her granddaughter be. The situation became a bitter sweet pill sensation when Bisi informed all their friends at the University who then began teasing and calling her Granny's wrapper or Virgin Mary. With many of her friends consequently abandoning her, life in general and studying became a living nightmare and would have spiralled out of control if she wasn't already a day student. Her inability to understand why she was victimised for being virtuous absolutely escaped her imagination especially for Kunle whose nickname was the pranking freak. The biggest relief was when the pressure began rubbing on Bisi and everybody knows Misery loves Company!

She should have been suspicious when Bisi's cousin did not proceed to the bedroom with her despite the door been wide open. With her only concern being to help her friend, and seeing her back crouched up on the bed she knocked once and didn't wait for an answer before she stepped in. She had just stepped inside when she felt a big and heavy blanket drop over her head, as she struggled to shake off the heavy material she heard movement from the bed followed by the door being shut with a loud bang. She was still struggling to remove the blanket when she heard Kunle's voice.

'I told you you'd come to me yourself.'

Apart from freezing for hearing his voice she vividly remembered his last statement to her. She was out celebrating with friends after their final paper at the University when Kunle walked up to her. "It's a bigger world out there and I'll be waiting for you to come to me yourself." Every one burst into laughter including herself because it was considered a joke until now.

'Who is laughing now?' He barked angrily at her.

Her first attempt to remove the blanket moved it up for her to see him through a lesser thick part but her second try got her fingers clammy and sticky at everywhere she touched. Shivering with fear she wished she'd listened to Mama's caution and stayed at home. Unable to separate her fingers she clenched her hands to form a fist and pushed harder at the blankets but it also bonded instantly. She'd suspected him using some kind of homemade glues with horrendous smell. The shivering escalated when she thought of the worst scenario but was suddenly strengthened by the realisation that her legs were still free. At first, she sobbed silently at her frustration but became frightened and tried hiding her emotions when she heard him chuckle at her despair. Whilst preserving her energy for the perfect opportunity she was ironically glad he could not see how scared she was.

She coughed for a while before speaking. 'The toxic is affecting my lungs.' She thanked God for the transparent part that let a bit of fresh air in.

'I asked you out on a date, you not only threw it back on my face but you got my dad involved and that was not funny. Tell me who at this day and age tells their parents when being asked out on a date?'

Lola's determination not to respond didn't last half as long she expected. 'Have you been drinking?'

Instead of answering, he belched out loudly. 'Dad gave me two choices, stay in Lagos and forget about the car and the flat he promised me or get a transfer to Ife till the dust settled on my little fiasco.' She saw him reach for a green bottle and gulped some of the contents down before another loud belch. 'I wanted to stay in Lagos and I wanted the car and the flat.'

'Is that why you kidnapped me?'

Another bottle dropped on the floor with some shattering noise. 'Kidnap? You came to me.'

She heard him get up and approach her, with the smell of alcohol becoming undoubtedly stronger. He stopped right in front of her, undid his zip, dipped his hand inside his trouser and started stroking himself. Lola watched him rise and swell, a part of her wanted to run but she couldn't, whilst the other half became amazingly curious. She had witnessed a woman delivering a baby but never seen a man swell.

'I heard you are still a virgin, engaged to Yusuf. What does he have that I haven't?'

At first she thought he fidgeted because he was drunk and unsteady then his breathing became erratic. He closed the gap between them and rested his forehead on hers whilst still rubbing himself. She began to feel claustrophobic and squeamish because of the toxic emanating under the blanket and strong alcoholic smell from his breath. With little or no gap between them, his soft pleasurable moans got louder whilst she became more stiff and frightened. She pushed her way forward only to stagger backwards when he retaliated. Whilst he continued to massage himself terrified Lola desperately prayed she escape from this obscene situation unscathed. His closeness made her realise how tall he was and how difficult it was going to be for her to overpower him. When she finally felt his manhood hardening and rubbing against her lower body, she knew she had to act fast, so she waited for his pleasure to consume him more before she slowly tilted her head back and knocked it hard on his nose. This time he groaned with pain as he ran his hand through his nose and went berserk when he saw blood. Furiously, he punched her left jaw which sent her sprawling across the room. She began to scream as loud as she could.

In a frenzied anger he walked up to her as she lay helplessly on her back unable to get up and violently tugged the end of the blanket so hard that she felt her neck click. With no success, he used one of the broken bottles to rip the material apart and narrowly missed her thigh but nevertheless expose her lower half. She felt some of his blood drop on her and wondered what was coming next. 'There is no one around to hear or help you, so shut up!' His uneven voice warned her with his gritted teeth.

She decided to scream louder to avoid slipping into unconsciousness and to enrage him when she noticed the panic in his voice and when the strong toxic smell of the glue began making her light headed. He began to panic and tried to gag her mouth only to literarily get his finger bitten. Then he attempted to lie over her but ended up getting some powerful kicks, one of which narrowly missed his groin but went bonkers when he was kicked in the face for groping her exposed lower part of the body.

'I'm going to teach you a lesson you'd remember for the rest of your life.' He yelled above her screaming voice and dropped more blood on her. He got on his feet, ripped off more of the blanket and tied one of her legs to the nearest bed frame with it. As he towered over her enjoying his view, he gently kicked her other leg apart followed by a gulp of more alcohol and a big smile on his face.

Lola had calmed her fit of temper to rest her throat and aching bones, she thought it wiser to save her energy for later.

He tried to take his trousers off but staggered and fell on the broken bottle. 'Yee!' He yelled out painfully before he finally succeeded in stripping naked from waist down.

Lola's body throbbed in panic when he towered over her with another full erection. She was howling and equally jerking her leg at the bed frame helplessly. She felt a nudge then he whispered. 'Shhh! I will be very gentle, I promise.'

She was still in a fit when she felt his big weight crash heavily on top of her with the impact violently crushing her head against the hard floor and killing her huge determination too.

With no knowledge that she was drowning in her blood, she wondered why she couldn't hear herself scream for help and why she could neither run nor feel any part of her body except for her head feeling like it had just split into two. All she could feel was this huge weight pinning her down and the desire to shift it off but couldn't command her body to respond accordingly. The combined toxic smell of the homemade glue, the blood she believed was from him and the alcohol coming from the man snoring on top of her made a perfect dosage of anesthetic to knock her out.

Dear Lord, I don't want to loose my virtue to any man this way. Help! Was her final plea before everything, including his loud snore, went blank.

Lola was sure the Lord heard her prayer but unsure of how. As she drifted further into unconsciousness and in total harmony with the unwanted weight above her, Mama's voice and the kids managed to save the day! But then again, she'd been unable to differentiate dream from reality just as her mind battled against her retiring body.

Apparently, her howling and scream got Bisi's cousin to seek for help and broke the news to Mama in the presence of all the kids surrounding her. The old woman immediately jumped up to her rescue and left the kids in Bisi's cousin's care, but she thought it best to bring the remaining children to the scene as a shield in case the situation got out of hand.

Mama was struggling to lift him on her own until the kids and Bisi's cousin arrived shortly afterwards to help her. The biggest shame was letting the kids witness the degrading state she was subjected to. Unfortunately kids could not be sworn to silence and it was only a matter of time before the news of the incident went round and got distorted as it went further.

She was hospitalised for some days because of her head injury and toxic inhalation, which the doctors said was all artificial. But the innocent kids who witnessed her demeaning situation were busy narrating what they saw with one of the youngest telling his mother he saw her wrestling with a naked man who won her with a very bloody pin fall.

As the news spread like wild fire so was the truth seriously distorted. Many people sympathised with her, but there was one person whose sympathy and understanding would have made her predicament less traumatising! Yusuf's mother – her future mother-in-law was of the same generation as Mama and could not understand why she visited a man that was not her relative unaccompanied, when already betrothed.

Everyone realised the sensitivity of the situation and had to tip toe around her, even after Bisi's cousin came forward to confess. Finally, Yusuf's mother who originally couldn't wait for Lola to marry her son asked for more time before eventually calling the engagement and wedding off some weeks later.

She only realised the water in the tub was going cold when she heard Akin's step coming up the stairs.

'Lola please open the door,' his desperate voice ricocheted sharply into her thought.

Wiping her tears for the first time since getting into the bath, she unplugged the bath before a final rinse.

'Are you okay?' His desperate voice induced her already peaked anxiety.

She couldn't answer even if she wanted to; her shaky voice was likely to betray her.

'I'm sorry if it reminded you of any bad memory …' He deliberately stopped hoping she would reply, but continued when he heard no reply. 'Please forgive me.'

She stared blankly at the door, desperately struggling to hold the tears from returning as she wondered if she could ever forget one of the saddest moments in her life.

With no reply from behind the door, he started twisting the doorknob. 'I'll break this door down if you don't speak to me,' with no answer forthcoming he began a countdown from five.

With anxiety replacing sadness she wondered what to do if he did succeed in breaking the door down but was still determined not to respond. She eventually concluded it was a gamble she would have to take, knowing how pretty solid the door was.

CHAPTER 8

It was over a week later when she finally saw Akin again, after their last encounter and his unsuccessful attempt to break the door down. He tidied up the mess before leaving her a note that he was going on a business trip and would return a week later which she knew would as usual roll onto one or two extra days. She made no attempt to reach him over his mobile phones because she had no clue about what to say or how to deal with their last encounter. Sorry would have been a good way to start but she felt no remorse for her action, Mama's saying of "if you can't forgive your loved ones then your enemies stand no chance" could be held responsible for her little reconciliatory thoughts. Above all, she wasn't prepared to let her past destroy her future considering the fact that she spent over two years to find a partner her family would consider suitable. She hoped Mama approved!

She was busy preparing her meal when she jumped as a result of being grabbed from behind, and he quickly apologised for making her spill water into the already served rice, fried plantain and stew. Akin immediately played down his mistake by stuffing a spoonful of watery, savoury rice into his mouth and gulped it down all at once. She was meanwhile more baffled at how she neither heard him open the door nor walk up to her. Sensing her aloof mood, he instantly spun her round, held her hands to prevent her fighting back, kissed her face and neck before he progressed to inhale the fresh fragrance from her hair. Lola at first was rigid because of their last meeting but quickly psyched her mind to be on the guard and was suddenly stuck halfway between responding and not. Half of her wanted to talk about it but the other half wanted to watch the new development before pouncing, so she decided to go for the latter.

Without releasing her, he looked straight into her eyes before he spoke. 'I'm really sorry about my behaviour the other night.' He hugged her tightly before she could reply and when he released her he placed his index finger across her lips to seal it for now.

'Come I've got something to show you.' Holding tightly onto her hand, he literarily dragged her towards the door. On opening the door he stepped aside for her to see the car closely parked to the entrance with a bright pink banner spread across the front screen stating clearly 'Lolade, will you please marry me?'

She was so ecstatic that she hugged him tightly and followed it with a passionate kiss. He returned her loving kiss as his mouth claimed hers before he finally lifted his head to breathe. For a slight second he wanted to change his plan and sincerely profess his undying love to her but he yet again changed his mind when he remembered the bet and gently guided her towards the car. As she trailed behind him wondering what was coming next she felt little butterflies in her stomach when she saw something sparkle from one of the wipers. On getting closer, she discovered it was an engagement ring. The most beautiful ring she'd ever seen because it was given to her by the love of her life and the price didn't matter! Exhilarated to her bones, she rushed back to his open arms for what she would describe as the longest and most passionate kiss of her life. They both lifted their heads up at the same time and gulped some fresh air down, after which he removed the ring from her palm and slipped it into her third finger.

Whilst she was busy admiring the ring and rejoicing about Akin's proposal, he was busy with incantations and final preparation to seal the *Magun* charm he'd just afflicted her with.

Little did she know that she'd just received her death sentence and had just become a walking dead woman!

Magun, which literarily means "don't climb or don't mount" is a deadly time bomb with a devastating calamity that had existed amongst the Yoruba culture for centuries long before the advent of forensics, DNA samples, Private Investigations, recording facilities or any technological advancement. Another modern name for it was Instant terminator or Sudden Immediate Death and could be in any shape or form with endless use and could be inflicted on anyone by anyone for whatever arbitrary reason.

This was one of the sacred powers of Yoruba ancestors with the most common one otherwise known as sexually assisted death in many forms.

Before death, the contractor might crow like a matured cock immediately after intercourse with the carrier, or somersault three times. Another common one is where the contractor would bleed to death, vomit, urinate, eat or drink water to death after intercourse.

The type of *Magun* afflicted on Lola through her engagement ring was otherwise known as Glue where the contractor and contractee became physically conjoined after intercourse till they both died slowly and painfully. With no stipulated incubation period, but only to mature and activate after sexual intercourse and remain conjoined to their last breath!

Generally, *Magun* was always mostly implanted on partners especially by husbands who'd suspected their wives of committing adultery.

He finally sealed it with the special handshake before releasing her hand just as he finished the incantations, cocked his head backward to examine the ring on her finger, and shook her hand to seal it again before kissing her lips lightly and escorting her back inside.

He presented two envelopes to her as they were about to enter the dining room, still in shock she accepted them nervously and began to open. He moved close to her and rested his head on her shoulder before imploring her to open both of them.

'Flight tickets to Nigeria!'

'Don't worry yourself about the date, they are open tickets as usual, it will give us enough time to plan properly.'

Unable to express her utmost appreciation in words, she screamed with delight before she turned around and clung to him, he returned the gesture by lifting her from the waist and twirling her all around. Shortly afterwards, he steadied her feet back on the ground as they both struggled to get their breath back.

'But I plan to go soon.' He saw the sadness on her face and rephrased his sentence. 'What I meant to say was I would be back for you.'

'You mean we would both travel home together?'

'Yes.'

She jumped at him again and screamed for joy once more. 'That would be the best thing to happen to me in a long time.' He supported her waist whilst she burrowed on his neck still recovering from the great news. 'Ooops!'

'What?'

'Who would be looking after your aunty then?'

'Her old carer is back.'

'Back from where?'

'I don't know, she was away for awhile for personal reasons and now she's back.' He shrugged his shoulders.

'But ...'

'Let's continue this over dinner.' He gestured as he gently turned her round to the dining table still clung to him.

Akin was unusually chatty during their meal but this time decided to call on one of his friends as a deliberate decoy to suppress his guilt and trepidation on whether his plan would work or not. He extended a piece of meat towards her whilst she reciprocated the gesture.

For the first time he doubted if she was actually unfaithful, his chest suddenly felt tighter on the realisation that *Magun* would always claim its price and that death was the ultimate for either one or both parties concerned. If Lola remained faithful the Magun would mature inside her and eventually kill her unless she broke the spell, but if she was unfaithful she and the cheating bastard would die slowly and painfully. He was told there was a big possibility that she might live and he'd rather she remained faithful and didn't have to die so he could have the power to remove the curse and be her hero, but the *Magun* with that particular certainty would take months to prepare and right now, time was his greatest enemy! A cynical smile crossed his lips as his mind cast back to Adam's unfortunate fate.

As she got up to tidy the plates and take them to the kitchen, he reached for her left hand to admire the engagement ring before twirling her around in her mini skirt. He smiled with gratitude for his effective plan before he gently pulled her to sit on his lap and rested her head on his chest.

'How was your trip?'

'Fine, but boring without you.'

'You never said where you went.'

'Wales.'

'Wales?' She questioned. 'I didn't know you had clients there.'

'I do now.' He shifted from his seat a bit and was glad she couldn't see his face. 'Yes it's a new lead.' He couldn't tell her he spent two days trying to track down a traditional herbalist that came highly recommended in fear that she might ask him some uncomfortable questions he was not ready to answer.

He decided to change the subject instead. 'Your hair smells different.'

Akin never ceased to surprise her, he could be gone for days or weeks but he always picked little things around her up fast. 'Yes my new moisturiser.'

'A different hair cream, smells like coconut.'

Impressed with his strong observation, she smiled before she corrected him. 'It is 100% coconut and came highly recommended.'

He buried his head into her hair to inhale the alluring smell. 'Is it more expensive?'

She nodded in reply.

His eyes travelled to her erect nipples which hardened his manhood by merely looking at them.

She felt the nudge, laughed at him and tried to shift to one side of his lap but he responded quickly by gently pushing her back to the same spot. Despite his awareness that he couldn't have intercourse with her even if she wanted him to, he was still annoyed with himself for his lack of self-control. Lola was now contrarily indulging them both unlike in the past when she'd sometimes pleaded with him for more time. To disorientate him further, she placed his hands on her already hardened nipples and he began stroking them gently by finally succumbing to his desires. Prompted by soft moan escaping from her h lowered his head to nibble her right nipple and was increasingly encouraged by her response as he took the two erect nipples in turn. With his zip undone he gently guided her hand into his manhood, its warmth and hardness which not only ignited Lola's whole body but pushed her to beg for more.

It was at this point that he heard the awakening call that immediately shrank his manhood in size and rendered him temporarily impotent. Under a different circumstance, the shock and disappointmen on Lola's face would have sent him into fits of laughter but he was more preoccupied with his narrow escape from the claws of the looming death he was about to bring upon himself. Amazing how his indulgence in a desire of the flesh could have meant his ultimate death!

She cleared her throat of any misgiving and began dressing herself up. 'Are you alright?'

He couldn't answer but nodded his head instead.

'You are sweating profusely.' She eyed him suspiciously and continued. 'Are you sure you are okay?'

He noted the sweat dripping from his forehead, face and his back. He smiled weakly at her before he replied softly. 'I don't know.'

Without another word she watched him excuse himself into the toilet and heard him secure the lock on the door.

Meanwhile, Lola who was worried waited anxiously for his return but soon decided to ignore him when he started whistling as usual in the toilet. She eventually got up and went upstairs to the bathroom.

She came out feeling refreshed and had just finished getting dressed when he strolled in.

'Thank God! I thought I was going to have a heart attack back then.' He settled on the edge of the bed and gazed at her curvy bum.

She gawked at him before grabbing her towel and walking past him.

'That's not the kind of response to give your future husband considering what could have happened to me.'

She stood still and shrugged her shoulders nonchalantly. 'I almost had a heart attack from worrying over you until you began to whistle as usual.'

'I see.' He reached for her hand but she snatched it off him to answer her mobile phone that was ringing.

'Was that Adam?' He asked after she switched off the phone and finally got hold of her hand.

She replied him with a cold repulsive stare and allowed herself to be seated on his lap as he wanted.

'You haven't answered my question,' he insisted firmly with a gentle stroke on her arm. 'Have you seen Adam in the past few days?'

Her repulsive look was replaced by a deep frown.

He looked back at her and smiled weakly. 'You still haven't answered my question.'

She tried to get off his lap but he pulled her back. 'No it wasn't Adam and I haven't seen or heard from him in weeks!'

'Good,' He hid his disappointment. 'I wanted you to tell him the good news.'

She tried to snatch her hand from him in vain. 'I will if and when I do see him.'

'I'm sure that's easier than you are making it.'

Lola chose to ignore his comment to avoid a fall out. She wanted more of his loving nature than letting any unnecessary innuendo upset them both. Hopefully things will improve for the better between them from now on. She thought.

He pressed her firmly down on his lap to prevent her from getting up. He pecked her cheek before he continued his enquiry. 'Tell me what you know about Adam.'

'I don't know anything about him.'

'The little you know then.'

She decided to reply when she looked straight at him and saw the seriousness on his face. 'His name is Adam Salvador and he has a Great Dane.'

'Where does he live and what does he do for a living?' Akin's persistent tone worried her.

She lifted her upper body to level her eyes with his and be more assertive. 'I honestly don't know the answers to your questions.'

'Could you find out?'

'How?'

He shrugged his shoulder. 'I don't know but I'm sure you can do better than that.'

'But why?'

'Why not?' He paused for a while. 'Just out of curiosity.'

'Let me get this straight, you want me to find out some information about Adam.' She jumped out of his lap to gawk at him and was surprised to see him nod his head in agreement with a strong determination written all over his eyes.

'But there are better ways than me getting close to him, Akin.'

'Yes I know but this is quicker, reliable and more effective.'

Lola was pensive as she pouted her lips with concern.

'Don't have any fancy ideas.'

'I still don't get it though.' She protested quietly.

Akin got on his feet and gently pulled her closer before cupping her face with his hands. 'Promise me you would try your best for me.' He kissed her mouth before she could protest.

'Promise me.' He repeated firmly when he withdrew his mouth from hers.

'I promise you.'

'Shall we take a covenant?'

Lola's uneasiness suddenly hit the roof. 'On what?'

'That you won't betray me.' Feeling her stiffness and without giving her the opportunity to protest, he showered her with more kisses on her face and neck before his mouth finally claimed hers again. 'That you will be faithful.'

She exhaled loudly before she tried to study him critically but he looked away instantly.

He pressed her hard against himself and smiled weakly. 'I was just kidding.' He teased by whispering into her ear.

Lola moved her mouth to his ear before she replied. 'I don't think you are.' She moved away to study his reaction but he wasn't letting go.

'If it will assure you, then let's do it.'

Still resting his hands on her hips, he looked at her for a while before he went further. 'Only you need to do it.'

With her mouth still close to his ear she whispered. 'How strange! I wonder what kind of a covenant that is.'

'A tantalisingly titillating one.'

Suddenly she remembered the grudge she'd been harbouring for a while and was uncertain of the outcome but was convinced it had to be said or there would be no peace within her if she continued to keep it to herself. 'Why not take a covenant with me that you are not a dad already.' She slowly got off his lap and sat opposite him to watch his reaction.

To her, his reaction of slight backward jerk was convincing enough. 'So when were you going to tell me?' She continued when he remained silent.

Akin's face remained focus and void of everything. His only concern was saying the right words that would still keep the ring on her finger. He had all along planned to deny this allegation if she ever asked him but he contrarily found himself cornered to admit the truth. Not funny at all! 'I was looking for the perfect opportunity.' He stretched out his hands to grab hers.

'Would there ever be?'

'No and I'm sorry for you hearing it from outside and not from me first.'

'So how old is he?'

He spoke with his head bent downwards. 'His name is Jake and he's seven year's old.'

'Seven? He looks about nine or ten to me.'

He instantly looked straight at her before he smiled weakly. 'Yes, everyone said that.' He wanted to ask where she'd seen them but was afraid of the discomfort that might bring.

Lola sat still, mesmerised and tried to cover her shame with her hand. 'What about his mum?'

'What about her?'

'Is anything still going on between you two?'

He frowned. 'No, haven't you seen her state?'

She was about to ask what he meant when she remembered he believed she'd seen them. 'Why does she always come out with you two then?'

'Because she's afraid of going out on her own.'

'In other words she needs your support.'

'No. My son needs my support.'

'Why didn't you marry her?'

'Things were different then?'

'Why were they different?'

'Well she was gorgeous and not addicted.'

'Yes, some men can do that to some of us.' She stated emphatically.

'Don't blame me, she dumped me for her ex.'

'Can you blame her? She possibly caught you cheating on her.'

'Do you seriously believe that?'

Alarmed by the surprise in his voice, she tried to say no more on the subject. No matter what she said or didn't would change the situation. He's had his son before meeting her and not during or after so she had to thread carefully. She suddenly remembered her first engagement and how everything went wrong afterwards. She asked her last question in a mellow voice that sounded different in her ears. 'Any more surprises?'

He shook his head sideways without looking at her.

'Good,' she got on her feet. 'Because I don't know how many more surprises I can take.' Without another word, she left the room.   What she couldn't tell him was he'd taken her for the biggest fool. There she was arguing with her friends and almost throwing them out of her house!

CHAPTER 9

Lola's return to work coincided with Rosie's second send off party; after the company's official party at the weekend. Roxanne decided to honour her by organising a surprise get-together with a host of close friends and family since they both go back a long way. She had initially secured a table for the group during lunch but the news somehow got to Bob and he was making it an issue that whoever exceeded the one hour break would face disciplinary action.

At exactly half five Lola was still printing some reports when her desk phone rang.

'Shouldn't you be on your way home?' Roxanne challenged her immediately she heard her voice.

'I'm just waiting for the printer to finish.'

'Excuses, did you get my text?'

'Hang on,' she took her phone from her bag and scrolled down. 'That's so lovely! And it's a set.'

'Pure Diamond earring and pendant set from me and Billy.'

'It's true when they say diamonds are girls' best friends.'

'Have you decided on what to wear?'

'No,' she stapled some items and filed it away. Have you?'

'You have no excuse to stay behind now that you've finished printing.'

'Was your phone call simply to make me leave the office on time?'

'Sure, if Bob denied us a good time by intimidating us I say we pay him back same way we can.'

'I'll agree with you just for now.' The two women bade each other bye laughing mischievously before placing the phones back on the rest. Without wasting another minute she picked her mobile phone with her handbag and was out of her office like a shot, especially after remembering she hadn't collected Rosie's present. She was heading downstairs when she bumped into Mr James who seemed to be waiting for the lift or for something else. As she returned his smile she wondered why he tried so hard with something that came naturally to many!

'Sorry I have not been able to ask my dad about Major General Anifolase.' She quickly admitted after they'd both exchanged greetings to save themselves some time.

'That's okay, he replied with another hard smile. Actually I wanted to invite you to my sixtieth birthday party.' He stretched a cream envelope towards her, giving her no opportunity to decline.

She took a long, hard look at the man's face to confirm if he really was, but he in actual fact looked fifteen years older. He'd moreover told her in their first meeting that he was nearly seventy 'Wow!' She smiled as she opened the envelope to read the content. 'That's the weekend after Father's Day.'

'Yes, but I haven't invited anyone from here.'

'But you are going to?'

'Nope.'

She wanted to ask him why but she guessed what his reply would be. Luckily the lift stopped on her floor and she gladly excused herself. He'd already invited her to two other parties both of which she did not attend.

'Please let me know if you are not coming, call me on my mobile from the invite. I really hope you'll make it this time.' He patted her arm gently. 'Don't get too drunk tonight.'

'Tonight? I don't drink sir.' Politely, she nodded her head with another plastic smile whilst waiting anxiously for the lift door to shut and get her to the car park quickly.

She jumped into her car, started the engine and was out of the building in no time but not only to get trapped in the traffic jam ahead, but also to see Mr James walk past her busy eating fish and chips.

Lola met the man slightly over a month ago in the staff room during the lunch break after missing to throw her empty sandwich container in the bin. All she could hear was soft laughter, some chuckles and an inaudible remark from the table occupied by four men on her far right corner. She was about to get up and correct her mistake when one of the men beat her to it and sat right in front of her afterwards. Instead of returning his smirk she sipped her decaffeinated coffee and equally focused on the other three men left in the room with her who all pretended to be deeply embroiled in an argument. With the break period nearly over and many of her colleagues in the newly created smoking room it was no wonder their voices echoed through the four corners of the large-sized room.

Finally, she settled her gaze back to the man and grinned to acknowledge his presence.

'You don't mind me sitting next to you?' The security man tried to lean back on the chair but quickly changed his mind.

She only beamed at him after noticing his mixed up accent.

'Thank God this is part time.' He covered his mouth as he yawned. 'You see what I mean … I can't wait to get to bed.'

Lola looked at him and returned his smile with a gentle nod.

'Today was my first experience of a full day here.'

'Really?'

'Yes, and I don't want to make a habit of it.'

'So you'd rather work part time.' She asked rather than stated because she had no recollection of any male part time on the payroll.

'Without any doubt.'

'Why part time?'

'Because I'm old and …' He looked at her and stopped.

'You don't look that old.'

'I might not but I sure feel it.' He eyed her jealously as he whispered. 'Will be seventy soon.'

'Really?' He nodded his head and grinned.

'Anyway, age is just a number.' She must have raised her voice as all heads turned in their direction especially those who just joined in from outside.

The man looked all around the staff room before speaking again. 'I used to know one Major General Anifolase who shared the same birthday with me.'

The way he pronounced it was enough hints but she still refused to be baited.

'Do you know him? I'm sorry but I heard you mention that name yesterday.'

'Major General Anifolase?'

'Yes, he was a very good friend of mine.'

Extremely irritated by his question but still managed to keep her voice calm. 'Really? And where would that be?'

'Yes in the Nigerian Army.'

'I see!'

Encouraged by her tone his voice got louder. 'We both served in the Biafra war together, shoulder to shoulder.'

She remained suspicious but still pondered if she'd ever heard her daddy or mama mention any of her relatives in the Biafra war or any war whatsoever.

'You've heard about the Biafra war haven't you?'

She wanted to answer but was stopped by the ever changing tension and pain covering the old man's face. He instantly swore under his breath and banged his fist on the table before hardening his jaw line so severely that his face became a mask of sadness, pain and torture right underneath his dark, wrinkly skin. Surprisingly, all her compassionate nature could see was a sad, haunted old man with a wide unsmiling mouth, tough, watery, sharp brown eyes that seemed to dance in every direction. Nature couldn't create a sadder face to look so suppurate even when laughing. He was old, definitely older than her Mama, but looked much tougher than he wanted people to believe.

'Biafra war cost me a once in a lifetime of happiness.' Slowly he shifted his gaze back to her and smiled stiffly before he concentrated blankly on the table in front of him. The longer he looked the quicker the tension on his face dissipated. He pointed his index finger up to explain. 'The only woman I've ever loved ...' He let the rest of his sentence drift as his voice became shaky, facing her squarely made the pain in his eyes too evident. He tried to smile but only succeeded in making his mouth wider. 'I bet you weren't born then?' His chuckle was ironically sad.

She wanted to speak but found her throat blocked by a big lump which eventually made her nod her head in agreement.

The Biafra war was a Nigerian civil war between the Ibo in the South and the rest of Nigerians. She could remember how mama described it, and the sadness that would overcome her when she remembered her family members she'd lost during the war. Especially her aunt who married an Ibo man and their desperate attempts to escape getting killed from both sides of the war making them stuck indoors all throughout the war period. Every house with glass windows had to be blocked with dark object to prevent light reflecting externally and avoid being targeted.

Lola cringed as she remembered how her great uncle Daddy Kahf narrowly escaped death during the war whilst working in the north. He was attacked by a mob of northerners who mistook him for a southerner and was about to mutilate him when another northerner that had stood shoulder to shoulder with him earlier in the mosque came to his rescue. He had been mistaken for a southerner because of his light skin and would have been an unfortunate additional statistics if not for the timely intervention of his religious alibi.

'Are you okay?' The man's face moved closer to hers. 'I guess you didn't hear my last question.'

She shook her head again to wait for her discomfort to diffuse as the silence dragged on.

The security man focused on her badge for a while before he spoke. 'I hope I am correct for assuming Anif to mean Anifolase or …?'

'Yes Sir,'

He edged closer to her with another forced smile. 'Which state are you from?'

'Born and bred in Lagos sir,' she lied and was surprised how well he took it.

'I was born in Abeokuta in Ogun state but moved to Lagos to join the Army; regrettably I lost more than good friends in that bloody, unnecessary war.' He squinted his watery eyes as he tried to assess her intelligence, when he spoke again it was in a whisper. 'I lost half of my heart too.'

The chill in his voice dishevelled her heart but she pretended to be stoic on the outside. To fully quench her panic she searched for his badge to know his name too.

'I'm finished for the day, which explains why I have no badge on.'

She quickly grabbed her cup, raised it to her mouth, took a sip and struggled to swallow the cold coffee. 'Mr Felix James.' he stretched his right hand out at her.

She slipped her hand into his and was received with a firm handshake that confirmed he was a physically fit and strong man.

'I'm sure that will be freezing by now.'

She tried to remove her hand from his tight grasp but unsuccessful.

'Are you here with your parents?' Mr James interrupted her thought.

'No.'

'Are any other members of your family here?'

She wasn't sure where this question was going, which made her more elusive. 'No, why did you ask sir?'

He noticed her discomfort and finally released his grip on her. 'Nothing at all.'

The smile spreading across his face told her he was lying.

Deducing her suspicion, he pretended to reflect before speaking. 'I just thought you might be lonely being on your own.'

She wanted him to explain what he meant but was discouraged by the sadness on his face yet again.

'Because I get lonely sometimes. Moreover, I'm as new on this part time job as I am in this area.'

'I see,' Lola's quick glance at his face saw something she couldn't explain and suddenly empathised and imagined her grandma at a stranger's mercy. 'You mean your family will join you later?'

He only shook his head sadly.

Where is your family based then?'

He studied her face for a while and smiled sardonically. 'My wife is dead, and my two sons are in Canada.'

'Canada! Doing what?'

'Working of course, one is a pilot whilst the other is a neurosurgeon.' He explained proudly.

'Impressive but why are they both in Canada and you are here on your own?'

'They were born over there, my wife was Canadian.'

She looked at her watch to politely indicate that she would be leaving soon after she realised he had no intention to speak any further on the subject. 'I see,' she stood up and he did the same.

He waited for her to tuck her chairs before he moved. Making sure he was close enough for no one to hear him, he said, 'Please don't let anyone know I am a Nigerian,'

'Why?'

He noticed her disappointment. 'It's okay if ten or hundred whites gather around, they are having a chat but if three blacks gather they are planning something bad.'

'Yes I know that but you can't change who you are,' she wished she could hide the passion in her voice.

'Yes I agree. They don't know and I am not going to volunteer. Moreover, I am not very fluent with the language anymore. '

'How is that possible?' How on earth could anyone claim to have forgotten his mother tongue? Unless she'd spent centuries away from home and his or her people, definitely not while mama is alive. She has never met anyone prouder of Yoruba culture and traditions than her grandmother.

She tried to convince him to try and speak it but he interrupted her again, 'let's leave it that way, shall we?'

'Okay.'

He tried harder to sincerely smile for the first time only to reveal a wide gap on the lower front line which was still nevertheless impressive for his age.

Lola's instinct warned her again that he was not to be trusted.

'Please don't forget to ask your dad about the Major General.' Mr James whispered after her just before she left the room.

She nodded her head in reply without looking back and wondered why her discomfort had suddenly grown stronger around the old man. Her instinct to distrust the old man increased but her sentiment wanted her to think of him as a lovely, upright, harmless man that became a victim of a senseless, stupid war like many Nigerians of his time.

Mr James's gentle tap on her window prompted her back to reality that the road ahead had cleared. She waved at him, accelerated and drove off.

Hours later, Lola was nicely dressed in a tight fitting floral print evening dress with a side bow that perfectly hugged her waistline and accentuated her hips. With the plaits out, her newly relaxed hair fell in harmony with her lightly made up face, the cliché was the new hair style, a centre parting with the right and left side thronged to create ringlets that made her look like a million dollar for she was naturally blessed with long, dark and beautiful hair. She looked in the mirror and was not only pleased with the face staring back at her but agreed that the time, effort and money was well worth it. The only regret was for Akin not seeing her first in her entirely new outfits, but then again he was miles away in Berlin meeting an uncle that was arriving from Canada. He'd promised to give her his contact details later.

'Why didn't you invite him over?' She asked him when he broke the news to her three days ago.

'I don't have problem with inviting my uncle over but I can't stand his son and that's why I'm going alone instead of with you.'

'Do I detect some resentment in your voice?'
'Yes!'

She studied him and he looked back at her. 'So how many days are you thinking of spending with them?'

'I'd say three days,' he indicated by waving his hand sideways.

'We'll see,' that to her meant five days.

'And if I get lucky, I might just send some cars home.'

'That will definitely take you more than three day then.'

'How can you say that? What's the big deal in exporting cars?'

She shrugged her shoulders. 'I have a feeling you'd tell me anyway.'

'Well it's as simple as A.B.C.'

'Okay it's now simple from the same nephew you couldn't stand earlier.' She pointed out critically as she'd usually been since he'd confessed about his son to her.

'What I didn't tell you was that he conned me, so he has to deliver or there is no old score to settle.' He explained with confidence.

Her gaze shifted to the wall clock before realising that April would be picking her up anytime from now. The earlier, unexpectedly prolonged traffic jam had seriously inflamed her ankle further again. Many colleagues considered her the link between herself and Roxanne in all respect, her dual heritage background balanced the other pair retrospectively, but above all, Lola valued her unequivocal opinion on matters more. She was the tallest and nearly a decade older when compared to Roxanne's of around sixteen years gap, but most importantly, she had so much admiration for both women for being mothers.

Roxanne being the closest to Rosie suggested they tried a newly opened club and restaurant in Brindley place that served Asian, European and African cuisine. Its dining and seating area was so beautifully designed that the canal all surrounded it with the best fascination being the tranquil water waves and the silhouette reflection amongst other attractions.

Lola paid the taxi driver with an agreement that April would foot their return fare before both were ushered to their table by an enthusiastic, clumpy and a professionally friendly teenager. They were not surprised to find their table close to the entrance with Rosie and five others already seated and waiting. She was flanked on both sides by her sisters-in-law named Aisha and Lisa, respectively. Roxanne who was facing her was also bordered on her right by someone introduced to her as Sally whilst Jade an ex colleague was on the other side. With April standing next to one of the two vacant chairs Lola had no choice but to occupy the seat facing her and next to the stranger called Sally. The two women regarded each other warmly as she sat down.

'So how are things with you Jade?' Lola asked after thanking the waiter for her starter.

'Cool, never better.'

'Glad to hear that.'

'I followed your advice, Kevin and I have decided to give our relationship another go; the twins are now in full time school.'

'And the little one?'

'Settling down all right and now sleeps through the night and I cope better at work because my boss is quite understanding.'

'What does your company do?' Rosie spoke for the first time.

'It's a medium-sized law firm.'

'You never said!' She shot a glance at Roxanne who both knew fully well that Jade had wanted to take A.B.C & D to the employment tribunal. 'I bet he put you up to the tribunal thing?'

Lola wished she could retrieve her question to avoid opening the cans of worm once again.

'It's a She actually and yes she did influence me because I think Bob shouldn't get away with what he did to me.' Jade's face suddenly became sad and gloomy. 'The man is a bully and a sexual predator. He is not worthy of the power entrusted upon him.'

'You are right. Roxanne being worried about the repercussion of such litigation on A.B.C. & D. does not mean you have to let him get away with his abuse of power.'

'Thank you Rosie, all we did was condoning his actions whilst he hid behind the company's image.' Jade stopped when a waiter brought bottles of a mixture of wines, a teapot of herbal tea for Sally, two glasses of orange drink and the main course menu.

Hungry Lola like the rest concentrated on her mushroom soup until it was time to order her main course. She wanted to ask a few question about Bob but didn't want to speak first, the woman beside her never seemed to stop watching her either.

'Have you finished packing Rosie?' April broke the silence by speaking for the first time.

'Yes, thanks to my sister-in-laws.'

'What happens to your house?'

'Aisha and her family are moving in. She winked at her sister-in-law who was busy with her spring roll.

'I thought you had only one brother.'

'Yes, that's Abdul's sister and Lisa my brother's wife.' She nudged the two women with her elbows simultaneously.

'I see.' April finally laid the matter to rest.

'When do you leave?'

'Next week.'

'It is a big step? One giant leap landing you all the way to Africa.'

'No not Africa, Ghana.'

'What's the difference?' April asked with irritation.

'Africa is a continent; Ghana is a country in the Western African region.'

Everyone else burst into laughter except her who was embarrassed for being corrected whilst Lola empathised with the ignorants but could also relate with the enlightened. 'How did you find your first visit?'

'It was wonderful.'

'I mean the society and the people in general.'

'The people were warm and nice like the weather.'

The first waiter brought Rosie's and Roxanne's similar orders whilst two more waiters followed with the rest of their main course and the next half an hour was spent in almost total silence with everyone tucking into their grubs apart from the cutlery's noise.

Lola looked around only to meet Aisha doing the same whilst dissecting a chicken perri perri shoulder.

'You said Abdul has got a job?' April continued after washing her meal down with her red wine.

'No I said he was taking over his daddy's accounting firm whilst I in the meantime assist with the office duties. I'm computerising the whole system for them.' Rosie looked at her closest friend in awe before she spoke. 'You know how much I love the sun but this sun came with a complete package. Tell me who would say no to a tall, dark and handsome man who wants to make a honest woman out of her?'

'You know what they say.'

'What?' Rosie put her empty glass of her favourite white wine down and smiled eagerly.

'That you never look back once you taste a black man.' Sassy mouth April remarked before scanning every one's faces for their reaction. 'My mother told me that when I was sixteen, I tried it at eighteen and I've never looked back.'

Rosie reached out to clinch hands with her as everyone at the table started laughing. 'Dead right!'

'Let's leave that as a personal choice, shall we?' Lisa, obviously offended spoke for the first time. 'I have never had that experience.'

'Haven't you tried it?' Rosie turned towards her with a conspiratorial smile. 'Don't worry I won't ever tell my brother.' She teased and nudged her.

Everyone at the table laughed and jeered so loudly that other diners turned to see what was going on. Embarrassed Lisa blushed and bowed her head as all the ladies enquiring eyes focused on her whilst she giggled continuously.

'Look me in the eye and say no you haven't.' Rosie continued.

Still laughing hysterically she finally raised her head and replied with a firm 'No.'

The whole group applauded loudly with some tapping on the table gently but loud enough to attract other diners. 'Then you don't know what you're missing, I tried it and got hooked.' Sally who had been quiet all along laughed so much that she choked on her drink and had to be patted on the back by Roxanne. She afterwards got on her feet and spoke. 'Maybe we should persuade Lola to try the other side as well?'

'Yes that's not a bad idea.' April agreed whilst everyone else cheered.

'And make my mother not only turn in her grave but come out of it and beat me senselessly.' She finally noticed Aisha laughing and relaxing at last.

She would be about her age but either very shy or really unhappy today. 'Roxanne you are on the minority's side, why don't you try the other side first?' Aisha's friendly gaze met hers again and they both smiled as they both reached for their glasses of orange juice.

She edged forward to catch everyone's attention. 'I haven't seen anyone I fancy besides I am not that adventurous.' Roxanne defended and resumed back to her seat. 'You never know, you might just like it more than the rest of us here.' She teased before glancing across the table to indicate that the majority had already tried both.

'I don't do rainbow relationship; I'm quite contended with Akin thanks.'

'Try telling Roy that.'

'Who is Roy?' April asked with keen interest.

'Roy the Company's financial advisor.'

'Oh he's gorgeous!' Jade remarked.

'He is single, tall, dark, handsome and, loaded.'

'How did you know all these?'

'You are not supposed to ask question April, just support me.' She implored and winked.

'How could you say he is dark when he is white? You've been obviously reading too much romantic novels.' She shot a quick glance at her two closest colleagues and friends before she continued. 'I know you two have your reservations about Akin but I am engaged to him now.'

'He hasn't stopped talking about you since he saw you at Aston University recently. He calls you his

African princess and begged me to organise another get-together so he could have an opportunity to introduce himself to you personally. He's seriously in love with you Lola.'

She frowned deeply with concern. 'I don't know what he looks like besides he doesn't even know me.'

'He said he knew all that mattered to him and he's every woman's dream man; just agree to meet him once more and see what we mean.'

Lola laughed at the desperation and sincerity in her voice. 'I don't believe you; those meeting you for the first time would think you earn a living from this.' She looked at April and was shocked by her guilty expression. 'So you knew about it too!' She leaned back on her chair and looked away for a while before she continued. 'Tell him I said Love is not enough and I'm not interested.' She finished her drink before she continued. 'In my culture, when a woman marries you automatically forget and forego your lifestyle and culture for your husband's.'

'Everything?'

'Yes April, even sometimes up to diet and dressing.'

'I was told that but I didn't believe it initially.'

'That's living someone else's life.' Lisa remarked.

'You can look at it that way but to me that's where cultural compatibility comes in. You won't need to forsake much if you've had the basics in common. Maybe you two can see why going out with the likes of Roy is going to be the biggest challenge for me.'

'A big one indeed!'

'The colour of my love is brown, neither black nor white. Excuse me I need the toilet.' She got on her feet leaving them to banter amongst themselves, she could without turning round hear the passion in April's and Roxanne's voices. As she walked she wondered why she felt overwhelmingly uneasy with the hair at her nape totally erect. She wanted to turn around but quickly changed her mind with the hope that it would all come out in the wash.

She was approaching the table when she saw everyone on their feet with Roxanne speaking. 'Let's propose a toast for Aisha.'

'We use pop drinks instead.' Rosie stopped her from filling everyone's glass with unopened champagne on their table. 'Aisha and her family are strong Muslims who don't touch alcohol. Harram!' Rosie concluded and beckoned on the waiter to bring the cake already ordered.

Lola joined everyone in the happy birthday song and watched the celebrant blow the candles off before cutting it and dishing it round. Just then she caught Sally and Lisa pointing in her direction, but decided to ignore them and look away.

Roxanne bit a mouthful of her cake and eyed her childhood friend with admiration. 'I can't believe you're finally going. I just didn't think it would come so soon or ...' She let the rest of her statement drift off as her voice became unsteady.

'... I would have buckled out as usual but when you moved in with Billy, I realised it was time for me to get serious with my life too after nearly thirty years of friendship.'

'Moreover we are going to be forty soon.' The two women regarded each other with warmth and affection as they remembered all the good times they've both had.

'And we don't even look it.'

'I'm going to miss you.' Roxanne edged forward to hug her friend as she fought back the tears. 'But then if you hadn't ventured to Africa then I might never have met Lola.'

'True or needed anyone to share the house with for a start. So we're all winners!'

'I got you this.' She said as she handed her the gift wrapped in a golden coloured wrapping paper.

'Ah!' Was all Rosie could say with sheer excitement after opening the package. 'You little devil, you've always known how much I wanted this. Now I have two sets. One from Abdul and-'

'From me and Billy.'

'This is a very pleasant surprise!' Rosie expressed to her sister-in-law who was helping her put the new set of jewellery on.

Roxanne meanwhile filled everyone's glass with champagne and their drinking glasses all clicked together as they all chanted. 'To Rosie for a rosier future!'

'We are all going to miss you.' Lola said after walking over to present her an 18-carat gold bracelet with her name inscribed on it and a hug.

'I would kill for a glass of wine or this champagne.'

'But you can't because of your medication.' Lisa concluded Sally's statement.

Lola smiled at both women as she settled back in her seat.

'I know but I can still wish can't I?' She enquired. 'I hear you've recently got engaged?'

Lola fought off the embarrassment and nodded her head with a smile before noticing that the two women were very similar in their brash and witty personality amongst other things, except for the distinct difference in the loss of life and vitality in Sally's eyes. Her eyes and face portrayed nothing of the beautiful, glorious woman she once was, leaving only traces and evidences of her nicely curved lips that would have committed havoc in the past. Without being told, Lola could see her being swallowed by sadness, ill health and would have taken a lot of her guts to be out on a night out like this. Her distinctively deep voice would definitely attract many men but could equally spark nasty controversy amongst many women too.

'Has been engaged changed anything?' She interrupted Lola with her inquisition.

'No.'

Without another word, she pouted her luscious lips before sipping her tea with an unsteady hand, something she just noticed before her attention diverted to April's discussion, when she looked back Sally was still starring at her intensely.

The serenity in the ambience was quickly replaced by a strange feeling as soon as their eyes met.

Her nervousness returned, but she quickly played it down by engaging in conversation and pretending to be cold. 'Lisa I'm ready when you are, it's nearly time for my you-know.'

She gulped the last content in her cup down before she replied. 'Give us another fifteen minutes or so.'

Sally thanked her before turning back to Lola. 'Have you fixed a wedding date yet?'

'No.'

'Why?'

She felt uncomfortable at her unnecessary inquisition but tried to hide it from her prying eyes. 'Because we would like to travel home for the two families to meet officially first.'

'The traditional stuff Rosie always talked about.' Lisa added.

'Have you got a date for that yet?'

'No, Akin can't take time off work yet.'

'That might be a long engagement then.' Sally remarked with some underlining bitterness.

'Might not because we've already bought our tickets – open tickets.'

Just then the dance floor started filling up with a handful of people. Rosie implored them to come to the dance floor. 'Sally, just for five minutes,' she pleaded.

'Alright then,' she concurred and followed Lisa.

She decided to do the absolute opposite of whatever Sally did. She'd only met the woman for

the first time and she already disliked her, which wa
quite unlike her. She hadn't really said anything
particularly bad, but the way she constantly gawped
at her was making her severely uncomfortable.

'I thought your ankle was healed.'

She froze at the realisation of whose voice it was.
No wonder she'd been feeling uneasy! She turned
around to find Adam standing closely behind her.

'You ladies were obviously having a good time.'
Without another word, he sat beside her but facing
her. 'You look ravishing!'

Sally was gawping at them from the dance floor,
Adam ogled. She didn't know which she preferred.

Never had any man's compliment embarrassed he
nor made her speechless until now.

His boyish charm was absolutely electrifying in a
grey dinner suit and bow tie. Despite being savvy
and dangerously attractive, his new hair cut
highlighted his triple curve hairline and his
rectangular shaped head. Apart from her never
seeing his hazel eyes so sensual and receptive, the
pairs were having some strange effects on her.

Their eyes remained stuck on one another with
one appreciating the other's beauty in joint silence.
With Adam's sensual eyes beginning to tease hers
she instantly looked away.

'You will dance with me.' He demanded instead
of asking.

'Adam there you are.'

Their wall of silence was interrupted by the
sexiest voice she'd ever come across. They both

turned and got up simultaneously. Lola was not disappointed with her physique and face either, a dual heritage, tall, elegant with grey pleasant eyes.

'Lola meet Karel.'

The two women shook hands and smiled briefly. Suddenly, Roxanne and April turned up and exchanged greetings with Adam and ultimately Karel before departing again.

'Ladies, your taxi is on its way.' One of the club staff stated.

'I could give you a lift.'

'No don't bother, I'm going with April.'

'It's still not a problem.' He insisted but Lola could notice his date's dislike of his gesture.

'We have to stop on the way to pick something up first.' She interjected gently.

'Alright, I'll see you another time.' He stated before leaving with his date for their table.

'That's your solution. He couldn't take his eyes off you again.' Roxanne whispered into her ears gloatingly.

'Meaning?'

'You can have a bit of both; he's neither black nor white.'

'I told her they were like two magnets the first time I met him but she said my eyes were deceiving me.' She giggled.

'I said the same thing when we met at the fundraising event.' April added laughing.

'Maybe she'll believe us now.' She summoned for the bill and gave her debit card to the waiter.

'We don't need a taxi.' Rosie interrupted them before glancing at her sister-in-law for her consent. 'Aisha will drop us all.'

'I'll drop the others off then.' Roxanne hugged her friend before bidding their farewells, but she insisted they'd all leave together.

'Well I suppose, tomorrow is another working day.' She concurred as she put her debit card and receipt into her purse.

Everyone thanked Roxanne with another hug for paying for their meals whilst Rosie asked her to thank Billy. Sally and Lisa led the way whilst Lola created as much gap as possible by being the last to leave the venue, the uneasiness was still there but she knew why, at least some of why.

CHAPTER 10

Lola rushed out of the house, locked her door and drove down the road, driving as safe and fast as she could in her attempt to get to the post office before closing time. The pain she felt in the first few minutes of driving seemed to have subsided as she accelerated more whilst the driver behind her continued hooting his horn to express his frustration with her slow speed. Sade had just called to inform her that her husband was travelling to Lagos soon and wanted to know if she had any item to send home.

'Yes I do.' She replied anxiously when she remembered her half brother's birthday was only ten days away. His presents as usual were the latest designer computer games already wrapped up which would have been posted if she was not on sick leave. Today was her second time of driving since she'd twisted her ankle and it felt as strange as the weather, but it nevertheless meant no more taxis or lifts from friends. The sun was shining with intermittent rains, yet with enough winds to knock some trees off. She was sure to hear more of it on the news the following day. The weather forecast from yesterday's news only predicted sunshine, no rain or severe wind!

She could have walked it despite the bad weather, but doubted if she would make it before the post office closed since it was Saturday. Moreover, she reckoned her anxiety to get to her destination quickly might do more damage than good.

As anticipated, Akin arrived back in Birmingham after spending five days in Berlin and had been quite understanding and very supportive in the past few days, working less hours, spending quality time together and planning the future as a couple. He'd been dragging her out of the house and taking her on long walks which had been really helpful to her healing process. She'd received more presents in the past weeks than he'd given her since they met, the only problem being the intimate side of their relationship. They are now engaged to be married and there is no better time than now! To her dismay and frustration, she complained to him and was surprised at his flimsy admission that he wanted that moment to be spectacular so they shouldn't rush. She eagerly expected this bravura moment within their first week of being engaged but they were now well over the third week and she was still waiting. She could have been more forceful with her demand if she didn't have the worst stomach pain ever that went on for a week, there was no vomiting, no diarrhoea, just some vicious, nasty cramp that reeled her, weakened her and totally confined her indoors. The biggest mystery was how two different medical professionals couldn't diagnose what her ailment was except to advise her to drink a lot of fluid to flush it all out, even after submitting every possible body fluids for further tests. She unfortunately felt sorry for Akin who was really worried about leaving her to herself and had inadvertently encouraged them to cuddle and touch more, but he had likewise claimed that his reason of not taking it further was his fear of triggering another mysterious stomach upheaval. She was always, nevertheless, irritated to hear his excuse despite the validity of his point, but it scared her to realise that her boastful years of a super-strong, bug free stomach had finally ended. What bothered her the most was how she caught it in the first place, but their love had been really solidified by this. As her carer, she had the first hand opportunity to see his sensitive, caring and loving side. To crown it all, he waited two more additional days to guarantee her full recovery and only left this morning. She was missing him already, something she very rarely did. It'd been three days now since she'd felt any sign of the stomach cramp whatsoever.

She sighed with frustration at the fleet of cars in the car park and drove round for a while with the hope of finding a spare space but no luck as expected with most Saturdays before three p.m.

She drove further from her location and still didn't get lucky. As she drove round again looking for a convenient parking space she looked at the time and realised she had just fifteen minutes to make it to the post office, hissing, she wished she had walked instead of rushing out of the house like a maniac with no time to make up or dress properly. A green mini came out of a corner ahead of her and she followed the direction, surprisingly the space wasn't big enough for her car. Already frustrated and more desperate than ever, she reluctantly squeezed into the space but not without blocking a black Porsche.

Without another thought she turned off the engine, grabbed her hand bag, her parcel and rushed into the post office. She had just stepped inside when the door was locked behind her by one of the staff.

Twenty minutes later she stepped out of the precinct glad and relieved that her brother's parcel will make it to its final destination well on time before his birthday. She walked faster as the gush of wind enveloping her made her shiver whilst praying passionately that she didn't have to face any flack or palaver from the driver of the car she'd blocked in. The only thing she wanted badly now was a delicious spicy food, the mysterious bug had denied her meals of her choice for too long and it was beginning to rattle her. The closer she got to her car the more it became obvious that there was someone sitting on her bonnet and on the phone possibly waiting for her. She began to panic.

'Me too, yesterday was superb; I enjoyed every bit of the time we spent together.'

She was immediately relieved after taking a few more steps closer. 'I'm glad you did Paige.'

Adam laughed before he continued. 'You know as much as I do, and the answer to that is yes! Yes! Yes!'

'Yes I agree, I'll beat and double your 100% love and devotion. Should have been but I've been blocked in by one irresponsible driver.' He looked around for anyone but didn't see her because of the angle she was positioned. 'I'm sure she is a woman and a careless one too.'

He laughed seductively before he called her name again. 'Paige darling.'

She alerted him of her presence by deliberately jamming the driver's door loudly. She wished there was a gentle way of nudging him with her car without inflicting any serious damage on him. *How could he sit on someone else's car?*

He turned round sharply before getting off the bonnet to come and have a word. With the phone now in his breast pocket he came round her side to level with her window before beckoning her to wind down.

She fumbled for the right button and had started winding the window down before she wished she hadn't.

'The driver finally returns.'

'Hello Mr Salvador.'

He stooped to ensure his face was parallel with hers before replying. 'Hello Lola,' making a strong emphasis on each of the syllables in her name. He began to appraise the car with admiration and wouldn't need spelling out that the car met his taste. 'To what do I owe this obstruction?'

'I sincerely apologise for that, it wasn't deliberate.'

He now moved closer by leaning his arm on the half wound down window. 'Does that excuse the fact that it didn't happen?'

'I said I'm sorry.'

'You are attracting trouble by doing that.'

'Doing what?'

He deliberately ignored her impatience by eying her. 'By leaving your house keys and letters with your address in the car. I'm sure car thieves will be laughing all the way to your home.' Her eyes suddenly lit up when she grasped the implication.

Surprisingly, she looked on the passenger seat to realise her folly. She agreed at being lucky for some drivers weren't that careless to have their car windows smashed. What was she thinking of?

'Their mere sighting of your keys is more than sufficient reason for a break in. For all it's worth …'

'For all it's worth is nothing because it didn't happen and you are wasting my time right now.' She interrupted him angrily but uncertain of why.

'Nice car though.'

She raved the car to move on when he beckoned her to wind down again. She annoyingly fumbled for a while before pressing the right button.

'One of your headlights has been smashed.'

'No! Never!'

'It's nothing serious though, I wouldn't worry if I were you.'

Without any more word, she pushed the door open to check the extent of the damage and was in no time by his side. He stooped close to the right headlamp whilst pretending to be having a closer look.

'Silly me, I must have imagined it.'

'Imagined what exactly?' The anger in her voice was unmistakable.

'With the sun's reflection you would think it was broken.'

'Possibly from a novice like me but not from a man of your expertise.' Lola prayed he didn't hear her stomach rumble so loudly.

'Do you fancy a light meal in a nearby restaurant?'

'Sorry no can do,' she snapped to hide her embarrassment.

'Lunch now or dinner later?' Adam appraised the designer face cap covering most of her hair apart from loose ends hanging on her shoulder, her bright eyes and pretty non-made up face, the coordinated jeans trouser and jacket complimented by a white cotton blouse. His look finally landed on her feet, those feet again! He looked at her straight in the eye rather than dwell on those feet and wondered why the brightness in her eyes always made her more graceful.

'None of the two.' She opened her car door as she struggled to control her exasperation at the amusement in his eyes.

Ignoring her irritation, he tried again. 'There is no dressing code,' he stated flatly.

Fastening her seat belt she added; 'Good I'm still not interested. Karel yesterday, Paige today, God knows who tomorrow.'

'Yesterday?' He questioned with a deep frown. She eyed him and started her engine before she spoke again. 'Good day Adam Salvador.'

As she drove off she felt both elated that she had her way and deflated that Adam gave up so quickly. Was she shocked he gave up so quickly or what?

Surely a man as gorgeous as Adam would consider it a waste of time and effort to push too hard when there were many fishes in the ocean, and he would not need to ask most of them before they jumped at it. Then her next question was why he asked her out after his awareness that she heard his conversation with his lady friend, she concluded he must have taken her for one of those ladies he could use and dump at his beck and call. She was certain this Paige would definitely be a better company than she could ever dare to be in that department.

Another rumbling sound from her stomach warned her to find a solution to the problem and stop lamenting. Regrettably, she wished she hadn't turned his offer down as she debated whether to eat out or go home and cook. She chose the former when she realised that time was her greatest enemy. Luckily, she found a newly opened Chinese restaurant with car park facilities nearby and jumped at it.

She was attracted by the poster on the tinted double-sided door and felt at ease when she walked in. A young, oriental waiter walked up to her with a smile whilst she was busy admiring the internal decor of the restaurant. 'Yes, this is my first time of coming here.' She returned her smile.

'Follow me madam,' halfway she asked Lola if she was alone.

After finishing her tea she began to study the menu and had beckoned on the waiter to place her order when another waiter walked up to her with one red rose. She looked at the stick with surprise before resting it back on the man. 'No thank you,' she spoke in total finality.

'Take,' the man urged strongly again.

'No I don't want it,' she replied with a smile and was hoping someone would come to her rescue.

Finally one of the waiters came to join them and spoke to the man briefly. 'He said one gentleman over there asked him to give you the red rose.'

'I see, who did he say?'

The waiter was about to ask when she heard the all too familiar voice always triggering her mixed reaction.

'We meet again Lola,'

'I'm afraid so.'

'Why don't you join me, please?'

The tantalising smell coming from the restaurant's kitchen had seriously wet her appetite and weakened her resistance to anything. With little or no strength to argue she complied with his request and followed him to his table. 'I didn't know you were into football.'

'No I'm not,' she began to wonder where he got that impression from. 'Oh the conversation I was having with April's son at the fundraising event!'

He nodded and smiled when their eyes met. 'Wasn't she also with you the last time we met?'

'Yes, her son was just telling me about the goal he scored that day.' They got to his table which was obscured from open view and looked at her again before pulling out the empty chair for her to sit. 'You know what kids are like?' She rephrased her statement when he wouldn't take his eyes off her.

'No I don't,' he replied bluntly as he sat facing her. 'Where is lover boy?'

'Working, might be joining me later.' Her heart gave a weird flip when his hand touched hers and she couldn't resist touching the flame emanating from that little part of her body. Today, she noticed his face was slightly tanned and it formed a sharp contrast to his intelligent and alert hazel eyes. 'And where is Karel or Paige?'

The waiter bringing her order stopped his reply and she wasted no time in tucking into her meal.

Whilst she was eating her meal in silence, Adam was busy studying every feature on her face like he would never see them again. He also realised that there was something forbidding and dangerous about her that excited him to the core of his bones. He lingered a bit longer on her enigmatic face before his eyes landed on her voluptuous lips as she asked the waiter for a drink. As the sun shone onto their table, Adam's pupils glistened gladly as his eyes roamed to her neckline freely before moving on the chain around her neck and finally the pendant. 'I'm sorry about the trouble I caused the last time I never had the time to apologise when we last met.'

She looked up to discover that nothing could escape the intense scrutiny between those piercing eyes. 'In fact I should be thanking you.'

He lifted one eyebrow and slanted his neck curiously.

'This is the result.' She stretched her left hand towards him.

He grabbed it but didn't take his eyes off her. With his lips thinned he spoke derisively. 'I didn't realise I was such a big threat.'

'Threat to what?'

'To have pushed lover boy to propose.'

'You are such an egocentric maniac.'

'Really? He must have seen me as a threat.'

'You?' A cynical laughter escaped her lips. 'We all have the right to flatter ourselves sometimes.' Lola moved her face closely to his and gestured him closer with her right hand. 'Adam Salvador, this face will only date a full breed Yoruba man and not just any Nigerian. My equal opportunities policy doesn't extend that far.'

He felt his stomach clench and twist. 'And sacrifice a lifetime happiness just to culturally belong?'

She tried to remove her hand but his grasp was firm. 'And that will be one concept of a relationship you would never understand.' She saw his facial expression tightened and withdrew her hand underneath his grasp. 'As for me, cultural compatibility is a big issue in any romantic relationship I have.'

There was a hint of resentment in the way he stared at her. 'I still maintain that I have my reservation about his method of proposal. What if the love is one sided?'

'Your prerogative! You can choose to bother yourself with the navel gazing whilst I concentrate on the end result. Okay?'

He could tell she wasn't finished so he replied with a nod of his head.

'Tell me what is wrong with wanting marriage from the one you love?'

'Nothing at all if the love is true and reciprocated.'

'Exactly, marriage is a natural progression. Moreover, my family won't accept anything less.' As usual, she finally looked away when the heat of his stare became too much for her to bear.

'Less in what way?'

'Anything lesser than marriage to them is unacceptable. What or who is Lolade Anifolase without the deep culture embedded in her?' She tapped her chest and her jiggling boobs reminded him of their first encounter again. She became equally embarrassed when she caught him watching but recovered quickly. 'And that is all they expect in return for their time and resources invested on me.'

Suspicious of where the conversation might lead, he ran his hand through his hair to catch her off guard. Yet, his curiosity took the best of him, 'You mean your parents or the whole extended family?'

'Yes, ideally but in my case, my dad, my grandmother, their family and other well wishers. Some of them might not be your blood relations but you have to accord them the same privilege and respect as your family members.'

'Why?'

'Because that's the way things are done.'

'Does it make it right?'

'No, it doesn't make it wrong either. Have you ever heard of the legendary Africa saying "that it takes a whole community to raise a child?" '

'Yes, too many times and sadly.'

'That's part of the concept.' She looked at him and noticed his insipidness. 'You don't get it?'

He smiled meekly. 'No!' He frowned for a while and forced a smile when he caught her starring at him. 'And I never have!'

'It's like here when a black or white man achieves something great and all well wishers intrinsically feel proud. A good example for us as kids was to always be of good behaviour even when our parents were not around because a neighbour or an uncle might catch us, then reprimand us on the spot and still report to our parents for a top up. Simply because of the inherent belief that this child belonged to us all and we're all obliged to protect him from harm and danger.' She stopped when she discovered that his face had been darkened with worry. 'Are you alright?'

Despite the paleness in Adam's face he forced a smile. 'I can actually relate to that experience, but that could be too much for some.'

'Some people could see it that way. I for instance lost my mother at the tender age of three and I never realised till I was around nine.'

'Really?'

'How is that possible? So who looked after you?'

'My grandmother.'

'Come on!'

'Honestly. I initially only wondered why my mother was much older than my mate's mums and why she was addressed as Mummy or Mama but I never pondered too much over it because anyone older than your mother is automatically addressed so and vice versa.'

'So you could have ten mummies.'

'Or daddies.' She added.

'Yes, and it might include your next door neighbour who is simply older than your mother.'

'And how would you differentiate them all?'

'You could say mummy next door.'

'How stupid is that?' He ran his thumb around the rim of the glass. 'I'd always hated that.'

'Some people can see it that way.'

'Especially when the family disowned their own because of whom he or she loved.'

'Exactly and I think it's too much of a price to pay for love especially when I grew up believing her to be my mother.'

'Fascinating!' He watched her lick her lips in hesitation and hoped he hadn't overstepped his boundary. 'But you must have been devastated when you found out.'

'That would be an understatement of the century.' A shallow smile escaped her lips but never spread to her face. 'Never even had the proper chance to grieve yet.'

Adam's first instinct was to hug and kiss her sadness away but equally anxious to know why and very scared of asking in case she changed her mind, so he held his breath eagerly. 'Why?' He finally summoned the courage when the suspense became unbearable.

'I don't know how to describe it. I discovered the truth about Grandma close to the time I was aware about my mother's death and I was trying to grieve when I reunited with my father after nearly seven years of separation. I suppose my ecstasy of having a mother and father for a change superseded the grief of my mother who died years ago.'

'Oh they were divorced before she died?'

'Not at all,' she was amused by the confused expression on his face. 'My mother and I travelled to Lagos to visit my grandmother whilst my dad planned to join us three weeks later but mum died before then.'

She could not believe how red his face went.

'And you never saw him till around seven years later?'

Lola nodded her head sadly.

'That was wicked of him.'

'Really?' She frowned and scanned his face. 'Why is that?'

'He should have put your need first.'

'And what exactly was the need of a three year old?' She eyed him to suppress her emotion. 'Should he rush home as planned and abandon his studies temporarily or forever?' She paused to swallow the lump in her throat. 'Or should he bring me back here to add more to the problems on his plate?' At first they looked at each other silently, but something seemed clearer to him and his face was relaxed. 'Don't forget he'd just lost his wife and was a student before a husband and a dad.'

'I see!' He looked deep in thought for a while. 'So you forgive your dad then?' His voice was meek.

'There was nothing to forgive; he did what he had to do according to how the situations demanded.'

Adam who had always wondered about the depth of her enigma began to understand and see the glimpse himself. The acuity in her was more than it met the eye. Above all, her objective, courage and strength was something he lacked when dealing with his father he hadn't seen for thirteen years or more. 'What is the biggest sin in a relationship?'

She angled herself for some strange reasons and looked straight into his eyes. 'You are a man, let's ask you!'

'Don't change the subject, we were talking about you.'

'That wasn't about me because I'm sure you've been there, done it and have the T-shirt to prove how many women you've hurt.'

'I don't hurt anyone, not knowingly anyway.' He joined her laughing. 'How long did it take your dad to remarry?'

'Should I answer that question because he is a man or my father?'

He only shrugged his wide shoulders.

'Not long enough, but then I was young and I now understand how lonely he must have been back then.'

'How did you feel about it? Did you feel betrayed?'

'Yes acutely. I was very bitter, it really hit me hard, and I was just getting to knowing him when he introduced this woman as his wife. Very hard, and that's why I am closer to my grandmother.' She averted his gaze for a while and cleared her throat. 'But it hasn't changed the fact that he is my father or diminished my love for him.'

'So I am right to believe every woman would want a man for herself?'

'Yes in an ideal world.'

'Would you forgive your partner for cheating on you?'

His dimension took Lola by surprise and was still thinking of the best answer when she remembered Akin and his son she'd only just discovered, but she was quickly distracted by a young woman who for a while had been looking in their direction. She watched the woman get up but was pulled back to her seat by her accomplice. 'I think your date is waiting.' She nudged in the young lady's direction and was glad of the diversion.

Without taking his eyes off her he replied flatly. 'What date? I am looking at her right now. Not even lover boy can take you away from me right now.'

'You would really like that very much, won't you? Just admit that you are jealous of him?' she teased.

'What if I am?'

'That's too bad,' she leaned back on her chair only to see the young woman at a close range. 'Sorry this lady is taken.' She stretched her finger with the engagement ring towards him.

'Adam!'

They both turned towards the direction of the noise, Lola saw a young beautiful woman tower over them full of smiles.

Adam got on his feet and embraced the beautiful blonde before giving her a peck on her lips.

'Paige meet Lola.' He towered over the two ladies comfortably and didn't take his hand off her back.

She did the same with her hand. She then acknowledged Lola's presence with a cold demeaning look before concentrating back on him with another beaming smile.

Lola, who instantly got the message that she was in the way decided to leave. Paige's expensive perfume not only engulfed the whole surrounding but was equally attracting a lot of attention from many men. She already felt inferior in her casual denims jacket and trouser in comparison to her trendy military styled jacket with a V neck top without her giving her the pompous look. 'I have to go now.'

Just then he stepped closer to Lola only for his guest to do the same. 'Do you really have to?' He sounded like a boy who had his favourite toy snatched from him by an adult.

'You know I do, I have to be somewhere with Akin remember.'

'Yes, that's true.' He wanted to hug her but restrained himself once again. 'You cannot begin to imagine the benefit and enlightenment from our discussion today.'

She looked at his face to try and understand what he meant but unsuccessful. 'Really?'

'Yes, thank you very much. It's been a tremendous pleasure.' He finally opened his arms to embrace her. He embraced her stiff body and began to relax when he didn't let go. 'You've really saved me from possibly the biggest mistake of my life. Maybe I will borrow a leaf off you and forgive and forget.' He whispered into her ear and pecked her cheeks before releasing her.

They were both interrupted by Paige who had been tagging behind them for a while.

'The programme has started and is boring without you.' She slipped her arm into his and blushed when he returned her affection.

Without another word she intensified her pace and was about to call Akin when April's number showed on her mobile phone to tell she'd just seen her approaching her car. She turned round to see Adam squeeze her bum after Paige's giggle distracted her. She could remember seeing her face before but couldn't remember where. Determined not to look back again she dialled her fiancé's number to find out where he was but was surprised to hear him say he was on his way home. He said he had something really important to tell her. That would be the first! She reflected as she got into her car and began to head home, where she ought to really be.

CHAPTER 11

Lola again blamed her third recurring early morning anxiety to her longest four and half weeks of sick leave and three successive sleepless nights of supporting Akin which many could find depressing. She should have known he would never call her to rush home for a good news, she'd rushed home in response to his call three nights ago only to find him looking gloomy and depressed, her first intuition was confirmed when he told her there was bereavement in his family.

She slumped onto the nearest chair with shock and disbelief. 'Who was it?'

'My mother.' He replied with a shaky voice. 'They want me home as soon as possible.'

'My God!'

'But she died in Accra.'

'You didn't say she was living in Ghana.'

'No she wasn't, she went to visit her sister and died after briefly falling ill.'

'Would she be buried in Ghana?'

'I don't know.'

'Why do you need to go to Ghana then?'

She got her answer with a cold, stark stare.

As she picked her handbag and her folder from the passenger seat she wondered how much more she could bear this week before she snapped. She concluded that the long time taken off work had been overshadowed by Akin's bereavement and the pressure of supporting him to the best of her ability.

His departure yesterday should have given way to a sound sleep but she surprisingly didn't, eliminating his bereavement meant the cause lied somewhere else and the only other place she could think of was work. Today was her fourth day of resuming for crying out loud! Hopefully she would be able to bounce back after the weekend that seemed so far away. The windy weather blew her hair up in the air and made her cover the little distance between the car park and her office quicker.

She shortly afterwards stepped into the big and newly refurbished reception and was immediately received by Sara's smile and hand wave for a quick word. Returning her warm smile she listened and watched the two ladies handle barrage of incoming calls before transferring them to their respective colleagues or taking messages.

'You look nice,' she eventually spoke amidst the transfer of a call to her manager.

'Thank you, this new colour really suits your complexion.' She complimented her back with a smile.

'This is for you.'

Lola initially recoiled and eyed the A4 sized padded envelope placed before her. 'Why not the pigeon hole?' She asked the two ladies behind the large oval desk who only smiled at her before carrying on with answering more calls. Sara stood up to show her where it was labelled "please do not fold."

'Where did this come from?' She examined both sides and frowned. The content felt like video cassette player but slightly heavier.

'It was delivered by a tall dark and handsome gentleman.' She replied before taking another call.

'Oh yeah? I'm sure he's much darker than me.'

She squeezed her face at Lola's sarcasm. 'Of course not.'

'Then take the dark features out.' The ladies all smiled before turning towards the noise coming from the B.D.U.'s office.

'Never mind, their systems are down.' She picked another call but the caller hung up on her. 'Which dumps the pandemonium on our lap with almost every call for Bob?'

Lola giggled quietly. 'Anything else about the mystery parcel or it's delivery man?'

She replaced the phone with a big bang and relief. 'He had the cutest bum ever.' Amy replied after being finally free of her caller following thirty minutes of making detailed notes of her complaint.

The two women looked at her amazingly before they all burst into laughter but wasn't surprised Amy wouldn't be able to offer any constructive description apart from good looks.

Lola excused herself after several minutes of her unsuccessful attempt to extract further details from the ladies. Her anxiety to get to her office and open the parcel was soon crushed by the relaxed attitude in the office; she simply wasn't in the mood for the kind of laughter and fun surrounding her today. She seemed upset that everyone was chilling whilst she'd been bugged with too many workloads, especially the reports Bob wanted on his desk by noon today. She'd reliably gathered from the girls that he wouldn't be in till around eleven with four meetings already lined up. Without wasting more time she decided to use the stairs and avoid as much people as possible.

'Morning Lola,' Roxanne's voice chased after her.

'What's going on?' She asked after returning her greeting and noticing the stress in her voice.

'The computer systems are down; three of our engineers are onto it. I reckon it had to do with the interestingly controversial email photos we received this morning.' She quickly answered her phone as she hurried past her on the stairs.

'What were the photos about?'

'Revolting enough to put a smile on some faces.'

She increased her pace to try and keep up with Roxanne who wasn't stopping. 'Who was it about?'

'Bob and he is not taking his calls.' She branched off and headed to the annexe before stopping halfway. 'Sorry Lola I'm expected in a meeting as I speak. These distractions are not helping the situation and most importantly I want to leave early enough to make my dentist appointment at four.'

She watched Roxanne disappear and walk on.

'I'll speak to you tonight my dear if my mouth is not too sore.' She picked another call on her hands free official mobile phone as she finally disappeared.

Relieved the joke wasn't about her this time she quickly planned to stop in the nearest office and look at the photos before they were blocked or removed but instead changed her mind and rushed to her office. The atmosphere in the office this morning confirmed to her that Bob's senior brother was very much preferred and was still musing over this when she saw a handful of people right by her office door all engrossed in a large printout held by Gary, the Personnel Manager, who had asked her out on numerous occasions but had always been politely declined. At thirty, the most eligible bachelor of A.B.C.& D. had dated and dumped more girls than anyone in the company, but Lola who had all along suspected a secret agreement between him and Bob had it confirmed by April who overheard the two men arguing and fighting over her. She further recounted hearing Bob telling him to be more seductive with his approach, but Lola was finally glad she didn't break her long-standing guiding principle of never dating colleagues despite his brain, braun, charms and some of his qualities that constantly reminded her of Adam. In spite of the awareness that her probability of opening the door without being noticed was zero, she was still willing to try. She had successfully keyed in her code numbers and was trying to quietly push her door open when he asked her about the leak.

'What leak?'

'Some staff's personal details are on the internet.'

'What do you mean details?' Lola asked in a panic.

'Like this,' he extracted the last two pages and handed it to her.'

She stood transfixed as her eyes scanned through series of her colleagues' names, dates of birth, addresses, and other details.

'When did you get this?'

'Just now.'

Still disorientated, she dropped the parcel on the chair normally occupied by colleagues and sat on the one next to it for support when her office phone rang. On the other end was her bank account manager who was just fulfilling his promise to call her back as earlier agreed regarding her complaint of the thousands of pounds missing from her credit card account.

She placed the phone back on the receiver fifty minutes later wondering what could be going on before deciding to make herself a cup of tea to calm her nerves and sooth her dry throat. She wondered why she was bombarded with so many unnecessary and irrelevant questions, would she be calling them if she knew the answers. With her P.C. loading, she settled with her drink and was about to open the parcel when April barged in from next door charging with excitement and full smile.

'You'll never believe your eyes with this!'

She raised one eyebrow with a dry smile before putting the brown envelope down again. 'Surprise me.' She said dryly and also wanted to visit the website Gary gave to her but the onslaught of email messages flooding in prevented her straight away. Her whole concentration shifted to the computer as more messages kept flooding in and her attempt to get on top of the situation became paramount.

Meanwhile, April who had cracked several jokes and asked her colleague several questions without any response decided to quit and come back later. 'I'll leave these here for you to look at when you're ready.'

'Sure,' Lola replied absent mindedly with her face wholly stuck on her P.C. screen whilst her mind was preoccupied with the implication of such confidential data leak to the individual staff and the company's image in general. Without another word, April left the photos on her desk before vacating her office with disappointment.

Lola neither heard her nor saw her leave and only looked up when she heard her door shut, but decided to deal with her later. For now, the confidential breach was more important than anything else except if she wanted to cause further damage to her already tarnished reputation.

Lola was answering a telephone enquiry from the Benefit Office about an ex employee's claim for incapacity benefit when Bob walked in with one of his guests. She was initially distracted by his hostile presence and conversations, but she eventually switched off and managed to continue answering the caller's questions. She was still struggling to pick on Bob's conversation when she suddenly noticed a deafening silence in the room and looked up to see their faces downcast as they both gawked at her simultaneously and then back onto her desk. With no other choice but to follow their gaze, she quickly terminated her conversation and stood up to join them in gawking at the degrading A3 sized coloured pictures April had left behind.

The first one was an obscured face of a male adult stripped down to his boxer short and tied to a lamp post. The next photograph showed the male's dilemma as before but fully naked with Bob's face and a FUCKER placard stuck on the lamppost above him and written on his forehead.

She could vividly recollect this particular incident at the car park and had to summon Roxanne who immediately called on Billy to his rescue. She would have opted to be hit by the fastest running vehicle to this! Her office was supposed to be out of bounds for gossips and innuendo, so blaming it on anyone else would complicate matters more. More so, Bob would never believe she had nothing to do with this, if only she knew those who tied him up in the first place! A secret Roxanne said he had consistently refused to divulge to his brother. 'No, where did that come from?' She managed to ask nervously but not convincingly.

Uncertain whether she pulled it through was one thing, the shock and horror on Bob's and his guest's face was a similitude of the world coming to an end! It inadvertently took him a while to compose himself and when he finally introduced her it was with utter contempt and disdain.

Lola's effort to diffuse the tensed atmosphere was not only impossible but hastened their exit and left her to pick up the pieces. She wondered whether she should be more concerned with her own plight or the guest's impression of Bob or the Company in general. With Bob's face as red as a beetroot, she wondered if anyone would believe she knew nothing about the pictures because she couldn't convince herself. Then she realised she was doomed!

Unsure of how to redeem herself she decided to revisit the site containing her colleagues' details. She remained focused on the screen for endless hours looking for any loop hole she could use to defend herself as she flipped from her emails to the site. For inspiration, she decided to read her incoming emails unlike when she only scanned through them earlier. The first message was coincidentally from one of the managers explaining the leak of selected members of staffs' personal details, in his own opinion he blamed the jammed high wave technology. The next email and other successive ones accused the Personnel and Payroll department of some sort of piracy and implored those concerned to seek legal action against their employer. She gasped with shock and horror at this implication on her career, but was subsequently calmed by one message from the Bought Ledger Department warning and imploring managers to be protective of the information within their means and concluded. "Above all we all know information is power especially if it gets to the wrong hands."

Her eyes unfortunately began to ache from the strain but taking her eyes off meant missing vital clues. Just when it was all getting to the boiling point, her phone rang and it was Bob asking to meet her immediately. With the conversation finished she still found herself clutching onto the receiver as her stomach began to somersault with worries and trepidation. Her frozen faculties only began resuming to normality after the sudden bleep from the other end made her drop the phone and hit the floor. Without an iota of doubt she swore she had a mini heart attack! Quickly, she called both April and Roxanne for words of advice or inspiration, but both were unfortunately away from their desks.

Okay! She breathed in and out for about five minutes like she was in labour but still didn't feel any better. Was this a trap? Then she remembered a representative from Personnel Department might just help her case. Quickly she pulled out her folder that she normally took to meetings and started flipping the pages for her personal career plan. Who would believe she was innocent with all the compelling evidence? As she grabbed her handbag, she relived all the nasty gossips she'd heard about Bob before getting on her feet to leave for the meeting.

Robert Morris ended his abrupt conversation with Lola before placing the phone on his rest and leaning his head on the reclining chair to reflect on the latest development. He had just faced the greatest humiliation from a subordinate with all the qualities he considered extremely inferior, she is black, African and a woman! His P.A. rang to inform him that his next appointment was running late because of diverted traffic in the city centre. As grotty as he was feeling today, he would have asked her to cancel and reschedule the meeting, but he wanted legal advice and clarifications on Litigation matters especially the Bonus payout, Insolvency, health and safety and t most importantly the directors and shareholders dispute. And he wanted them now!

The company was just springing up to one of the top five of commercial law firm in the region. He just didn't want to approach any law firm, he wanted a referral from reliable source and most importantly independent of his brother and his spies. With employment matters, he'd been already advised to make the undesirable member of staff redundant but he was waiting for them to tie enough ropes around their necks so they would not be in a position to refuse his generous offer no matter how little. His first target and mission was controlling and managing the payroll system, he was already secretly taking the course and would be taking over very soon!

He adjusted his tie and was about to return to the file when his mobile phone rang. He listened for a while before he interrupted snappily, 'What do you mean nothing?'

He frowned at the response from the other end, 'are you telling me there is nothing like parking fine, driving offence, and county court judgement?'

'None whatsoever, but we've got something on the fiancé.'

'Forget her fiancé, I know he's in prison and he's one of us.' Bob interrupted angrily as his voice vibrated through the other end. Angrily, he yanked his tie off and slammed the phone down at the same time. Another useless P.I.!

He leaned back on his chair and shut his eyes as he planned of how to execute the rest of his plan.

Like a prompt he sat upright and reopened the file he'd requested from personnel department. He's been trying to pronounce her name correctly for the umpteenth time, after reading and digesting every detail in her file so many times that he could write a dossier about her except her name. Gently he pulled the file closer to try again, Lolade Anif-olase, he commended himself with a smile for getting it right, before progressing to her middle name which was proving to be too challenging to his liking. O-lu-wa-ti-mi-le-hin he managed to read proudly, but still wasn't convinced he got it right. Her name rolled off his tongue one syllable after the other but didn't sound right in his ears. Getting their names right always and somehow convinced them that he actually cared about them and it was nothing personal!

Bob does not consider himself a racist but just intolerant of blacks and Africans and he makes no bone about despising the likes of Lola who wants to be self-righteous. To him, a righteous Nigerian only exist if the price tag was low, all you need to do is increase the stake. The higher he raised the stake the more adamant she became and the more his brother was jumping on his bloody back. An expensive experience he acquired some decades back was not to let Billy too close. He was already running out of choices when he brought Wonder on board but the moron proposed to marry her and refused to carry out his assignment. Now he decided to grab the bull by the horn, and finish the task himself! By the time he met Lola for the interview he had wished he'd taken the opportunity his brother granted him to employ one of the previous successful applicants. His flimsy excuses about the previous applicants made him smile cynically, one successful applicant was turned down because of her feeble handshake, another was not cheerful enough and then one was described as being too soft. Billy knew his problem was because they were all black; he just refused to admit it and he was sure his brother knew too. Fortunately, Lola was at an advantage over other applicants because she was employed through a scheme that was totally out of his control. This, however, did not prevent him from scrutinising her, but her exemplary records and achievements could not be swept under the carpet. Regrettably she was the best of the candidates and good with her job too!

He was interrupted by the knock on the door.

'Please do sit down,' Bob said as he pointed to one of the expensive dark mahogany chairs facing him. She stared at his large, wide, oily forehead and the aggressively receding hair line.

With no one else in the room with them, she clutched her bag for life support as she nervously sat on the edge of the chair closest to her and wondering why she thought he'd play fair.

Pretending his mind was occupied with the piece of paper in front of him, he cleared his throat before he spoke. 'I gathered the Personnel Department are having their monthly meeting so I reckon it might be a long wait before a representative does arrive.'

She gave a big sigh of relief. Their eyes met and they assessed each other suspiciously.

'Have you been to the website?' He asked after the silence stretched between them and became unbearable; needless to say she was still caught off guard.

She presumed he was talking of the same website and nodded.

'Do you think the company values your contribution in these past years?'

It was obvious to her that he had played this scene many times over with many other women like herself. 'I guess so.' The half of her proclaiming innocence now echoed curiosity whilst the other half became highly suspicious.

'Which of your roles have you enjoyed the most?' He wasn't the sort to send for a woman to praise her.

As she tried to stare back at him, sunlight shone through the window into the room to highlight the nastiness and hardness of his face, but equally made her blink out of weakness and fear when his wicked eyes finally met hers.

'All of it.'

'What section or role would you say you mostly struggled with?' He knew she wasn't stupid, only a genius could plan something like this for so long. He lowered his head and pretended to be studying the file on his desk, hoping that would encourage her to speak freely.

She frowned as she thought deeply about his question and realised it was not different from the previous one. 'I enjoyed them all.'

Bob digested it with disappointment and followed it with a long, imposing silence before lifting his head. Realising it wasn't as easy as he had planned; he went straight to his point. 'What areas do you think you require training on?'

She sat still pretending to think when she realised the question wasn't different from the previous two.

He finally interrupted her. 'In the past one hour, these names have appeared on another Web site. He pushed the white paper her way and watched her reaction closely. 'Everyone on that list is dead, married or no longer working with us.'

As she reached for the paper her fingers touched his and she cringed almost to the point of cutting the offending fingers off with a sharp object. She read the first few lines and felt her stomach lurch with mortification and fear. Like an innocent person at the mercy of a judge about to receive a death sentence for an offence he or she knew nothing about, she made an involuntary sound that made him look at her. Their gazes met and she noticed him gloating at her but she quickly averted her stare back to the piece of paper in front of her. Everything began to seem surreal and poignant but nonetheless senseless.

'Miss Anifo-…' Bob tried to call her last name like a well-learned litany, but failed. She sensed his frustration before he pretended to clear his throat and looked straight into her eyes with a renewed hatred that had had just been recharged. The realisation of knowing that it was always there and had never for once gone away suddenly began to bother her. 'You've really planned this well, haven't you?' His tone now changed like a judge finally having the opportunity to pass his sentence on a criminal after so many mistrials. 'How many more websites should we expect our personal details to feature?' Bob fixed her with a level stare as if hoping she might reflect on her wrongdoing and confess.

She blinked and hated herself again for doing that. Gently she lowered her gaze back to the paper like she had missed something vital out, but the whole page was blurry just like her mind. None of this was making any sense! He wanted her to admit to something she didn't do. With her face stuck on the piece of paper for what seemed to be forever, she took a deep breath and hoped it was her last.

He snatched the paper away from her and waved it in her face. 'Have you any idea the embarrassment this has caused the company and the danger you are exposing the staff to?'

She wanted to speak and defend herself but changed her mind when she remembered what Roxanne always said of him. 'Bob doesn't have a dialogue he holds a monologue.'

With no response, his eyes swiftly sought hers; she gave him the satisfaction for a while and cast away her look when his red eyes were consumed fiercely with an abhorrence she couldn't bare. 'You'd better pray we don't get lawsuit from any employee.' He flung the paper at her and the edge hit her right in the eye that not only blurred her vision further but made her eye watery.

Without an apology he got up and picked the paper from the floor. 'The likes of you always express their gratitude and kindness by fraud of some sort.' He waited for a counter reaction and continued when she still remained seated and silent. 'Your trouble is you see yourself as an equal to us, because we've tolerated you. You strut around the office like a goddess ... or queen of universe ... self-righteous, arrogant ...' He discontinued with a wave of his hand.

She instantly realised the depth of his detestation not only for her and what she stood for but also noticed that his demeanour was becoming belligerent and his voice was getting louder. He relished each word with judicious hatred!

She decided to respond with the same note of repulsion and distaste. 'The likes of me? I beg your pardon! Do you think I chose to be born in the midst of the likes of you or would I have come back to this country if I knew the likes of you still existed?'

First it was shock then horror followed by anger before immediately replacing the colouring of his face with a swift, plastic smile. 'I'm glad we understand each other.' His expression froze for a while before clearing his throat yet again. 'Let me rephrase myself in case you have not understood.' He paused and tried to force a smile but without success, when he spoke he wasn't shouting but his voice had an underlying aggression beneath it. 'I have been suspicious about you right from day one even though my spineless brother wouldn't listen to my warnings.' He looked at her like a piece of dirt he wanted off his precious shoes. 'Can you begin to imagine how we can assure those employees whose names, addresses, date of birth and N.I. numbers have been publicised that it was nothing?' He paused and thought briefly. 'How can we assure them that their privacy had not been already invaded?'

She restrained herself from saying anything with a definite assurance that more was not only coming but his ultimate aim was to provoke and corner her.

He moved closer to watch her closely before speaking. 'By the way we sincerely apologise for our mistakes, it was due to our untrustworthy payroll manager's attempt to tarnish the Company's image and violate the data protection act and regulation.'

Lola detected some incoherencies and more underlying bitterness but was perturbed by the wicked, twisted smile in his voice and face.

'I hope the money is worth all the trouble because the Company has decided to let you go on compulsory leave till the investigation is over.' He stretched his hands towards her to demand for her office keys.

She became more mortified than ever and didn't see the point in listening anymore by swiftly pushing her seat back to leave.

Without giving her the opportunity to respond, he equally stood up and tried to level his five foot five inches height with her five foot seven without any shoe, 'I demand you hand the keys to your office over immediately.'

She decided to take advantage of height she'd always carried with pride and dignity by yanking the tiny bunch out of her handbag and dumping it on his desk without taking her eyes off him. To her favour her high heels made her more arresting and him much smaller despite his tip toe. 'Very soon it's going to be our credit card details and then bam we are going to have our identities cloned by Nigerians in Nigeria whilst the rest of you all swing on the trees and eat bananas.'

She wouldn't mind if he was having a go at her personally but she reckoned he'd gone too far and needed to be stopped. Not only was she profoundly shaken by his vehemence, hatred and insult but angrier with the amount of his saliva landing on her face. Above all that was a low blow! With her posture more arresting than ever, she gazed at his large, wonky, shiny forehead, big sunken eyeballs, then on the long, shapeless hooked up nose before finally resting on his overlarge, drooly mouth. Without moving her face she wiped the saliva off and drew her longest hiss before turning round and walking out.

'You have my pathetic brother to thank for the paid suspension and don't be under any illusion that my brother will believe you over me. It's all going to be your words against mine.' Bob's calm voice trailed behind her with a hint of harsh finality.

Unable to explain how she got to the ladies, she leaned on the cubicle door to compose herself as she reflected on what had just transpired. Uncontrollable tears rolled down her cheeks as she relished the barrage of lies, torrents of accusations and bullying he'd subjected her to, and more tears flowed freely.

After a heart wrenching weep, she decided to head home before anyone caught up with her and was halfway to her office when she ran into Mr James emerging from the opposite direction. 'Are you all right baby?' Without waiting for her reply he led her towards her office which was also the way out.

'He just sacked me!' She wanted to explain further but found herself tongue tied as more tears pushed their way through.

He drew her closer to console her but she broke down completely as her handbag and it's contents landed and spread all over the floor. They both bent down to pick them up but she was too despondent to think straight apart from sob more.

'What are you doing here?' Bob's angry voice caught them off guard as he eyed the pair revoltingly whilst Mr James quickly picked her bag and guided her back to her feet.

'Relieving Jimmy.' He opened the bag for her to dump her belongings she'd picked up in it.

'Where is he?' He snapped.

Lola wanted to proceed home but was restrained by his tight grip. 'He went to the toilet.'

Whilst Bob wanted an eye contact she couldn't.

Just then Jimmy approached in the adjoining hallway and started running when he saw Bob's angry face waiting impatiently.

'I specifically ordered you to stay here, you incompetent bastard.' His thunderous voice echoed all around. 'You'd better all conduct yourself professionally; I'm taking an important visitor round.'

She watched the terror on Jimmy's face.

Just then his P.A. showed up to inform him his visitor had finished his telephone conversation and was waiting.

'Bring him over here.' He moved closer to Jimmy and pointed his chubby finger in his face. 'I'll deal with you later but you can go back to your post for now.'

Mr James wanted to continue escorting her but was literarily barked at. 'I want to have a word with you now.'

The old man flashed his dangerous smile. 'Okay boss.' There seemed to be some kind of silent communication between them. 'The young lady is upset.'

'Keep your nose out of this matter Felix.' He wasn't shouting but his firm voice was still loud enough for her to hear. 'My guest has arrived.'

To avoid aggravating the situation, she went ahead and neither waited for him to complete his sentence nor for Mr James's response. She was just by her office when Bob's loud voice turned all charming and pleasant to his guest. 'Did you manage to get all the information Mr Salvador?'

'Yes, my secretary is faxing it through as I speak; I was hoping we could go through it together.'

Lola froze and turned round at the deep, familiar voice. As her sad and sore eyes met Adams' she prayed for a stop to all her embarrassments. Whilst he smiled at her, she hurried on with the intention of leaving the premises and its vicinity immediately.

She was completely shocked by what was to come next! A loud, big bang shook the ground she was standing upon with everything around her in flames. The last she saw was her office window shattering and glass flying everywhere, and then feeling something hit her hard on the head. She slumped to the ground, bleeding and was amazed at how quickly the three men got to her side.

Bob's voice vibrated through the immediate surroundings as more colleagues started streaming out of their offices. 'You stupid cow now what have you done? Turn the building into rubbles?'

Adam wasted no time in gathering her into his arms. 'Can you call the ambulance?'

He was baffled by the panic in his voice. 'We don't need an ambulance for her; we have qualified first aiders on this floor.'

'Yes you do! She is slipping into comma.' His firm voice ricochet through his surroundings just as April arrived at the scene. Shaken, she quickly called for the ambulance on her phone.

She bent down to assess her colleague's bloody face after passing the details to 999 then onto Adam's panic stricken face. With Bob still towering over them with his fist clenched and an impertinent look, it was obvious he felt insulted and undermined by Adam's insolent outburst and authority.

'Yes?' Adam asked interrupting her thoughts with terror and rudeness. With no regards to the heavy blood stain on his shirt, he gazed back at the lifeless, yet precious body he cradled gently.

'Sorry, the ambulance and the fire crews are on their way.' April managed to explain before rushing to the toilet to throw up. She could never stand blood no matter how minute and what she'd seen gushing out of Lola's face was enough to pass her out for days. In the past, she'd passed out on numerous occasions over much less blood and here she was still standing instead of wrenching her guts and spleen out. She wondered why as she doused some water onto the pale face starring back at her in the mirror, maybe it was the guilt of abandoning a very good friend in dire need!

No sooner had April rushed off that Amy one of the qualified first aider on the floor arrived. Then she sent for another first aider to check on April when she remembered her phobia of blood.

The magnitude of the situation was not only beginning to hit Bob but was also terrifying him as he swore under his breath and equally sweat like a pig. As his worry spread faster than the fire burning in Lola's office, he smiled apologetically at Adam who reciprocated it with scornful stare. He realised he'd bitten more than he could chew!

CHAPTER 12

Adam sat upright on the hospital chair with his hands overlapped and his arms leaning on the arm chair rest. With a big sigh of relief, he took another long, look around the large room with fewer appliances, no ventilator for a change and less plaster on her face. He twitched his nose to ward off the antiseptics that had invaded his nostrils through the ward and the hospital in general.

He was not aware of the meeting with Bob from A.B.C. & D. Ltd. until Leslie Brown called the office that he'd rather be with his wife. Apart from his recent promotion as a senior partner in one of the fastest growing legal firm in the region, he was also covering for his boss due to return next week and he'd already had everything up to his eyeballs. He was half way to his briefing when the receptionist walked straight to one of the managers and whispered to him.

'Not again!' Kirk his most senior manager in the room angrily banged his fist on the table.

'What is it?' Adam asked, trying desperately to contain his anger.

'Les is running late.'

'Leslie Brown? Then phone client and tell them.'

'No, he'd phoned the office that he couldn't make the appointment because he'd rather be with his wife in the hospital.'

Adam glanced from one surprised face to the other and finally onto the receptionist.

She looked at Kirk first before looking at Adam. 'Mrs Brown was having their first child.'

Kirk burst into laughter with most of his other colleagues.

Adam got on his feet to tower over everyone in the room and gently patted the table. 'Leslie Brown chose his priority and ours right now is this Company.'

'Yes boss,' echoed by many in the room.

'We've got a business to run.' He faced the receptionist before he continued. 'Can you get me the customer's file please?'

'Kirk what can you tell me about the company?'

It was during the briefing that Adam realised it was a new client but a familiar territory. His attempt to forget or overlook their strong link suddenly became a struggle. As he closed the file before him to embark on the visit, he was paradoxically thrilled when an inner voice told him it was fate doing him the honours and justice. When he finally set his eyes on Lola he strongly believed he was killing two bird with one stone and couldn't wait to be officially introduced by Bob but the excitement was quickly quenched by a loud explosion. He only believed it wasn't a bad nightmare when the impact not only knocked her to the ground but violently shook the ground underneath his feet.

The blast really frightened him, talk about a cocktail of emotion! Luckily, the paramedics responded very quickly and were able to resuscitate and stabilise her on the accident scene before taking her to the hospital. April was able to supply all her necessary details to the paramedics before he volunteered to accompany her. Whilst ignoring the amusement on everyone's faces, his eyes met hers when he informed the paramedics that her only allergy was cats and dogs mostly. On the way to the hospital he later on called Dr Mason to ask if there was anything else to add but he insisted on speaking to the paramedics instead. But his relief was short lived when Lola convulsed with fits and had to be resuscitated again. She was immediately taken to the theatre for operation and was returned to the ward several hours later. He quickly seized the opportunity to go home, freshen up and change into something more casual.

Having waited for what seemed to be eternity, he wasn't surprised when his round the clock vigil turned daylight into evening and finally into night. Adam had never been so excited about anything or anyone until she regained consciousness, even though the mixture of joy and relief disorientated him for a start. He was bizarrely thrilled that she was finally speaking on the second day after the ordeal and didn't care that her first words were complains of severe headache and blackouts, which in no time brought a doctor and a nurse to her bedside for another assessment. Lola kept dozing off halfway to answering the medics question and didn't take much longer before she became fully sedated with the new set of medication.

Adam sat still, mesmerised with relief and disappointment; watching her sleep peacefully for hours before he decided to go home and have some rest. Whilst watching her breathe softly, he hoped she open her eyes again and smiled at him. It then dawned on him that she didn't need to open her eyes for him to remember how teasingly trusting they were. Finally admitting that it was one of the qualities he admired greatly about her encouraged a wild thought to cross his mind just as he got on his feet to leave. After deliberating over a bizarre thought for nearly ten minutes he ultimately decided to follow his heart; he walked up to her, pecked her side of cheeks free of plaster and stitches but lingered more on her lips before bidding her goodnight. He imagined it to feel like kissing a log of wood but the response her soft, inviting lips stirred in him amazingly surpassed his expectation.

The memory followed him all the way home and continued needling him till bed time. It reached a critical point when he kept turning and tossing in bed despite being physically tired. All that kept replaying on his mind was helpless, bloody Lola in the middle of the blast and the deafening noise that followed it. Hours later, with still no sign of sleep, he angrily yanked his bedcover off and decided to get a glass of water in the kitchen which he gulped down in two go and was still upset. With nothing but contempt for the likes of Robert Morris who had no regards for other people's lives apart from their stupid ego and narrow-mindedness, he would so much like to knock some evil out of him and replace it with some senses, decency and humanity but first and foremost Lola had to fully recover. Talk about timing! He wondered what would have happened to her if he wasn't around, he would have deliberately delayed all the medical assistance required to reduce her chance to survive. He was told she'd obviously suffered from amnesia but they couldn't establish how bad she'd suffered until they carried out further test.

He was accustomed to opposite sex reacting to his height, look, suave and his intellect, most of them either wanted him for his body or his money. And he reckoned it would be an injustice not to admit the leverage these qualities gave his self-confidence. An assumption that he only had to snap his finger for many people to be at his beck and call was again put in practice with Bob's P.A. who was more than eager to help but was also all over him like a rash. It diabolically surprised and bothered him that it was the other way round with Lola and worse of all he was unable to resist the magnet that constantly drew him to her.

Adam was, on the third day, glad she'd been transferred to a private room as he'd asked Dr Mason for the favour yesterday and felt more at ease with no prying eyes or distraction unlike the open room she was previously in. On top of her bedside cabinet were three colourful bouquets of flowers, now placed in separate vases by the hospital staff and three get well cards from him, Roxanne and April.

He eagerly sat up when he heard her muffle some words but was disappointed to find her eyes still shut as she continued to breathe softly. His eyes quickly summed her helpless and hopeful position on a single-sized bed with drip stuck on one of her arms, a bandage wrapped around her head with her eyes tightly shut. Noticing a few grazes on her face, especially her cheeks, he edged forward for a closer look. There was a scar right between her eyes but it didn't affect the natural upward slant in her eyes, which equally assured him that her bright, brown eyes would still glow like pricy gemstones if she opened them now, as they always did whenever she was happy. Her neither flat nor pointed nose was thankfully not affected either. Surprisingly, his eyes continuously lingered on her well-proportioned mouth and her delicately radiant full lips, clearly outlined at both ends but still secured the real beauty of her neatly arranged white set of teeth. What mystified him the most was how her dimples and high cheekbones enhanced and still summed up her beauty.

Whilst seated and still reading the same paragraph of the weekly magazine for over thirty minutes, the same nurse who made the sinister remarks yesterday and afterwards burst into laughter when he corrected her walked into the room, smiled at him before going to examine her. He realised he was just being touchy yesterday, who else would she have asked for Lola's underwear. If they presumed he was her partner then he was naturally expected to bring some, and it was up to him to decide whether to pick them from her house or buy her some new ones. Picking them from her house meant rummaging through her stuff and that might not look credible in the future, especially if *loverboy* hears about it. But then again, he truly deserved it, if he judged him by what he already knew about him. Having decided to buy it himself, he began to worry about how she would react if she found out and secondly getting the right size meant emphasising on some parts of her body that were already stimulating him. As he watched her add a few lines onto her case file at the foot of her bed, he heaved a big sigh of relief when she finally excused herself without any disturbing comments like yesterday. She had earlier informed him that Lola woke up some hours ago crying, that explained why he'd like to stay as long as he could, today. Sade, her next of kin had been informed and was expected to visit from Reading with her mum from London tomorrow or the day after. An uneasy feeling overcame him when he tried to imagine what would happen if *loverboy* turned up from one of his mysterious trips. Despite his knowledge of taking chances he knew he could get away with it for now. His inability to take control of the situation was beginning to irritate him amongst many other things, but he still felt he owed it to her and himself. If not for anything but for that unique, exceptionally alluring and captivating aura he'd never experienced with anyone before. His biggest concern was how her aura was gently pushing him to face the darkest abyss in his life, despite having the ultimate choice to end it all right now he unfortunately couldn't. Well as they say, the sweet i never as sweet without the sour taste!

He finally accepted defeat and put the magazine away before focusing back at Lola's peaceful face sternly. He shortly afterwards looked away from her and concentrated on the ceiling to prevent his mind getting too carried away. As he covered his mouth to stifle a yawn he prayed she woke up sooner rather than later, because he might not be able to move tomorrow's important appointments, and he wanted her to see him first.

He must have dozed off and dreamt of her whispering his name softly. He was turning around for more comfort when "Adam!" penetrated through

Suddenly snapped from slumber, he remembered where he was and what for. Edging forward from his seat, he wiped his face with his hand for clarity and saw her hand move. Within a snapshot he was by her bedside, holding her hand and looking straight into her eyes without any inhibition.

Lola batted her eyes at him, giving him the full benefit of dazzling irises shielded by lashes so long and full that they were often mistaken for fake. She would remember this face anywhere and time. Strikingly handsome, honey glazed skin, his jet black hair neatly cut. His striking, hazel coloured eyes flecked and the curve of his lips was full of smiles and inviting. 'You'll need to move closer because I can't shout.'

Still holding her hand he did and he found the closeness ticklish, as if that wasn't bad enough he instantly noticed she had no bra and decide to gauge the two moulds on her chest with his mind. His best way of describing his bodily response was sensational.

'Am I in the hospital?'

'Yes.'

'What happened?'

'You bumped your head in an accident.'

'When?'

'Yesterday.'

'At home?'

'No, in the office.'

'In the office?' She tried to frown but failed, followed by a painful moan.

'Yes, why are you surprised?'

'Yes, why was I in the office when I'm still on sick leave for my injured ankle.'

He held onto her hand and began stroking it whilst she ran the other one through her wrapped up head.

'My head hurts so badly, I can't feel anything on this side.'

'I know.' He reached for the bell and pressed it hard whilst looking into her eyes with so much sincerity that her heart nearly melted.

'Where is Akin again?'

Despite trying his hardest not to upset her he wanted to tell her the truth, but the situation was saved when the nurse walked in with some medication and it did favourably douse his wild sensation to some extent.

By the fifth day of her admission, it had been medically established that the blast did not do any permanent damage to any part of her body or brain apart from some months' gap in her memory. Adam reckoned it was around two to three months to be precise. The doctor advised him to try and make her revisit known places and incidents to help her fill the missing gaps.

Her most frequent question regarding Akin's whereabouts was also finally answered when Roxanne and April visited her on the same day with the biggest get well card ever seen. Whilst April was busy reading her colleague's get well messages decorated all over the card, Adam was about to knock on the door when he heard voices from the other side.

'You told us he was in Ghana with his aunt for four weeks.'

'His only aunt known to me is on a wheelchair.'

'Yes, I could remember you commenting on her disability.' April added.

'Any idea of when he exactly left?'

The two women looked at each other's face before speaking simultaneously. 'Around a week ago.'

'That means he has around two more weeks left to return .'

'No, you were supposed to join him.'

'Really?' Lola frowned when she tried to remember something.

'When?'

'You never said.'

Lola's next question shocked everyone in the room. 'Did I tell any of you that I was pregnant?'

'Not your style.' 'I don't think you two have had se …'

'Keep your voice down.' Roxanne finally cautioned. 'And if you were, it would have shown in the tests carried out so far.'

She held tightly onto her abdomen before finally letting go. 'True but my uterus burns like mad. And I wonder why. Burning uterus or stomach cramp wouldn't have anything to do with pregnancy?'

'Don't think so.'

'What can be the cause of such then?' She looked helplessly at her guests.

'The best thing is to book an appointment with your G.P.'

'Sure.' She sipped from the drink they brought for her. 'I am seriously relying on you two and Adam to fill me in.' She rubbed her palm over her stomach for a while before she continued. 'No flesh, just give it to me in raw bone I'm begging you two please.'

'Do you remember being engaged?'

'No way!' She raised her left hand to confirm the ring still stuck on her third finger.

'Lola, you too were planning to travel to Lagos for a traditional ceremony.'

'Oh my God!' She held onto her head like it was going to fall off whilst her eyes widened with disbelief. 'When was I supposed to buy the travel ticket?'

'You already had it, open ticket you said.'

'The thought of it alone made me miss home terribly.'

'You are not fit enough to travel!' The two women echoed together.

Adam's knock triggered some anticipation as all eyes focused at the entrance. His eyes quickly locked Lola's as they both froze in their respective positions totally oblivious of their surroundings or anyone else until the shrilling voice from another room. They both looked away simultaneously with his eyes dancing mischievously whilst Lola's heart missed a beat. Suddenly his face sobered as he smiled at the two guests before speaking in his warmly caressing tone just like his eyes. Without another word the two women looked at each other and decided it was time they left, all Lola's effort to convince them to stay failed.

After their departure, she sat up and he sat beside her before embracing and pecking her forehead. He offered her the drink she asked for and held the cup for her.

A few minutes later, she decided to confirm what she'd heard. 'You didn't tell me I was engaged.'

'I thought you knew already.' He lied.

She believed him and quickly continued to confirm all she heard from her colleagues, which led to his job, how he came to be at A.B.C. & D. on that fateful day, and the kind of day he'd had. 'Roxanne and April called you my hero.' She concluded as she locked his gaze for his reaction.

Adam was as much touched by the way and timing she said it. It was one of his rare moments of being bashful, poignant and equally lost for words.

'Can you lie me down please?' Her voice penetrated his thoughts sharply.

He quickly reached for her pillows and moulded them to her desired shape before guiding her gently onto it.

Lola was still talking when she dozed off, he as usual watched her for a while before covering her up, pecking her and finally taking his leave. He wondered how long these stolen kisses were going to drag on for.

The following day, Lola seemed a bit withdrawn and more sleepy than usual even though she'd welcomed him as usual with her bright smiles that melt his heart. She told him the scar on her head was itchy and he warned her to resist scratching it or risk infecting it. She complained of a terrible headache and requested him to read one of her favourite novels that he'd bought her some days back until she slept off. There wasn't much talk about the two of them today except the novel he read her. After reading three chapters he suggested they talked about what he'd read so far and was shocked to find her deeply asleep.

Adam left the hospital and bizarrely drove past Lola's house when he noticed her living room light was on. His first thought was Akin but he quickly dispelled it because of his latest update about his location. Shortly afterwards he saw the old man trying to console Lola on the day of the blast coming out of her drive way clutching to some folders. Quickly, Adam closed the gap and challenged him, but the old man initially refused to be intimidated, until he snatched the folders and would have grabbed it back from Adam if they hadn't both seen a police patrol vehicle on the prowl. He wasted no further time to explain the implication of his action especially when the police vehicle slowed down before them. Coincidentally, the police vehicle stopped next to Lola's house, acknowledged their presence before knocking on the same door. To avoid suspicion from the officer, he suggested that Mr James should drive them away in his car, the old man instantly obliged without an argument.

'Who sent you?' Adam asked after settling comfortably in his car.

He told Adam off the record what he'd overheard and what he wanted to do with the information.

'How did you hear about this information? And why should I believe you?'

Mr. James flashed his fake smile. 'I am a Bounty Hunter.'

'A bounty hunter? In what way?'

'Information-hunter.'

'I see, you are a blackmailer.'

'SHHHHH. Not so blunt.' He tried to speak calmly but the panic written all over his face reflected in his voice.

'Is there a market for this information?'

'Of course there is.'

'Explain it to me.'

'My source wants some privileged information to blackmail Lola and I've got not only the information but the evidence with it, tell me how much you wouldn't pay for such a treasure.'

'Tell me why I should not suspect you as the mastermind of this problem and yet again pretending to find the solution?'

The old man put his hands up and down before playing a recorded conversation.

'How much do you want for this information?' Adam asked after listening to the tape.

He spread five fingers towards him.

'Five thousand pounds! What do I get in return for not grassing you to the police?'

'You wouldn't do that.'

'Why not?'

'Then those who planted the explosion will walk freely and she might not be that lucky next time.'

'And you claim to have that evidence too?'

'Yes, enough evidence to get her out of this cobweb and convict those bastards behind it.'

'I've got all I need thank you,' he waved his mobile phone at him.

'If you can live with the consequence. I'm an old man trying to make provision for my pension and I'm open to offers.' He persuaded him.

Adam rubbed his forehead in desperation for a bright idea. 'A thousand pounds.'

'That's too little, not enough!'

'Consider it a goodwill gesture; I'm just taking your words for it.'

'You love her don't you?'

The two men assessed each other for a while before he corked his head and pretended he didn't know who he was talking about. 'Who?'

'You know who.' Mr James smiled and tapped his nose.

He gave him one of his complimentary cards. 'Phone me tomorrow to arrange a meeting.'

'Are you coming with the money then?'

'If you are coming with all the information and the tapes, take this as a down payment.' He handed him the bundle of twenty pounds note from his pocket without counting it.

Mr James wouldn't stop calling him, his excuse was as he called it "guarding his interest and confirming he hadn't changed his mind" which got to a point that he deliberately left his phone with his P.A. who after nine calls had to ask Adam who he was. He was due in court all day so there wasn't much time for unnecessary telephone conversation and had received another nine calls from Mr James basically asking the same questions by the end of afternoon. His latest excuse was that he didn't feel safe with the rest of the information on him and he would also want to change their meeting place. Despite his busy schedule, he managed to fulfil his agreement and meet him in his chosen environment with the hope of making good use of him in the near future. With that end wrapped up, he knew things could only get better. His generous offer of one thousand five hundred pounds must have impressed the man because he afterwards offered to buy him a drink but tired and miserable Adam politely declined and exchanged for another date.

He was so anxious for an early night that he cancelled his date, but home unfortunately did not offer him the solace he so much desired until he called to check on her progress and he could tell from her voice that she was deeply upset that he didn't visit her today. He'd rather she openly admitted it than sulking but that would inadvertently acknowledge some kind of feeling that might complicate matters more, unlike him that missed her today and hoped to tell her to her face. Surprisingly, one other reason he didn't bother visiting today was because Sade and her mum would be visiting her today instead of tomorrow.

Lola surprisingly called him the following morning that she would like to see him as soon as he possibly could. He promised to be there in an hour's and was surprised at how well she received him. He would have got carried away if not for the timely arrival of Sade and her mum who mistook him for Akin because of their cosy sitting arrangement and became disappointed when he could not reciprocate her greetings in *Yoruba*. They brought her some traditional meals which was different to his take away. With the three of them deeply engrossed in their conversation, he decided to excuse them.

'Are you coming this evening?' She asked him immediately he rose from his seat.

He would have automatically said no to check her reaction but he realised she might not be in a position to banter so he instantly agreed. Evening also came with its own disappointment, whilst April and Roxanne remain comfortably seated, he politely decided to excuse them but not before enquiring about her family whom he gathered were already on their way back to their respective homes. He was relieved about the news even though he didn't know why.

On the seventh day of her admission Adam knocked on her door for a visit and was particularly looking forward to finishing the chapter he started two days ago.

'I've been discharged!'

'Good,' he replied as he settled on the bed beside her. He slipped her hand into his and began stroking it gently. He wanted to embrace her but stopped because he knew what effect that would have on him. 'How is the scar?' He asked instead after noticing the change in the dressing.

'Fine,' she examined her dressing through a small mirror. 'Not bad, I could easily cover this with a hat.' She stopped from putting her towel in her bag and looked at him. 'What's it Adam?' He instead slid her other hand into his and pecked her before facing him fully. 'You can't fool me, what's wrong? You are far too quiet to my liking.'

'I wouldn't advice you to stay in your house for now.' Despite his frankness, he wished he could put the gravity of the situation in a simpler way.

'I miss my home.'

'I can imagine but there is something I'd been meaning to tell you.'

'What's wrong?' The fright in her eyes stopped him short immediately. 'Is anything wrong with my house? Have I been burgled?'

'Yes!' He replied immediately. That would have to do for now since he couldn't bring himself to tell her right now that her life was in danger.

'But why?' With a shaky voice she stared at him to prevent the tears rolling down. 'Was that why you missed one day?'

He didn't answer but looked at her with a blank expression.

She clasped her hands over her face with tears running down her cheeks. 'Was that why you'd been discouraging me from asking to be discharged?'

His admission with a nod brought more tears.

'Why have you kept this secret from me?'

'Why not?' In a pensive mood, he stroked a strand of hair on his forehead before closing the gap and hugging her.

A young black nurse with a round cheerful face walked in with her prescriptions, a letter for her G.P., her discharge letter; get well tips and advice booklet followed by an outpatient appointment for the following week.

As he drove out of the hospital, Lola insisted he took her home but he refused bluntly. He finally succumbed to her plea when she started crying after arguing that she had a right to see the state her house was in.

When he finally pulled up in front of her house he reminded her to be careful and not to be too distraught. He knew straight away that he couldn't leave her on her own because he wouldn't forgive himself if anything happened to her again, but that ultimately meant his date was cancelled again. Yet he wasn't complaining for missing another date with paige, he lifted his brows as he wondered what had come over him. As he got out of the car he sighed with frustration and hoped she appreciated all his efforts.

As she turned the key through the keyhole she doubted him strongly until she looked into the study The books on the shelf were all on the floor; one of the drawers of the filing cabinets was emptied. 'This break in is about my job!'

'Why did you say that?' Adam hoped she didn't notice the fear in his voice.

'Because everything in this cabinet was entirely about work and the office.'

'Do you suspect anybody?'

'I used to suspect Bob but I'm not sure anymore.' Her eyes landed on her missing P.C. and she felt her temple throb. 'Glad my laptop was with me.'

Adam began to wonder if Mr James lied to him or he'd made another trip before or after. If it was after why did his P.I. not know about it? Unless … 'How many windows are in the back?'

Whilst waiting for her reply he saw a visible shoeprint that led to the bathroom. He quickly followed his instinct. 'Bastards!' He remarked when he saw the broken window.

Lola was swiftly beside him to see the shattered glass all over the floor, she wanted to get inside but he pulled her back. 'Police evidence.' Staring at him with disbelief she melted and started sobbing.

Adam watched her sob only for a while before he acted against his decision not to hug her. 'Calm down, it's not as bad as it looks,' he urged with his arms wide open which immediately progressed to bawling by the time she was in his arms.

He dialled 999 and was lucky to get through to the right department; it was from his conversation with the police that they remembered to check the bedrooms upstairs.

He was upstairs in one quick stride with Lola closely behind. The first room was her bedroom, considerably big with a king-sized bed surrounded by wardrobes apart from the window positioned at the foot of the bed. On one side of the wall was a portrait of her and Akin both of them dressed in suits. Whilst trying to observe his surroundings for any clue her natural scent from the room filled his lungs. 'Does anything look out of place?'

She didn't respond immediately but instead looked thoughtful.

He stepped inside, pulled the curtain for any sign of forced entry but didn't see any, and then he noticed one of the wardrobe's doors slightly ajar. 'May I?'

She only nodded at him to go ahead.

The wardrobe had four equal shelves all filled with colourful traditional outfits. Lola moved forward and reached for the jewellery box which had been obviously tampered with. She flipped it opened and looked blankly at first, picked three little velvet pouches and emptied them on her bed. 'Thank God!' She gasped with relief as she replaced them and saw an A5 sized blue envelope. She pulled it out to find two more envelopes that had already been opened. The first one she pulled out was her return ticket from Lagos to Birmingham and the next one belonged to Mr A. Ajibola.

Adam looked at her face for a reaction but none seemed to be forthcoming. 'I thought you said he'd travelled.'

'Yes, Ghana.'

'How can he be in Ghana when his ticket is here?'

'Because this is only Birmingham to Lagos.'

'Couldn't he use the same tickets?' Their eyes met and he noted her irritation. 'In fact ignore my last question.' He left her to check if anything was out of place in the next two rooms, then he realised she might not detect any recent changes because of her amnesia.

She checked where they kept their passports and found his Nigerian passport with her two passports.

'What is his passport still doing here?' She asked. 'Maybe he decided to use his British passport then.'

'Which means he would need to travel to the Embassy in London for Visa on his British Passport when he could have easily used this' Adam simplified the situation. 'With the little notice he had.' He looked at her reaction so far and she seemed to see his point. 'Only an idiot wouldn't think twice about what his choices are and I know he is no one.'

She remained thoughtful for a while before she spoke. 'Yes, I agree it's too much hassle, it doesn't even make sense.' She touched her head because it throbbed and decided it was time to relax.

It was around 2 a.m. in the morning when Lola heard bangs on her door; she got out of bed and walked to the next room only to find him fast asleep on the bed spread eagle on his back. She wanted to tap him gently but couldn't resist watching him, snoring softly and deeply asleep. His first three buttons undone, shirt sleeves rolled halfway up that exposed a mat of dark hair she was tempted to touch . She quickly tapped his foot gently, and he responded without moving.

'Someone is at the door.'

'And?'

'I think it's the police.'

He quickly sprang up to get the door. 'You'd better come with me.' He urged when he was almost at the bottom of the stairs.

'Why?'

'To tell them what you know.'

'I don't know what I know.'

Adam instantly retraced his steps to wait for her and catch up with him when he remembered how fragile she still was.

Lola checked the door to confirm who was behind it before finally letting the two officers in. A very lanky middle-aged male officer with two lazy eyelids and a funny moustache was accompanied by a young strawberry blonde female officer who wasted no time in going straight to the questions.

CHAPTER 13

Lola was awakened by the noise from downstairs; she jumped out of bed and quickly reached for her dressing gown.

'Who is there?' She waited for their silence and could still hear them smiling and laughing with radio noise in the background. Uncertain of what to expect, she rushed down the stairs like lightning to find two strangers in her living room.

'Hello Ma,' a chunky, dirty hand was stretched towards her. 'Adam sent us round to fix your window.' He added when he noticed her reluctance.

She finally slipped her hand into his with a big sigh of relief. 'Where is he?' She asked after returning his greetings.

'Where is who?'

'Adam.'

'We haven't seen him since he let us in.'

'I'd better let you get on with it.' She said as she went to the kitchen. 'Does anyone want a drink?'

'Yes, one cup of coffee, and tea both white and no sugar please.'

'Coming right up.' Whilst waiting for the kettle to boil she called him to confirm about the two men. He said he'd left her a note because he didn't want to disturb her sleep but she explained she couldn't have seen it because she was forced out of bed by the noise. There was a slight awkwardness before he asked if she fancied lunching out and she responded positively so he told her to be ready and waiting in exactly two hour's time.

'Two hours? That's too long a wait!'

'How soon can you get ready then?'

'An hour.'

'Then an hour it is. I'll see you shortly.' He closed the folder he'd been reading and headed for the bathroom. With a promise to inform Lola at the right time he wondered why Mr James agreed to sell that information at just one and half thousand pounds when he could have made a lot more from the juicy information contained herein. He planned to gently ease her memory back to her experience at work; he hoped she remembered it all and soon!

Forty five minutes later, Lola was ready and waiting in a flattering, gypsy patterned blouse and a vintage, tie belt cargo skirt with a matching hat. As she put her hat on, she looked at her face in the mirror and wondered how she would explain the entire ordeal to Akin when he arrived, but no blames were hers if he left no contacting details and had not bothered to do the same. With all the grazes nearly gone and her scar healing tremendously well she couldn't really complain. Whilst in the hospital she gave her mobile phone that was crushed during the blast to Roxanne to help her fix but she'd all along forgotten until she reminded her some days back. If he'd tried the mobile without success what about the land phone, there was no message from him whatsoever. She had been successfully able to confirm from his friend and cousin, Bola, that he was abroad but they weren't sure of his date of return which was less to say when she contacted his forwarding details in Ghana and Nigeria. The only person she hadn't contacted was his aunt with dementia, despite her doubt that she could actually help.

After hearing Adam's voice downstairs she took a final look at herself in the mirror before rushing to meet him and nearly tripped when she caught him watching a big portrait of herself with her dad in complete African attire. She halted her movement for an in depth observation whilst he remained transfixed and focused despite the rapid changes in his expression. His smile was immediately replaced by a frown that hardened his jaw line and made his bone structures visible; she could easily see how quickly his expression had gone granite cold. Afraid not to be caught staring she retraced her steps, faked a cough and pretended to have just come down.

Lola noticed he was as nervous as her and didn't know how to respond to her greetings in the presence of strangers. In the end, he took her hands into his and pecked her on the cheeks whilst appraising her outfit .The twinkle in his eyes told her he was impressed.

They were leaving instructions to the builders who insisted they waited for them to finish, making her decide to while away the time by fixing them a light meal. Truly to their words, she was still struggling with her sandwich when the builders completed their job and left them behind. He didn't even give her the opportunity to ask for the charges before he mentioned that they'd already been paid. As they stepped out, she smiled to express her gratitude whilst he acknowledged it with a slight bow of his head.

'Where do you want to go?' He asked after settling behind the wheel beside her shortly afterwards.

'You are the one behind the wheels.'

'How about the pictures?'

'No, I don't think I can handle the noise for now.'

'Sorry about my lack of consideration.'

'No problem. Can we go to a restaurant first because I'm hungry?'

'Yes, sure I know of one that was recently opened.' Without another word, he started the engine and drove off.

Adam drove for miles unending. With summer officially a few days away, the weather was very beautiful and hot with the drive to the country side creating a gentle breeze that kept her dozing off and on. Neither of the two said much as they enjoyed Lionel Ritchie's three times a lady track, but kept catching Adam glancing at her every time she wasn't dozing off. She felt a surge of warmth run through her veins just when he reached out to hold her hand. As she slipped her hand into his she felt a jolt of an unexplainable feeling from her head to toe and she shuddered slightly.

'Are you okay? He appraised her with a mocking look.

She left her eyes shut to blot out the effect his touch was having on her but managed to reply with a shake of her head for fear of saying something bizarre.

'Did you sleep well?'

She nodded her head again.

He noticed her demeanour. 'Are you trying to shut me up?'

She felt his eyes on hers and smiled with another nod.

When she finally opened her eyes, the car was at a standstill by a fish and chips shop heading back to Birmingham. His hands clasped tightly around the steering wheel but his hazel eyes were angry and critically appraising her.

'Is something the matter?' She wiped her hand through her face and sat upright.

'You were having nightmare and ...'

'How long have I been asleep?'

'I've been driving for over two hours.'

'I see.'

He turned around for her to return his gaze. 'You were talking to Mama about your womb. Who is Yusuf and what is wrong with your womb?'

Her first reaction was as he expected, shock, horror and finally composure.

'Have you ever had any abortion?'

'No! How could you say such a thing?'

He apologised for upsetting her before he continued. 'And you are not pregnant?'

She shook her head. 'What exactly did I say?'

'How the hell should I know? You were speaking in *Yoruba*.'

'Why are you angry?'

'You try being in my shoes and tell me how you'd feel.' He stormed out of the car without another word. She was deliberating whether to go with him when he returned with two portions of fish and chips and drinks. He gently placed them on her lap, started the engine and drove off.

Lola not only became unsettled but also lost her appetite. Frustrated and close to tears, she decided to close her eyes, relax and shut all her troubles out but she instead kept changing position every now and then. She opened her eyes when the car suddenly stopped to find Adam starring and facing her.

They locked gaze briefly before he broke the silence. 'Can you at least eat?'

She shut her eyes and shrugged her shoulders nonchalantly.

'Okay tell me about him.' As the silence between them stretched, he expelled a gulp of air that told her his patience was wearing thin. 'Please?'

She opened her eyes to check his countenance. 'Yusuf was my first love I should have married.'

'How old were you then?'

'Twenty, why?'

'And you were pregnant with his baby?'

'There was nothing as such with Yusuf.'

'What do you mean nothing as such?'

She wanted to pour her heart out but wondered if he would believe her and if she told him that Yusuf was her first love who broke her heart because his family poisoned his mind against her, more questions would ultimately follow. Focusing on him, she remained thoughtful for a while before turning her back on him and shutting her eyes whilst hoping she could do the same to him too. She would have been married possibly with her own baby or babies if she had not been stupid to have rushed to rescue Bisi that evening. With her whole future turned upside down she was forced to relocate to save face, all for some unfounded rumour. Founded or unfounded the evidence witnessed by the kids were compelling and kids would innocently recount their experience no matter how absurd, because telling them to lie would only compound the problem like it did for her as Yusuf's mum alleged. If only Mama hadn't come with the kids from the neighbourhood that day or if only the incident happened on a different day or she'd cooperated with Bisi's brother. Would she have been happy with Kunle or would she really return to her place of birth if the incident did not occur? For once she began to understand what her dad had been telling her all along that she was better off getting married before travelling abroad because of the difficulty of finding a compatible spouse for a *"well cultured, home rooted girl like mine,"* his exact word and voice echoed in her ears. Despite the vastness and the diversity of the different cultures in Nigeria there were some fundamental similarities, individual uniqueness and yet strong differences.

In her three years of return she had made new remarkable friends like Roxanne and April, then a fiancé who haven't spoken to her in almost three to four weeks to say the least after a benefit of doubt that she might have no recollection if they'd spoken before then. She wondered if she would have gone out with Akin if she was in Nigeria where she would have been exposed to opposite sex with the same cultural orientation and ideologies. He was the only Nigerian that had asked her out, in fact the only African! She wished she'd continued to say No when he was pestering her. Since her hospitalisation, all she could recollect about Akin was his irresponsible and selfish nature that was totally different from what her friends told her and the worrying things were the proofs supported all they said. Him not contacting her this long matched the kind of fiancée she remembered and would have simplified her problems without the namby-pamby from April and Roxanne. She would have immensely appreciated Adam's contribution, but he'd deliberately avoided saying anything concrete apart from the rhetorical analysis that made her wonder if she pressurised him into the engagement.

She noticed the car was moving and glanced sideways to look at Adam gripping the wheel tightly with his jaw clenched so hard that she could see his teeth frame. Extremely good looking, nicely built frame with no superfluous flesh, caring, generous but with a cultural clash unless she resigned her fate to speaking English and adopt the lifestyle for eternity.

She could really live with that if she set her mind to it but what about hers and his family! She thought of her parents' efforts and sacrifices, then her grandmother and immediately concluded that no relationship was worth turning her back on her family for. The alienation from both sides would not only isolate them but would constantly challenge them. It could be the driving force for some but she knew that would be the complete opposite for her. She glanced at him again and suddenly realised she didn't know much about the man beside her. 'Adam what's your best memory about your dad?'

He gave her the worst granite look.

'Sorry, I've just never heard you mention him.' She apologised before they were both consumed with another long silence.

His austere stare was telling her something she couldn't understand.

Lola cringed with defeat and didn't bother looking at him again.

The next thing was feeling a hand stroking her cheeks before opening her eyes. 'Did I have another nightmare?'

'No, are you hungry?'

Without brushing his hand off, she agreed.

He finally removed his hand from her face and squeezed her hand before getting out of the car to wait for her to do the same.

As they stood at the entrance of a restaurant one of their managers approached them, greeted him warmly before directing them to a secluded table and handing them the menu. Lola felt warm and secure in the environment as she read the menu; suddenly she looked at him and smiled instead of saying thank you to him loud and clear.

Adam told the waiter they were famished, they both smiled as he quickly departed with their order.

'I bet you come here often?'

He looked at her for a while with the hope of reading the meaning behind her question. 'I suppose you are right, considering it's newly opened.'

' 'A good way to avoid the stress in one's life.'

His reaction clearly showed she had pressed some kind of a button, whether good or bad remained unclear and was about to speak when their starter arrived.

He thanked the waiter and quickly poured himself a cup of strong tea but did not take his eyes off her. This was followed by a desire to laugh but that too suddenly became suppressed. 'Is it that obvious?'

'Yes that obvious for an idiot like myself to source out!'

Shortly after finishing her carrot soup, Adam's main course of warm lobster with roasted potato and salad arrived and he persuaded her to have a taste from his plate.

'Is that prawn?'

'Yes, why?' he asked after giving her a suspicious look.

She begged to taste and liked it, she then pleaded to swap with his meal and he obliged without any hesitation. He tasted hers, liked it and wasted no time in getting down to business. They didn't realise how hungry they were until they began to eat and he went further to order an extra plate of fresh lobster in case she wanted more. He finished quicker and watched the gratification on her face as she gulped the meal before she caught him.

They ate in total silence but with occasional deep, meaningful stare and smiles that made Lola's heart jump and equally send some coded messages to an embarrassing part of his body.

Adam looked at her with admiration as the silence between them lingered. 'Have you thought of work recently?'

'Yes, most especially what would have happened to me if you weren't there?'

'I think and worry more about the source of the bomb.'

Lola exhaled a deeply laboured breath before pouting her lips.

'Do you normally receive parcels from work?' He asked hesitantly.

'Yes, but very rarely.'

'I suspect it was an inside job.'

'Yes I know so too but the question is who?'

'Do you think it was meant for me?'

'I thought that was obvious.'

She leaned back on her chair and breathed heavily before looking at him again.

He edged forward and squinted his eyes. 'I take it you've worked in all the Accounts Department.'

'Yes and Personnel Department, why?'

'Because I'd like to know why anyone would letter bomb you.' He reached for her hands and grabbed both of them. 'A.B.C. & D had invested so much into you then.'

She nodded.

'That gives you an edge of being easily employable.'

She rubbed her hands together and bashfully replied "yes".

'How did you get employed by them?'

'I was recruited through a Black Graduates Trainee Scheme where I had to spend three months in about four or five departments so I could see the Company in a bigger perspective.'

'Tell me about work.' He asked further.

'What exactly do you want to know?'

'A normal day for you.'

'That depends entirely on the day and how close we are to month end.'

'Okay, let's start with the month end.'

'Payday is the sixth of the month so cut off date for commissions and overtime is 12 p.m. of the last working day of the month.'

'So everybody get paid the same day?'

'Yep.'

'It must be difficult to get all the paper works required together.'

'True, but that's where planning comes in.'

'How?'

'We have around two hundred and fifty employees on the payroll and majority of salary is constant which means I only have to worry with the variable figures and I know most of them. More so, each department should notify me of any changes in their department before the deadline too. The quickest way is to compare each department previous month to the current.'

'Did you have previous payroll experience prior to A.B.C. & D?'

'Only in voluntary capacity.'

'What would you say is your biggest concern in the department?'

'Right now or in the past?'

'Both.'

'If I can remember correctly, that would be the commission from the B.D.U.'

'Why is that?'

She gazed at him thoughtfully as she leaned her chin on the back of her hands whilst he just lifted one of his eye brows and smiled instead.

'We seem to be duplicating a lot of invoices.'

'You mean sales invoices?'

'Yes.'

'Why?'

'I know the answer to that but all I can tell you is that the sales ledger department had to invoice all the Sales Order forms authorised by the head of the B.D.U. whether the accounts department agreed with it or not.'

'What you are telling me is that the B.D.U. deliberately exaggerates the sales figure to get more commissions.'

'Exactly, what I am not telling you.'

'That could be interpreted as fraud,'

'I wouldn't go that far but that is why I was also i charge of the B.D.U's commission and salary?'

He frowned for a while. 'I'm sure they weren't happy about that,' he stated rather than ask.

'Absolutely, and no other reason why most of them disliked me.'

'That must be hard for you.'

Lola looked at him long and hard, she tried to say something but none came. She continued to bite her little finger instead.

'Now tell me what happens when sales order forms are being deliberately duplicated.'

'I thought that was obvious.' She snapped at him.

He slightly recoiled but wasn't deterred. 'The enc was obvious but I want you to take me through it step by step.'

'The Sales Ledger Department receives sales orde forms from the B.D.U for invoices to be raised. It could be from any of them but it has to be authorised by the manager or any of the directors.'

'Don't they need to attach the customer's Sales Orders?'

'Yes ideally, but not in all cases.'

'How does it get resolved?'

'At month end Sales Ledger always had piles of Sales Requisitions without Sales Orders waiting to be invoiced.'

'What's the difference between the Sales Requisition and Sales Orders?'

'Sales Requisition is internally generated to interpret the customers Sales Orders.'

'In other words they are both the same apart from one is internal and the other from customers?'

'Correct. So when the Accounts Department finally closed the system at month end their sales figures would be miles apart from that of the B.D.U. Then the M.D. stepped in and asked for the invoices to be batched in the system.'

'But where is the sense in that?' Adam asked.

'A fantastically higher sales figure.'

'I see.'

'At first the M.D. was on our side, but he was soon convinced that some orders were sent through the internet, some of our customers signed for more than one year's contract which had to be invoiced quarterly, or bi annually.'

'So he caved in.' Adam completed her sentence.

'I'm afraid so, some of the B.D.U. were falsely alleging the management of deliberately cunning them out of their commissions.'

'And is that true?'

'Of course not, the M.D. is a very nice and honourable man.'

'So how do you deal with duplicated invoices?'

'We rely entirely on our customers for that and will be classified as disputed.'

'Which might contradict what your colleagues wanted?'

'Yes and a lot in the past.'

'And now?'

'The B.D.U. staffs only get their commission after the customers paid up, which made my time at Sales Ledger useful. '

'Did it work?'

'Yes it did, we are all happy, the management gets realistic sales figure, no more aggravations from customers to credit control or vice versa. The Accounts Department stopped chasing the invoices that could never get paid and above all it drastically reduced the hundreds of credit notes we used to issue monthly.'

'What would you consider your greatest achievement?'

'I just told you!'

'Why?'

'Because that was my idea.'

He smiled and lifted an eyebrow for more.

'Okay, being able to get a challenging job that was equally financially rewarding.'

'Bob told me that the management was not happy about the soaring salary figures.'

'He told you that? Did he tell you who was responsible?'

Adam shook his head sideways to disagree.

'Rumour has it that he wanted to push for a management buyout.'

'How?'

'By running the company into debt and I'm beginning to believe them.'

Adam sat still with an impassive expression as he tried not to divulge anything confidential yet.

'The monthly salary figure had nearly doubled just within five months.'

'Obviously the management should know why.'

'Yes they do, but Bob never sought any of the management's approval before recruiting.'

'But Billy could have stopped it if he wanted to.'

'As you know Billy is an ailing man.'

'Has there been a physical headcount of employees?'

'Billy was thinking about it but then he changed his mind as usual. Something needs to be done.'

'Well it's not going to be me, everyone hates me well enough. I don't really care as long as I get a properly signed P46 or P45 and a contract of employment before adding them on the payroll system.'

Adam shifted from his seat and sat upright whilst watching every move she made. Her yawning was perfectly timed as the extra lobster meal he ordered arrived. 'I don't think I can eat anything for now.'

'And I am sure I can't finish this,' he remarked as they both burst out laughing like teenage school kids. He looked up to find the waiter still waiting. 'Leave it for now.' He gently pushed the plate over to her side and she did the same, so it went on for a while until they stared up at each other simultaneously and both froze with their hands still on the plate. Adam's eyes remained focus on her voluptuous curved lips whilst totally deaf and blind to everything around. Suddenly a bit of normality returned when he slightly looked at the lobster and took a bite before offering her. She refused by shaking her head and suddenly stopped when a waiter stood beside her with some flowers. Her eyes caught Adam's smiling face just before she spoke.

His smile deepened when he stared back at her. Gratefully, he took the bouquets of flower from the waiter and stretched it her way.

As she received the bouquet she temporarily forgot the hurdles and rifts she'd placed between them. Flattered and overwhelmed with gratitude she edged forward and pecked his cheek, but Adam walked over to her and asked for a peck on his other cheek; she bashfully rose to oblige and was not prepared for what was to follow. She was about to sit down when he gently turned her round to face him, put her arms around his neck and bowed his head to claim her mouth. Lola's eyes desperately pleaded with him not to but thought that saying it out loud would be hypocritical since she approached him first. Gentle at first on her lips but she soon discovered there was a savage appetite within him that needed to be satisfied as his tongue began to tease and probe deep. Apart from the few eyes that were watching, she felt a unique sweet, melodious sensation spiralling through her veins. Her arms were free yet she couldn't resist the sensational music awakening in her body and soul. Adam progressed to her neck when he felt her hands stroking his nape and only stopped when she began trembling in his hands.

'Are you all right?' His voice deepened by the sensation.

'Please take me home right now.'

Now it was his turn to be bashful, with his hand firmly around her shoulder, he gently guided her to his car and came back to pay their bills with the lobster pre-packed.

'Do you realise I am engaged to someone else?'

Adam froze and gripped the seat belt for a while before throwing her a demurred look, but still didn't reply till he started the engine and drove off.

Lola kept glancing sideways at his face that looked like a shield, hard and muscular with his jaw fully protruded.

There was no communication between the pair throughout the journey to her house; the friction between them was so much that it could be cut through with a knife. They both wondered how such a lovely time could suddenly end with so much disaster.

As Adam approached her house, the urge to justify his action grew stronger and he knew there was no peace for him until he cleared what was on his chest. As far as he was concerned everything happened for a reason even if he couldn't explain why. He parked his car in front of her house, turned off the engine but secured the central lock so he could buy himself some time to explain a few things to her.

'Yes, I was aware of your engagement. You told me in the same restaurant about three weeks ago.'

She scanned his face for any sign of ambiguity but was disappointed. 'Really?'

'Yes, apparently you actually thanked me for it.'

'I don't believe you.'

He shrugged his shoulder instead of convincing her.

Believing he was goading her she covered her ear with her hands for a while before speaking. 'Can you let me out please?'

He removed one of her hands and replied. 'I know I am the last person you want to see right now but believe me when I tell you your house is not safe.'

'I see, I should go inside pack my stuff and move in with you and just pick up from where you stopped.'

Adam only smiled when he detected that her cynicism was mixed with regret. 'Seriously Lola.'

'So is fondling another man's fiancé.' She interrupted him angrily.

'That fondling as you called it was the best ever in my life.'

Her first reaction was a mocking giggle. 'Good.' She teased before noticing the sincerity and seriousness on his face and voice.

'What do you mean by that?'

'That means you don't make a habit of snuggling other people's wives.' She fumbled with the door handle and remembered why she was still in the car beside him.

'Here we go again always trivialising important discussion.' He wanted to touch her but held his hand back. 'You can't tell me it didn't mean anything to you. How can feeling so right feel so wrong?'

'Please let me out.' She insisted with an unsteady voice.

'Promise me you will be safe.' He looked at her face for a response but none was forthcoming then he focused on her lips seductively.

'Adam stop it.'

'Why? What have I done?'

Still looking far away, she could obviously see that he has a lot on his mind and he was battling with himself on whether to share some of them with her or not. 'Just let me go please!' The plea in her voice said it all.

Adam on the other hand wanted to open up to her but doubted if she would believe him.

'Be very careful inside that house of yours.' He advised in a similar final tone. 'I need you alive.'

Once inside, the portrait Adam was gawping at earlier caught her attention. She stopped to watch it closely and hopefully see something new and different. Maybe he'd never seen African outfit before! Many people that had seen the picture were ever so full of compliments.

Maybe he hates Nigerians! She could easily recollect his demeanour when he met Sade and her mum at the hospital some days back. The thought of such possibility shocked her so much that guilt and fear of such repercussion made her sick. She finally dismissed such a nasty thought and was glad that she didn't bother to enquire about what got him so upset, knowing fully well that she almost did.

He is mixed race not Mediterranean! She was somehow relieved and calmed by such realisation but couldn't say why. As she decided to go to bed, part of her felt guilty that she should have done more to enquire about what upset him. It got so bad that every step on the stairs gave her more pangs of guilt as his disappointing look suddenly became more vivid.

'Maybe someday it would become glaring before it's too late.' His last remark continued to repeat itself on her mind. And she realised Adam was one man she would really love to hate for being so marvellous to her. Complete package doesn't come better than that and has so far done nothing wrong. The feelings he evoked in her was second to none. She reluctantly repeated his question as to how feeling so right could feel so wrong as she flung herself onto her bed with frustration!

CHAPTER 14

Today marked his fourth week in the prison and the sixth week of his alleged engagement to Lola. Unfortunately for him nothing had gone according to plan, his solicitor that promised to file an appeal for his immediate release had not contacted him for an update since sentence had been passed. Sally, his wife had only visited him thrice which must be quite hard for her considering her health, but Lola had neither written nor phoned, that to him made visiting far fetched. He hoped she'd received his letters, which explained why he gave the two letters to separate people. Worse still, he'd woken up everyday hoping this would be the day she was going to turn up and confront him, that would give him the opportunity to explain everything to her because all he'd succeeded in doing so far was covering one lie with another. With tears in his eyes, he shook his head regrettably as the memory once again all flooded back!

"Mr Akinwande Ajibola.' The judge had a long rest after succeeding in pronouncing his name before glancing through the audience in the courtroom. "Considering your wife's medical condition and all the supporting evidences makes me sympathise with you two … However, drug possession and trafficking is against the law in U.K. and should not be taken lightly. You are hereby sentenced to ten weeks imprisonment …"

Akin could hear no more, he could have sworn he died and resurrected whilst the sentence was being passed as his eardrums vibrated continuously. The loud, hollow noise not only made his chest heavy but his throat progressively narrower until his saliva tasted like bile in his mouth. He only believed he was still alive when the sweat that rolled from his face burnt through his thigh, he'd never felt so scared and depressed at the same time. The judge considered his sentence of ten weeks imprisonment as "an act of mercy" in "light of his wife's illness." So this is his Nemesis for dealing with a crook! He'd been double crossed!

The police officers discovered a stash of around fifteen grams of cannabis in his glove compartment. He later admitted and pleaded guilty to charges of possessing cannabis for his wife's personal use on the said date but denied ever selling the drug to anyone. Luckily for him, there was no trace of drugs in the samples he provided which further supported his argument that the said cannabis was meant to neutralise his wife's recurring nightmares, depression, constant aches, pains and to restore calm from the side effects of prescribed medication. His lawyer who corroborated his plea that he had personally witnessed his client's wife of many years in traumatic incidences, only started using drugs as a form of self-medication after the fatal accident that led to life-threatening illnesses and seizures. He concluded his argument that long prison sentence would have a drastic effect on his wife's already frail health and concluded by pleading for leniency.

If only he wasn't speeding! He sped past an unmarked police vehicle on a twenty mile zone and was flashed to stop but didn't because he was only a few yards to his home. Totally disregarding the incident, he turned off the engine and was just collecting his house keys when he heard a knock on the passenger window only to be faced by a young woman in a white top.

'Is this your car sir?'

He got out and locked his car before replying. 'Why?'

'PC Paula Anderson.' She flashed her badge. 'Can you confirm if this vehicle is yours sir?'

'No it's my wife's.' He scratched his stubs as he always did when nervous.

'Can I see your driver's licence sir?'

He took it out of his wallet and stretched it towards her before he asked his question. 'Is there a problem?'

'You were caught speeding at forty miles in a twenty miles zone sir.' She waited for his reaction and continued when he didn't respond. 'That was pretty excessive sir.' She stopped to listen to her radio. 'Does this vehicle have a valid Mot?' She continued earnestly.

'As I said earlier, the car belongs to my wife.'

'I can confirm to you sir that your Mot ran out a week ago.'

He studied her thin, mean lips and suspected there was possibly more to this palaver than met the eye. 'I see.'

'Would you come with me sir?'

Akin was already trailing behind her when she stopped to receive another radio message and responded by reading his car registration number to her colleague on the other end. 'Sir, we've just been informed that a vehicle similar to yours had just left a crime scene. We need your permission to search the vehicle sir.'

He finally gave in after rounds of argument, uncertain of what they were searching for but did not expect drugs.

After the search he was subsequently arrested for possession but was fortunate to have been granted bail because of his wife's medical condition. If only he had listened! As the old adage said, "*that you can't fool all of the people all of the time*" had finally manifested in his life.

The court clerk's voice reignited his nightmarish trance as he impulsively joined everyone on their feet for the judge to leave for his chamber.

He looked at the bed with disdain for the umpteenth time as his mind drifted to his comfortable beds in his own home and the ones he shared with his women.

'One wife and many mistresses!' His cell mate, Craig had looked at him with disbelief earlier today.

Akin nodded his head.

'How do you manage that?'

'Pretty well.'

'You were in relationships with two different women at the same time.'

He nodded again before the reality began to dawn on him.

'And then an old flame turned up?'

'Making three?' He continued after another nod.

'Do they know of each other or what?' Bewildered Craig asked surprisingly.

'Never.'

'Are you a sex machine or what?'

These were the same questions he'd been asking himself since he'd been in the confinement that had given him more opportunity to reflect on his past and fight off his isolation within these four walls.

His mistrust in women had been sealed by someone close to him since his youthful days. He shook his head to rid the memory off his mind. Then he asked himself how many women's heart had he broken? He began to count and the first few women to cross his mind made him cringe with shame and degradation especially when he remembered how close one of them was to committing suicide. Feeling so unpleasant, he decided to selectively pick his list from Birmingham and skip the ones before then.

First was Bea, one of his first female friends in Birmingham whom he regularly met at the bus stop every morning and evening waiting for the same bus as him. For a while they didn't exchange a word until the day she thanked him for helping her with the correct change she needed to get on the bus.

Things went back to the old way till one dark, winter evening that hundreds of commuters were all stuck in city centre waiting for buses that had all been diverted to another destination because of bomb scare. After waiting endlessly, commuters took matters into their hands and started walking out of city centre whilst others were phoning for lift from relatives and others for taxis. She finally walked up to him and asked if he was interested in pairing and sharing the taxi fare home with her and he obliged eagerly. They began talking immediately and she invited him into her home that same evening, and henceforth started sitting next to each other in subsequent journeys and conversed happily. He asked her out some weeks later but she told him her heart belonged to someone else and never stopped talking about him every time they met until she finally asked him to visit her home again and he wasted no time in getting intimate. Shortly afterwards she asked him to move in with her and he gladly obliged to every night of explicit passion for five months before she told him she was pregnant.

Thrilled by the news and still hung over the most intimate and cherished time of his life, he proposed to marry her but she said she wasn't interested. Ten months after having Jake she had another baby boy named Jack by emergency caesarean. Three months later she told him she was going back to her ex who had just been out of prison for drug related crimes and didn't take long before she became addicted too. He wanted to walk away but couldn't leave his children until she was finally locked behind bars for some serious drug-related offences. Which left Bea's mum to become the two boys' carer until her release from prison some months back and to Akin's surprise she wanted to renew their relationship. Her argument was she and the kids needed him, she'd also promised never to dump him again because she claimed to have learnt from her mistakes but he didn't buy it. He wasn't willing to let her break his heart again.

Bea had barely been locked away when he met, Sally, his wife in a flower and gift shop that she'd inherited from her parents' retirement. Sally chased him relentlessly until he finally gave in to go on a date with her. On their first night out she told him all about herself except that she hoped to inherit more than one hundred grand, a lovely bungalow and a horse riding school when her parents died, thanks to Sharon, her best friend and assistant. Three months later they were pronounced as husband and wife at the Marriage Registry.

Some months later, Sally was hospitalised for months following a miscarriage and a serious horse riding accident. At first, doctors predicted she wasn't likely to survive and that if she did, her standard of life would be very poor. Initially, Akin wanted to abscond as Sally's health deteriorated but her parents words of encouragement and support convinced him otherwise especially when he realised he had everything to live for if she died. So he hoped, and for three years, her parents paid for the best healthcare money could buy in any part of the world with him right by her side until they died in a train crash whilst touring Europe and left him to continue playing the role of a loving, caring and supportive husband. A fortnight later, Sally's parents' solicitor paid them a visit at home to read the will. Her inheritance had drastically shrunk to fifty thousand pounds and he would only be entitled to half of it if they remained married and he was her main carer. Another conditional quarter of a million was in trust for each of them! Talk about tying a bone around the dog's collar! Akin looked from the solicitor's Adam's apple travelling back and forth his long over tanned neck then to his grinning wife before resting on the Will whilst wishing he could grab it and shove it down his throat.

With Sally's health improving dramatically and after some bedroom negotiations, she agreed to wave off the twenty hour care condition stipulated on the Will. He loathed himself for being conditioned to stay and was scared he might despise himself if he left, so he decided to occupy his time with other attractions like gambling and womanizing. The two main roots of evil!

Then he met Bob at an exclusive betting club he owned who later taught him a few gambling tricks and introduced him into drugs dealing. He was now grateful for standing firm against Bob's persuasion to take drugs, but was stupid enough to have been persuaded to become a dealer, but he retrospectively understood his coercive ways and hated himself more for it.

'It will relieve your wife's severe seizures, aches and pain.' Bob's voice echoed in his ears once again after all means of persuasion had failed.

Akin remembered giving him a look that asked "how the hell did you know?"

'I carried out my investigation to be certain you are not an undercover.' His lips only stretched instead of a warm smile.

'Fair enough and what have you found out?'

Bob patted his shoulder and smiled. 'Nothing to worry about.'

He still didn't accept the invitation despite mounting pressure, until Sally, in one of her excruciating crisis begged him to get her some alternative medication to relieve her of her agony. To improve his wife's standard of living he instantly approached Bob who later introduced him to some of his acquaintances. One of them was Mia, an interestingly, beautiful woman who rose fully to his challenges by introducing him into a higher social level and pleasing him with everything he dreamed of including money, time and affection. Around six months later, she demanded he broke off with Sally and when he refused she ended their relationship and later cried out rape. He couldn't believe his ears when the police arrested him for questioning some days later with a promise to investigate further. Two months later Mia hinted she would drop the charge if she got ten thousand pounds and also keep the pregnancy. He personally wanted to meet with her and ask her why she was doing this after several months of unforgettable eroticism, but Bob who somehow got to hear about it advised him to drop it before volunteering to lend him the money which he later blackmailed him for. Somehow, she became depressed after delivery and things got from bad to worse for her before she moved to London, at least he had a beautiful four-year-old son that was worth ten grand debt he hasn't completely recovered from.

After a lot of effort, he struggled to pay Bob half of his debt but had managed to pile more up because of his compulsive nature. With Sally still stuck in hospital admission, he was already vulnerable when he met Fiona, a pretty young and vibrant recovering gambler already known to him from Bob's exclusive club who seemed to know what she wanted from him. In her words they both had scores to settle with Bob, and so she led him on till he gullibly fell in love without realising she was using him to get her ex boyfriend jealous and eventually back. Bob told him first but he laughed it off and the only time he believed her was when he overhead her conversation with her ex about him. When he confronted her, she denied it, it was shortly afterwards that a fight ensued between the two men before Bob intervened.

Then Bob invited him to A.B.C. & D. for a job interview where he met Lola again after several, previous meetings but was now properly introduced to her. He was quite pleased to have an opposite sex with the same cultural background even though he wasn't particularly after a meaningful relationship considering his track records of four children from three women and his well anticipated inheritance. Some months later, Bob walked up to him and asked for the balance of his debt and agreed to write it off if he could clinch a date with Lola who according to him was a self-righteous woman in desperate need of gentle persuasion. She unfortunately turned him down initially but Akin knowing what was at stake persisted. Some months later, after a series of staged, coincidental meetings she finally agreed to go out with him. This coincided with him winning a twenty five grand bet and ultimately reducing his debt with Bob to twenty thousand pounds. Shortly afterwards, Bob requested for his personal details and later demanded he opened a bank account with her as a couple, but Lola wasn't ready to go that far with him just yet. She wasn't aware he knew Bob personally but was regularly updating him about her boss's unnecessary meetings and enquiries, which encouraged Akin to reject some of his unsuitable offers flatly after he discovered what a priceless gem she was.

After series of Bob's requests met walls of defiance from Lola he asked Akin to break the relationship up but he blankly refused, his reprisal for defying Bob landed him in prison and he absolutely cursed the day he met him. Akin had just had enough of his influence in all aspects of his life; having realised that the more he concurred to his demands the bigger and deeper his crisis got. His debt to Bob was around fifty thousand pounds when he was awaiting sentencing and all for what? He was extremely upset for letting her down on the day she twisted her ankle which wouldn't have happened if he was there as promised and agreed. This means she wouldn't meet Adam under those precarious circumstances and might have not needed *Magun*. Bob was fully aware of Lola's plan and he deliberately jeopardised his and hers by asking him to escort him to Aberdeen after spending the whole night containing Sally's seizures and fits. He often wondered how Sally's worse fits and seizures always coincided with when he had important outings with Lola. To him, the *Magun* would help him secure her till he was ready and done with Bob and or even Sally; he had hoped to sort it all out by now!

His unfortunate realisation that the house of card was crumbling coincided with the time he began to fall in love with Lola's inner strength, kindness, consideration and her *Yoruba* pedigree that happened to be the most important of all. He had finally succumbed to his conscience to come clean and confess his misdemeanours to her when *Teddybear* showed up. He was sure his timing had something to do with that evil Bob again, but now he'd show them all. After all Bob had him where he wanted him and he'd got them where he wanted them by moving one step ahead. To imagine what could have happened between them if he hadn't interrupted them was unthinkable. He could not believe the jealousy that possessed him when he caught him out trying to drop her a bunch of flower. Instantly, he realised it would not only be too shameful to have a *Teddybear* for a love rival but that they both needed to be taught some lessons.

What made him panic the most was what would become of them if he did time; leave everyone to live happily ever after? No way! He had come too close to confessing his sins and nothing was going to stop him and worse yet, he had the gut to tell him he recognised his face, how dare he? Women! Can't live with them and can't live without them.

He was already suspicious of the two of them when he showed up unannounced at the football fund raising competition, having got tired of lying about business trips, family problems and was prepared to introduce her to Sally if needed. So as not to forfeit his half of the bequest, he might just wait for her to die before marrying Lola. Indeed, there were family problems but not the kind of ones the women in his life would understand.

He drew his breath slowly as if death was finally coming for him. With no other alternative, he might just forego the legacy all for Lola who to him was a reasonable, caring person and quintessentially a wife material who would make a lucky bastard like Teddybear happy someday. And that lucky bastard should be him and not anyone else! His jealous admission of how kind, considerate and well cultured she was tasted like piles of bile violently rammed down his tiny throat. He'd just realised how much he loved Lola for all the right reasons and Sally for all life's comforts. For a start he wanted to get Bob off his back for good and divorcing her for now was not an option unless he was willing to forfeit his inheritance. Given another chance, things would definitely be done differently if not for the time constraint on then. He was tired of people messing with his life and had to start from somewhere. That unfortunately was Lola and if *Magun* was to claim him what was rightfully his when he was ready, and not on Bob's terms anymore, he'd be more than delighted.

His engagement was a symbol of using one stone to kill three birds by stalling off Bob's threat and to hopefully reduce his debt and finally end his blackmail. Whilst *Magun* to him, was the mechanism to suspend their relationship until he was ready to free and consummate with her if she could be faithful for another three months or so

. Ten weeks sentence to him seemed really harsh and inhumane, but was extremely pleased with the precautionary step of the *Magun* as a backup.

It sometimes crossed his mind that he could be wrong but he always consoled himself that the truth shall come out in the wash. Even if she was in the past, she certainly wouldn't now! Discovering that she'd received a bunch of flower from an admirer was more than a proof for him and also cast a big shadow of doubt over her story that they met accidentally through a dog. Never for once did it cross his mind that there could be a remote possibility that she was faithful whilst he'd been driven and blinded by jealousy!

As far as he was concerned, their secret relationship only came to light because he caught them right in the act, they were too cosy from the little he was opportuned to see. He'd chosen to hold his horses till he sorted a few things out and the defining moment was when she threw his sexual advances back at his face and topped it up by kicking his balls. How long did she expect him to hold on for? His first reaction was to force her but then he thought of the repercussion of such an action especially his recent encounter from the authorities. Then it dawned on him that time for talking was long gone and the only thing left was action.

He could never forget how bad her stomach cramp got when the *Magun* started working. After days of seeing her in agony, he nearly ran away because he was so scared the doctors would eventually detect something unusual but was very relieved when it was put down to some virus. The only reason he didn't abscond was because he thought he would look too suspicious. Sally's agony was nothing compared to what she went through for nearly two weeks or more!

He eventually rolled onto his back waiting for sleep to take over after coming to terms with his predicaments and finally agree to endure the harsh prison life. His rumbling stomach instantly reminded him of the change in his diet. He gazed at the ceiling whilst imagining the alternative outcome if he had confessed to Lola as earlier planned. He had his solicitor to thank for that, despite his strong assurance that he would either have a community service or a suspended sentence.

He was suddenly distracted by a loud noise from Craig, who was screaming and crying from his sleep 'Bob No! Bob No! Bob No!' Akin got out of bed to watch his inmate sob before he began sucking his thumb and finally settling back to sleep.

What the hell was Craig shouting Bob for? Akin rolled back onto his other side and hoped the Bob mentioned was different from the one he knew.

Looking back he could confirm Bob never intended to offer him any job in the first place, all he had in mind was just for him to meet Lola before he started scheming things up.

When he discovered she was a Yoruba girl, his feeling could be compared to the thrilling experience of when his feet touched the soil outside Murtala Mohammed Airport in Lagos after many years here in England. Words could not describe what seemed to him like ancestral warmth but was inadvertently love at first sight, with his initial intention of friendship. For him, the only regret was not having the guts to approach her on their first meeting, maybe a lot of things that went wrong in his life wouldn't.

A twisted smile crossed his face. He'd reluctantly agreed on getting physical with their relationship as she demanded because he suspected Bob might be pulling the string. After all, he was her boss and Bob wouldn't work closely with someone he couldn't control or manipulate. Conclusively, if the pair thought they could easily toss him aside, they, especially Lola should think again. Bob had on the other hand been controlling his life since he'd known him and he'd been seriously thinking of a way to get back at him! He was interrupted again by a soft plea from his cell mate who was still fast asleep.

How could you claim to love someone so much without tasting the forbidden fruit?

May be because it was still forbidden. If only he'd been strong enough to resist Bob initially and at least had a bit of faith in her. He should have realised that their first meeting had been before she started working for A.B.C. & D. which was definitely not designed by Bob but by fate!

In reality, blaming everyone else but himself was still sweeping his problem under the carpet but he should openly admit that he was a compulsive gambler. His open admission propelled him to sit up and sob helplessly which eventually woke Craig up.

'I'm a compulsive gambler!' He repeated after he asked what the problem was.

'Alright.'

'It's wrecked my life.' He was interrupted by a soft snore from his roommate once again and would have called on him if he didn't hear the warden footsteps approaching. He quietly lied on his back to avoid any unwanted consequences.

The last decision he made was to telephone Lola and tell her the truth because only that could set him free! Then he realised this freedom would still not get him out of prison.

CHAPTER 15

It was her first outpatient appointment with the hospital after the accident, and her concern about the outcome had been uppermost in her mind for days, especially getting into the scanner and the result to expect. She was more anxious to have her stitches off which would eliminate the hat she'd been wearing since the accident. Today, she opted for a trendy face cap.

Later, the doctor echoed the same thing the hospital staff had been saying all along that she had nothing to worry about; the scan result confirmed that her fall left no permanent damage. Her health had dramatically improved within a week and should in that respect expect full recovery soon. The only downfall was no one's ability to predict when she would regain her memory.

They were soon joined by a female consultant who echoed the same encouraging verdict before requesting to see her in a fortnight's time.

They left the hospital exactly two hours later with a relief that she hadn't taken much of Adam's time even though he didn't complain. Until today, she'd seen so little of him since they last argued about the contentious hugs and kisses, but he'd always called her to check all was well every morning, afternoon, night and also a goodnight text message before he went to sleep. She felt a bit awkward that he still cared this much about her despite the nasty way she'd treated him on their last meeting. Having truly enjoyed all the benefits there in but didn't want the emotional responsibilities it was trying to stir in her. Half of her wanted the safety, security and enjoyment that came with Adam's aura but disliked herself for looking forward to his visit, phone calls or text. She'd initially thought his absence would go without her flinching but she'd never been so wrong! In spite of the solid barrier she'd erected between them she had a lot of warmth, affection and respect for him, and honestly doubted if Akin would ever be as reliable or committed as him. She was somehow saddened by that realisation and also for comparing the two men but quickly consoled herself with the old adage that said out of sight is out mind. With ease she quickly convinced herself that everything would be in place if and when he eventually returned. She missed loosing her memory for the sheer curiosity of not knowing how it was between her and Adam. Did she feel like this about him then? If she did, did Akin know about it and if he did ... She decided to change her thought pattern when she felt a violent thump for overstraining herself.

'Are you alright?'

She was touched by the concern in his voice and was diabolically irritated that she observed it. Apart from loathing her sudden recognition of this development, she was anxious to know more. Her apprehension was the shock the outcome might have on her. Even at the hospital today, both the staffs and the patients all turned their heads towards every direction they went whilst admiring their partnership except for one beautiful woman with long curly blonde hair. 'Why do I have the impression that the female doctor doesn't like me?' She asked once they were outside the hospital building and was surprised when he only responded with a chortle.

'What did you say to her?'

Snapped from a deep thought, he responded better with a deep, warm smile. 'Why?'

'She kept squeezing her nose every time I asked questions.' Rebelliously, she stood still whilst Adam unknowingly approached the car park, which gave her the opportunity to notice how his grey stripy suit suited him perfectly. 'That sneaky smile on your face tells me something else.'

He finally turned around when he didn't notice her beside him and gestured for her to come closer. 'We only exchanged greetings that's all.'

With her arms on her hips, she approached him slowly whilst equally observing his facial expression. 'Why do I feel there was more to it?'

He shrugged his shoulders and smiled again.

'Adam, she was my consultant for God's sake.'

He let her level with him before whispering into her ears. 'And she was my girlfriend before that.'

'Then you should have warned me.'

'And when exactly would have been the best time? Unless you wanted me to come and tell you whilst you were in the ladies providing your urine sample.'

Defeated Lola studied his face for a while and noticed his crude attempt was all to encourage her drop the subject.

'What's the matter?' He frowned and looked at her thoughtfully before picking his words carefully. 'She was an old flame who broke up with me for not wanting to take our relationship further.'

The sincerity underlining his tone made her believe him but it equally left a painful lump in her chest.

'Are you alright?'

She nodded her head.

'We are still in the hospital you know.'

'Very funny.' She eyed him jokingly and was glad he didn't notice her jealousy.

He opened the passenger door for her to step in before turning the ignition key.

The next ten minutes was in absolute silence with everyone for their thoughts until their phones rang at almost the same time. Whilst she spoke to her grandma, he was giving instruction to one of his colleagues in the office.

Since Adam's conversation had come to an end, he had no choice but to listen to her conversation and it immediately became apparent to him who she was talking to.

'Which of our discussions Ma?'

'Mama but I haven't forgotten.' She replied, sounding as much rueful as she could muster.

'Your youngest brother said he was still waiting for a return phone call I promised him.' She nervously placed the phone on the other ear. 'But why hasn't he called me himself?'

'He said we spoke three and five weeks ago.'

'Mama honestly I'm okay and I apologise for loosing his number.'

Adam's knuckles went white with frustration as he turned the wheel and had to listen to her repeating the same excuse again 'Can you give me his number again?' She scribbled the numbers as quickly as she could before she half stated and half asked. 'He leaves in three days time anyway.'

As the conversation ended she glanced at Adam and simultaneously heaved a big sigh of relief. 'That was close.'

His mocking stare made her quickly shy away and concentrate on her great uncle's number instead. 'Do you have any idea of the area using this code?'

His harsh stare continued, whilst she chewed her bottom lip with a deep fervour that Mama would call her tomorrow again to confirm if she'd spoken to him. But her immediate concern was how many more errands she'd forgotten and how long she could keep her memory loss secret from her immediate family. Whilst seriously doubting if her grandma hadn't suspected something was amiss already, an idea occurred that she should call her again tonight to update her about her great uncle and to equally allay any suspicion she might have.

'Why don't you just tell them what happened?'

She eyed him with disbelief. 'And kill everyone with worry?' She began jabbing the numbers on her mobile phone. 'My dad might just be able to handle the news but Mama simply couldn't, moreover I'm much better.'

'True, apart from the crucial week's gap of memory loss. Only God knows how many more important things you've missed out.'

'Which will hopefully be restored sooner than-.'

Adam noticed her switch to Yoruba immediately the phone was picked up from the other end by a young boy who told her granddad was praying. She felt a jab of guilt as she decided to hold and while away the time by engaging him in the usual kind of conversation about school. The boy only answered her questions about his parents' well being just before he said his granddad was finished.

Adam observed how her tone was quickly subdued when she finally heard his voice on the other end. He heard her mention address and bank details as she continued scribbling in her makeshift journal she'd always carried with her since the accident.

'But you addressed him differently whilst talking to your Nanny?' He asked rhetorically after disconnecting the phone.

'Correct.'

'You called him daddy what?' He lifted his eyebrow but didn't take his eyes off the busy road.

'Daddy Kahf.' She smiled. 'Oh Yes, I grew up hearing people call him so, but was told it was a nickname from those who doubted and challenged him.'

He giggled and shook his head. 'What does Kahf mean?'

'Kahf means Cave and is one of the chapters in the Quran. Part of it was the story of some time travellers stuck in a cave for a long time and was evidently very popular with this great uncle of mine.'

'How?'

'He once told me it was the longest chapter he knew by heart first and I also heard from Mama that he used to confine himself to bizarre places for meditation and prayers when he was much younger.'

'And now?'

'He could prescribe just a verse to ten individuals with different problems.'

'But does it work for all these people?'

'Yes amazingly so.'

'I see, more to him than that cultural mummy and daddy thing?'

'Yes. He is a physician and an Islamic scholar with his own uniquely weird identity amongst my relatives on both sides.' She cringed to hide her own guilt and embarrassment as she tried in vain to remember the last time she prayed.

'Wonderful, why not just uncle?'

'Call someone older than your own parents an uncle? I could get away with it now but not as a child and it's more acceptable nowadays.' Her laughter was satirical. 'And how would I be able to distinguish one uncle from the other if nothing was added then?'

'Why not add their names to the uncle?'

'What? And let them tell me the history behind my conception or my mother's shortcomings?'

'But you said she was dead.'

'But she lived once.'

'Now it makes perfect sense.'

'Can you drop me at Merry hill please?'

'I have a meeting nearby too.'

'And I have to post some items today unfailingly. Daddy Kahf reminded me of some things Mama would have asked from me.'

'But you are not sure if she actually did?'

'No, but something tells me she did. Please we're so close to it.'

He grimaced and nodded at the same time.

She heaved a big sigh of relief when he followed the signpost to Merry Hill. 'Thank you! Thank you! Thank you!'

After some minutes of silence, he pulled up safely by the entrance of the mall before giving her a white envelope he took from his glove compartment.

Suspecting what the content was she still decided to ask anyway. 'What's this?'

'Something I should have done a long time ago.'

She ripped the envelope opened to find piles of new twenty pounds notes. 'Meaning what?'

'A small token of gift.' He bashfully shrugged his shoulders. 'Use it to buy some things for mama or Daddy K ...'

'I could never take this from you; you've done absolutely more than enough for me. You are such a wonderful guy and I really pray you meet someone as nice as you some day.'

Grimaced again, he stretched past her to open the passenger door before he spoke contritely. 'I'll pick you up at the same spot in ninety minutes time.'

Realising her last statement came out incorrectly and trying to rectify it might worsen the situation. 'I'll see you in ninety minutes time.' She dropped the envelope on her seat, rushed out of his car and quickly set the alarm countdown on her mobile phone.

Her first point of call was the herbal shop where she hoped to buy her grandma's vitamin supplements, herbal teas and favourite beverage. After buying a few extra items as a backup she left the shop twenty minutes later and decided to go straight to the post office and post them to her great uncle. She was certain there would be many items she'd bought for her at home but couldn't remember them right now and wasn't prepared to risk not sending anything to her beloved Nan since his flight was early morning. She would have to compensate the stuffs she missed out with money that could be easily transferred over if she ran out of the ninety minutes.

A frustrating sigh escaped her when she discovered the long queues in the post office but smiled with relief when she checked her watch and realised she still had plenty of time. Fifteen minutes later, only four people had been served and emotions began to run high. The pelican faced man standing two positions behind her was shouting that the ration during the war was much quicker than this. Suddenl the queue moved quicker when more post office clerks filled more counters and she was next to be served. After explaining to the post office clerk wha she wanted, he gave her a little slip to fill in and told her to step aside, so he could serve someone else.

The lady behind her must have heard one of her questions to the clerk when she stepped forward, turned to her and said, 'Recorded delivery items to Nigeria is a waste of time and money,' whilst waiting for the two books of European, first and second-class stamps she requested for.

'Even with insurance?'

'That only stretches the impossibility.' The woman moved closer to Lola and whispered into her right ear. 'Better still use a courier company and there are quite a lot now.'

'Exactly what I suggested to my colleagues who wanted to know but I had to confirm.' Lola adjusted her face cap and became more sensitive about her accident but still managed to turn towards the woman with a smile. She quickly caught glimpse of her sky blue eyes, the full blonde hair made the strands of grey hair on her temple and forehead suit her face even more. Her searching, friendly eyes suddenly met Lola's assessing pairs, simultaneously they both smiled and looked away immediately afterwards.

'The postage comes with insurance of the item up to certain value, but you can pay for additional insurance.' The post office clerk who had been busy glancing through a manual finally explained.

'In that case keep your receipt till your item gets to the other end.' The woman smiled exposing a tiny gap in the lower front teeth. 'Is it going to Lagos?

'The enquiry was on behalf of a colleague whose friend now lives in Nigeria but this parcel is going to Milton Keynes.'

'I know Lagos very well; I have relatives living in Ikeja.'

'Ikeja? Where exactly in Ikeja?' Lola asked before thinking.

She tapped her forehead gently. 'It's escaped my mind, but I know it's very close to Allen Avenue'

'We live on Allen Avenue.' She hoped she didn't give any clue away that only her dad and her siblings lived there whilst she lived nearby with Mama.

A short silence ensued as they continuously measured each other up, but Lola prayed she didn't get too familiar to ask about the few grazes on her face despite her feeling familiarly graceful and fascinated to the older woman. When she smiled, her amazing big blue eyes not only warmed her heart but encouraged her to ask the stranger more questions.

'Here is your stamp and your change madam.' The post office clerk interrupted them again.

'We'll talk more-later.' The woman offered as she faced the post office clerk to collect her stamps and change before finally stepping aside for her.

'Can you put the parcel on the scale please?'

Lola concentrated her next five minutes or more on the post office clerk and her parcel, pocketed the receipt and was looking forward to continue their conversation but was disappointed to note she was not in the post office. She approached the exit for a wider view in the belief that she was still waiting outside but felt thwarted and saddened that she was nowhere to be seen. Whilst still searching around, her mobile phone alerted her that she only had thirty minutes left. Right in front of her was the men's designer shop with some half price poster, she impulsively decided to enter and do what she'd never done before. To show her gratitude to Adam for his unwavering support in the most turbulent time of her life, she asserted herself. She's known him long enough to know his taste, preferences, and size, more than Akin's? Her regular intrusive voice probed again and instantly reminded her of the mystery man and the bizarre dream she had early hours today.

She was about to go to bed when Sade, her cousin, called to inform her of her husband's arrival from Nigeria a day before with some presents. Lola gathered from her husband that Akin's three phone numbers in Nigeria led to nowhere.

'So no one picked any of the three numbers?' She asked to confirm that she heard him correctly.

His affirmative answer made them pause for a while before the phone was transferred to her cousin. The two women chatted for over thirty minutes with most discussion on Akin, Adam and the latest news about members of their family before they bade each other good night.

She was already dozing off when Adam's phone call soon followed with one giving the other a low down of their day's event whilst tucking into his bed. She apologised after he complained of her dozing off on him halfway through their conversation and remember him mentioning the time as half eleven before promising to call her the following morning.

She suddenly jumped up from sleep, fully awake and terrified of her surroundings, sitting up she tried to recollect what had happened. She was reminiscing in the park alone when from a far she caught a glimpse of Akin approaching her, and he began looking more like Bob as the gap between them closed, but he eventually hid behind a big tree instead of coming straight to her. Lola was full of smiles whilst eagerly waiting for him to come to her when she unexpectedly found herself on the floor with Akin on top with her stomach suddenly on fire. Whilst screaming the pain intensified and her fiancée frantically tried to quench the rapidly spreading fire until he got up and left her to answer Bob's call. The smile on their faces suddenly became disturbingly vivid as she remembered the two men leaving her to continue suffering and screaming when apparently another man came out of nowhere to douse the fire. She couldn't remember her saviour's face but there was something about his hands that was familiar and comforting in her dream.

Lola tried to convince herself that it was nothing more than a dream but the sweat dripping down her face refused to erase the nightmare off her mind. She gradually passed her hand down her stomach but was surprisingly welcomed by a sharp persistent pain, and might have successfully convinced herself that she was still dreaming if her bedside clock hadn't stated 3.10 a.m. Clutching her quilt cover closer and tighter to her chest she solidly leaned against the head rest and began pondering about the meaning behind her dream, nightmare, premonition or whatever else she could call it!

The past three months had been the worst period in her life; well maybe or she could be more specific with as far as she could remember. It had been a rollercoaster of one event after the other with a more serious disaster lurking in every direction she turned. She thought of calling her grandma to interpret the dream but refrained herself because of the distress it would cause her for the timing. Despite her doubting that Akin would be able to interpret it she still wondered how he would react to it, but she'd at least know his where about first. She'd already sought Sade's opinion out on whether to report him missing to the police, and she'd suggested she tried his workplace and his friends first. She couldn't tell her cousin that she could only remember been introduced to one cousin and another friend. Lola felt she'd coped really well so far without many complaints until now, her old belief that Akin's impromptu trips and last minute change of plans was preparing her for days like this had finally crumbled. She wanted to call Sade again but changed her mind to avoid disturbing them; moreover, there wasn't much they could do for her all the way from Reading that couldn't wait till daytime. Infuriated, confused and lonely she decided to call her grandma later in the day. She was fortunately still analysing the dream when sleep took priority over all her worries. Her alarm's bleep brought her back to reality and also reminded her of the little time left.

She'd paid for her purchases and was wondering what to do with the remaining fifteen minutes when she remembered the wrapping paper for her presents. She quickly popped into the greeting cards store adjacent for the finishing touches and was a few step away from their meeting point when she saw his car approaching. They both smiled for their perfect timing as he pulled up beside her.

'Great minds think alike!' he remarked as she sat next to him. He waited for a safe time to pull out and didn't wait for her reply before he continued. 'How was shopping?'

'Great.'

He looked at her and wondered what the smirk was for. 'Were you able to get everything?'

'No.'

If her abrupt contradictory reply bothered him he ignored it and drove on with a scowl instead. The rest of the journey was in silence except the Motown collection CD playing in the background.

Adam was not happy about the outcome of his impromptu meeting. His scheduled meeting with his P.I. was cancelled but Mr James timely call filled it. He was supposed to get him some information but he'd instead turned around to ask for more money upfront. He'd been closed to getting the old man arrested a couple of times and today was not an exception. Getting tangled in Lola's mess was accidental and he had instinctively volunteered his help but he never expected so much cans of worms opening up all around him. His open and secret surveillance about her yielded nothing to implicate her, likewise the facts before him. But he couldn't imagine the magnitude of her offence to have warranted so many circumstantial stitch ups both in her personal relationship and at work, but he was as determined as ever to find out no matter the cost! He sincerely hoped she would appreciate all his efforts someday.

'It's time.' Lola interrupted him.

'Sorry.'

'The light has changed to green.'

Without another word he put his car into gear and sped through, which coincidentally was the extremely long road leading to her house. He in no time pulled up in front of her house and stopped the engine. His instinct told him not to bother escorting her inside because of their individual sombre moods moreover, he had some phone calls to follow up with Mr James. His thought was again derailed when Lola's hands gently brushed past his thighs, when their gazes met she was smiling and holding a gift. 'What is it?' He asked with a frown.

'Open it.'

Still focusing his attention on her, he examined the box carefully, and then shook it before ripping the wrapping paper off at once. In it was a pair of silver cufflinks, a shirt and a matching tie. 'I'm amazed at you, Lola. Just one more thing,' he grabbed the collar to check the size before nodding with thanks and approval. 'Thank you!' Still smiling, he reached out, hugged her tightly, and placed a peck on her lips and each side of her cheeks.

He stopped but held her face in his hands and wanted to kiss her all over when his phone rang; keeping one hand still on her face he answered the phone with the other.

His swift mood change gave Lola a clue to excuse him.

'I'll excuse you for a while.'

He didn't protest but instead waited for her to leave the car and shut the door.

She was absolutely relieved that his perfectly timed phone call saved her from another emotional upheaval and embarrassment. A strange, sweet sensation went through her body when he held her face, her lips and cheeks suddenly became ignited with feeling she was ashamed to admit to herself let alone acknowledge. As she turned the key in the keyhole she conclusively interpreted her sensational feeling into her unconditional and uninhibited love for Akin whom she missed so dearly—her mind suddenly went blank because of the shocking sight before her, she instantly froze as her gaze raked over her living room. Oh no! I've been burgled again! She tried to comprehend the situation but the violation not only boldly stared back at her in every nooks and crannies she looked but repulsed her guts. Quickly, she rushed outside to escape but only to run into Adam's embrace.

'What now?' Without resisting, she stayed within his embrace and continued sobbing uncontrollably. 'Are you going to tell me what's wrong?' He asked with as much patience as he could muster.

She tried to explain amidst the sob but couldn't get a word out let alone a sentence. Gently, Adam turned her round towards the door only to notice her resistance, she eventually obliged when she felt his hands tightly around her.

'Not again!' Adam muttered under his breath but loud enough for her to hear. 'What the hell is going on?' His scowl disappeared when he saw the state she was in. 'Come here love.' He gently turned her to face him and continued rubbing her back to calm her. For once, the thought of kissing her crossed his mind but he restrained himself after remembering the last controversial fondling as she called it. More so, he didn't want her to see him as taking advantage of her. If only his feeling could be so sensible and logical around her instead of him constantly battling it out!

CHAPTER 16

Billy Morris leaned against his comfortable chair facing his huge, oak desk whilst emitting sense of power and authority despite being a semi retired managing director. Hot and bothered in a casual pair of jeans and a grey long sleeved polo shirt, he got on his feet to stretch his long legs that always made him seem taller than his five foot nine inches. The recent trouble both at home and work had taken a serious toll on his already fragile health as more strands of whiteness showed in his thick, glossy hair. Lately, the truth was beginning to unravel after weeks of critical assessment and upheavals in his home and relationship, yet with his biggest question still unanswered.

'What has disputing Lola's presence got to do with anything?'

'Because Bob claimed she'd been suspended the previous day and if it's true I'd like to know why she was in the office the following day?'

Roxanne pushed her reading glasses slightly down the bridge of her nose and locked his gaze to reflect on his question. 'And if she wasn't?'

'How do you mean?'

'What if she was really suspended on the day of the blast?'

'Why would my brother tell me otherwise?'

She angrily slapped the novel on the empty sofa beside her. 'I told you yesterday, the day before and many other times that he lied to you. Read my lips, your brother is a very big, nasty liar!'

Surprised at her sudden outburst, he sifted his hand through his hair whilst his pleading eyes still hooked deeply into hers. 'But why?'

'Do you know who's causing the biggest problem?'

Without a word, he gently walked up to her and sat beside her still looking deeply into her cobalt blue eyes for a miracle answer.

She tapped his shoulder firmly. 'You are.'

'Me?' His eyes widened with surprise before it suddenly calmed down. 'Now you are being ridiculous.' He decided to thread carefully after noticing her cobalt eyes darkened, something that rarely happened. She wasn't being shrewd or manipulative, but being absolutely honest even if it was going to kill them both!

She bounced up to stoop and level her face with his. 'Yes, you are the one who had never listened to all the hints and complaints. Your brother says one thing everyone else says the other and as usual we are all wrong and he is right. We are dumb and he is smart. We are all bad and he's good!' She stood up, walked away and stopped halfway. 'No wonder he always described you as his broad-minded, gullible brother, he laughs at you behind your back.' She turned round to pick up her novel. 'Excuse me I need some fresh air.' She strutted out of the room without looking back.

Billy watched her tiny waist wriggle seductively and remembered how it used to tantalise him, but realised how things had changed. Was it the effect of his health or the same lingering, divisive subject? She so much wanted him to believe her, he did but his problem was understanding his brother's motives. Head downcast, he agreed the resolution was entirely his and no one else's. He'd always loved and trusted his siblings to a fault especially after letting his sister down decades ago. This is quite precarious! Just like being stuck between a hard stone and a big rock! According to Roxanne, Lola was suspended on the same day as the blast, which totally negated and contradicted his brother's explanation that she'd been suspended for insubordination, incompetence and fraud the day before the explosion. The surveillance cameras that could have shed more light unfortunately had no tape in it. If she was truly suspended the day before the explosion why was she let into the building the following day? If she did at all turn up, why hadn't her pass been disabled?

The only other person that could have shed more light was Lola who now had amnesia. He held her in high esteem for being one of the most hardworking, diligent, honest and loyal employee he'd ever had, but business as usual had to come first. She was recruited through a scheme to specifically employ five graduates from the ethnic minority in his attempt redress the imbalance of racism scandal originally instigated and perpetrated by his brother. Secretly, he admitted that the only plausible answer was that of Roxanne whose only crime was loving him whole heartedly for twenty odd years or more.

He met Roxanne shortly after Marianne, his girlfriend, of five years went missing which coincided with the peak of the rift in his family. Wit Sherry and Bob gone, he then decided to get serious with Marianne who'd supported him throughout the difficult years with his family. As childhood sweethearts from the same neighbourhood in Tamworth, they relocated to neighbouring Lichfield pooled their savings together to buy a derelict building that Billy refurbished into ten Bed and Breakfast. With the B&B thriving they employed a chef, Rosie, and a cleaner whilst Billy was secretly working on their next project, a twenty bed hotel as a surprise when she suddenly disappeared. With days rolling into weeks, he was forced to abandon the surprise hotel project and face the already established B&B. After a while, he received her letter with recent pictures that she was fine and had met someone that ignited her love life. Every doubt in his mind was totally eliminated by another letter supporting the first, but it initially put him at a total loss and immediately propelled him to call a staff meeting and update them. With Rosie promoted, she took on most of the administrative roles, chef's working hours were slashed whilst the cleaner was made redundant. Ten months later Rosie tendered her first resignation to travel across Europe with her partner but did him a favour and introduced her best friend to relieve her.

He could vividly remember standing by the filing cabinet when she knocked on his square boxed office to introduce her new successor. He immediately reached for her C.V. Rosie handed him some days back.

"Boss, Roxanne Green my best friend that I already told you about." Rosie shoved her shy friend towards Billy so hard that her bosoms brushed past his arm on the filing cabinet.

He instantly stepped backwards and stretched his other hand for a handshake but that physical contact left its print on his mind forever. As his big hand wrapped hers over, his heart leapt several times and many more when their eyes met. He later on convinced himself that it was because of her striking resemblance to his sister, except that Roxanne was much shorter, but with the same bubbly, blonde hair style and an exact pair of cobalt blue alluring eyes the last time he saw her. He more or less left Tamworth to start afresh and hopefully rid himself of his guilt.

Rosie supervised her friend for a fortnight before embarking on the journey of a lifetime. It was only a matter of time before the young, hardworking, caring and a very passionate Roxanne added her own enthusiasm to the new role transferred to her. Billy really appreciated every little contribution that eased his daunting task of weathering the severe storm engulfing his life both at work and home. Basically, she offered him comfort and the restoration of his hope in life, which was all he needed the most then! With Roxanne's strong support, he eventually overcame his crisis, and had lost interest in the proposed hotel he had nearly finished restoring by vigorously seeking a buyer. The six months it took to find a suitable buyer also coincided with their relationship progressing to a "hot passionate level". The interested buyers wanted to buy the two properties, but he was initially reluctant to sell the B&B until Marianne turned up and demanded for half of the B&B's current value. Even though he finally gave in to her persuasion whilst secretly hoping and praying she relocated with him to start afresh again. He'd meanwhile broken off with Roxanne!

To his utmost surprise she rejected his invitation with a lame excuse, but realised she wouldn't bulge after weeks of persuasion. Without wasting much time he joined his share of the proceeds from the established B&B with the completed hotel to buy A.B.C. & D. in Birmingham. Having realised his folly and being dumped twice by the same woman, he tried to find Roxanne and not only ask for her forgiveness but to also offer her a few thousand pounds to appease and persuade her. All his effort was without success.

Whilst still searching for Roxanne, Marianne came back for the third time and begged for his forgiveness again, Then he knew he was doomed when his old feelings resurrected and it all felt like she'd never left him or he'd never cried over her for days or nights unending! They got married a year later to equally celebrate the christening of their baby girl- Saffronne. They stayed married for eight more years until she died in her sleep.

After her death, he grieved over three women even though he knew the other two were alive. He was certain he could feel and hear their pain because he let two of them down when they were young, innocent and inexperienced! They had now frustrated all his efforts by changing all their contact details from the face of the earth until five years ago when Roxanne finally tracked him down.

On their second meeting, Roxanne told him she'd specifically returned to Birmingham from Spain to find and tell him he'd fathered her fifteen-year-old son named Dale. He was still overwhelmed with shock, trepidation and most of all anger for keeping it a secret for so long and hadn't recovered when she told him he was anxiously waiting for them in the car. He still couldn't explain what propelled him to lead the way outside but was met at the entrance by a young man of almost his height but a spitting image of Roxanne. Dale didn't wait for any introduction before giving him the most remarkable hug that instantly eroded all his past anger and frustration. He always felt proud and fulfilled whenever he reminisced the result of the most passionate and erotic period in his life, especially after the D.N.A test confirmed he was the biological father.

She had since then immensely contributed enormously to his life and had been his rock especially throughout the period of his early retirement, illness and hospitalisation. His brother would have definitely got away with murder if Roxanne hadn't been in his life. He instantly remembered Marianne's main excuse for leaving him was because he didn't ignite her love life! Billy endeavoured to suppress the emotion those few words still stirred in him.

But his concern about the affairs of his company had never been so critical with so many unpleasant revelations requiring urgent attention. His forehead creased as he wondered what next would go wrong. On the other hand, his doubt in his brother's capability had sky rocketed, and his early retirement seemed suddenly short lived. He blamed himself for believing he was a changed man when he reappeared a year after Roxanne resurfaced.

Billy was seven and his brother four when his gambling parents became separated because of their addiction. Two years later they had a step mum named Flora who soon filled the ever growing feminine gap in their lives and everything was perfect until she had the adorable Sherry who then became the centre of attraction. To make matters worst Bob shared the same birthday with Sherry. She always received all the attention and presents especially on her fifth birthday when he didn't get anything because Flora realised her husband was still a compulsive gambler and had lied about attending counselling sessions. Dad had so far succeeded in hiding it from her and the rest of the family except Bob till then, which worsened the situation at home for everyone.

Years later, Flora went out with her daughter one day and never returned home but was kind enough to drop a letter to tell everyone she was fine. She also stated her main disappointment at his dad's gambling addiction that had superseded the welfare of his family. Her ultimatum was for him to tackle the problem if he really wanted them back, but his dad never did. Billy squeezed his forehead as he did decades ago when he zealously wished he could do the same with his brother. With Flora gone, Billy had to grow up quicker and provide for his broken dad and his handful brother.

It was eight years later when dad confided in him that Sherry had been in frequent contact and would be moving back with them sometime, which happened three months later. The reunion as he remembered was quite emotional especially for his dad who couldn't believe what a dazzling young woman his daughter had become, he began spoiling her with everything again. As he rejoiced with his dad he wondered why Bob was again umbrage and began to wonder what role he played in splitting dad and his step mum up, despite his strenuous denial Billy not only disbelieved him but always made his doubt known to him.

It finally slipped out of Bob that he lured his dad back into gambling just to convince Flora and eventually get rid of her. Surprisingly, he recovered quickly from the shock but it also starkly reminded him of their growing up, when an egotistical, reckless, nincompoop Bob wouldn't care what he destroyed as long he got his way. He'd been trying without success to split him and Roxanne up, as he did with Sherry and T.J.

Wishing he'd nipped the problem in the bud then, he straightened the three wrinkles on his forehead to suppress his guilt, especially when he started bullying their little sister. Sherry left her mother to be with her brothers but fell in love with a pleasant, Nigerian gentleman called T.J. who went through hell. Initially, Billy did not believe her claim that their brother had joined a racist militant group; he thought his actions to be harmless sibling prank and fun. He looked back and seriously wished he had intervened when his sister complained he was going too far and pleaded for his help, instead of assuring her that Bob was simply protecting her. He finally realised how cynical his bullying tactic had become when he assaulted T.J. and threatened him with a knife if he didn't break up with his sister. Despite seeing Bob's true colour, he still refuted all the signs

A pleasant smile brightened his face as he clearly recollected the day fate turned against his brother after challenging the brave and courageous T.J. to a fight. His consistent refusal not only provoked Bob more but made him taunt and bully Sherry more until she was goaded to instigate a financial reward to the winner. T.J. finally agreed after another challenge from Bob who in contrast to everyone expectation said he would get back to them for date.

It was exactly three weeks later when he walked in with ten friends to tell them he was ready to fight now, surprisingly T.J. rose to the challenge immediately. Bob wasted no time in striking the first three punches that strangely was the only glory he had that day. Everyone watched him crumble under T.J.'s heavy punches until Sherry intercepted and stopped the fight when he was bleeding heavily. Three days later, his disgraced brother reported the incident to the police with more self-inflicted bruises to gravely incriminate him; unfortunately all his friends that lost their betting denied witnessing any fight whatsoever.

It was almost two months later when Bob decided to take the laws into his own hands by setting T.J. ablaze. It landed him in hospital for weeks receiving treatment for a third degree burns on his shoulder, right arm and upper part of his body.

Billy remembered the gratifying smile on his brother's face when T.J. was screaming and rolling on the floor for help. He was hospitalised for weeks with Sherry visiting him day and night but was shocked like everyone else that he left no forwarding address when he was discharged. His sudden departure left Sherry heartbroken and on hunger strike for weeks when she realised she would never see him again. Her physical weakness and mental state convinced Billy she'd given up on life until she found out she was pregnant. Most of her pregnancy period was spent in hospital admission until her mum took her back to Scotland with her. Whilst his determination to track his troublesome, absconding brother was waning he received a postcard from Sherry telling him he had become an uncle.

He heard voices and looked up wondering whose they were but only saw Roxanne approaching with a recorded cassette player. 'Is that Bob's voice?'

'Shhhh!' She nodded her head and gestured him to continue listening. 'Here lies the answer to some of your questions,' she turned the volume up and sat on the desk to join him.

They both gave a big sigh of disbelief simultaneously just as the tape came to an end. 'Do you want to listen to it again?'

Billy pursed his lips in anger and swore under his breath before reiterating the words his brother used to describe him. Bearing the consequence and reprisal of his brother's action in mind he tried his utmost best not to get emotional. 'I don't believe this!' Bewildered, he looked up at his fiancé who was still gloating in her 'I told you so' look. 'That bastard called me pathetic and feeble.' He buried his head between his hands as he always did when troubled.

Bob has done more damage to him than anyone else. He was beginning to understand why Sherry never forgave him for standing by and doing nothing and also why she blamed him for costing her the love of her lifetime. He finally realised that the betrayal she felt then was reliving itself in him right now and they both have Bob to thank for that.

'I don't expect you to fight my battle for me but I can't accept you letting him get away with it by standing back and just watching. But unlike him I'm only your half sister and it wouldn't take a genius to know who to choose between us. As usual I'm on my own again.' Sherry's last, bitter words reverberated vividly in his mind. The last he heard about her was when she relocated to Walsall then to Worcester after his cards and presents were returned to him unopened.

How he wished he had done something then, he lamented as he toyed with the cassette recorder and tried to suppress the anger brewing in him. She was his little sister, and he let her down but he'd let himself down even more. He regretted not having the inclination to nip the problem in the bud, worse still, contrary to his expectation, his admission didn't relieve him of his guilt and the mere fact that he'd tried so much in finding her without success offered him no consolation either. Every disappointing year had made him understand how much she must have loathed him then and now.

Billy had recently given up hope and expectation that she could find the kindness in her heart to respond to his birthday cards if she couldn't bring herself to forgive and forget. He had been recently told that Sherry was now retired and back in West Midlands for good. He smiled whilst trying to imagine what she would look like now knowing she'd always been a stunner.

He was deeply hurt when he didn't hear nor receive any condolence message from her for Marianne's death or during the time he was hospitalised. That was the turning point in his life, even though he'd been weary of his brother and had kept him at arm's length until he sought his financial assistance despite being scared of loosing him completely.

Now, look how the bastard repaid him! He could not believe the level of anger that had suddenly enveloped him. Thank God! Earl, his lawyer, would be advising him all the way on every legal step and implication. His first plan was to legally reduce his powers and roles in the company because he could no longer afford a renegade in the company he'd worked too hard to establish and accomplish.

He sure wouldn't blame Lola if she chose to drag the company to the employment tribunal for racism, bullying and health and safety violation amongst other things. But before she could get around to doing that he had to come up with a plan to disconnect A.B.C. & D. from his brother and also come up with another good image for the company. Only God knows how many more law suits to expect.

'Are you happy now?'

He'd forgotten he wasn't alone until Roxanne's voice interrupted his thought. He raised his head to face her but decided not to disclose his plan to her for her own protection. 'More than happy my darling.'

He opened his arm to embrace her, when she stooped to hug him back he pulled her in tightly before exhaling deeply. She tried to wriggle out and see his expression but he wouldn't let her. He squeezed her tighter as he released his anger and frustration when he remembered his promise to his doctor. He pecked her hair and looked straight ahead before whispering 'what would I do without you?'

CHAPTER 17

Lola managed to wake up early this morning but without much enthusiasm. Whilst waiting for the police officer's visit to interview her about yesterday's burglary she decided to put her rubbish out before the bin men arrived. On her way in she observed how lovely the Friday was, with no clouds, lot of sunshine and a slight breeze that had started clearing the summer humidity since last night.

She got back inside and slumped on the only sofa unscathed by the burglar before turning the television on. An ongoing advert instantly reminded her of her pigsty living room before she remembered Adam's advice not to touch anything in case the police wanted to gather any finger printing evidence whilst equally stressing his fear of her safety.

Yesterday's incident gave her an insight into his gentle and comforting nature when he responded to her unstable emotion, his calm and soothing voice had consoled her when she was crying endlessly. He tried his possible best to persuade her from staying any longer in her house, but she remained adamant about staying put. He eventually got angry and they yelled at each other before he rushed out of her house. Just before he turned the door handle, he stopped and said she should inform him when the police arrived only if she felt it was necessary.

Good riddance to you! Lola thought dismissively as the door shut loudly behind him. She'd wanted to do this long before now but something beyond her means always cropped up, she was this time determined to see it through. She was interrupted by a phone call from her landline; despite the cordless by her side, she deliberately took her time in answering because she was certain it was Adam.

And she couldn't be more wrong!

It was Chucks, one of Akin's close friends that had just arrived from Nigeria. 'You've finally decided to call me.'

'What do you mean you haven't heard from him since when?'

'When exactly was the last time you've heard from him?'

'Okay Chucks I'm calm. Are you sincerely telling me that it's been nearly six weeks since you've seen or heard from him?' Lola's panic spiralled as the phone slipped off her hands. 'And you said that was the day you dropped him in my house?' She paused with the hope of remembering any vital clue on the said day but her memory let her down as usual. 'Who sent me text messages from Lagos two and three weeks ago then?'

'Yes, everyday in those weeks I mentioned.'

'No I haven't received any this week.' She answered his question affirmatively.

'What do you suggest I do?' She quickly grabbed a pen to take his numbers down. 'You want me to give you till tomorrow to get back to me?'

'Chucks that's too long.'

'Yes I agree, I survived weeks without knowing but it's different now that I know.'

'Okay, I'll wait till this time tomorrow as you suggested before I inform the police.' She struggled to calm her shaky voice. She replaced the phone before she noticed that tears had already gathered in her eyes. Twenty four hours wait was nothing compared to the weeks of nothing.

Akin had been gone for six weeks according to her friend's calculation. She couldn't remember the first three weeks but she received his text message for the fourth and fifth week. She dreaded the worst! How could she justify her ignorance to herself let alone to anyone else? She wiped more tears away from her face despite her annoyance at her memory loss and all the vital clues that could have helped solve the riddles surrounding her life. With more tears flowing freer than ever and with nowhere or no one to turn to she dejectedly placed both hands over her head and face towards the ceiling for some divine intervention.

She was snatched out of her disheartening slumber by the doorbell and wasn't much surprised to find a police officer at her doorstep. Her first instinct was to send the officer away but logic took over when she thought of how suspicious that might seem, moreover she wanted to tidy her living room up as quickly as possible. She swiftly stepped aside to let the over six foot officer bow his head inside.

The police officer introduced himself as P.C. Ian Welsh, took as much notes as she answered his questions before snooping and touching around still taking more notes.

'I heard you were recently involved in a bomb explosion?' P.C. Welsh asked out of the blue without looking at her.

She recovered quickly from the shock before answering with a weak 'yes'.

'Have you now regained your lost memory?'

'No, is it related to the burglary?'

'You tell me.' The officer stood upright and eyed her from head to toe. 'Mr Morris told us that you keep companies with people of questionable character.'

She began to suspect his hostility. 'Bob or Billy?'

'Your Managing Director, Bob Morris.' He continued after flipping over some pages of his jotter whilst waiting for her explanation. He also described you as "the most negative, problematic, incompetent and uncommitted team member with severely underlined personal problems."

She leaned her temple on her palm. 'Did you ask him why he hasn't fired me yet?'

The officer flipped over the page again for some guidelines but ended up saying no and returning it into his breast pocket.

'May be you could ask him next time you chat with him.' She watched him scribble a few lines before she continued. He'd say that wouldn't he?' She found a perfect opportunity to return his scowl. 'I'm sure he didn't tell you I don't have many friends or did he give you names of my so-called people of questionable character?'

'Yes actually,' he immediately reached for his jotter and frowned. 'Mr *Akinwande Ajibola.*'

'Yes? Have you heard anything about him? Is he alright?'

P.C. Welsh instead smiled to ignore the concern in her voice and her barrage of questions. 'I take it you don't know he is currently behind bars.'

'I'm sure you are talking of someone else. My Akin is in Ghana or Nigeria.' She stopped when she noticed his humouring stare and her last conversation with Chucks .

He folded his arms and smiled weakly. 'I'll see myself out.' He walked towards the door and was about to turn the handle when he turned around. 'You can tidy up now. He placed one foot outside before he spoke again, 'good day Ma.' He tipped his head slightly before putting the other foot and finally shutting the door behind him.

Her eyes remained stuck on the door even long after the officer had gone. 'Damn!' She cursed loudly. 'Just when I thought I could handle this myself! Akin behind bars?' She continued ranting. With her head burrowed between her thighs she wondered how the hell Bob knew about him or what people of questionable character was he referring to? What crime did he commit? 'Adam where are you?' Crying, she yelled out with anger and frustration.

'I wish I knew.'

Lola looked up sharply to find an intruder leaning on a walking stick and was still dumb struck when the woman spoke again.

'Sorry, the police officer said I should try and catch you before you went out.' She added quickly to downplay her intrusion and ignore Lola's surprise.

She appraised the short, round, and frail looking woman with the sun's reflection making her auburn hair shine more, especially the parted line in the middle. She was obviously blessed with good mouth and nicely curved lips that would have committed havocs in the past. 'We've met before haven't we?' She guessed her age to be about thirty five, but the illness had taken control and overshadowed the once upon a beauty that she previously was.

'Yes, at Rosie's send off get-together.' She dropped her handbag close to her feet on the floor as she crouched heavily on her walking stick desperately struggling to regain her breath and strength whilst awaiting her invitation to be seated.

'You're Sally aren't you?' Surprised for remembering her name she quickly cleared one of the sofa for her to sit. She was anxious to know what she wanted but still slapped the sofa with her palm and invited her to sit instead of asking.

She nodded and slumped into the sofa with a gracious smile. 'Akin asked me to give this letter to you.'

'My Akin?' Their eyes met. Lola saw her lips thinned angrily and her eyeballs flamed up but she ignored it and still forced a smile before taking the letter from her. As she tore the envelope to start reading the letter she caught Sally looking at her surroundings with suspicion, reservation and ill feeling.

The letter was dated three weeks ago with the address of a prison in the Midlands. 'What kind of a sick joke is this?'

'Have you finished?' Sally ignored her question with an enquiring expression.

For the first time she returned the spite by eyeing her before concentrating back on the letter which was apparently written in Yoruba. She began to sweat immediately the reality dawned on her. 'My Akin in prison?'

Trying so hard not to show her flaring temper, she threw Lola a tentative smile that fools would mistake for niceness. 'Well, I don't know about that but this is the Akin that sent me to you.' She opened a cream coloured leather album to show a picture of herself with Akin.

'Why you?'

Sally looked at her condescendingly before flipping over the next page to show her another picture of the pair.

Lola too positioned herself and repaid her with a similar scornful stare. She had already risen to the challenge when she noticed the next picture in the album.

'This looks like your wedding?' She'd already asked before noticing the banner behind them stating happy married life to Sally and Akin Ajibola. The picture was that of a younger, leaner Akin kissing a much prettier and livelier version of Sally. The next picture portrayed a promising, happy couple who looked vibrant holding hands, smiling and in love.

Sally's lips thinned as she closely watched her ever changing expression before nodding her head. 'I was four months pregnant here.'

She decided not to succumb to her curiosity and ask what happened to the pregnancy. 'I had no idea.' Her sincerity sounded so weak that she could hardly hear herself.

'I didn't think you knew.' She replied in the same whispering austere tone.

Lola cupped her chin with her right hand and gazed at her. 'How ...?' She stopped and shook her head fiercely instead.

'We've been married for nearly seven years.'

'That was not what I wanted to ask.'

'I apologise for my premature assumption.'

'That's okay. Whilst trying to anticipate her next statement, she stared at her sombrely.

'How did you know where I live?'

'I apologise again.' She opened a page in the album and stretched a brown envelope towards her. 'That was his first letter to you.'

Lola edged forward to receive the letter she'd so much looked forward to but now meant absolutely nothing. 'So he knew I didn't receive his first letter.'

'Not sure, but he insisted on seeing you.'

'Before or after writing the second letter?' She slapped the brown envelope against her palm whilst struggling to hold her tears and steady her voice.

'Before or after, what does it matter?'

With her gaze fixated on the letter that she believed was certainly no longer hers she suddenly looked up to find Sally gawking at her intensely. 'How long have you known about Akin and …?' She completed the rest of her sentence with a gesture of her hand as she uncannily felt strange to comprehend their relationship.

A faint smile spread across her thin lips whilst her eyes raked through Lola's solemn face. 'I had him investigated and had to see for myself at the football fundraising event.'

'But he wasn't with me that day.'

She smiled then coughed; the deep scratchy, hacking cough of an ex chain smoker clearing her chest of the residue. 'So I noticed and I also found out about this other woman and her two sons.'

'Two?' She frowned.

'Do you know her?'

'No, he told me about a woman with a seven-year-old son.' Lola's face became downcast with ignominy for her constant dismissal of Roxanne and April's warning.

It was now Sally's turn to frown and look at her pensively. 'What did the woman look like?'

She looked at her to indicate their similarity. 'Like a recovering drug addict.'

'It was Bea.' She said with firm assurance.

Instead of Lola replying she embarrassingly ran her tongue over her dry lips to hide her guilt from the series of confrontation with her closest friends on the same subject. 'I suppose I won't be needing this anymore,' stretching the brown envelope back at her.

Sally deliberately ignored the letter. 'Don't you want to visit him?'

The edginess in her voice encouraged Lola to be astoundingly impassive before she shrugged her shoulders and raised her face towards the ceiling. 'Can you write his address here for me?' She explained in clipped words and a fierce stare. She had no intention of visiting him but was not going to divulge it to her either.

Disappointed by her noncommittal reaction she tried to scrutinise her face for any kind of response but soon gave up in realisation of its futility.

She neither knew what to say nor how to say it because remembering a lot was entirely different from remembering everything. Exhaling deeply, she checked her wrist watch and got on her feet. 'Mrs Ajibola ...' she stopped and instead tapped on her watch to signify her time was up.

Sally sensing her reluctance pouted her lips that made her face more gauntly 'I'm sorry I've taken so much of your time.' She prolonged her unsuccessful attempts to get up but Lola played it cool by not offering any help. 'I suppose you won't need to contact Chucks anymore.' There was a hidden meaning in her question, but Lola chose not to answer.

'Was the first letter given to Chucks?'

They locked gaze in mutual silence before Sally finally denied and broke the silence. 'Maybe another time?' She finally added after recovering from her heavy breathing and now on her feet.

She made her strong refusal apparent by fiercely shaking her head sideways consistently before stepping aside for her guest to lead the way.

'Thank you for your time anyway.' Sally finally said just before stepping out.

She was still securing the locks of the front door when tears flowed recklessly and without any reticence. She leaned on the door and gradually slid to the floor only for more tears to follow.

That explained his sudden appearances and disappearances and the so called family pressures! On his frequent impromptu trips to Nigeria, she could remember asking Akin to drop some parcels to her family but he always refused with some lame excuses, and if he did he always came back to apologise that he lost the package at the checkout point, forgot them or that his distant relative hijacked them. She remembered that the first letter she read was still on the table and quickly reached for it. Was she been irrational? Of course not! Why did he give the letter to his wife to deliver? The only obvious reason was to let her know that he was already married. How could she be so gullible not to have suspected that he was married! Wonders shall never end! This was the man she hoped to spend the rest of her life with. She immediately confirmed his handwriting by comparing the letter with his other documents already with her. What was his point in writing it in Yoruba? She asked herself again, but was suddenly interrupted by one of her portraits with Akin dropping from the T.V. cabinet closely by her feet. They both wore the same traditional outfit made from the lace material bought and paid for by her dad. She admired her posture and elegance in a wrapper and *buba* complemented by headgear while he was wearing a complete *agbada* and a hat made from the same fabric. It was a happy day for both, now the picture of the man beside her had changed everything. The image staring back at her with full on smile almost changed her mind for one second but rage overpowered her as she grabbed her shoe beside her and smashed it on the picture over and over again until a broken glass pierced through her palm. With her bloody hand and tears blurring her vision she dashed straight for the stairs and far away from the messy downstairs. She could have washed her hands downstairs but that would again remind her of the break in. As she angrily ascended the stairs, she felt a strain on her ankle and began hopping on one leg whilst leaning on the balustrade and simultaneously wishing she'd never woken up or gotten out of bed at all. This was much harder than she could bear and could for once in her life appreciate a shoulder to cry on! She wanted to scream for Adam but remembered what happened the last time she did. After attending to her wound, she crashed into her bed crying and asking herself why. 'Why me?' She cried out loudly.

She eyed the ring that now meant nothing to her; this was an object she wore with pride and dignity.

She wanted to flush it down the toilet immediately but something warned her against it. How could she get it so wrong? How could she have fallen for the wrong man on earth? What was to become of all his promises and their plans for the future! She felt anger brewing up inside her again but another voice asked her to be thankful to the creator, for things could have got worse if she was pregnant. What if his name had already been added to her property deed or they were already married? What would she tell her family then? Mama would not say a word but just throttle her. Above all, Lola was glad she still maintained her chastity against all odds.

Good riddance to the troubles in her life! She definitely wouldn't hear the last of it from her friends, and indeed they sure did warn her, she was just the fool who wouldn't listen. She was certain her grandmother would have seen through Akin if she'd set her eyes on him at least once. As tears streamed down her face like a burst pipe she finally curled up in her bed and wallowed in the worst self-pity, self-loathing and destructive situation ever imagined.

She must have dozed off as she found herself in a park full of people and noise, especially kids playing and having fun, she sat on a wooden bench eating fish and chips and watching the kids when she saw Akin approaching. Her heart melted with love and desire when he returned her smile but he suddenly disappeared from her view and the next thing was her frantically rolling on the floor with her stomach and womb literarily on fire. Akin appeared from nowhere and began quenching the fire when Bob turned up, took him away and left her screaming with pain. Unexpectedly another man appeared and placed his calming hands on her stomach area and had nearly put out the fire when she jumped up from her sleep. All she could remember was the ring on the man's finger smiling at her.

With sweat streaming down her face, her mouth and throat felt dry. She looked around to be met by the only familiar things in her bedroom with her bedside clock ticking. The clock had just gone past midday.

Whilst wondering she placed her hand on her stomach and was surprised to feel the heat. She was still pondering over her dream, premonition, nightmare or a combination of them all when she heard some ruffling and shuffling downstairs. Petrified and confused she remained put as the noise increasingly became louder until she asked herself what she would do if the burglar came upstairs. Quickly, she dialled Adam's number but was unfortunately only able to leave a panicking message before jumping out of bed to dial 999 and explained what was happening to the operator as loud as she could. Knowing fully well that there was no entrance to the bedrooms except through the stairs, she positioned herself at the top of the stairs anticipating the burglar's next step. It was another ten minutes before she was certain the burglar had left and was still shaken when Adam returned her call that he was outside her front door. On hearing his voice she began mumbling and crying without making any sense to herself let alone anyone else.

Adam yelled from the top of his voice that he would break the door down if she didn't comply. She eventually got up and tried opening the door for him, but her anxiety was so critical that she could not insert the key into the lock and had to drop the keys through the letter box to him. She was confused when he finally stepped inside and his attempt to calm her down was met by heavy resistance. After inflicting several frustrating punches at his chest he overpowered her with a gentle bear hug and numerous comforting words. Having been subdued she berated him for abandoning her all day and was gently hushed up with a promise that he would never leave her again. He frowned as he wondered how he would achieve his promise but would have made bigger promises to calm her down instead of reminding her that she literarily threw him out yesterday and the day was still young.

'What happened?'

With no reply but still clinging tightly, she shifted position before burrowing her wet face in his chest.

'Was this here yesterday?' He finally asked after ensuring she was well settled.

She looked up at him with a pair of red, puffy eyes. 'What?' She let her gaze follow his as they moved towards the first corner in the living room.

'Don't touch it.' He urged as she tried to bend and get it.

'No, it wasn't or I would have seen it when Sally was here.'

He frowned. 'What did this Sally come for if she couldn't help you clear this mess?'

Her stark stare made him raise his hands up in the air. 'I think I'm going through the worst phase of my life and today is the worst so far.'

Without taking her words seriously, he bent over to examine the scarf closely and wasn't surprised to see her do the same.

'That looks like Mr James's scarf.'

'Yes I was going to say the same.' Adam had mistakenly concurred loudly.

'Do you know him?'

'Yes, the man at the football fundraising and right beside you when the bomb exploded.'

'Okay, we are definitely talking of the same person.' She sucked in the air and released it slowly as if her life depended on it. 'There is a dog's odour coming from the scarf and I can't remember if he has a dog or not.'

Adam straightened up and watched her amazingly before trying to sniff it. 'Sorry it smells homely to me despite the chaos in here.' What Adam couldn't tell her was he was with Mr James when she called and that he never owned a dog. Depending heavily on him for the recent updates about Lola's situation had brought them closer especially after he told him he was a Nigerian too. His thought was soon interrupted by the door bell followed by a loud knock.

Lola opened the door for the police officers, this time P.C. Welsh accompanied by a female colleague introduced as P.C. Cathy Mann who was almost as tall as him. After the female officer took note of all the answers she provided, they checked the toilet and examined the shattered glass scattered all over the floor.

'Mrs Walwynson next door claimed she saw a man with balaclava running away from your garden.' P.C. Mann stated whilst her colleague excused himself to go outside. 'Can you show me the scarf?'

'Over there.' Adam led whilst the ladies followed.

She took a pair of gloves from her pocket and slotted it on before bending over. 'Do you know who owns the scarf?'

'Not at all.'

She got on her feet and took out her note pad again. 'Have you ever seen a similar scarf on anyone you know?'

'No.'

'It's just bizarre that a burglar with gloves on would forget his scarf.'

'What are you trying to say?' Lola asked nervously.

She rolled her big bulgy eyes before scanning their faces for any clues whatsoever. 'Mrs Walwynson said the burglar's gloves prevented her from knowing his ethnicity.' She waited for their reaction and was about to expand on it when P.C. Welsh walked in, collected the scarf in a transparent bag and labelled it.

He handed Lola some booklets and a reference number if she needed to contact the helpdesk. 'We shall contact you shortly,' P.C. Mann then followed her colleague after a warm handshake with both of them.

CHAPTER 18

'This is really a bachelor's apartment.' Lola remarked amidst mixed feeling before putting her last luggage on the bedroom allocated to her. Like the outside, the inside looked compact, classic, modern and contemporary with the handmade glass windows been the best features. The bedroom and hallway walls were painted with subtle, relaxing colours. Her bedroom was more than adequate with a remote controlled heater and fan, double sized bed and mild flowery beddings.

'I'll let you unpack before showing you round.' Adam leaned on her bedroom door with his hands in his pocket whilst observing her with a renewed interest. First thing she placed on the bedside table was her jotter containing every recent detailed event and addresses. 'Don't you have a diary?'

'I do but I like to duplicate things here.' She held up the blue A4 notepad and slapped it fondly.

'Why?'

'Just playing things safe, moreover I can't afford to trivialise any information till I fully regain my memory.' She looked at the jotter before focusing back at him. 'You know why?'

Adam raised his eyebrows looking befuddled.

'Because information is power.'

His face lightened with humour as he tapped his temple lightly before bursting into laughter, which surprisingly amused her too.

'Do you have a guest room?' She asked after they'd both stopped laughing.

'You are in it and a study. But the two rooms are en-suite with their individual bathrooms.'

'Making two bathrooms and a toilet downstairs?'

'Yes this apartment is mainly used for business purposes.' What he didn't mention was that his mother recently bought it for him as a birthday present.

Something in his voice told her that was not entirely true. 'Before they were completed I used to wonder who would buy them at such ridiculous prices but I never knew they were very well designed and so beautiful.' She opened the wardrobe and hung some blouses in it.

'Feel free to have a look around at your convenience,' he said half-heartedly to check her reaction. 'Unless you want me to show you around now.'

She winked at him and smiled in appreciation. For just that split second she felt something that prevented her from looking away. He seemed much taller and better looking than she'd always believed. His firm, upper body anchored by broad shoulders which accentuated his nicely fitted black trouser and cream short sleeved polo T-shirt. The deeper she thought the more his physique attracted her. His not too casual dressing appealed to her immensely.

'You are right about the price but you know it's because of the city centre location and it's suitability for young and single-minded career people. It's even a walking distance to Broad Street.'

'I would never have imagined you as a hedonist.'

'Hedonist?' He reflected on the word for a while. 'I don't think so, but I consider myself a socialist.'

'Okay, how many times a week do you go clubbing?'

He disagreed by shaking his head sideways. 'Sometimes I visit clubs strictly for business purposes.'

'You still haven't answered my question.'

'It depends on my mood and my stress level?'

'Does that mean you get stressed often?'

'No, not really. But my parents cause me more stress than my personal love life.'

'I didn't know your parents were still together.'

Adam regretted mentioning the subject, the keenness in her voice and face propelled him to play it down gently. It had been a taboo subject he'd successfully locked away in the darkest part of his heart for years, and had been gradually resurfacing since he'd gotten to know her. He studied her face for a while before smiling bashfully. 'You've never asked.' Quickly for diversion, he stepped inside her room and picked up the remote control for the heating and air conditioning system. 'Are you happy with the room's temperature?'

She looked at him and nodded. .

'This is how you regulate the temperature in case you need to.'

Lola watched with fascination before she asked to have a go.

'What do you fancy for dinner?'

'What have you got?'

Adam watched her smiling face and noticed a dramatic improvement in her demeanour. The pitch in her voice seduced him without touching her. 'You as my guest will have to choose for us.'

'Are you really sure of letting me choose for you?'

'Yes why not?'

'Okay you're cooking.'

Adam was relieved of her banter mood. 'Then we'll both die, not of starvation but of food poisoning or something similar. Don't you want to eat out?'

She pondered for a while before shaking her head sadly. 'Can I cook then?' She asked instead.

'Yes sure, but you'll be the first woman to do so in that kitchen.'

'Don't your lady friends cook?'

'I've never brought any of them here.'

'I see.'

He eyed her suspiciously. 'To answer you properly, some cook, some don't but that has never been a prerequisite until now.' His cautious smile gave her the impression that what he didn't say was until he met her.

She hated herself for feeling jealous about his girlfriends, but quickly shrugged it off by wincing at him even though half of her wanted to believe him whilst the other half would like to confirm her suspicion. 'Have you ever been in love?' She quickly covered her mouth as she wondered what has gotten into her.

'Looking back now I thought I was.' He remained pensive for a while. 'I always thought that my true love and I would just fit together perfectly with our likes and dislikes, more like a soul mate.' He stopped to check her reaction.

Lola wanted to tell him she always thought the same but changed her mind. She instead looked back at what she had with Akin and realised that it was nothing more than lackadaisical relationship! The only regret was not finding out sooner, it scared her to be back on the dating market again. But what bothered her mostly was how long she could continue to stall Adam especially now that she was becoming fond of him, seeing more of him and liking what she sees. Akin had apologised in his letter and had yet again insisted on her seeing him. It was for their interest but mainly for her own good and well being. What a nerve he had!

She felt Adam nudge her gently and had no idea how long he'd been speaking. 'Sorry I missed that.' She looked deeply into his eyes as he did hers but shied away first to avoid been conquered by the cocktail of emotions in his eyes.

'I asked if you'd made up your mind on what to cook?'

'Not until I've checked what you've got in your kitchen first.' She finally emptied one of her suitcases. She opened the outer zip and took out a pair of house slippers and brownie.

'What could have made you look so scared and upset?'

'Let me check your kitchen first.' She deliberately avoided his question and his gaze. 'Was it that obvious?' She whispered before slipping into her slippers. They both reacted when her arm slightly brushed his as she walked past him to the kitchen.

With a nod of his head he added in the same tone. 'Yes, pretty obvious.' He quickly followed her to the kitchen and caught her hand in his. 'Let me in, don't shut me out please.' She avoided his gaze again and instead pretended to be admiring the big and spacious kitchen with loads of storage facility.

Already the brief encounter of their bodies sent awakening calls to Adam's senses. He fought the urge to comment on how beautiful she looked today and apart from the sparkle he noticed something was definitely different about her today. Was it because he'd seen her broken down in tears or because she appreciated his support after their first row yesterday? Maybe it has to do with the scar on her forehead healing rapidly. But his thought of her mouth, her voice, and those two melons pointing right at him became extremely hard to shake off. She quickly busied herself with the cupboard above her when she noticed the passion in his eyes again.

He eventually placed his hands on her shoulders and swiftly turned around. 'You don't have to tell me what is eating you but please let it go.' Looking deeply into her eyes, he stopped to watch the impact of his words on her before he continued. 'I-you don't want this trauma to turn you into what you are not.' He released her shoulders and turned her back towards the cupboard with him. 'Now what shall we eat?'

She moved to the fridge and he stood watching her. 'From what you have I could manage to make rice and a sauce, omelette with bread or potatoes, fish and chips.'

'I'm so glad we are spoilt for choice.'

'Why?'

'Because I don't want to leave you miserable and I don't want you making fish and chips either.'

She turned around to ask what he meant but changed her mind and took the bigger of the two cooking pots in the cupboard out instead. 'That leaves us with two choices then.'

'You choose for us.'

With the rice boiling, she quickly used the hand blender on the little tin of tomato plum and onion, poured it into the saucepan containing the already heated oil mixed with the available spice and let it cook to a bubble. She then added the frozen prawns, stirred it and turned the heat down for everything to marinade. She took the salad out of the fridge and was mixing it when her mind drifted to Adam's last comment before leaving her for his study.

If only she knew what to do with Akin. She realised she still had to hear his side of the story but she wasn't prepared to run to him yet. If he knew he was going to be locked up why did he buy them a return ticket to Nigeria? Sally said he was due to be released in a week's time but her resolution had been to follow her instincts and let things take care of itself, it was time he did the running in this relationship. But what if Akin and Sally had divorced? Then how did she get hold of the letter written by Akin to her? And if they were an item she still had a right to know about her existence rather than him making that decision for her. She wondered if she could ever trust him if they got back together? As far as she was concerned, trust was everything in a relationship. Even if Adam wasn't her family's ideal son in law, he'd been the most supportive and helpful man she'd ever known. He had no rivals in the looks and caring department. She might face the possibility of being isolated from the rest of her family because of their cultural difference. Her father might just come around, but Mama would carry the grudge to her grave. And Lola wasn't sure if she could afford that on her conscience!

She turned to open the fridge for any drink when she noticed Adam standing by the door watching her in silence.

'How long have you been standing there?'

He instantly shut his eyes before sucking the sweet aroma of the sauce in. 'Hmm! Long enough.' Stepping into the kitchen, he took of the lid of the saucepan and inhaled more of the sweet aroma before tasting a spoonful and many more. 'Beautiful, cultured and a good cook makes the stake much higher.'

She wanted to ask him what he meant but decided to leave it till later because she already knew.

With Adam filling his plate two more times, Lola decided to have her meal in the kitchen as well. Because they were both hungry, they had their meals in total silence and were both finished in no time.

He urged her to put the dirty dishes in the dishwater but she refused, and argued that it wasn't a lot. She was washing the plates whilst Adam was rinsing when she heard her phone ring and ran to pick it but missed the call just as she located the phone from her handbag. 'It's dad! I hope he calls back because I have no credit.' She tossed the phone on the dressing table with frustration. 'No matter how much you try, things would still be forgotten.'

'You can use mine.' Adam offered her his phone from behind.

'No thanks I need the international credit to call Lagos.'

'Yes I know.'

'Are you sure?'

'Yes positive, it's strictly for international calls.'

She reluctantly received the phone and began dialling her dad's number with scepticism.

'You can speak for as long as you like.' He left her for the living room.

'Hello dad … yes, I spoke to Daddy Kahf.'

'Yes I did that as well. Okay I will call her later. No this isn't my number, no it's not Akin's either.'

She began smiling. 'Yes, I'm at another friend's house right now.' Then she frowned. 'Dad you know that's not fair! Of course I remember the daughter of whom I am. In fact you haven't got a clue what hell I've been going through in the past three months or so.'

Adam knocked on her door when he heard the distress in her voice. .

'Dad I'm in someone else's house and using his phone ... I see! Sade's mum told you about him. Well you'd better go back and ask her under what circumstances she met him.' She put the phone on speaker and yelled out Adam's name.

Without entering he signalled if everything was okay. 'Do you remember meeting Sade, my cousin, and her mum?' She asked him after nodding to his question. .

He pretended to be pensive before nodding. How could he forget the pokerfaced woman that kept on looking at him like he was a rapist or a paedophile? She also reminded him of the wicked step mother he once had? 'Oh yes, at the hosp ...' she quickly hushed him up to prevent her dad from hearing the "hospital".

'Yes dad, he's here.' Still holding the phone she massaged her forehead for a while and when she spoke it was in a whisper. 'Adam Salvador. Why do you want to speak to him? Okay I'll ask him.' She put the phone away from her ear and asked Adam if he wanted to speak to her dad.

Adam closed the gap between them. Holding her hands he whispered in her ears. 'What do you think?'

Engulfed by his unique masculine smell and aftershave, she was forced to look straight into his eyes and only struggled to shrug her shoulders. 'It's entirely up to you, but be prepared for the unexpected.'

'And I shouldn't forget the daddy affair.' He added in a whisper.

'Hello, I'm still waiting.' A voice pierced from the other end.

Adam impulsively took the phone and spoke. 'Hello Sir.'

'Hello how are you?' A rumbled voice asked from the other end.

'I'm fine thank you Sir.'

'I' gathered you've met my sister.'

'Your sister?'

'Yes Sade and her mum.'

'Oh yes sir some weeks ago.'

'Are you Adam or Akin?'

'Adam Salvador sir.'

'They'd mistaken you for Akin.'

'A day hardly goes by that my remarkable friend wouldn't talk about her wonderful, loving dad.' He deliberately steered him away from his last statement.

Instead of a reply from Mr Anifolase, he chuckled and laughed quietly at his last remark. 'Anyway, where does your Salvador come from?'

'Lagos sir.'

'I'm glad to hear it. I would just like to say a big thank you for all you've done for my daughter.'

It was now Adam's turn to chortle.

'Tell Lola I'll call her tomorrow.'

'Okay sir.' The other line went dead but Adam still found himself clinging to the phone as if his life depended on it.

Lola who was still massaging her forehead to reduce her stress level and avoid scratching the healing scar finally spoke. 'Your knuckles have completely gone white.' She began to massage his fingers to ease his tension and increase blood flow. 'Dad must have automatically assumed you meant Lagos in Nigeria.'

Instantly smiling, he gently snatched his hands from her and covered hers instead. 'How did I do?'

'You were absolutely brilliant!'

'I told you to trust me.'

'Okay I shall try my best from now on.' She flashed him her rare impish smile that always made her dimples deeper and Adam felt his heart make a flip-flop as usual.

Still in a jolly mood, he kissed her hands before raising them to his shoulders and placing them there He gently stroked the dimples and he felt them smiling at him. Turning her face sideways, he slowly placed a long peck on each dimple, feeling a buzz of excitement all over he straightened up. 'I'd wanted to do that since I set my eyes on you.'

She fluttered her long lashes and shamefully bowed her heads.

Adam gently tipped her face up and looked straight into her eyes fighting every urge of excitement all over his body and most of all resisting taking her to his bedroom and making sweet, zealous love to her.

Whilst guarding her face and stroking the scar beside her ear, he removed her hair bubble and let her slightly long hair down before slowly planting short, passionate kisses on her forehead, her eyes, the tip of her nose, neck and deliberately saving the best till later. The more he kissed her the more he wanted and the more she expected with her lips slightly parted and waiting for him. Finally the raw hunger took over; he kissed her soft lips long and hard before his tongue pierced through her mouth. Tasting, taunting, teasing and probing was suddenly okay after he felt her hand gradually moving to stroke the hair at the nape of his neck before progressing to his back and the rest of his body. Suppressing the tremor in him he pressed her closer to feel his hardness against her luscious body whilst his hands continue to roam all over her back and other parts. She trembled slightly with pleasure, whilst the uncontrollable passion flooded through her veins. Meanwhile, her body continued to respond well to his hands intimate demands.

With both gasping for breath he lifted his head and quickly resumed to nibbling her lower lip till she quavered and pleaded for him to stop. The feeling from Adam was raw, unadulterated, untamed, the response from her was stimulating and beyond his wildest dream. If he was dreaming he didn't want to wake up.

'Adam please stop!' She quickly stepped backward and was about to leave when he caught her arm.

He leaned back against the wall, struggling for words. 'I'm sorry you always make me feel this way.'

'That's just your third leg talking.'

'The response from you wasn't bad either.'

Lola lowered her head to the floor to hide her embarrassment and shame.

He tipped her chin up to look straight into her eyes again. 'We make a lovely team; it's nothing to be ashamed of eh?'

'Adam I can't give you what you want.'

'To me, what your body and soul tells me differs from what your mouth says.'

'I don't believe in sex for the sake of it and I can't marry you period!' She wanted to kill and obliterate whatever feeling she had for this man in every possible way and as soon as possible.

'My dad said five things make a lasting relationship. One is friendship; the other is compatibility, trust …'

'And?'

'I forgot the rest.'

'Too bad, we are not compatible then.'

'We are,' he argued. 'You remind me of my mother a lot.'

'Adam your mother is white!'

'Yes I know, strange isn't it?'

'You're blinded by fantasy.'

'No I'm blinded by love?'

'No you are blinded by lust.' She watched the disappointment spread all over his face gently before she continued. 'Look at us! We don't need light when you take picture and we don't need darkness when I do, which makes us …'

'You are not that dark.'

'And you are not that white either.'

'Concurred. We're both in the middle!' There was a chortle in his voice when he spoke again. 'Which brings me back to our compatibility subject again?'

'Meaning?'

'You say the glass is half full and I say it is half empty, they are basically the same thing.'

She yanked her arm off him when she felt the current of his body through hers again.

'Lola my point is I've never been this mad about anyone.'

'Take antidepressant for your madness.' The passion in his voice and the transparency in his eyes frightened and triggered her to say the first nasty thing that came to her mind. 'You'll be telling me you love me and want to marry me next!'

His expression became suddenly surreal before he expelled air that was tightening his chest. With his lips sealed to avoid saying the wrong thing, he nodded his head severally before he smiled. 'Yes, very true.' The more air he expelled the more constricted her chest and breathing felt.

She on the other hand, found her emotions lost and trapped in the surreal atmosphere with it's poignance forcing her to quickly snatch herself out of this illusion. 'I need to shower and I suggest you do the same; cold shower for you.' Without looking back she left for the bathroom with him still standing on the same spot mesmerised.

Cold shower it is! Adam dragged himself away from the wall and headed for the bathroom after saving the last number she dialled on his phone. He might just be desperate enough to need it one day!

Lola's anger had reached boiling point when the heat from the hair dryer burnt her ears; she turned it off and rubbed her ears angrily but was amazed that the hot water had relieved her itchy forehead. This time last week, only God know how many layers of bandage she had around her face.

How low would she need to get? She sighed with frustration. She should have stopped him earlier. How could she when she was having the best time of her life? All she needed to do was look at him and all her senses would let her down. She would never till now imagine how her own body could betray her so much, nor believe so much excitement could be derived just from kissing and touching. Imagine his cheek trying the biggest trick in the book telling her he loved her. She began to wonder if moving into his apartment was the right thing to do. They had been quarrelling and arguing about this since she came back from the hospital. She had initially rebuked him for overreacting but she sincerely dreaded another break in right underneath her nose. More so, what if the burglar decided to harm her next time? The thought of it alone frightened and prompted her to another option. She was thinking of asking Akin for his house keys initially but meeting Sally changed that. The other option would be to go and live with Sade, which wouldn't have been a bad idea if she was close with her husband, but her whole family would consider such a step as interfering in her marriage. Staying with her aunt would be her family's ideal but would be her last resort.

She was still brooding when she remembered the state the kitchen was, she quickly chose a kaftan from the wardrobe and dashed to the kitchen.

Lola had finished cleaning the kitchen when Adam peeped to ask if she would come out with him.

'No, thanks for asking anyway.'

He stepped inside and seemed to choose his words carefully. 'I apologise for my actions!' Even though he was genuine but there was no underlying remorse in his voice. She was unable to explain why she looked up at him and still didn't speak. Meanwhile, her cheeks, face and everywhere he'd touched still burned with so much passion that it could boil an egg. She felt like reaching out to him and telling him it was okay but another frustrating voice wanted to scream at her for feeling so strongly for him. Love shouldn't be so blind. This is totally wrong! Did she say Love?

'Lola, I am really sorry for getting so carried away and I don't want you to think I took advantage of you because you were in my house.' Adam interrupted her thought contritely.

She looked straight at him for his timely interruption yet again. He stood aimlessly for a whil before focusing on her as if he just remembered something important.

He continued when he heard no reaction or response from her. 'You will be all right won't you? He asked with a professional tone as he continued scanning her face.

'Yes thank you,' she said the first thing that came to her head and hoped that would prompt him to leave.

'Then I'll see you shortly, I really wish I could postpone this meeting …' He eyed her adoringly. 'Make yourself at home.'

She watched Adam leave with a heavy and worried look and wondered where the vibrancy of the man that escorted her into his apartment earlier had suddenly varnished to.

He strolled back in without her noticing. 'I meant all I said earlier.' He walked towards the door and stopped at the doorway. 'I do not regret what happened between us today either. And it's obviously not the third leg talking now.' He moved on without giving her the opportunity to respond.

She was only able to look at the door after it was slammed. With him out of the way, a big sigh of relief escaped her but was immediately followed by sudden sadness and emptiness telling her that not going with him was a big mistake.

She touched her burning cheeks and face and wondered if she would ever be the same again or look at him the same way. What if he was being honest? Why did she never feel this sensational buzz whenever she was with Akin or when he touched her or even came near her? Lost and confused, she decided to crawl to her bedroom for proper reflection but must have dozed off because she jumped up from sleep after another door slam. The first thing she noticed was her bedroom door wide open.

'Adam!' She called out repeatedly, but still didn't get any response, so she decided to seek him out and ask him what he wanted.

She walked up to the nearest door and knocked for a while before gently pushing the door wide open. She stepped into what looked like a study with the two large oak desks, a desktop and lap top connected to the same printer and fax machine. On one of the desks was a young woman's picture full of smile, her blonde hair was short and spiky, she recognised seeing the face before but couldn't remember exactly where. Adam obviously had her smile.

She was snapped back into reality by the fax machine's papers jamming halfway to printing some incoming messages. Her initial urge was to quickly sort it out but something prevented her, she was eventually forced to manually feed the paper through when the papers quickly ran out and noise from the machine got worse. Having quickly scanned her surroundings for more blank papers she got closer for another look when she noticed a folder on a secluded filing cabinet with her handwriting on it. Still doubting her eyes, she decided to have a closer look and got the shock of her life. The first piece of paper was a note she made a day before the explosion. The subsequent pages contained the names and salary details of every employee on A.B.C.& D.'s payroll that was stolen from her house but wasn't sure when. It immediately dawned on her that the timing of her burglaries mostly coincided with when Adam was out with her.

Except the last break, an inner voice pointed out.

Which he set up so he can seduce you after you've run to him.

If that was the case why did he bring you here? Another logical voice inside her asked strongly.

Because he underestimated you or maybe made a mistake.

That's not Adam's style; he is very thorough and meticulous. The logical, defensive voice echoed in her head.

Tell me what the file is doing here then? Think of all the troubles you've encountered since you've met him, and don't forget there are still weeks of memory gap with no one around to fill you in. What if he's trying to kill you? Or had already tried and failed within those weeks?

She began sweating profusely whilst her conscience battled between logic and the facts. She tearfully ran back to her bedroom with the file and shut the door behind her. The shiver running down her spine had totally incapacitated her physical and mental ability. She leaned on the door for support even though her legs had ultimately gone weak to support her weight. As she slid to the floor, she began feeling claustrophobic but quickly propelled herself back up and dashed straight out towards the door. She stopped when she got to the door and felt much better but swiftly decided to run back to her room and hide the file in case he returned. Still disorientated, she grabbed the file only to discover some of the papers were loose and dropping out on the floor. As she picked them up not to leave traces, she grabbed her biggest travel case and stuffed the file in it too, but suddenly had an irresistible urge to pack all her belongings out, alive and safely. With one suitcase still unpacked, she grabbed all her clothes from the wardrobe, filled her case in no time and was out of Adam's house within minutes. She thought of leaving him a note as she left but changed her mind purely to save enough time for her safety.

She picked up the phone, wanted to dial 999 and report the incident but changed her mind for fear of insufficient evidence or incriminating herself further. So she decided to call Roxanne who unfortunately made it categorically clear that she was busy in the hospital, whilst April's phone rang continuously without her picking it up. She tried her cousin and was informed by her answer phone that she was on holiday again, Akin suddenly slipped into her mind but it was quickly discarded. She instantly decided not to waste further time by calling her aunt since she was sure to get access to her property no matter what.

With all her belongings hurriedly packed, she finally decided to travel to London and spend some time with Sade's mum. Luckily for her, her aunt doesn't like Adam so his charm could not work on her. She convinced herself as she stepped down on the foyer desperately trying to wave any taxi down without any regard to the risks involved. Her greatest concern was to avoid pandemonium and getting out of the vicinity before Adam showed up. She was relieved when a private taxi pulled up near her and asked for her destination.

'Anywhere away from here.'

The Asian driver looked stupefied at first but smiled awkwardly before he spoke. 'You have money?'

'Of course.' Without wasting much time, she dumped her luggage in the back seat and jumped into the passenger seat with the smallest luggage.

As the driver set the car in motion, she had her head tucked away for fear of Adam catching a glimpse of her.

She straightened herself up after leaving the vicinity as the gentle breeze fanned her face. How stupid she'd been by playing right into his hands! She'd trusted him and had even kissed him. The thought of the sensations he'd aroused in her nearly made her keel over and throw up. Talk about dinning with the devil!

The news on the radio pierced through her thought with a bomb scare at the Birmingham International Airport and some flights delays.

'Take me to Birmingham International Airport please.' Lola pleaded as she rummaged through her handbag for some documents. Adam had strongly insisted she took all her important documents out of her property, she was glad she did.

'Are you alright?'

She heard him but needed to be sure before responding.

'Did you find your purse?' The cab driver continued agitatedly.

She finally took the wallet out and kissed it passionately before nodding her head with a big grin.

'Thanks for reminding me,' she quickly tucked it back into her handbag to be sure.

The driver heaved a big sigh that made Lola turn sharply towards him.

She replied with a shrug of her shoulder.

'Did you not say Birmingham New Street Station before?' He scanned her face and noticed her deep frown.

'Yes and I've changed my mind to Birmingham International Airport now.'

'Sorry, I had to be sure. I'm just having a bad day with passengers who don't want to pay.'

'Don't you worry about that with me.'

'Okay Birmingham International Airport it is then.'

CHAPTER 19

Sherry was already feeling Lagos heat and the humidity as soon as she stepped outside the Murtala Muhammad International Airport in Lagos but quickly remembered it always came with the territory here. She was waiting for her luggage when T.J.'s phone call asked her to call him after collecting her luggage.

'What?' Sherry shouted after informing him that she'd collected her luggage and was heading out. 'How would I recognise the driver?'

'How could he recognise me when he doesn't know me?' She protested.

'What do you mean I should keep coming? You promised to pick me up.'

'How would he be able to distinguish me from the three other whites around?'

She was still consumed with anger and disappointment that she didn't see him right before her. She screamed with joy and relief when she finally set eyes on him. It had been a year ago that she'd set her feet on Lagos soil. Tunji Salvador, her host and husband was parked a few minutes walk from the airport terminal.

Unlike last year, Sherry fell asleep as soon as she got into his car, even though he had deliberately picked her up to allow room for discussion. He'd planned to take her out for a meal but she'd insisted on going home to freshen up first.

She quickly went for a shower after arriving at the flat she always shared with him whenever she was around. Coming out of the bathroom with a towel wrapped around her chest, she inspected the three bedroom flat with caution; looking pensive she nodded her head with appreciation. Finally, she acknowledged that a lot of efforts had gone towards preparing for her arrival unlike last year.

'But I didn't know what your plans or intentions were last year.' He spread his hands in the air. 'What did you expect with only six day's notice?'

'And I already explained to you that it was an impromptu visit.'

'So you expect me to move mountains with one week's notice for an adlib visit?'

'I could have stayed longer if I was warmly welcomed.' She rubbed her hand on the wall beside her and pushed her bedroom door opened for a closer examination. 'What about my visits prior to that?'

'You insisted on staying in hotel.'

'And you made no effort to persuade me.'

'How could I when you'd already made your mind up?'

Lost for words she eyed him before looking at the room once again. Apart from the complete makeover of the flat she'd had a new set of bedroom furniture starting from wardrobe to the dressing table. 'These wardrobes are really nice and solid.' She deliberately changed the subject.

'Yes, real Mahogany. Do you like it?'

She acknowledged with a nod and a smile.

'That's the difference between a proper planning and an ad-hoc one.'

She eyed him warily again and stroked the smooth, veneer finish of the wardrobe instead.

'Welcome home.' He embraced her warmly before kissing her lips. She returned it with a more passionate kiss before inviting him to sit beside her. 'Can I have a very cold drink?'

Tunji shouted for the house help and left the room when he didn't hear any response but was surprised to see her fast asleep when he returned with her drink. He quickly reduced the air conditioner and left the room.

It was already midday when Sherry finally made it out of her room. She could remember him talking to her yesterday after she requested for a cold drink but couldn't recollect what her responses were, and was still sound asleep when he bid her good bye this morning. Despite being jetlagged and tired from the long hours' flight her new, comfortable bed was the biggest factor in the longest and deepest sleep in months. And that was what she dreaded the most when she left her home in Solihull yesterday. The bed she slept on gave her back ache for three months after arriving back in England many years ago. Adam's phone call temporarily suspended all hopes of further sleep but was surprised she finally did.

Already hot and bothered, wearing only a sky blue camisole and navy blue short she sat on the reclining chair on the balcony to enjoy her surroundings. The noisy floor beneath her echoed the tiny voices of the nursery school children singing their nursery rhymes from the top of their voices with excitement. She was busy singing along when Mercy, the house help quietly placed a tray of cold Pap and moin-moin before her.

'Oh I love baked bean cake.' Sherry remarked enthusiastically before requesting for a bowl of cold water and sugar to mix the pap with.

She was just finishing her meal when Mercy placed the newspaper on the table and a glass of water with iced cubes.

'Thank you,' she reached for the cup and sipped it as she harmonized herself into the nursery rhymes, cars tooting their horns amongst the busy traffic and lastly a church service brought closer with the help of a microphone. She listened to the woman's testimony of how she amongst her family of five divinely escaped a terrible car accident unscathed. As she got passionate with her narration Sherry wished she could meet the woman and commend her bravery especially after being given up for dead and about to be buried. The Lagos she returned to had been transformed in all aspect of infrastructure despite the increase in noise and pollution level which had never deterred her from returning.

'Can you bring my handbag please?' She asked the housemaid after the woman speaking on the microphone finished her story. She wondered how T.J. claimed this flat to be his sanctuary with the noise levels surrounding him, but then again, she slept soundly regardless. Just then, she heard another loudspeaker calling Muslims for the afternoon prayer.

She thanked her after receiving her handbag. Tunji walked in and immediately began mocking her for her sleepiness. She started laughing in return as she reached for her reading glasses but decided to remove the brown envelope brushing her hand first. She resisted the urge to open it but placed it on the table and hoped the gift would be received with thanks this time.

'You slept for quite a while.' He remarked instead and deliberately ignored the envelope.

'Who's counting?'

He sat on the arm of her chair and looked into her eyes. 'I've always admired you for that. You should be called Sleeping Beauty too.'

She faced him squarely and smiled. 'The bed was very comfortable.'

'I went to the factory to specifically request for it. Backache becomes a thing of the past with the quality of the mattress.'

'Quite right, I've never slept so deeply outside my home.'

'It's because this is your home too.' He was glad to notice the relief on her face. 'What's this?' He reached for the envelope after numerous hints from her and thrust it back on the table when he recognised the handwriting. 'What's with the brown envelope this time?'

She shrugged her shoulders and pretended to be a ignorant as possible. 'Adam didn't say, he just asked me to give it to you.'

He gently pushed the envelope back at her. 'Then I'll accept it if he brings it himself.'

'At least accept this first.'

'Sherry it's still a capital NO!'

'He's just as stubborn as you, what do you want him to do when you keep slamming the phone on him every time he called?'

'And I've repeatedly told you that the line was ba the last two times he called.'

'Okay, agreed then why haven't you tried calling him back when the communication lines were restored?' She eyed him and shook her head for his silliness. 'You've got no excuse with the four numbers you alone have.'

Tunji Salvador realised she had him well cornered but was not prepared to back down yet because he wanted her to intensify the pressure on their son.

'T.J. we need a miracle because I am exhausted.' She removed her glasses and wiped it clean before putting it back on. 'You've so far refused to meet him half way despite all his efforts. You keep insisting you want him over here but would you personally and willingly swap your comfort zone to be at the mercy of a hostile father?' She got on her feet to walk away but stopped after taking a few step 'You've deliberately shut him out for the past thirteen years and you are both becoming set in your ways as the years roll by. What would happen if any of us dies?'

'God forbid it! Such a bad calamity shall not befall me by God's grace!' He barked at her so she could see the sadness and loss in his eyes.

'Your son had survived the last thirteen years without you!'

'I paid him the last visit, remember?'

'Yes, thirteen years ago.' She gestured the number by counting her fingers. And every time he sends money …'

'I don't need his money.' He closed the gap between them and swore quietly but loud enough for her to hear.

Sherry suppressed her anger till later for not understanding the meaning and wasn't prepared to give him that satisfaction yet. 'I know, but he's fulfilling his obligation as your son and you turning it down are simply being ridiculous. You should be enjoying the privilege as any proud father should.' She shook her head regrettably. 'Isn't that part of your culture?'

'It is also my culture for kids not to have acrimony against parents.'

A crooked laughter escaped her lungs. 'Any wonder where he got it from. All I know is I'm tired of being the piggy in the middle.'

'Did you tell him this?'

'Yes I did and I'm saying the same to you.'

'What's changed?' He hunched his shoulders high and spread his hands out helplessly.

'For once he apologised and told me the following day that he'd adopted this Nigerian ...' She decided to move on instead of completing her sentence but he jumped in front of her to stop her.

'As his father?'

Sherry looked away as soon as her eyes met his frosty stare and only answered with a nod of her head.

'Have you met him?' The disappointment in his voice was more than crystal clear.

'Yes.' She felt guilty for lying. 'And if it's any consolation I think he's a crook and this wouldn't have happened if you'd met him halfway. I always arrive here with great expectation but always leave disappointed, how do you think that makes me feel?' Her voice quavered as she held back her tears. 'I've spoken to him and he'd complied with my requests but my only question is if you are inadvertently or otherwise punishing him for my brothers' sins. And that T.J. boiled down to the fact that I am not a *Yoruba* woman. Now if you'll excuse me.'

He stepped aside for her to move on, and waited for her to get to her bedroom door when he spoke. '*Se ka pe nisinyin?*' It was a question she couldn't pretend not to have heard.

Suddenly static and smiling she turned around and handed her phone to him. 'You can do the honour yourself *Baba*.'

'*Mai ti lo o!*' He pleaded desperately as he dialled the number and waited for it to go through.

Sherry stood by him as he requested. It would take the combined United Nation's army to move her away from his side right now.

'Answering machine.'

'Then leave a message.' She whispered softly.

'Bamidele daddy said hi.' Disappointed, he quickly turned the phone off before looking at her.

'Let's try his land number too, just scroll down to the next number.'

T.J. smiled at her desperate voice before growling with frustration for complying with her wish. 'Engaged … answering machine too.' He frowned as he listened to the instruction. 'Bamidele it's your dad from Lagos saying hi and I'd already left a message on your mobile. Take care and God bless you.' He disconnected the phone and winked at her smiling face. '*Se nkan ti mo so wa okay?*'

'More than okay, apart from calling him *Bamidele*.' She turned round and hugged him which he topped up with a light kiss on her lips.

'But it's what I personally named him.' He slightly moved back with his hands resting on her shoulder. 'It was a good thing you included it on his birth certificate.'

'But it's the last name on his birth certificate.' She defended. 'It was a good thing we talked about names before I realised I was pregnant or before you disappeared.'

'Must we talk about that now?'

She scanned his face and pecked him when she saw the old pain resurface on his face.

He responded and hugged her deeply. 'I feel so relieved now.'

'So you should.' She sucked in his natural odour and held her breath as long as she could. 'I'm glad to hear it.'

'Welcome home once again.'

'And I say thank you.' Sherry looked deep into his eyes and found the warmth and affection still as strong as ever. 'Now I believe you.'

He turned her towards her bedroom. 'I'm going to the bedroom are you coming?'

She giggled seductively 'T.J. you haven't changed at all.'

'Neither have you,' he coaxed.

'I'll join you soon.' Sherry shouted after him just before the door was shut behind him. Before surrendering her body to the desire, she needed to review the burden she'd been carrying back and forth for over fifteen years. She would need a strategy of how to rekindle the relationship between her son and his dad despite missing his touch and the passion between them. She's had some other relationships but always felt what she had with T.J. was special and wondered why, but more importantly, her numerous failed attempts to erase it. She'd often succeeded until she looked at her son before being enveloped by a renewed and refreshing pain and passion. She'd reluctantly admitted that the grudge between them had to be ironed out and she would like him to revisit England and possibly prosecute her brother for the crime he committed decades ago.

Despite being glad and grateful for finally convincing him to return their son's phone calls she didn't want to return home without sorting everything out this time.

She was sixteen, young, innocent and naive when she met Tunji Salvador nearly thirty years ago, who was not only her first and only love but also taught her the act of love making. For a year that they dated he was subjected to the worst name callings, pranks, humiliation, bullying and the last straw was the third degree burns he sustained without provocation.

Her two half brothers, Billy and Bob, considered her stupid and bullied her with Bob more brutal with his tactics. He was only forced to stop after the situation got out of hand. The more she relied on their brotherly love and guidance the more he misled her. At a point in her life she shuttled between Aberdeen and Tamworth just to prove to him that she belonged and had still not divulged the secret agreement between them. Her mum and senior half sister, Ruby, warned her to keep away from him but she didn't listen. She wondered if he ever felt guilty for all he did to her, which was why she took up travelling as a hobby with Ruby after Adam went to University with his cousins. After many years abroad, she returned home to finally settle in Solihull and run a fitness centre. She can now boast of five big and successful fitness and relaxation centres in the West Midlands region alone.

It had taken her decades to realise that T.J. was only being human when he made his decision to turn his back on her and had often wondered if he would have acted differently if he knew she was pregnant. She'd also at a point tried her best for her son to have an in depth understanding about his paternal cultural background, but something along the line went missing and totally wrong that resulted in achieving the complete opposite.

When Adam was younger, she'd been to Lagos a couple of times to resolve their differences but both parties maintained to be victims. With one party demanding sympathy and apology from the other and having totally forgotten that the biggest casualty was an innocent, young boy.

She could neither believe she'd known him for thirty years nor that they would ever get intimate again after years of bitter exchange of words, resentment and even hatred. It took her nearly one hour to summon the courage to enter their bedroom and wasn't surprised to find him deeply asleep. She was relieved and more amazed that he kept to his word of letting her come around in her own time. She shut the door behind her and moved closer to the bed listening to him breathing deeply, yet softly. Trying her best not to shake the bed, she gently slid underneath the light, white silk cover and continued watching him. Coincidentally, the first thing she noticed was the scar on his arm. Succumbing to her curiosity, she gently pulled down the cover to expose more of the charred and patchy scar around his shoulder, upper part of his arm and on his side. She gasped with horror as usual, just like she did in the previous years but soon realised it wasn't different and she would always react this way.

The burning smell and the discharge from the affected area nearly three decades ago suddenly seemed vivid like yesterday. Her mouth felt distasteful and the tears felt closer when she remembered his helplessness, agony, pain and sorrow whilst in the hospital. T.J. used to cry, she would join him and they'd both cry together. She had begrudged him for decades for abandoning her, but this was a very pricey love, how could she really blame him for walking away from them decades ago? What if Bob had really killed him like he meant to? *Wouldn't you and Bamidele live your life?* One of his usual unanswered questions echoed in her head.

T.J on the other hand had pre-empted her reaction and had wasted no time in getting undressed and slipping underneath the light, silk cover. He was still waiting for her when sleep quickly took over but knew when she joined him. He pretended to be sound asleep and give her all the time she needed as he promised her. 'Are you satisfied now?'

She jumped from hearing his somnolent voice and mistakenly pulled the cover further away from him. In hearing no response he opened his eyes and sat up to observe her face closer.

'Why are you crying?' He watched the tears rolling down her face and moved to close the gap between them before hugging her by the shoulders.

'Don't cry for me Sherry.' He wiped the tears and hugged her more.

'I can't believe my half brother did this to you.' She rested her head on his shoulder for a while and blew her nose with the handkerchief he provided.

'I'm really sorry.' She said tearfully.

'For being alive or what?'

She eyed him sceptically before pointing with her mouth towards his scar 'For what Bob did to you.'

'My peers returned home from abroad with qualifications and certificates, I did mine with combined honours and a terrible scar.' He gazed at her for a while and looked away before he continued. 'Do you want to look at it again?'

Her uncertainty towards his intention made her stare blankly at him but she finally nodded.

He sprang to his feet to expose the scar whilst she just starred. 'It took me a while to be able to look at it and undress where there was light. If only you knew how far and long I've come to be able to do this.'

Without a word, she touched the scar and wondered if he felt anything. 'Did the skin grafts help?'

'I think so but I'm used to it now.'

She was still stunned when he sat on the bed beside her and noticed she was still in her underwear. He stroked her cheek and she kissed him first. He responded before slipping the bra strap off her right shoulder and then the left one. She giggled and he looked at her.

'That was exactly what you did the first time we did it.'

'When was this?'

'Nearly thirty years ago.'

'It's because it tickled.'

'You are always ticklish.'

'I know.' She giggled again.

'It took me years to get this image off my head.' He returned her kiss and gently pushed her to the bed whilst he towered over to admire her beauty.

'And I've only come to realise what agony you've been through because of me.'

She moved to face him and were both enveloped by the softness of the bed. As they exchanged hot passionate kisses and one thing leading to another, she decided to cast all her inhibitions aside and enjoy their every moment of glory together from now on. This to her was a new dawn and beginning with all the required strength and wisdom to weather the storm in Tunji Salvador's life and household. That to her was the matured Sherry talking and coming to terms with reality. She knew something would have to give; she just wasn't sure what it would be yet and at what cost.

CHAPTER 20

It was several hours later when Adam finally walked back into his flat to retrieve the information Mr James had earlier requested for. He instantly called upon his guest whilst heading for his study, and automatically assumed she was sound asleep when she didn't respond. Inside his study, he immediately noticed the coloured papers in the fax machine but decided to deal with it later to avoid further lateness. Without giving it another thought, he stretched over the filing cabinet and wasn't surprised to find it unlocked but shocked to find it empty. Baffled, he walked over and noticed only a piece of the paper on the floor but with no sign of the folder. He stood up to appraise the room again and found another piece of paper stuck behind the door. He quickly reached for it and knew exactly what had happened but had no idea of the gravity. Without wasting any more minute, he dashed straight into her room and was surprised to find another piece of paper on the floor but no sign of Lola. Assured she'd seen the folder he surveyed his surroundings only to discover the dressing table she filled earlier with her personal effects were now all gone except the jotter. His worst fear was confirmed when he opened her wardrobe to find all the clothes she'd previously hung gone with her suitcases.

His first reaction was to go straight to her house and try to explain but something strange and unexplainable prevented him from doing just that yet. Weakened at his knees he sunk slowly onto the bed he saw her lying on some hours ago to gather his thoughts before facing her. Realising he might only have one shot left buckled his nerves up against him and made him admit that the best possible way was for him to mentally revisit all his actions beginning with his last encounter with Lola.

He recollected his most titillating snuggle that forced him out of his house in a panic and made him reel in his car with anger and frustration. Angry that she didn't believe him when he professed his true love to her and frustrated with himself for feeling so strongly towards her. He decided that taking her out on a romantic meal would be a perfect opportunity to open up more to her. He suddenly jumped out of the car to physically ask her and avoid being turned down over the phone but was surprised to find her curled up in her bed fast asleep. Befuddled, he stopped and watched her for a while before leaving her door wide opened and retracing his steps back to his car with disappointment. He could remember lamenting in a self-pity wallow and regret when the only thing that kept flashing to his mind was how complete he felt every time she was with him.

He was snapped back into reality by a phone call from his aunt, Ruby Mason, who called to ask him when he would be able to drop by and take Bravo for another walk. He promised to call her back as soon as possible and for once didn't wait for all the pleasantries before terminating their conversation and immediately setting off for Lola's house.

It took him a while to step out of the car and approach her door. After several minutes of banging on the door endlessly and mercilessly he decided to enquire from Mrs Walwynson, her next door neighbour who confirmed she had not seen Lola since they both bade her goodbye earlier. She explained further that she would have noticed any movement in or out of her house because she'd been tending her front garden all day. Despite his disappointment, he believed the pensioner who had never missed a thing in the neighbourhood except when she visited her husband in the old people's home. He dejectedly walked back into his car to think of his next plan. Whilst hoping she turned up, he started flipping through her jotter from the last page to while away the time. Desperate to break this ridiculous stalemate he bravely dialled her number with his hands wobbling and increased adrenaline. Whilst holding his breath for her to speak first, it hit him like a bull's eye that he'd fallen deeply in love with Lola and it scared him to admit the feeling to himself let alone anyone!

'About time, April!'

'No it's me Adam'

She drew the longest hiss he's ever heard before the line went dead.

Whilst desperately retrying her number, he compared the pain in his heart to kicks of metal boots between his legs that consistently increased with the number of silence encountered. After several failed attempts, he decided to give April a try to save his heart from further torment. Thanks to the jotter, her number was staring straight at him. He could certainly count on April's support based on her account of his zealous reaction and effort at the explosion, a view Mr James had already confirmed more than once to him. Whilst her line was engaged, Adam could never remember any of his cars ever taking so much frustrating punches whilst waiting to get through, not even for his biggest contract!

After what he'd describe as the longest wait in his life he finally got through to her. 'April Franklin?'

'Yes speaking.'

'Adam … Adam Salvador.'

'Yes?'

Adam felt a lump in his throat and was reminded of his first telesales job with his manager standing right behind him. 'I've been trying to reach Lola …'

'And?'

He deliberately ignored the hostility in her voice. 'And I thought she was with you.'

'I'm sorry she's not.' She paused for a while before she spoke again. 'Well … bye.'

Adam was shocked to hear the line disconnected and had landed another frustrating fist on the dashboard before he realised it. He quickly redialled her number and was surprised he got through. 'I'm sorry for being impertinent; do you know where Lola is?'

'Yes I do.'

'Can you tell me where please?'

'It doesn't matter anymore. She's where you can't reach or hurt her anymore you bastard! I would have made sure Trevor locked you up for stealing our company's information if I didn't miss her previous calls. The poor girl was in such a state she'd have to run thousand of miles away to Africa to feel safe.'

'You mean Nigeria?'

'Yes what difference does that make to another manipulative scumbag like you?'

He'd always known her to be smart-alecky on the few occasions he'd met her but was still surprised she could be this sassy. Adam instantly realised he had been automatically assumed to be the burglar that stole the information from Lola's house. The shocking discovery that he had been tried and vindicated behind his back made him whistle unconsciously whilst the phone momentarily dropped off his hands. He was not surprised to find the other end dead when he finally picked it up as he suddenly remembered his dad beating the living daylight out of him decades ago for whistling exactly the same way he just did.

With his hands above his head and his mind void he stared blankly ahead whilst whistling continuously. He had never in his whole life felt so incriminated or worthless for being magnanimous and also to the point of being so desperate to exonerate himself when he was innocent in the first instance! He felt like a complete failure for someone who always prided himself for being prudent and proactive. Just when he thought he had made a clean break with his nasty and tormented childhood, he fell in love with a woman that epitomised what he'd passionately despised and avoided for nearly two decades. Why does Love have to be so complicated? Should he wait for her to come back? What if it was too late then? Could he really wait that long? Well, it would be a risk he'd have to take! He concluded as he found himself at a total loss. He was about to start the engine when he impulsively pressed the green button on his mobile phone without hearing it ring.

'Bamidele!'

The voice he heard from the other end prompted him to rub his palm over his face to be sure he was not dreaming. He wanted to reply but found his tongue tied to the roof of his mouth.

'Yes dad!' Adam finally managed to reply to the only person that called him that name. It all felt like yesterday rather than thirteen years when he severed that link.

'Why haven't you replied my calls?'

He'd promised to return his call when he was better prepared unlike now that everything seemed to be on top him.

'It seems we've called you at a bad time.' He excused himself before he continued. 'Is everything okay with you?'

'Yes dad.' He shut his eyes with the hope of shutting this dream out. 'How's mum?'

'Bamidele I'm here.'

He sneered silently when he heard his mum's voice. He suddenly remembered the long and hard battle they fought before she reverted back to calling him Adam. 'How is the weather over there?'

'Why don't you come and find out yourself?'

'Nice one mum, there I was fooling myself that you were fighting my cause.' He remarked in a monotonous and cynical tone.

'You know very well that I am. But your dad is keener than you can imagine.'

'Let me not keep him in suspense then.'

'What are you trying to imply?'

'Can I speak to dad first?' He applied the same sombre tone to neutralise the panic in her voice. 'Mum give the phone to dad please.' He implored firmly when she insisted on probing further.

Tunji snatched the phone off her before she could put her next sentence together. 'What did you want to say?'

'I wanted to tell you to expect me around three to five days time.'

'Here in Lagos?'

'Yes in Lagos.'

'Why three to five days time?'

'Because I'm hoping to meet a business associate first.' He lied through his teeth.

'I see, which area in Lagos is this business associate of yours?'

He desperately scouted for a location in Lagos and was surprised that none came to mind. 'Top secret dad.'

'Okay then let us know your exact flight details and your arrival time okay?'

'Okay dad.'

'Let me give it to your mum now.'

'Bye,' he waited for the phone to be transferred to his mum before he continued.

'I hope you're not lying about this proposed trip.'

'Have I ever pulled such a stunt before?' He deliberately smiled to confuse her.

'Yes actually!'

'Well mark my words that your son is a different man from today.'

'Okay we shall see.'

'We shall truly see.' Adam replied amidst laughter before he continued. 'I'll get back to you on the flight details later.' He switched the phone off and went into a deep frenzied thought.

He couldn't believe how easy it was to just pick up from where they'd stopped over a decade ago. But then again he had been the begrudged party who had deliberately and systematically frustrated his dad's every attempt all along. He could remember absconding the last time he visited England and had nearly got him arrested simply because his understanding of life was shallow and selfish! He realised that judging and blaming his dad for all that went wrong between his parents was not only a big oversight but immature. Livid that it'd taken him this long to realise his folly, his stomach churned when his mind suddenly flashed back to some of Lola's sensible advice and cultural insight. She didn't resent her dad for abandoning her in Lagos when her mother died and there he was despising his dad for something much less. In fact death does conquer all! What would have happened if his dad had died when his uncle set him ablaze? Would he in fact mourn him? Yes he would have and possibly idolized and adored him. Would he still begrudge him? No. How about forgiving him? Yes he would and yet he abhorred and blamed him for living. How diabolical! He was still evaluating which of the scenario was more severe when his phone rang again. With enough surprises to last him a lifetime, he cautiously checked the name on the screen without a care of missing the call and was still contemplating on whether to take it or not when the caller hung up.

The only person that meant anything to him right now was *Lolade Anifolase*! He called her name in soft litany. The power of emotion that tried to suffocate his heart diabolically worried and pleased him immensely.

He was interrupted by another phone call and the name this time showed up on the screen.

'You promised to call me back hours ago.' Mr James's soft voice seared through his ears from the other end.

'The information you requested for wasn't in the folder.' Adam lied and was surprised at how good he was getting at it.

'It was there the last time, maybe you need to check again.'

'Or I can bring the folder over to you?'

'That will be much better actually. When are you bringing it?'

'Are you home now?'

'No, but I will be in another thirty minutes time.'

'Okay I'll see you in half an hour's time sir.' He was quite certain the old man was already home but would like the thirty minutes to set his gadgets up as usual.

The old man's invitation into his home made Adam realise the distinction between moderately liking gadgets and becoming obsessed with them. The old man's archaic and modest collections were more than enough armory for many small countries combined and would have certainly cost him a fortune. He once told him that a burglar lost his limb when he tried to sneak into his house through the kitchen window. Just when Adam thought that was nasty he showed him a big scar on his wrist where he was impaled by one of his gadgets he tried setting up. Initially, he was precariously fascinated but had overtime come to realise the complex nature of such an old man, but to actually understand why would be an entirely different matter. His reticence on most of his questions actually confirmed his nightmare that the old man was an errand boy and if he was, he wondered how dangerous his master or boss was.

His P.A's call came through. 'Yes Donna?' She always understood when and what to speak from his tone.

'Just to inform you that I'll be going home in about an hour.'

'How long do you think it takes to get a Nigerian visa?'

'You mean on your British passport?'

Something in her voice told him she was relieved he was finally facing up to his responsibility. 'Yes of course.'

She detected the smile in his voice but chose to ignore it. 'Let me confirm from Jack and get back to you.'

'Jack or Neil?'

She was pensive before she replied cautiously. 'I would say Jack.'

'Okay, find out from both of them,' his reply coincided with the car engine switching off.

Minutes later, as he approached the front door to his flat to collect some recording appliances for his meeting with Mr James a tiny fraction in him wished Lola was waiting for him inside.

'Yes Donna.'

'Jack says three to five working days.'

'Tell him he has two days to deliver.'

'Okay, anything else?'

'Yes tell him lives depend on it.'

'And the flight?'

'Three working day's time. And one more thing.'

'Yes boss?'

'Leave your communication and recording device on this evening.'

'Bye Mr Salvador.'

'Same.' He'd always admired his only member of staff he couldn't fire even if he wanted to despite his knowledge of her colourful past when she was his mother's cleaner in his younger days. As his most loyal and versatile employee, he'd always relied on her for many things including his girlfriends' birthdays, anniversaries and other memorable events in his life especially when he was dating three women simultaneously.

Adam swapped his belt for the one with a hidden tape recorder, his wrist watch, his pen and his special mobile phone all had the capacity to record voices varying from fifteen minutes to two hours and any movement within a minimum of a mile radius. And the last but not the least was his cufflinks connected to another communicating airwave device. The more he got to know of Mr James the less he left anything to chance. Especially around the man who had not only opened his eyes and mind to things he would normally take for granted, but had also stressed his disbelief in coincidences. Regardless of his age and fragility, the discerning man had the most dubious and money grabbing mind he'd ever encountered. He was well aware of the implication of what he was embarking upon but was doubly convinced it was the only way Lola could believe his innocence, and subsequently exonerate her.

His instinct told him things might go nasty after ruffling Mr James's feathers, he just prayed he could contain the situation without outside help so it could all go as planned.

CHAPTER 21

Lola dumped her jacket with her hand luggage into the baggage compartment overhead before settling in the middle row seat allocated to her. She would have ideally preferred a seat by the window despite being grateful to have come this far so quickly. She'd had to wait for several hours before successfully boarding the flight to Amsterdam from Birmingham and had eventually connected with the flight to Lagos. It was such a privilege to enjoy the benefit of a dual nationality and just travel with her valid passports instead of going through the embassy for visa first. She had luckily and narrowly missed the abolishment of automatic citizenship normally granted to Nigerians born in the U.K.

She leaned back on her seat to ease the apprehension and suspense she'd been subjected to in the past couple of hours! Considering she was the last person to board from Birmingham to Amsterdam and now to Lagos had been emotionally nerve racking. Crying from the moment she got off the taxi had made her eyes red and sore whilst her heart and body wrenched and ached like dynamites about to explode. She shut her eyes to relax the throbbing pain in her head, eyes and stomach despite the soaring noise surrounding her. Her mind had been purely occupied with why and when Adam stole the folder from her house. She'd desperately wanted to be proved wrong that the file wasn't hers or A.B.C & D's because she could have sworn Adam was unique and different from all the men she'd met but she was yet again wrong!

First it was Yusuf, then Akin and now Adam. The three men had left painful, remarkable impression in her heart and had permanently dented her life for different reasons. Yet the first two men had certain air of strength, determination, courage and principle but Adam had it all to the maximum.

Yusuf, a successful lawyer was older by four year was her ideal man in every way. Apart from the two families being close for generations, he was honest, caring and religious, a quality she personally lacked but could always remember Mama favouring that above every other quality he possessed. She'd always stressed that family that prayed together stayed together.

She had grudgingly obliged to his request of postponing any intimacy till their wedding night and would have been happily married if she hadn't single-handedly responded to Bisi's call many years ago and subsequently subjected herself to the most ridiculing, controversial and incriminating circumstances. His family's argument that she might have been under duress or intoxicated to have forgotten what actually happened made it difficult for him to extricate her from the compromising scene already described by young and old in the neighborhood. The fact that she not only bled but lost consciousness didn't in any way help her case, they'd already concluded the source of the blood. His mum finally admitted that she didn't want to risk performing the traditional ceremony if she wasn't a virgin. In other words, all the wedding preparation should be jettisoned.

And so was their narrow mindedness! Mama eventually concurred when she finally realised that the conversation between the two families had halted and Yusuf was shortly afterwards engaged and finally married.

To save face, her dad grudgingly granted her heart's greatest desire of returning to England, the genesis of her being and creation. This she believed purposely connected her to some of her deceased mother's last journeys. The timing coincided with the most independent, difficult, saddest and loneliest period of her life. Her perception continued to change as she understood the British way of life coupled with the greatest challenge of finding a compatible partner her family had expected. Akin was like a God sent after months of loneliness and mismatches from concerned relatives and friends. Their first and several subsequent meetings were at the Birmingham central library she regularly visited for her post graduate assignment and dissertations. They've often acknowledged each other's presence in mutual silence until he finally walked up to her on her graduation day to congratulate her and her family. He had indirectly impressed her dad positively. Then she met him again at her office for an unsuccessful job interview. Their friendship grew as he poured his heart out about himself, his family in Nigeria and Ghana and his wheelchair bound aunt now suffering from multiple sclerosis but with no surviving children. He felt it his natural duty to look after her. Yet, he always felt threatened when Adam or any other man got close to her despite his prolonged and impromptu absences. She had been foolishly supporting him without knowing that he was already married and had another son from another woman. He was a smooth talker that had lived in his own fantasy world for too long that he believed in his own lies and had on many occasions forced her to abandon her plan just to please and support him. The letter he wrote from the prison finally opened her eyes to what a walkover she'd been and often explained why she was sometimes taciturn.

Anger brewed inside her when she reflected over the challenges she'd encountered in the past few months and wondered if she would have still twisted her ankle or met Adam if he had returned her car as earlier promised and wouldn't have needed to be running thousand of miles away. It hurt her to admit that she was wrong to believe Adam sincerely cared about her despite his unique hazel eyes mirroring his strength of character, body, mind and soul, and his peculiar composition of being sometimes patient or domineering, but always thoughtful and kind. There were times he would only tease, talk and probe, but his strength of character always warned her that he never messed about and wouldn't tolerate being messed with either. If her analysis were correct she wondered what he was going to do with the folder and if wrong she still wondered why. With her eyes still shut, she rolled onto her side and curled up comfortably but suddenly questioned what she actually felt towards him. Underneath the betrayal, she felt deeply embarrassed to admit to herself that she had extreme passion for the man she was not culturally compatible with but might also be her greatest enemy. But her greatest problem was her family especially her dad's usual echo of; "I don't want a son-in-law that would be calling me by my first name or the ones that don't understand my culture." .

Lola was forced to open her eyes on the shocking realisation that she'd regained her memory! But her attention was immediately attracted by some snigger around her, she glanced straight into a young, black lady and her white partner holding hands, snuggling and laughing at each other. She immediately shied away when their eyes met as a pang of envy and jealousy ran through her veins when she remembered why she was running thousands of miles for doing nothing wrong. She had in her own way loved and trusted the three men and they'd all broken her in places that couldn't be fixed. Could she ever trust another man?

Who needs men when all they do is break your heart? She lamented silently but was quickly welcomed by a voice from the plane's crew asking everyone to tie their seat belts before explaining the emergency procedures. As the plane took off she wrenched and quickly dashed for the toilet as soon as it was safe to get up.

She was immediately approached by one of the cabin crews who wanted to know how she could help. Uncomfortable Lola complained of dizziness and asked to lie down. The stewardess accompanied her to the back row and sat her comfortably on the last seat before getting her some ice cubes and other first aid paraphernalia.

Whilst lying down, she felt a twitch on her finger and started twisting the ring around when she remembered the day Akin tied the engagement ring to her car window as a symbol of his love. Her joy that was second to none ended with disappointment for the lack of intimacy on the said day and subsequent ones. Her nightmare once again became reality as she was suddenly gripped by the stomach ache she thought she'd cured. She felt paralysed with the most acute pain she'd ever experienced in the whole abdominal area and tried to scream but couldn't. She felt much worse than any period pain ever imagined and if labour pain was worse than this may God help every mother during childbirth! As she reeled and moaned in pain, she wondered if labour pains always affect stomachs, abdominal areas, legs and other parts of the body.

Crouched up, she then tried to seek help by attracting anyone's attention and kicking the seat in front but only succeeded to wriggle violently. She was eventually restrained from falling off her seat by a firm, familiar hand.

'Lolade.'

She opened her eyes and couldn't believe who was staring directly at her but was still too weak to speak or react.

'Can I sit with her?' Daddy Kahf asked the hostess whilst supporting and focusing fully on Lola.

The air hostess refused blankly.

'He's my great-uncle.' She pleaded weakly as she clutched to her abdomen painfully.

Before the befuddled air hostess could speak, Daddy Kahf settled beside her to support and closely observe her. After watching her for a while he implored her to open her eyes before silently reciting something and rubbing his hand all over her head and face. Pleased with the result, he placed his hands on her chest, felt nothing, moved lower to the stomach and abdominal part and quickly snatched it away before frowning deeply. 'Please get us some ice.' He watched the lanky brunette rush out of their earshot before whispering to Lola. 'Did you pray today?'

Embarrassed and ashamed she nodded her head hoping he didn't press her further. She'd not prayed in months!

He doubtfully looked at her with a deeper frown as he continued rubbing his hand all over her stomach and abdomen. 'When exactly did you pray last?'

She expelled a gulp of fresh air to suppress her deceit and immediately looked away as she suddenly remembered this was why she'd always avoided him.

'You are not pregnant?' He looked straight into her eyes for assurance.

Lola finally stared back before shaking her head with a fierce negative response.

He placed his hands on her stomach again and was equally compelled to snatch it away quickly. Looking befuddled, he muttered to himself but loud enough for his niece to hear him. 'Well, I can feel something in there.'

It was now Lola's turn to look stupefied and wanted to argue but changed her mind when she saw the air hostess approaching.

'Can I have a glass of very cold water please?'

The flight attendant swiftly returned with a big jar of water with ice and a plastic cup.

Daddy Kahf filled the plastic cup up and started reciting silently into it before giving it to her to drink afterwards. He watched her gulp it down at once before speaking. 'Tell me how you feel now.'

'Much better thanks.'

He rested two fingers on her stomach whilst muttering some words silently for about five minutes before taking out a little hard covered book from his breast pocket and handing it over to her. 'You can start by reading this, I need to do something.' Without waiting for her response he got up and excused himself.

With the pain drastically subsiding she read the words on the cover with disappointment before placing it on her lap. He was nicknamed Daddy Kahf because of his strong belief in the chapter of the

Quran that it could cure any predicament and ailment. She had, after all these years hoped and expected differently. The few times he'd scolded her was because she was late in saying her prayers which made her avoid him when she grew older.

'I didn't give you the book to place on your lap.' The anger in his voice pierced through her thought and made her jump. 'Don't tell me you are not strong enough to read that.'

'Sorry Uncle.' She reluctantly picked the book up that would have been impossible for her ten minutes ago. 'I expected you to have covered the first few pages by now.' He edged closer before flipping the first page open. 'No miracle is closed to an opened mind and neither is any opened to a closed mind.' He observed her smiling. 'I can see you are getting better already.'

'Yes sir.' She agreed before edging forward from her seat and smiling impishly back.
'Read this for now and tell me what you think.'

'Suratul Kahf &the mystery of life. Sceptically, she eyed the next paragraph and flipped many pages before another title called "the Companions of the Cave" caught her attention. Holding on the page and debating whether to read it or not, she caught a glimpse explaining how these men's life still remained a mystery that could only be understood by believing and knowledgeable few. Already challenged, enchanted and captivated, she began to silently and earnestly read about the sufferings of these virtuous, faithful and patient men. These believing youths hid in the cave to avoid persecution, men put their cases and needs to Almighty in prayer. They put themselves under his protection and disowned all attribution of partners to Him. Whilst their dog watched the entrance they all fell asleep with no knowledge of what was happening outside and as if they had died with their ideas and knowledge.

They woke thinking they'd only slept for a day or so and appointed one of them to go to the market for food. The market was in uproar when the marketers discovered that his dressing and speech was old fashioned and the money he hoped to spend was long gone out of circulation. News spread all around the market and eventually to the king who not only requested for their presence but also asked them for narration of events. The sleepers who could not determine their duration in the cave explained that they'd just woken from sleep after praying for Almighty's help and mercy from persecution. The king, a believer later corroborated their story that he was young when he'd heard about their disappearance. He went on to express his utmost amazement about their youthful look despite sleeping for around three hundred solar calendars or years. A memorial of a place of worship was built to honour them.

The next paragraph was about two men. One was provided with two gardens of grape-vines and surrounded with date palms. As his crops increased so did his wealth and power, so he became materialistic with no thanks to the Creator of heavens and earths. One day he took his companion who bestowed him with his wealth but the less affluent man was unmoved as his trust was with the Almighty. He instead reminded him, as he usually did that all his wealth were vanity if he denied the Almighty that created him out of dust then out of A sperm-drop before fashioning him into a man. But his wealth made him transgressed that he doubted if his wealth would ever perish. He only regretted his folly when all his wealth and possessions were destroyed.

She wanted to continue reading but was interrupted by an overwhelming surreal feeling that paralysed her whole body and speech. She finally looked around to notice her great-uncle reciting some prayers as he slowly and slightly slid down her engagement ring. With her hearing sharper than ever she tried to resist the pressure but was pinned harder against her seat as she simultaneously felt some heat zap out of her stomach. The throbbing aches and agonising cramps in her legs and abdomen suddenly ceased. Smiling cautiously, he placed the same hand on her stomach to feel and hear the thundering noise that caused her to fart endlessly. Whilst she was relieved that many passengers didn't hear it because of their earphones, she was still embarrassed by the offensive smell, but even worse because her physical weakness prevented her from excusing herself or from suppressing the uncontrollable urge and noise. Still motionless because of her weakness, she seriously wondered how she would have coped if she was on her own. She, nevertheless, expressed her utmost appreciation to her great-uncle with her gracious, gracious smile.

If her great-uncle was worried, he didn't show it but instead faced her squarely to examine her finger and the ring. He whispered softly before asking for the ring.

Lola removed the ring and suddenly jerked violently as she felt a surge of heat evaporate from all parts of her body before farting loudly and finally blanking out. He looked around to observe if anyone heard the offensive sound or saw what happened, but was relieved to find many passengers asleep and the rest busy with their televisions and earphones on.

'How is she?' The lanky air hostess returned to examine her.

'She's sleeping now and hopefully for the next two to three hours.' He stopped from fastening his seat belt to watch the long-limbed woman feel her pulse before grinning at him.

'I'll check her again in an hours' time, alright?' She left to have a word with another colleague whilst pointing to them.

An hour later, he finished praying and glanced sideways at his great niece still fast asleep. *Alhamdulillah!* He thanked God in Arabic silently for his perfect timing and wondered what would have become of her if he wasn't around. The paramedics would have possibly administered some painkillers that would have shifted the problems to a different level with a more devastating repercussion. He once overheard his great-niece asking his sister why men hated their children.

'Don't be foolish to believe they don't love you all, it's because some men see expression of love or affection as a weakness.'

'But why?'

Sister slapped her hands on her knees before she replied, 'Not everything in life has straightforward answers, sometimes things need to be accepted and you'll understand better when you get older.'

'I promise to say I love you to my children every time.'

'And that proves what?'

'Is that why daddy looks at me strangely sometimes?'

'What do you mean strangely?'

'Like he … he … hates me.'

'Can you hear yourself, for God's sake?' Daddy Kahf heard his sister's snappy and defensive tone challenge her. He was prompted to come in when he saw her being calmed and gently pulled to her grandmother. 'I don't want to hear a thing like that from you ever again, in fact you should not even think it.' She ordered softly but firmly before planting a kiss on her forehead. 'Okay?'

Lola nodded obediently and apologised with adjuration before leaving the room. He remembered her apologising again after stumbling into him as they crossed each other. Steadying her gently, he led her to a corner before asking what the problem was.

She held back more tears that he presumed had earlier blurred her vision. 'I think I've upset Mama.'

'Whatever made you say that?'

'Because I told her I think daddy hates me.' She blurted out before bursting into uncontrollable tears.

He implored her to stop crying before consoling her as usual with some Quranic recitation about the role of a father and how she constantly reminded her dad about the loss of her mother because of their resemblance. She wiped her tears and lightened up with a smile just as she heard her deceased mother. Then he noticed how a young, sensitive girl he once knew was quickly growing into a distinct effervescent, intuitive lady with a lot of gut instinct. She as a result of that conversation taught him to compliment his immediate family and children more than ever before despite his shortcomings.

As the eldest man in the family, he was unfortunately summoned to break the news to her dad when her mother died and was also regrettably in charge of the funeral arrangements. Every one that had been affected by her mother's death had been proud of the young, ambitious woman leaving Nigeria for England some years back. He had personally prescribed a daily prayer for her and had reminded her to always remember the daughter of whom she was, after which she'd personally assured him of doing everyone proud.

To now fathom what his niece could have done so wrongly to deserve such a severe curse of *Magun* absolutely eluded him. In all his years as a physician he had only experienced such gravity about thrice and only from women who later confessed to combine professional prostitution with their marriage. In his spiritual rendition, his niece was still a virgin and if she was, why and where was she inflicted? Who would have reason to doubt her faithfulness and inflict her? Could he have been wrong? If he was and he doubted that, has she conveniently forgotten her cultural and religious background to have started sleeping around or what? He quickly cautioned himself from his reckless thoughts and rechanneled to a more constructive dimension.

He looked at her face and closely examined the scar on her forehead and beside her face before being forced to glance away because of the enormous burden revealed. The past three months had been hell for her! If what he detected was *Magun* and a very lethal one then it was only a matter of time before someone died, if it hadn't happened already. With a shake of his head, he banished such horrendous thoughts happening to his great-niece.

He took out his counter and began supplicating silently for distraction but his mind kept wandering back to the young lady already fast asleep and now snoring softly beside him. She would require some days of quarantine but he would need to speak to his sister first. Hell will definitely let loose after that!

He gently felt her already stabilised forehead and stomach before heaving a big sigh of relief. He then grabbed her hand to feel her condition, nodding his

head proudly he made some notes before letting go.
He decided to wait till she woke up.

CHAPTER 22

Adam turned over for more comfort and to continue sleeping but was immediately awakened by the announcement from the plane crew that they would be landing at Murtala Mohammed Airport shortly before advising everyone to tighten their seat belts and remain seated. He was again overtaken by drowsiness but was quickly interrupted by a gentle tap on his shoulder as he tried carrying on. He turned slowly to face a strawberry blonde air hostess with the shiniest forehead he'd ever seen advising him to fasten his seat belt immediately. With the final clasp, he returned her warm smile with a grin and waited for her to leave.

With all traces of sleep finally gone, he checked his watch and couldn't believe he'd slept that long, the last thing he remembered was finishing the light snack he'd requested for.

Donna's assurance that therapy and tablet would work if he took it just before boarding was absolutely accurate! Flying anywhere in the world had never bothered him but the apprehension of the circumstances surrounding this particular visit was extremely uncharacteristic. Mr James phoned him on the early hours of yesterday that he'd been tipped that planes in the major International Airport across the country had been planted with bombs. Adam suspecting he'd known about his intended travel and wanted to discourage him only shrugged it off after managing to advise him to inform the airport authorities immediately. His misgiving about the old man was recently confirmed that all he cared about was to continue milking money off him; their last meeting was still fresh in his memory.

Adam had left his flat to meet Mr James as agreed but was surprised to meet his absence. Furious, he continued knocking on his door until he received his phone call apologising and postponing the meeting to two hours later. He quickly ran to do some errands and rushed back to the office to sign some important documents. He returned to Mr James's house fifteen minutes before schedule but was invited in and suggested their meeting be postponed till the following day because he had a guest. Adam suspecting his tricks insisted on waiting in his car outside.

'Our discussion might take some hours,' the old man defended.

That's okay, I've got all the time in the world,' he lied. He was in all honesty keen to visit his aunt Ruby and his visiting cousin but instead had to endure his suspicious eyes burning the back of his neck as he headed for his car.

'Have you got the information I asked for?' Mr James tapped on his car window thirty minutes later.

'Yes, but I need to know what you want it for?' As he surveyed his surroundings wondering where he came from he pushed his door open.

'I told you I need to know how much Akin Wonders got last month.' The old man's snappy tone underlined his voice.

'And you haven't told me who Akin Wonders is.'

'And I already mentioned how much that will cost you.' He walked back towards the house.

Adam stretched his arms to properly adjust his special cufflinks before speaking. 'I can't cover for you anymore,' and quickly caught up with him as he pushed his flat's front door open.

'But you have to. I still need to extract some vital information from …'

'Here you go again, always asking and taking but not willing to give and when you do it's not free.'

'But I'm the one risking my life and credibility here.'

'Sorry no.' He settled at the empty chair closest to him.

Mr James banged his fist on the table to reinforce his determination but ended up moaning with pain instead.

'Are you okay sir?'

He responded with a nod and tried to smile but looked more petrified instead. 'Please, give some more time,' he pleaded some minutes later.

'Lola's credibility is on the line.'

'It's not Lola's that you are worried about is it?'

Adam didn't respond but smiled with his lips and checked if the pen in his breast pocket was still recording.

'So you haven't got a choice but to let me proceed.'

'Oh yes I do, today Lola's house was burgled again.'

'When?'

'This morning.'

The old man laughed croakily before speaking. 'You are my alibi, we were together Adam.'

'Yes we were. Whilst you were busy collecting another thousand pounds.'

'What's that got to do with anything?'

'I was coming to that if you'd let me.' He cleared his throat and edged forward before he continued. 'The burglar left your scarf, hat and one of your gloves.'

'You know damn well it wasn't me.'

'Agreed, but the police would consider you a main suspect, possibly an accomplice and if they believe in your innocence they would be definitely wondering who would hate you so much to frame you?'

'You haven't told them those items belonged to me, have you?' With the desperation in his voice so obvious, he got closer to plead with his sad eyes.

'What about the poor innocent Lola whose only crime was doing her job diligently?' They locked gaze for a while. 'Would you be a false alibi if someone you cared about was in her shoes?'

'You can't seriously think that mentioning my name to the corps would solve everything.'

'But at least some and it would most importantly end the thousands of pounds you've extorted from me.'

'Okay I will refund you your money.'

'How much?'

'Three thousand pounds.'

'What of the first three grand?'

'Give me a break, those were long gone.'

'You are no longer the one pulling the strings so if I were you I'd worry about myself first.'

'Alright, why don't you turn off all the recording appliances and let's start all over again?' The old man pointed his wrinkly hands at the pen in Adam's breast pocket and his shirt sleeves before lifting his hands to examine the cufflinks thoroughly. 'These ones are much better than mine.' He smiled bashfully at his guest's mesmerized expression before he continued. 'They must be really expensive,' and nodded severally in appreciation.

All Adam could do was nod with a relief that he had no knowledge about the recording device in his waist belt.

He bent closer to the recording appliances and shouted from the top of his voice. 'I, Mr F. James admit to everything we'd discussed so far on tape but would like to tell him more off the record.' He sat back and looked at him. 'Happy?'

'What's the point after turning all the appliances off?'

The old man smiled at the realisation that he'd disconnected all his appliances. 'I don't like being coerced.'

'But you like dishing it out.' Adam pushed a pen and some clean A4 papers towards him. 'You'll have to do better than that sir.' They locked gaze for a while. 'We can start from you making a statement.' He added by deliberately ignoring his contemptuous gaze.

An hour later, Adam read the two sheets of paper carefully before correcting some spelling mistakes and asking him to clarify some other inconsistencies.

'Let me make a copy.'

'I'll come with you.' Adam sprang up to follow him but was advised not to.

He returned shortly with a mahogany wooden box that was switched on by battery charger. 'I don't think you should make peace with your dad yet.'

'Is the photocopying machine warmed up yet?' Adam knowing him so well refused to be distracted at this crucial moment.

He smirked at him briefly before concentrating back on the machine and eventually taking the documents. 'What do you think my chances are?'

He pretended not to understand. 'With what?'

'The evidence planted in Lola's house.'

'The police are still conducting their investigation.'

'I wonder why two police officers came to the office yesterday.'

'And?'

'They spoke to Bob instead who as expected did and said everything to discredit her.' He suddenly scanned his face for any clue. 'Please don't encourage her to travel now.'

'Why?'

Mr James hesitated for a while. 'Let's just say it will seriously support Bob's fabricated lies and accusations.'

'In all honesty, Bob's days are seriously numbered.'

'My advice is that you leave no stone unturned when dealing with Bob, he is an extremely dangerous man.'

'I knew that a long time ago.' Adam swiftly returned his gaze as they both considered the weight behind his statement but none chose to comment.

He wondered if the old man suspected how his name made his skin crawl but faked a yawn before getting on his feet.

Mr James quickly followed his guest and whispered to him. 'Are your parents still exerting pressure on you to come home?'

'Yes, more than ever.'

I still don't think you should go to Nigeria yet.'

'Why is that?'

'It's best to iron out the differences over the phone first for more bargaining power.'

Adam remained pensive till he got to his car.

'Can I expect that information tomorrow?'

'I will endeavour to bring it tomorrow.' Glad he'd pulled it off; he started the engine and drove off.

Getting back home and discovering that Lola had left with the wrong impression of him changed all his decision and would have still not bothered him if April hadn't called him all the most undesirable names under the sun. The poor woman has had more than her own share of nasty coincidences.

Lucky that his flight was a direct one, he would have buckled out if Donna wasn't with him till he boarded, especially when his flight was delayed for hours. He was glad he'd finally grabbed the bull by the horn as he still doubted in his ability to see the journey through even after the plane had taken off. What kept him going was the adversity of a bleak future without Lola and the fear of his family ostracising him if he delayed their dispute longer, especially now that his mum was on their side too. He still wondered if he was right to act against Mr James's advice, but the closer he got to landing the more certain he was and that not giving him any information about his flight details was for the best.

The following day, he phoned April to request for her address and posted some edited version to her just as he reported the latest development to the police officer investigating the case.

Adam's dad always maintained he would understand his firm actions someday but he never believed him until now. He was somehow remorseful for begrudging him because he abandoned his mother long before he was born.

He was told he was three when he met his dad and the big fight over him then was circumcision. His mum considered it unnecessary and him too old for it. His dad wasn't having no for an answer and the fight went on forever with Dr Mason having to play the mediator yet, again. His mum finally gave in when he was five years old and insisted he witnessed it. True to his words, his dad returned to England and stood by them for three months which was the only time he ever remembered his parents being civil to one another, speaking in one voice and beginning to bury their differences.

Many years later, his parents patched all their differences up that they became close again, his mum forced him to Nigeria when he was ten only to fall out with his dad again and leaving him stuck in the middle as usual.

His two faced step mother would only smile and be nice to him when his dad was around. What angered her most was his determination not to call her Mummy like everyone else in the household. But the biggest problem was from his two wicked half sisters who constantly jeered him that his maternal uncle tried to kill their dad by setting him ablaze.

Adam remembered crying his eyes out every time he was accused until he had no more tears to shed, then his step mum joined in and finally the whole extended family ostracised him when they knew how his dad sustained the burning scar all over the upper part of his body. His only friend in the household was aunty Wura, who was his dad's niece and also his interpreter and mentor. He never forgot her name because *Wura* meant Gold and she was truly a gem. Apart from helping him to foil his half sister's evil plans and teaching him how to be one step ahead, they were both subjected to the most unimaginable ill treatment every time his dad stuck up for them.

With time, he'd grown so fond of her that he always followed her everywhere. His face went pale when he remembered once sneaking out with her whilst on a shopping errand without her knowledge.

Whilst trailing her, he somehow lost her and found himself at the wrong place at the wrong time. It was the *Eyo festival*, a traditional festival unique only to Lagos indigenes and would usually take place in Lagos Island alone. The indigenous male household representatives would partake wearing a white veil, a straw cone-shaped hat and a big stick which would be used to beat any woman with any footwear and men wearing a hat within their vicinity. Adam had already disguised himself with a face cap and was busy trying to keep track of his aunty when he ran into the Eyo group and would have been thwacked if not for her timely intervention. And the greatest favour she did him was keeping his waywardness a secret between the two of them until three months later when the tailor living a few houses away recounted everything to his step mother who eventually told his dad. His step mother found the perfect opportunity to finally complain about him by lying that she couldn't control him and should be sent to boarding school for thorough discipline and he remembered spending one academic year in a boarding school.

At the end of the academic year, his parent's differences were not only irreconcilable but had also deviated to trivial matters. He became a ping-pong that was stuck in Nigeria to his mum's utmost dislike whilst his dad wouldn't have him anywhere else and he personally refused to live with his step mum, so he absconded! He could have gone to the Consulate but his friends warned him they would call his parents which he didn't want, especially since his mum refused to physically visit him. His friend's mum grassed him when she caught him squatting in her son's room; it surprised him to have lasted that long because he thought his light skin would easily give him away. He smiled when he remembered the five days of hell he subjected them all to!

So to appease all the parties concerned, his dad and Dr Mason who was now an expatriate in Lagos reached an ad-hoc agreement for him to spend the long-term holiday with him and his pregnant aunt.

His mum finally returned against her partner's wish to sort things out which led to his parents having another massive row. Her argument was his dad tricked her in believing that he was going to look after him, so his dad relinquished his hold. Since he wasn't keen to live under the same roof with his step dad he absconded again but his uncle knew exactly where to find him. Shortly afterwards Aunt Ruby had her third baby and his mum extended her stay to give her sister a helping hand and hopefully resolve the stalemate.

The long holiday soon finished and his parents were still at loggerheads, a phone call that his grandmother had a massive stroke changed it all! With her only two children stuck in Lagos, his mum volunteered to return to Scotland with an amicable agreement with his dad that he permanently lived with Dr Mason and his family. That inevitably made everyone happy!

About a year later, his mum now single again finally returned him to England after her mother's death. He was thirteen and he honestly didn't know what he wanted anymore because he could vividly remember crying when he heard the news. Proudly, he's nowadays the peacemaker between his oldest cousin and his parents.

But the only person that meant anything to him right now was Lolade Anifolase! He called the name in a soft litany whilst the power of emotion trying to suffocate his heart worried him immensely. He could literarily feel his blood heated up in his veins and he realised it was time for him to eat his humble pie. Everything he had repulsed, fought against, rebelled was Lola, if only his heart could choose someone else with less complicated culture. So much so that his dad would enjoy this, to be or not to be!

Adam was already feeling the Lagos heat as he queued before Nigerian Immigration control after arriving at the Murtala Muhammad International Airport. He surveyed his surroundings to compare the hustle and bustle of nearly fifteen years ago to now, the excessive heat, crowd and noise was still the same apart from the much improved orderliness. He shook his head on the realisation that it came with the territory and became apprehensive as the queue to the immigration point shrank quicker than he expected. The ebony skinned lady smiled and deliberately scrutinised his passport when he claimed to be an indigene. 'Where is your Nigerian passport?'

'It expired.'

She remained silent for a while. 'Do you know where you are staying?' She finally asked.

'Yes, Lagos.'

She scanned his face intuitively. 'As all indigenes know, Lagos is a very big place.'

'True, I think I can still remember that.'

'When were you here last?'

'Nearly fifteen years ago.'

She quickly glanced through the passport for his details. 'Then you were thirteen years old.' She closed it and handed it to him.

'Yes, something like that.' He confirmed and grinned when her face glowed with another smile.

'Can you speak the language at all?'

'Yes I can try,' he prayed fervently that she didn't ask him to speak any word.

She studied his face for a while before she stamped his documents and pushed it towards him. 'Anyway, enjoy your stay.'

'Thank you, I'll try.' Without moving, he pocketed his documents before courage took over. '*Odabo!*'

She smiled warmly again before replying. 'Bye to you too and enjoy your stay.'

He had barely moved away when his mum's number showed up on his mobile phone. 'Hi mum, yes, just been cleared by the immigration and coming straight out.'

He laughed before his next reply. 'So sorry mum no other luggage apart from my hand bag and laptop.'

'Even if I wanted to, I wouldn't know their sizes or preferences. I'll meet you outside shortly.'

Adam's heart began pounding heavily as the most intriguing question continuously played on his mind. Was his dad with her? Did he want him with her? If they were together how would he handle the situation?

Swallowed by the crowd's rambling noise from all angles and uncountable probing eyes piercing through his extremely light skin, he followed the exit sign. He slightly felt out of place except for his jet black recently cut hair, his height and the fact that he'd been here before. He was already sweating because of the heat despite feeling the air conditioner blowing on him everywhere. He was about to call for his mother when he heard his name piercing through the clamour loud and clear. Surprisingly, she was running towards him with her arms wide open when he turned to his right. He was busy twirling her when he observed two other men closing up on them. Just before answering her question, he noticed one of the men smiling at him as his dad.

His hand gradually slipped off her shoulder to face his dad whilst anxiety made his racing heartbeat sound like rain dropping on a big drum. His main reason for holding back for so long suddenly seemed feeble to him. With two giant strides, father and son stood facing each other, with a much lighter, taller, leaner and younger Adam about to prostrate when Tunji grabbed his upper arm and extended his hand for a handshake before embracing him. 'Just as I expected you to be!' The crowd watching the emotional reunion cheered, clapped, whistled whilst some of them began chanting *Dobale! Dobale!*

He felt his dad raise his hand to the chanting crowd before asking out of curiosity. 'What are they saying dad?'

'They said you should prostrate!' Still in a tight embrace, laughing heartily, he waved at them to be quiet and the noise subsided with most of the crowd quickly switching to other attractions. He broke up to look at him before his embrace tightened. 'Welcome back to Lagos.'

'Yes, welcome back!' Sherry added.

'How was your trip?' He asked quickly without giving him the opportunity to reply his greetings.

'Fine dad,' he replied bashfully whilst trying his best not to smile unlike his mum who couldn't stop.

'You see, I told you it would be fun.' She handed her son's luggage to the fourth person accompanying them.

'Thanks mum.' He raised one of his eyebrows mockingly as the trio assessed one another with something much deeper than warmth and affection. Adam was an exact replica of his dad except for his well and above the shoulder's height, his glowing light honey skin and the layers of black, thick curly hair.

'He's much leaner than you described.'

He returned his parents comment with a warm smile.

'*Egbon* give us something to celebrate now.' One scruffy short man with a spotty face appeared from out of nowhere with his hands outstretched.

Tunji Salvador dipped his hand into his pocket and thrust some new Naira notes into his hand. He immediately implored everyone to move when he saw more men approaching them. '*Egbon* don't forget us here too.'

He nodded his head towards the fourth man that had been quietly observing the trio when he saw more men touting their way before gently pushing the other two along. 'Isa we will wait at the end of the first turning on the right by that billboard.' He shouted after the man rushing off with the luggage.

'*Egbon!*' Adam and his mother enquired jokingly.

'It means *senior* but was used colloquially.' He explained as he gently hurried them towards the meeting point already agreed with his driver.

'That's news to me.'

'Me too!' Adam added.

'We live to learn and learn to live.' His words of wisdom were assimilated in absolute silence as they all paced towards the meeting point when they heard Isa hoot the horn.

They'd got close to the car before Adam broke the silence. 'I don't believe it!'

His parents stopped to ask what the matter was.

'Oh nothing that jeep is exactly like mine.'

'What colour is yours?' He gently guided his son to sit beside the driver.

'Silver,' he replied just as Isa stepped out of the car to open the doors for them.

After shutting the doors he sat behind the wheel awaiting further instruction.

'To the office please.' Tunji stated before asking his son the next question and equally throwing a handkerchief at him. 'I hope your other plans can wait.'

'Yes of course.'

'You didn't tell me you'd bought a new car.' Sherry edged forward before tapping his shoulder.

'It was just a week old and we've only spoken once after then.' His mind suddenly went blank as he remembered Lola's reaction when she sat in it. At first she'd congratulated him, before she'd asked if she could bless the car and he was busy trying to understand the concept when she instantly changed her mind.

'Adam are you okay?'

'Yes Mum, why?'

'You'd suddenly switched off. I asked who was looking after the vehicle now.'

'Donna of course.'

'What about that lady you told me about?'

Adam turned around to remind them of the presence of an outsider.

'Don't worry; he's your dad's cousin.' She edged forward again and whispered into his ears this time. 'You still haven't answered my question.'

'What was the question?'

'I asked about that lady you singled out.'

'She's here too.'

'We could have given her a lift.'

'Mum, I didn't say we arrived together, she was well here before me.'

'I see.'

Adam turned round when he heard a chortle from behind just in time to catch his parents wink at each other but was more surprised about his dad's question.

'Is this woman your partner?'

'No.'

'I was going to advise that mixing business with pleasure could be lethal.'

'I would have still done it with her anyway.' His honest reply was only meant to be a murmur but his parents unfortunately heard him.

'Seriously?'

Adam turned round to watch her reaction but was interrupted by his dad.

'So how's business?

'Great dad.'

'Your mother told me you'd just bought a flat in City Centre.'

'True.'

Mr Tunji Salvador stopped when he noticed the driver had stopped by his office and had opened the door for him to get out. 'You can close for the day.'

'Okay sir.' The driver half prostrated and left.

'Isa,' he called him back and waited for their eyes to meet. 'Shhhh.' He put his finger across his lips to indicate keeping his mouth shut before stuffing his hands with some Naira notes. 'Go and have some fun.'

The driver thanked him again with a smile before bouncing off.

'What do you think of Lagos compared to your last visit?'

He rubbed against his nape whilst trying to think of an appropriate answer.

But his dad continued. 'We'll go through the back entrance.' He took another bunch of key out of his glove compartment and gestured to Adam to pick his luggage from the booth before unlocking a graffitied sapele door with one of the keys just a few yards away from where his jeep was parked. As he followed closely behind his mum he noticed how the sunlight revealed a metal burglary proof door that immediately led to some stair cases and finally a shutter with code numbers. He slowed down to retrace his step and was beginning to wonder what it would be like at night when his dad told him to shut the shutter properly after him. With some long strides he could see his dad leaning against the wall holding the door for his mum to enter and hanging on after seeing him closely behind.

They were in no time in his dad's office where he sat on his executive swivel chair hidden behind a large mahogany desk and pressed the phone on his desk. Not too far on the right was a computer and its printer.

Shortly afterwards, a light knock on the door preceded it gently opening to reveal a young lady, with a high flying eyebrows and a pair of the laziest eyes he'd ever seen. Adam could easily compare her figure to Lola if he didn't look at her face.

'Nike, meet my son Bamidele who'd just arrived from England.'

She diffidently muttered her greetings silently and quickly concentrated back on her boss.

'Apart from being my P.A. she is equally a daughter to me.'

Adam focused at her for an inkling of the bizarre biological connection. But he panicked instead when his mind drifted to his next meeting with Lola and their over extended nuclear family discussion.

His mind was back to reality when his mum tapped him gently. 'You've drifted off again.'

'Is anyone hungry?' He asked them before facing his P.A. 'Nike please shut the door after you and let no one disturb us.' Tunji Salvador watched the click of his office door before glancing from Adam to his mum. 'Well, we are alone now and I think there are lots of pending issues to resolve between the three of us.' He stopped to assess their reaction to what he'd said so far. 'Has your mum or anyone else ever told you that I knew your mother was expecting before leaving?' He studied his reaction but was surprised he remained still and impassive.

Adam gazed from one parent to the other before replying 'no' weakly.

'Am I correct in assuming we were all hurt but dealt with our pains individually instead of collectively?'

The other two nodded their heads in agreement.

'You are no longer a baby, if you at any time disagree with me please feel free to express it.'

'What happened to "adults are always right and parents know better" that you always said?'

'That still stands but today, you have my unequivocal permission to express your opinion without any reprisal.' He edged forward but didn't look directly at them. 'I know you mostly bore the brunt of the bitterness, the row and lack of compromise between your mother and I for a long time.' His nose and eyes flared and his voice faltered. 'We sincerely apologise for that.' He looked straight at his son and slapped his hand hard on his chest. 'In fact I as your father earnestly ask your forgiveness for my absence in your life when you needed it most, especially whilst in Nigeria.'

Adam's face had all along been downcast, but suddenly looked up at his dad when his voice shook terribly with emotion only to reveal the similar pain he'd been personally carrying for years until he met Lola.

'I suppose I struggled to accept and live with the third degree burn your uncle inflicted on me decades ago and your presence then kind of made it harder to forget…Even though you are my flesh and blood.

The only simple term to put it would be that you unfortunately happened to be the grass that suffered where two elephants fought.' His metaphorical way of expression not only hit the bull's eye but immediately calmed the tension between father and son. With both men close to tears, they locked one last, painful gaze in mutual silence that secretly agreed to forgive and forget their past mistakes and prepare for a better, trusting future. 'Have you got anything to say before your mum takes over?'

'Yes just about two or three questions.' He shot a quick glance at his mum and only continued after his dad prompted him to continue. 'Why now?'

'We would not all be sitting here discussing if your mother was not finally on my side. And getting this far had been three consistent years of secret meetings and negotiation between us. Sherry had issues about my second wife.'

'Second wife? How many wives have you got now dad?' The objection and anger in his voice surprised his parents.

'Two.' He got on his feet to open the fridge door. 'Drinks anyone?' He asked instead and returned to his swivel chair with a tray full of various drinks, water and three glass cups. He poured himself a glass of water and opened a bottle of Malt for Sherry who was still calming her son down.

Adam was instantly on his feet but swiftly cautioned himself when he remembered where he was. The air conditioner in the room was suddenly inadequate to cool his temperature down. 'Did you know about his two other women?'

'Of course but let him explain first.'

He yanked one handkerchief out of his breast pocket to wipe all around his neck and face whilst he fixed his cold, disappointing gaze on his mother.

'Adam let him explain.' Sherry implored firmly again.

'I'm jealous of how protective you are of your mother but I want you to analyse the situation for me.' He deliberately stopped for his son to be calm. 'You were two years old the first time I heard about your existence and I was already married to Tosin, your stepmother, who was already expecting. I'm sure you still remember Buki and Bunmi, your half sisters?'

Adam's face hardened and his jaw line became evident. How could he forget his dead-pan face evil step mother who never forgot to remind him of how he came to being or how she pushed her two daughters to tease and taunt him?

'Now I want you to advise me on how you would deal with the situation.'

'I haven't got problems with her and my half siblings.'

'You do because you can't even bring yourself to mention their names.'

'Okay, I can't. They all bullied and alienated me except aunty Wura who ended up becoming their enemy for helping me.'

'It all came out in the wash after you left and everyone was accordingly dealt with. I had also over the years realised my mistakes and I promise to make it up to you and your mother.'

'You once told me you couldn't cope with two wives.'

'Yes.'

'So what changed your mind?'

'She did and because her circumstances were exceptionally compelling.'

'Big deal,' Adam humoured forlornly.

'I owed her a favour and that was what she wanted in return.'

Adam looked annoyingly at his mum who seemed amused at something so serious. 'Anyway, you don't seem bothered so what the heck?' With a shrug of his shoulders he finally joined his dad with a bottle of Malt, gulped it down within seconds and was replacing the bottle when he noticed the last bit of a signal between his parents. 'I suppose you wanted me here to exhibit me to your extended family?'

His dad nodded his head before adding 'amongst other things.'

'Why here?'

'Why not here?' Sherry enquired.

'Would you still want to come to Lagos if I'd been to see you in England?'

He wanted to say he would because of Lola but shook his head sideways instead as he struggled to banish her from his mind.

'Are you alright son?'

'Yes dad.'

Moreover if you were truly a Salvador, you'll have to return someday and what other time is better than now?' He got on his feet and stretched. 'Anything else?' He glanced from one face to the other.

'Yes there is,' Sherry added as she rose to face her son and held his hands. 'Adam we did the traditional marriage.'

'What? To be his third wife?' He yanked his hands off, shook his head despondently before he turned to leave.

'I am nearly forty six for God's sake!' Sherry shouted to stop him from moving further away and continued her explanation in a soft and slow pace. 'Third wife as you said is just a number that didn't exist, but as for me we are both number one.'

Looking befuddled he turned around to face them. 'How does that work?'

'In reality Sherry and I meant to marry before….'

Adam quickly nodded his head as his dad's face suddenly saddened.

She would have arguably been my first wife if we were already married but she nevertheless had my first son.'

'Or any child for that matter,' Sherry interrupted.

'But in reality she is your second wife because you were never married?' Adam summed it up.

'Yes, but will be accorded due respect and honour as the mother to my firstborn and she wants in.' Tunji Salvador explained so passionately and effortlessly that he didn't realise how he physically got to his son's side.

'Me?' Adam interjected proudly when he finally noticed how tall he was. 'So what would have happened to mum if I wasn't born?'

'For a start there wouldn't have been the need to rekindle our unfinished passion that was prematurely extinct by your uncle. And I would secondly have had the scar for nothing or might never have had it.'

'How precarious!'

'So is love.'

Adam walked beside his dad like contemporaries and felt so guilty that he had most of his adult life despised him for nothing. 'And complicated.'

'It doesn't have to be once you accept that love itself is the irony of life.'

'And as they say, love conquers all!' Sherry added from behind them.

'When you fall deeply in love, you'll understand it better.' He stopped to place his hand on one of his shoulders.

He looked straight into his dad's eyes and saw the delight and victory of it all reflecting in him. His mind suddenly drifted again to his conversation with Lola when he asked how she could possibly forgive her dad for abandoning her in Lagos. 'Thanks dad,' was all he could mutter without making a complete fool of himself.

'What for? We are all fugitives of love who understands the concept better and deeper with age and time.' He smiled blithely at him as he pushed the door open.

'Whao! That's so deep.'

'Life is deep my dear son.'

Adam was so thrilled and moved that he couldn't help hugging his dad.

'How dare you?' Was the next question from a well known and yet a distant intruder who instantly split them up and stood right between father and son.

Adam watched his dad's back violently pushed against the wall and suddenly felt like the young boy that was once bullied by the same woman except for the fact that this was real, live and he'd grown. In any other circumstances he knew what to do but this was his step mum rough handling his dad. 'Dad, are you okay?' He moved closer to examine him.

'Oh yes son. Only if you want to save me from the seventh child of a seventh wife.' Tunji pointed at the man with a fat nose who'd seemed to appear from nowhere. 'That's her driver and he is one of her half brothers.'

'Seven wives at once in a man's lifetime! How shocking!' Adam suddenly felt like a saint when he remembered his triumphant time of dating three women simultaneously.

'It is really,' his dad continued before turning to the woman in his face. 'Tosin have I ever failed in any of my duties as your husband and your crown?'

Instead of a reply, she pushed him harder against the wall and poked insulting fingers before his eyes.

'Is there anything we can do to help?' Sherry nervously stepped beside her son to ask politely.

'Yes, ask her to tell us how many of her five brothers are still monogamous? Even her youngest brother who'd just turned forty already has four wives.'

'Whao! Machine!.' Adam exclaimed in time enough before his mum quietened him up.

'*Omo ale*!' She turned around and spat at Adam scornfully.

'I would have married her if the circumstances were not beyond me!' Tunji sneered at her. 'Take a good look at him and tell me he is not mine. He is more legitimate than those four girls who will end up bearing another man's name. Buki is now Mrs Ogun only God knows what names others are going to end up with whereas my Bamidele will forever be a *Salvador*.' His cynical reminder did not only put Adam back on the spotlight but boosted him and his proud dad's pedigree.

Instead of her calming down, she undid her wrapper to expose a black Lycra legging that slightly covered her knee and roughened him up further. She looked back at the pair scornfully before kissing her teeth long and hard. '*Awon Olosi Olori buruku!*' This was subsequently followed by what Sherry and her son could only describe as trouble dancing of a caged, wild animal.

Adam as a kid had heard the abusive word too many times to forget its meaning. He instead scanned her appearance before concluding she was all out on a mission to cause trouble and trouble only. As the wrapper dropped on the floor he noticed she had no jewellery on and he could remember her obsession with jewellery too well.

'*The only wretched and ill-fated person here is you Tosin.*' He replied and pressed her nose with his fore finger really hard before turning to the other two. 'Son learn from this, she's come to provoke me into hitting her to discredit me because she knows I couldn't but her time is now up.' He guarded both sides of her face and warned her sternly and quietly in Yoruba. He then whispered into her ears but was met by further resistance.

When next he spoke his voice was firm and each of his words were in litanies. 'If you poke any finger at me again I swear to God the Creator of the universe that I, Tijani Olatunji Salvador will snap it into pieces.'

Adam watched her drop her wagging fingers instantly.

'Consider our marriage over if after the count of three you do not let go of me.' He continued when she didn't respond. 'And any more insults to any of them will cost your whole family hearing about this fracas.'

Adam once remembered hearing that tone from his dad as a kid finally realised they were not empty threats when she surprisingly let go after two counts. She immediately burst into uncontrollable tears and burrowed her face into his chest.

He hugged her with one hand and used the other to wipe her tears with his handkerchief. Finally, she stopped crying and turned around when he whispered into her ears again but unable to look at any one straight in the face. He then beckoned on Sherry to come into the fold but she declined. This went on back and forth between the trio for some minutes whilst Adam watched the scene with fascination before she finally joined in.

'Sherry and Tosin,' he deliberately paused for the words to sink in. 'You are now fully aware that this meeting is very much different from the previous ones and so the hostilities between both should be buried forever. Because you are now henceforth my wives according to my custom and religion and I solemnly promise before my God and everyone here that I would try my possible best to be fair and just between the pair of you as long as you continue to work towards the common goal. And may almighty God make it easy and bless us all. Amen.' He grabbed their right hands and bound it together with his. 'May peace, joy, blessing, success and above all fear of God reign more in our lives from now on and forever, Amen.'

He beckoned Adam to join in by placing his hand over his and glanced across everyone's faces before he whispered something silently for a while. 'Can we all say Amen again?'

Everyone including Adam echoed the word in unity.

With a big weight off his shoulders, he not only saw the relief all over his dad's face but admired him immensely. He pecked Sherry's forehead first before doing the same to Tosin on the left. 'Okay ladies, let's exchange greetings.'

They both peeped out like they've never seen each other before, only to mutually lock gaze and slowly looked away with no words actually exchanged.

Just when Adam thought he'd seen it all, his dad smiled, whispered into the women's ears before lowering his hands on their hips and finally beckoning him to lead the way. 'Come on, there are people waiting for us.'

Adam looked back to see his mum and step mum in reflective mood whilst his dad looked glee and cheerful. His glance now shifted to his so called step mum's brother's face and he smiled at him unlike some minutes ago when he looked terrified as if Armageddon was here and now!

CHAPTER 23

Lola finished praying but remained on the praying mat wondering about her affliction rather than promise to observe her five daily prayers that she'd abandoned since leaving Lagos three years ago. Her grandmother had always scolded her and now with a renewed hope that she'd learnt from her mistake. *Magun!* She wondered quietly with her head bowed. *Magun!* She repeated as more tears dropped on her laps. Gently, she tapped her chest out of amazement as she studied the strange environment known to be one of her great uncle's consultation rooms and instantly eyed the huge bed, the long bookshelf filled with Qurans and other religious books, her luggage stacked beside it, the small wardrobe and finally the open praying space. How in God's name did she catch *Magun?* What could she have done to deserve this and most importantly how long had she been a carrier? She didn't keep many Nigerian friends and would have strongly suspected Sade's party if she'd actually attended because that would have been the biggest Nigerian gathering lately.

Daddy Kahf refused to reveal who'd afflicted her but mentioned he would soon turn up for a reprieve, which to her would equally mean believing men could actually get pregnant and have babies. And if he was right, what would anyone gain from afflicting her when she'd never been unfaithful or promiscuous? She strongly suspected Akin but she equally wondered why he would want to marry her or still bother to write her from prison afterwards? Could he have been wrong with his diagnosis because *Magun* was more lethal and dangerous than AIDS? As her head became riddled with more questions than answers, she looked around the whitewashed wall for distraction or answers if possible.

She'd been quarantined in the outskirts of Ikeja, Lagos capital that bordered the neighbouring Ogun state for nearly a week. He lived literarily a couple o kilometers away from Ogun State. Apart from feeling claustrophobic since her arrival five days ago, she'd done nothing but prayed and telling her uncle she was tired and bored might sound ungrateful. She above all missed her home in Birmingham and her space, but would most importantly like to seize the opportunity to see what was happening on the street here. Not that she particularly has any friend around here; she'd reliably gathered that most of her closest friends have relocated either because of marriage or work. She'd had enough of all the strict rules and regulations, tired of being a full vegan without ingesting salt, sugar or oil except raw fruits that had all taken its toll on her.

On the second day, her medications took effect as they made her so emotional and delirious that she begged Daddy Kahf to leave her alone to die. The only thing he'd stressed was the need to exorcise and cleanse her. Then she felt very lonely and wanted her parents or Mama, even her stepmother would have been okay but was told again meeting any member of her family would counteract her recovery process. That was when it truly hit her that she was going to die a slow, agonising death alone from *Magun,* that she'd until now believed to be nothing but a Yoruba myth. Imagine not seeing one's families for three years because of the long distance and still couldn't when the distance was now narrowed to a few kilometres because of some unexplainable complications. Thank God for telephone invention!

She was by the third day getting sick of drinking too many *Quranic* mixtures. Some traditional herbs tasted worse than a mixture of faeces, rotten sewage and nasty urine together. She'd cried endlessly, and had survived the worst nightmares, keeled over the most horrendous stomach aches, pains and cramps. Having wrenched over the worst foods ever known to have been ingested by man she consoled herself that she'd never been forced to retake her own puke. But the good things were; she felt better than she had been for months, slept soundly, no more nightmares and burning sensation or cramps inside her womb, stomach, and the humiliating, blasting fart had all stopped.

Yesterday, she was getting bored of being housebound that she decided to while away the time by looking in the mirror but was shocked of the gaunt, dry, sad face starring back at her. Determined not to cry she began to reminisce her little sanctuary in Birmingham again when her grandmother and dad walked in after the necessary precautions even though her affliction wasn't contagious. Their setting eyes on her for the first time in over three years was so upsetting that Mama cried openly and was sure her dad shed tears secretly. Their shocking reaction finally triggered her tantrums when she noticed Mama trying to sneak the mirror out, but she eventually insisted on leaving it in her wardrobe after she confirmed that looking at the mirror would only upset her more. Thankfully, the situation was eventually controlled.

The rumbling noise from her stomach craved for cooked rice, fried plantain and a fresh fish stew Mama promised her when she was crying yesterday. Her mind drifted back to her last decent meal in Adam's house and how much they both enjoyed it before the snug and their final fallout. She quickly shrugged it off but nevertheless remembered her home in Birmingham again and one of their lovely meals at the newly opened Restaurant where Adam gave her a passionate kiss before she ranted and finally sulked at him for what should have been a very romantic evening.

Was that being unfaithful despite suffering from amnesia?' She'd confessed to her uncle a few days back and he'd told her yes it was, but he embarrassed her further by asking if she enjoyed it. Despite seeing the answer right on her face she still wanted to deny the unique, sweet alluring feeling that captured her brain to her toes before her panic and request to be guided to his car but failed miserably. She'd instead asked him how she would find a date without any physical contact and his reply was yet again unsatisfactory, but was able to deduce from his explanation that it might be acceptable only if they'd intended to marry. Did he or anyone realise how lonely, scared and confused the past months had been for her? He nodded that he did but further interrupted her with one of his parables.

'I don't understand sir.'

'It means I stand no chance if you can't be honest with yourself.'

Lola glanced at him before staring ahead and was deep in thoughts again. Apart from Adam putting a smile on her face she always felt this exciting buzz all over her body whenever he was around her and above all, she knew him more than she did Akin. Could there be a logical explanation as to why the folder was in his flat? Did she jump the gun by not giving him the opportunity to explain? Her uncertainty of whether she'd left her jotter in the taxi to Birmingham Airport or in his flat could not convince her whether he would have actually called her if he wanted to. Despite her conviction and innuendos, not hearing from him so far left a big vacuum in her heart. She also missed brownie and the thought of going back to his house for her doll surprisingly gave her a feeling of a sweet bitter sensation. Does she really need to hear his side of the story?

She was interrupted by a knock on the door and had subconsciously answered before realising it. She turned round to see Daddy Kahf peeping through with a smile and instantly went on her knees.

'How are you feeling?' The old man had asked after the exchange of greetings.

She forced a smile before replying fine sir.

'Did you sleep well?'

'Yes sir.'

'Is any part of your body giving you concern?' He stepped inside to assess her physically before checking her eyes and demeanour. 'Sister will tell you what we need to do next.'

'Is anything wrong sir?'

'No nothing,' he replied quickly. 'It's just that the next stage will be better explained by a woman.'

'And my mother would have done it?'

'No, we would only need the oldest female in the household.'

She locked his gaze to confirm but quickly looked away as a sign of respect. 'Okay sir.'

'Daddy Kahf said we can take you home.' Her dad spoke from behind him.

She didn't realise how weak she was until she tried to jump for joy. 'Really?' She asked instead.

'Yes,' her uncle added with a smile.

'You'll need to excuse her and Sister for a little chat.'

Lola cautiously watched the two men leave the room immediately Mama entered with one of her brother's assistant carrying a tray of dishes all covered up. She was suddenly apprehensive because of the pending news instead of being excited over the meal she'd so much yearned for.

Mama sensed her reticence and greeted her instead.

She instantly went on her knees as her grandma started praising her ancestral pedigree. 'A special treat for my princess,' she pulled off the white napkin covering the big tray with a hearty smile.

Still on her knees Lola stretched and opened the nearest dish, a traditional vegetable stew immersed with ground melon, varieties of fish and seafood amongst other spices. Next to it was white rice and finally ordinary stew of freshly cooked fish. She served her Nan and was serving her rice when curiosity took over. 'Uncle said you had something to discuss with me.'

'Yes when we get home.' She signalled to her brother's assistant in waiting to take her luggage to her son's vehicle.

Lola couldn't pester her but scanned her face briefly before looking away after suspecting its gravity for it not to be discussed here. The anxiety of the unknown subject made her loose her appetite and forced her to push her plate away.

Mama stopped her meal and looked at her surprisingly, but after all her pleas fell into deaf ears she summoned on her son to bid his farewell.

Lola was wondering why her dad drove instead of the driver but didn't bother asking. With little or no traffic jam, most of the journey home was quick and quiet except when the three of them laughed and commented on jokes from the car radio or when the hawkers on the motorway caught up with their vehicle to advertise their wares. With jus a few minutes drive of the journey left, Lola was forced to peep out of the window to call for the sweet hawker after Mama suddenly began to cough. She was haggling over the price when her dad's phone rang, He was about to answer it when Mama dissuaded him despite her situation.

Bayo Anifolase grudgingly complied with his mother's request sulking but not for long. 'Before I forget, you had a phone call today.' He looked at his daughter through the rear view mirror.

'Me, did you ask the person's name?'

'Yes, he said he was a cousin of Mr James your colleague at work.'

'That old crook asked me to check from you if you knew any Major Anifolase during the Biafra war.'

'The man must be really old.'

'To say the least,' she burst out laughing and suddenly stopped when she remembered something vital. 'How did he get your number?'

'Only you can answer that. I thought he was your friend?'

'Kind of,' she replied with reservation as he took the last turning to their home.

'Hmm, home sweet home!' Lola finally commented as she looked at the house she could hardly call home. She was already at the university and still living with Mama when her dad and his immediate family moved down here and rented his previous house out to one of government ministries. What first caught her attention were the orange and tangerine trees she remembered using as shades whenever she came round for a visit or hosted her friends. As the new gateman opened the gate to let his sport's Mercedes in, Lola surveyed her surroundings for something both old and new as the memory all rushed back.

Mama tapped her gently. 'We are going straight to my flat, leave the luggage to the gateman and others.'

'You finally got what you wanted.' She whispered into her ear at the same time her dad stopped the engine.

She remembered her grandma lobbying to move in with them before she left for England but was eventually moved into an adjoining studio flat last year following a knee injury. They both exchanged looks, followed by a nod as they stepped out of the vehicle simultaneously and headed for the house. She only looked back to see Mama talking to the gateman and one of the house help who had both gone to the booth for her luggage. She stepped inside and waited for Mama to catch her up but noticed her dad following closely.

'You are going to have a shower with this immediately.' Mama pointed to the small Keg in her handbag.

She was angered by the news and wondered when this fiasco would end because she had planned to extract the suspended information from Mama immediately they entered. 'Okay ma,' she grumbled when she saw her dad's presence.

'Would you like her to stay upstairs or here with you ma?' Bayo asked.

'Let her stay here with me.'

'But she will be inconveniencing you.'

'I don't mind moving to the guestroom next door; apart from the need to monitor her recovery we have a lot of catching up to do.' She moved up to Lola and patted her back with a smile.

She watched her dad retreat with a wry smile that told her something was up.

'Let me excuse you ladies, I need to pop over to number forty and conclude our plan about his daughter's wedding.'

'Okay don't be long my darling, extend my regards to his wife and kids.'

'Yes ma,' he slammed the door and rushed off. He couldn't wait to be out because he wanted to be away when his mother spoke to her.

Bayo Anifolase trekked another forty houses only to be told his friends of many years was not back from his trip. He headed back home and initially blamed himself for a wasted journey but immediately consoled himself that the exercise was good for him. He passed through the gate and was about to open the front door when he was approached by restaurant owner next door that a gentleman was in her shop waiting for him. He was still trying to accustom to the news when a young, bulky man of almost his height caught up and prostrated flat before him. 'Please get up,' he insisted, as he bent to meet him halfway. 'From where?' He eventually asked after his guest had been given a bench to sit on.

'From Mr Bamidele Salvador sir.'

'Were you the one that spoke to me this morning?'

'Yes sir.'

'But then you said Mr James.'

'Correct sir, they both sent me to Miss Lola sir.' As a means of diversion, he stretched Lola's notebook towards him. 'This was from them sir.'

Mr Anifolase obviously getting irritated by the confusion ran his hand through his stubby beard before taking the book and flipping it open immediately to glance through the pages that were full of his daughter's handwriting and notes. His anger subsided after reading some of the contents from different pages; he looked up to find the stranger's eyes fixated on him. 'Any other message?' He asked finally.

'And this one too sir.' He handed him a white A4 sized envelope. From Mr Bamidele Salvador sir.'

He examined the envelope from side to side before flattening it between his hands and only spoke when he was satisfied that the parcel didn't look or contain anything suspicious. His uncle aroused his curiosity after warning him to be careful when dealing with his daughter. 'What would you like to drink?' He asked after remembering to have spoken to one of Lola's friend named Salvador.

'I'm okay sir; my sister-in-law had offered me some drink before you arrived sir.'

'Did you say your sister-in-law?'

'Yes sir, she's married to one of my senior brothers.'

'I see, what is your name?'

'Isa sir.'

'Where do you live Isa?'

'Palmgrove sir.'

Bayo Anifolase psyched his appearance and age up before taking some Naira notes out of his pocket and handing them to him as a goodwill gesture. 'Is there anything else?'

'Nothing sir,' Isa got the message and was on his feet but suddenly stooped again with a smile. 'That's Mr Bamidele coming sir.' He pointed towards the man peeping behind the gate.

'Let him in,' he stood proudly and shouted at the gateman before switching his full attention to the man walking humbly into his premises. He was still wondering what the missing link about him was that he didn't notice him prostrating flat before him.

'Hello sir,' Adam greeted first still fully prostrated.

'*E dide*.' He finally suggested and gestured with his hand.

As he rose from prostration, he remembered how he used to rebel against doing just this in his younger days. But was never the less prompted by Isa who was now on his feet to occupy his seat.

When Adam looked briefly into his shrewd face he noticed his critical eyes assessing and prompting him to speak first. 'I spoke to you last week with Lola sir.' Feeling nervous and sweating like a pig, he hoped his instinct to trust him was correct.

His suspicion about him was equally confirmed by his light skin as their eyes met once again. '*Se iwo ni Adam Salvador ti mo ba soro lori phone ni last week pelu Lola?*'

'*Be –ni sir!*' He replied in a broken Yoruba.

'*Se ko gbo Yoruba ni?*'

'I only understand the basic *Yoruba*, I left Lagos when I was thirteen years old sir.'

'I see,' he nodded and scanned him again. 'How did she get that scar on her forehead?' He suddenly asked.

He bowed his head to contemplate after realising this was a win or loose all situation. 'She had an accident at work that led to amnesia.' He didn't want to be the bad news bearer but he had to.

'Were you there?'

'Yes sir and that's why I'm reperesenting her in court.'

'So you are a lawyer.' He nodded to appreciate and confirm the little his uncle had already told him. 'Anyway it's been nice talking to you.' He extended his hand for a handshake which Adam received with a gentle and polite bow. 'I'll make sure she gets this.'

'I was wondering if I could have her number sir.'

'Whose number?'

'Lola sir.' The respectful and polite posture instilled in him years ago all suddenly resurfaced and proved to be vital.

Impressed with his demeanour, he decided to assist him despite the negative hint he'd been getting from his daughter. 'I honestly don't have her number but try her on my number tomorrow.'

'When is the best time sir?' Adam looked at his pensive face and suspected him to be slightly younger than his dad.

'Anytime. I'm going to leave the phone with her all day tomorrow.' He noticed the relief on his face and immediately concluded to dismiss them or risk putting his daughter on the spot. 'Anytime tomorrow should be alright okay?'

Adam half prostrated to express his gratitude and bid his goodbye.

Without another word Mr Anifolase responded by waving his hand before heading for his mum's flat with the envelope and her notebook but was disappointed to find his daughter deeply asleep. He quietly sat on the chair right behind the door and watched her as he wondered where he'd gone wrong His daughter had constantly nagged him about her wish to continue her studies abroad but he kept promising to think about it. At eighteen she had become an exact replica of Tolani, her mother that not only brought the memory too close for his comfort but also made him secretly admit that he had failed in suppressing the memory her presence evoked. At this time, half of him wanted her to travel abroad and continue with her studies without caring about the educational platform whilst the other half was willing to bow to family pressure that she was too young to be left abroad alone. But the disgrace, the humiliation and controversy with Yusuf quickly made everyone's mind up, with the main reason being to give her room to get over the debacle and possibly start afresh without the scandal's hindrance. Despite his strong belief in his daughter's innocence, he empathised with her predicaments and wondered why he couldn't really see where she'd gone wrong. But it must be asked of where and how she contracted *Magun*, and above all its implication on her future or should he simply say where did he go wrong?

Would this have happened if her mother was alive? Apart from her death shaking everyone concerned to the core, he didn't realise the extent of the devastation and the vacuum it left behind until Lola recently repeated that her mother's death robbed her of knowing the most important person in her life that no one could ever come close to replacing. He was not only shocked and frozen the first time he heard her, but was forced to chase and eventually join her in looking at her favourite album in her bedroom. They both watched the fondest memories of mother and daughter with keen interest and mixed feelings. Would Tolani commend him for a job well done or would she be disappointed? For once he accepted that he should have been there for Lola more than he actually was, but the mere fact was they were both grieving because she'd lost her mother and he lost his wife. He wished he had been more patient with her every time she asked him questions about her mother; after all he was the only one she could ask. His daughter was to him, too keen to have everything about her mother out in the open but he wasn't ready to face the fact that Tolani was gone from his life and from this world forever. The more he hoped that time would heal the pain and fill the vacuum she had left in his life, the more he realised it as a mere wishful thinking especially now that he'd finally accepted that she was one in a million! He could never have a wife's package as complete as Tolani whom he had unknowingly taken her devotion, love and adoration for granted. Her face had been tattooed in his memory since their last meeting before they boarded the plane. He could vividly recollect being irritated at the airport because Lola had been unusually clingy whilst Tolani had been unnecessarily emotional, especially when she ran back after their final farewell to give him another hug with tears running down her cheeks whilst Lola cried to split them. He teased her to smile but they both burst into laughter after Lola mimicked their utterances and actions.

With a final hug she said she loved him very much, picked Lola up and didn't look back till she disappeared from his sight. If only he knew she was not coming back to him, he would have been more responsive and would have told her how much he loved her. It might not have done her a lot of good then but would have surely done him a lot more good now. Not only had he had been selfish, but had taken her for granted believing that she was his wife and would be with him forever, and that death would not come so quickly because they had so much things to share, to do, so much quarrels and so much battles to fight, and above all so much obstacles to overcome!

After so much thinking he decided to get close to his daughter and speak what he should have said many years ago. 'I'm sometimes frightened to look at you closely because you're the painful reminder of my lost love, a tiny consolation that she was alive through you makes me love you both even more and equally miss her terribly!' After his loud confession he wiped his tears with relief and determination to make up for his past and present mistakes by being more helpful and responsive to her needs.

He gently placed the envelope and the writing pad on her dressing table before facing her bed and making a solemn promise to his deceased wife. 'Tolani I promise to make you proud of me through her.' He wiped his face thoroughly before quietly leaving the room as he entered.

Lola turned around ten minutes after hearing her dad shut the door, having heard everything he said by pretending to be asleep. She bizarrely felt her pillow wet and eventually understood what Mama meant by Death is really the greatest conqueror! She initially wanted to jump out of bed and apologise for all her past tantrums and outburst, but was restrained by an inner voice that he definitely wanted to do this alone. She was suddenly overwhelmed with guilt for believing she was the only one grieving and feeling the vacuum of her mum's death, little did she know that they both shared and harboured the pain secretly but just couldn't openly acknowledge it! But she most importantly understood the depth of her father's love and that his mood swings had nothing to do with her personally but his individual way of coping with her mum's loss. How wrong could she have been to assume he hated her!

Yes, she felt guilty all the time for her inability to thank her mother personally for giving her life but never acknowledged the blessing of having such lovely kith and kin family who have all fulfilled her mother's role whole heartedly. She was most importantly ashamed for bringing the whole household to their knees by no direct fault of hers.

She had some hours ago cried to sleep because of Mama's news, which actually confirmed her suspicion that her dad deliberately stayed away to give them the opportunity to discuss the next step her great uncle mentioned earlier.

On getting home, Mama persuaded her to immediately have a shower with another cocktail of herbs from her brother and didn't wait for her to dry before offering her another concoction to drink.

She pulled face at the content as she wondered what it would taste like since it was odourless.

Mama observed her reluctance and moved closer to encourage her. 'This is purely an extract from the Quran.'

'Then why is it so dark like coffee?'

'That is the cooked sugar inside it.'

She believed her grandma and quickly gulped the mixture down whilst waiting for an aftertaste but was disappointed. 'Tasteless and odourlesss.'

'Good, my brother said the past months had been really tough for you.' She took the glass cup from her and continued without waiting for her answer. 'Does your womb still burn?'

'No ma, I just feel weak and drained.'

'That's expected anyway.' She gently sat her down and whispered. 'Daddy Kahf can't wait for you to be back on your feet.'

'Me too,' she stopped to sneeze as she'd been doing lately.

'He said you can be free to go out in two to three days time.'

Something in her tone made her look sharply at her grandmother. 'What's the catch?'

'You need to get married.'

'Yes, I know but why the rush?'

'For a universal language ... A natural means of communication between people of opposite gender. Something that you would eventually do in your own time only we want you to do it now.' She stopped to examine the impact of what she'd said so far.

'Mama I haven't the slightest idea.'

'How do you consummate a marriage?'

She shockingly jumped on her feet. 'Daddy Kahf gave me two days to find a man to sleep with.'

'Marriage first.' Mama nodded and urged her to resume her seat beside her.

'I've kept my virtue all this while because I haven't met the deserving man and you now want me to throw it all away and marry just anybody?' She snapped her fingers to complete her sentence and witnessed one of those rare occasions that words failed her grandmother. 'But that contradicts the principles and trainings you instilled in me.' She added after she nodded again. 'What if I refuse?'

'My jewel, you can't refuse.'

'I'm nearly twenty four and have been jilted twice because of this same self-righteousness and I'm sure I wouldn't have had this *Magun* if I'd cooperated with some of these men ...' she stopped and sobbed instead.

Mama stood up to wipe her tears. 'I know, it seems really complicated if you look at it that way.'

'But that's how it is and I can't do it Ma.'

The older woman opened her mouth in shock and started stroking her back. 'Please my precious. I pray to God to witness the day you get happily married in good health and not in ailment.'

'I can't see that happening if I carry out your instruction. Maybe there is another way.' Sobbing, she rolled onto bed and told her grandma she was tired but eventually dozed off before her dad woke her up again.

Her thought was suddenly interrupted by a phone call but she ignored it for fear that the caller might insist she took the phone to her dad since she believed he'd forgotten it. She finally decided to answer it when the noise continued to disrupt her thoughts but the caller unfortunately hung up just before she spoke into the mouthpiece. She randomly thought of Adam Salvador and wanted to contact him for his explanation about the folder as she became more convinced that he truly cared about her according to Daddy Kahf. But then, his advice was purely on the good things she said about him. Did she really know any bad things about Adam? Apart from the different cultural background, she couldn't remember one except the powerful emotion that could erupt inside like a volcano if she wasn't careful. If only she'd waited for his side of the story instead of panicking and running away, maybe Daddy Kahf was right about her being delirious and paranoid then. Obviously love is not enough to sustain a relationship, but could she ever imagine herself getting intimate with someone she didn't feel for or someone she hardly knew? Well, Daddy Kahf and Mama would need to drug her first or leave destiny to take its course as she'd concluded earlier. With her mind preoccupied she'd absent mindedly replaced the phone before noticing the white envelope on her dressing table and her colourful notebook. Cautiously flipping it open confirmed her hand writing which sent her on a personal odyssey of Adam's flat as the last destination. Still gobsmacked, she carefully picked the brown envelope and felt it for anything suspicious before checking where it was posted from but was surprised to see no stamp nor address except for her name. With the bomb experience vivid on her mind, flinging it out of the window quickly came to mind but she restrained herself because of the certainty that her dad would have done all the necessary checks before now. Finally, she emptied the content on the table in one go with the first document facing up being a Nigerian birth certificate of Adam Bamidele Salvador born to Tijani Olatunji Salvador and Sherry Jeanette Morris on the tenth of October nineteen-

'Oh my God!' The shocking discovery knocked her off her feet for a while. She looked back at the piece of paper in her hand to ensure it was real. *Bamidele! Often called and shortened to Dele! Meaning come home with me*! A unisex name for children born away from one or both parents' natural origin.

'Adam a Yoruba man! I'll be damned.' She tried to recollect if he'd ever hinted this valuable information to her or the oversight was from her, but there was no indication to support it. Why would he deliberately omit such vital information? Her new discovery was quickly doused by her last experience in his house but she quickly rose above it by picking four sheets of A4 paper stapled together. With so many documents enclosed she decided to come back to it later but managed to read the last paragraph and was surprised to see the signature of Mr F. James. She quickly reached for her folder to compare with the sample signature and was surprised to see no difference. Right behind it was a West Midland police slip with an allocated reference number issued to Mr A.B. Salvador and dated two days after she left Birmingham. Another was a full picture of Adam around thirteen years old with his classmates and on the back was written "my send off picture before leaving Lagos for England." Just then, a business card reading *SalvaTel Nigeria Ltd* slipped off and fell onto her lap, the address was in Ilupeju, Lagos with a telephone number of Adam's handwriting at the back of it. In another smaller envelope were two cassette tapes which she quickly slipped into her cassette player.

She was initially wondering what was being discussed but soon heard Adam asking questions and some inaudible answers, and had almost removed the tape when Adam asked about her break ins.

'Bob wanted the personnel file for one reason and reason only.' He coughed to clear his throat before he continued. 'Because of the name *Akin Wonder*, who apparently was Lola's fiancé but was also one of Bob's errand boys. You don't get it do you?'

'No sir.'

'After the bomb blast, Bob personally changed Akin's home address to Lola's home, the National Insurance and every other details were still the same except for his signature.

'Was that what he wanted the folder for?'

'Partly yes, to copy the signature and file the new details in the folder so she could be well implicated for fraud!'

'But Lola should be able to see the name on payroll.

'Akin Wonders is a fictitious name.'

'Then it can't be linked to her.'

'It would have been if all the records were backdated to many months.'

'That's why he wanted the folder!'

"Now you get it! Amongst other things he'd use to incriminate her.'

Lola angrily turned the cassette player off with a big sigh. What an fallible lie! After reflection, she concluded there was no indication that they were cordial or friends except when he attended a job interview and she was sure they never met on the said day. She finally picked the A4 piece of paper and began reading, but couldn't concentrate because of her troubled mind. The more she tried to think of the taped conversation the more Adam's discovery overshadowed it. How stupid she'd been! He must be laughing at her for all her insult about the cultural differences. She would need to know if he dropped the packet himself.

Just then, the phone rang again with no name showing on the screen. 'There is only one way to find out.' She whispered as she nervously pressed the answer button.

'Lola?'

'How did you know it was me?'

'Because your dad promised to leave the phone for you.'

'There I was thinking he forgot it.'

'Didn't he tell you I called?'

'No, I haven't seen him, I'd been … sleeping.' She hesitated about telling him the truth.

'You didn't look like your dad in any way.'

She giggled. 'They said I was a striking image of my mother.'

'I'm my dad's carbon copy.'

'Mama, my dad and his uncle are all like that.'

He laughed heartily. 'Like clones?'

She laughed too. Something she'd never done in almost a week. 'Yes, like clones. Wait till you meet the other two musketeers in my family.'

He chortled before a long silence ensued. 'So how are you?'

'I've been ill since I arrived but much better now.'

There was a prolonged silence but she seized the opportunity first. 'Adam, I'm really sorry for being a jackass.' She stopped when he heaved a big sigh. 'I will forever be grateful for all your help and support but most importantly for believing in me.'

'You are very welcome.'

'But I don't believe what Mr James said about what Bob wanted the folder for.'

'So what else did you think those burglars wanted after you'd openly admitted the break-ins were work related?'

'I have no idea but God knows what could have happened to me if you weren't around at the explosion.'

'Who's been telling you all these?' He wished to tell her how desperate he was to see her.

'No one, I remember it all now … how you stood by me at the hospital,' she whimpered. 'Which means you heard my aunt's comments.' She continued after a while.

'I thought she was joking.'

'Adam Bamidele Salvador, you are not a very good liar. I can still remember your expression and connected it to the same one the day you and Akin nearly had a fight. Am I correct or not?'

'I didn't know you noticed.'

'I didn't until now. How did you get involved with Mr James in the first place?'

'I'll tell you that tomorrow when you lie next to me. Do you now believe me?'

'Yes, of course.'

'Really?'

'You mean the evidences in front of me?'

'I meant us.'

There was a prolonged silence before she spoke. 'Adam we need to talk.'

'Of course,' but do you now believe that I meant it when I said I loved and would like to marry you?'

She held back the tears and would have denied him but she remembered her last conversation with Mama.

'Are you still there?' His quiet and sexy voice made her heart skip a beat and rendered her speechless. 'Lola, tell me you've missed me.' His intonation and words gave her emotional fever that instantly made her forget about her immediate problems.

Her attempt to admit the truth to him nearly stifled her throat.

'I've laid my cards on your table long time ago but you seem to have troubles with trust and expressing your feeling but I'm sure we can't make any progress without it. Eyes never lie and I know what yours tells me but I won't pressurise you into what you don't want. An unreciprocated love is too painful and I think I've got more than my share of that already. Your eyes have never denied loving me but your excuse had always been the difference in culture.'

She was moved to tears by his admission but more by the pain and rejection in his voice. 'Adam I've sincerely missed you in every imaginable way and I love you with all my heart but I have a confession to make first.' She tearfully spat the words out before her emotions took control.

'Is there someone else or have you met any old flame?'

'No.'

'And your family are not trying to match make you?'

'No, are yours?'

'Yes, the old man is.'

'Not bad.'

'Then why are you crying?' He continued after a while. 'Those two to me are the only problems we can't solve, our love for each other is second to none, and we are compatible ...'

Lola liked the word he used. 'What if it's anything else?'

'We'll sit down and talk about it.'

'And if we still disagree?'

'I'll have the veto power.'

'What happens to fifty- fifty?'

'I don't care who rocks the boat as long as I still wear the trousers.' Adam decided to borrow a leaf off his dad for once. If it took his parents decades to resolve their differences, he'd better lay his cards on the table straight away. 'That is not negotiable.' She'd secretly admired him for his constant uprightness. 'What if this love is tested by something …' she paused when she heard a phone ring in the background. 'I think the caller could be one of your newly match made suitors.'

'I like that.'

'Like what?'

'I like your voice when you are jealous.'

'I'm not jealous.'

'Okay. I know what I'm talking about. Can I just stress that they haven't got the effect your presence and voice has on me.'

'Which is?'

'I get excited all over and weak at the same time.'

'I thought that only applies to us women.'

'Speak for yourself; mind you men are humans too.'

'Probably a few of you are.'

'Are you in bed already?'

'No, just got out of bed. Why?'

'I was going to read you a bedtime story.' His voice was husky and sensual. 'Just kidding, but you sounded a bit down.'

'I wish that was my only problem.'

There was a prolonged silence until he heard her sob again. 'You are not pregnant?'

She wanted to agree but thought deeply about the implication of her reply. 'Hell no.'

'That to me was the most favourable no I've ever heard. I'll see you tomorrow. Sleep tight and dream about me.'

'And you?'

'I've been dreaming of you for months, another night wouldn't make any difference.' He faked a yawn before he spoke again. 'I think I should let you rest now my love.' He ended the call to attend to the knock on the door.

Lola still held the phone to her ear long after he'd bid his farewell and cried more. How would he look at her if she told him what was wrong with her? Could he keep the secret to himself if things didn't work out between them or would he return to England for good or pick up from where they stopped? In a different circumstances, she would be honoured to get intimate with someone she considered a complete package but *Magun* had changed all that. Adam's presence had nullified all her threats to her family, but who in his or her right senses would believe she was innocent and be willing to take that kind of risk for the sake of so called Love. Relieved and equally confused, she realised tomorrow can't come soon enough despite all the uncertainty and challenges it might bring.

CHAPTER 24

Lola woke up with mixed feeling and wondered why despite the bustling and the screaming sunshine around her. She was initially awoken by the cock's crow that sounded so far away and yet familiarly strange around five o' clock in the morning but must have dozed off again.

It was nine thirty when she looked up at the wall clock again, and was getting dressed after her bath when Adam rang her mobile phone to say he was outside. She promised to meet him immediately. Quickly, she applied her eye liner before rushing to the main entrance, and was about to tell the gateman to let him in when he hugged her from the corner behind her and finally kissing her passionately on the lips.

'People are watching.' She looked diffidently around to find next door's kids gathering round, sniggering and smiling.

He pecked the tip of her nose. 'I don't care.' He smirked and waved at the few adults gawping at them. His dazzling eyes gazed down at her, unwavering and direct. 'Is it me or you've truly lost weight?' He shot her a wry smile.

'I told you I haven't been well.'

He embraced her tightly and heaved a big sigh of relief before moving slightly backwards and holding her face in his hands and looking straight into her eyes.

'Nice tan.'

'Thank you.' He kissed her lips lightly and was about to repeat it when two fighting hens dragged themselves around them. The kids became more amused as Adam stamped his foot to break them up but the bigger and the more aggressive hen chased after the weaker one.

'Mama breeds chickens.' She grabbed his hand and led him back inside with his other hands resting comfortably on her hips.

'Should I call you Dele?'

'Call me anything but just don't ever do a runner on me again. If there is a problem, we talk about it. Alright?'

'Alright.' She concurred and were both busy chatting and laughing when they bumped into Mama coming out of her flat. 'I was just coming to ask what you would like for breakfast.'

She felt like a thief caught stealing from the cookie jar. 'Mama this is Bamidele.' She said bashfully instead of a reply.

Adam was saved half way from prostrating flatly by Mama. 'Hello my son.'

' Hello ma.'

'How are you?'

'*Adupe* ma,' He avoided Lola's surprising expression.

'May God bless you?'

'Amen ma.'

'What will you eat?'

Adam studied her calm, trusting face for a while before blushing and quickly recovered from his own embarrassment. 'I'm full ma,' he glanced at her round, smiling, intelligent face and back to Lola's for support.

Mama smiled and nodded before switching to Lola. 'How are you feeling today precious?'

'Fine ma,' she giggled. 'We'll have anything.' She gently dragged him away with a relief that they'd crossed the first hurdle successfully. 'So you do speak Yoruba.'

Adam locked the door once they were inside and smiled embarrassingly. 'Just a bit.'

He backed the door and pulled her to him before pecking her. 'You've suddenly gone tense.'

She looked back at his piercing eyes, darkened with a renewed interest and pride. Adam an embodiment of the businessman bachelor, debonair, particular and sharp 'I told you I've not been well, didn't I?'

'Oh yes.' Pensively, he led her to her bed and sat her on his lap. 'What's wrong with you my darling?' His eyes sucked hers in before embracing her with a forbidding intimacy that made her shiver. 'You know what?' He kicked his sandals off and was removing her slippers when he reminisced how their first meeting triggered the passion that still ran through his mind with pleasure. 'Let's just lie down.' He gently pushed her back onto the bed with their faces looking up the ceiling and a renewed determination to wait for her to overcome the hurdle, no matter how long. 'I have to tell you some things about my maternal uncles but … have you regained your memory?'

'Yes.'

'When?'

'On the plane.'

'How much do you remember?'

'I suppose everything.'

'Do you remember our first meal together?'

'And how your next visit triggered a confrontation with Akin?'

'Was it really my next visit?' He sat up and frowned.

'Yes it was.' She looked up at him. 'And you came close to knocking him out for calling you *Olosi*.'

'I only held back because of my love for you.'

'You were in love then?'

'I was in love the first day I set my eyes on you …' His roaming gaze reminded her of the embarrassing moment she caught him starring at her breasts.

To hide her embarrassment she tickled him gently.

He liked it and he reciprocated. Adam could be as smart with words as his hands; her heart somersaulted just for remembering the effect of his hands on her body. She hadn't had much intimate experience with men but she seriously doubted if any other man could ignite her body and soul so potently with just a touch.

Still sitting up, he gazed down at her whilst she maintained her position doing the same with the raw tenderness she picked from his emotion. He lowered his head to meet hers and claimed her lips with a hungry passion but withdrew to look at her when her lips remained sealed. Both burst out laughing afterwards. They stopped laughing simultaneously and stared at each other in mutual silence with their eyes narrowing slightly. Still smiling but in a slow and calculating movement, he kissed her forehead, the tip of her nose before finally claiming her lips and was glad when she welcomed him. As they swapped breath, their lips conjoined and tongues tangled up as one, their sensuous feeling both spiralled uncontrollably like a raging inferno. Adam led the way in igniting the flame of passion she'd successfully suppressed, she responded with her arms wound around his neck and continuously aroused him by twisting the curly bit of hair at his nape.

As they both moaned quietly, he progressed to nibble her soft, succulent lips in return for new awakening pleasure that trapped them in their momentous bubbles. Deaf, dumb and blind to everything around them except the pleasure of touching and feeling until a shrilling cough pierced their bubbles.

Adam jumped up first whilst Lola immediately sat up to face Daddy Kahf standing at the guest room's entrance adjoining her bedroom.

'The door was unlocked and I knocked on several occasions.' The teasing look on his face was more than embarrassing as Lola checked her dressing was fine. He moved inside and closer to them. 'It's time for your medication.' With his attention fully focused on Adam, he placed a transparent keg containing some dark liquid on the table beside them before stretching out his hands at him. 'And you are?'

'Adam Bamidele Salvador sir.' He quickly got on his feet before slipping his hand into his with a slight bend of his head. Apart from the austere command he imposed, the striking resemblance to Lola's grandmother and dad confirmed it, Adam also complemented his trusting, sharper, smoother and well-balanced facial feature, and initially panicked for his inability to tell what he was thinking from his facial expression but his aura was serene.

'And what is your intention towards my great niece Adam?'

'I want to marry her sir.'

For some seconds he gazed at Lola whilst still rocking Adam's hand with his reputable grin. 'And what was her response to your proposal?'

'She hasn't answered sir.'

'And she lets you fondle her in such a manner?' He squeezed his brows enquiringly. 'How old are you?'

'Nearly twenty eight sir.'

'The same age as me when I got married, good. Where do you live?'

'Ikeja sir.'

'I mean in England.'

'Birmingham City centre sir.'

'It must be noisy there.'

He curved his mouth downward to indicate it was okay, a gesture he'd seen his dad do so many times.

'What's your daddy's first name?'

'Tijani sir.'

'And your mother's?'

'Sherry-Jeanette sir.'

'Sherry Jeanette.' He repeated the names whilst looking deeply into his eyes before nodding his head with approval. 'And your family have no problem with you wanting to marry a Yoruba.'

'I am Yoruba too sir.'

'And a Muslim …' He deliberately let the rest linger as his eyes focused on Lola who was apprehensive about his intention.

'I'm now a Muslim sir.'

'Now?' Daddy Kahf released his hand and swiftly headed for the door. 'But not a practicing Muslim?'

'I meant … I've always been a Muslim.' His prayer of not being asked about the religion was answered when he spoke again.

'Excuse me for a minute.' He headed for the adjoining door but stopped halfway. 'We, especially my sister would be most pleased if you could do us a big favour …' He turned to look from Lola's drained face to her guest and back again. 'If you can stop her from committing suicide.'

Adam stared blankly at the door being shut when he finally understood his statement and back at Lola with shock, horror and disappointment. She, on the other hand had never felt so violated, humiliated and embarrassed at once. Her uncle had literarily done all the asking for her without the courtesy of introducing himself!

Unable to look at him directly, her face remained downcast in shame, degradation and humiliation as she took all that transpired on board with trepidation. At nearly twenty four she wondered when her family would stop prying into her affairs and was sure Mama wouldn't have put her brother to it if her English was fluent!

Adam's gentle tap of her shoulder brought her back to reality. 'Tell me he was joking.'

'You've met my dad, Mama and now the third musketeer in my family.' She finally lifted her head to face his gaze. 'I wish I could but Daddy Kahf doesn't lie.' She looked at him scornfully. 'I hope you are pleased now. Just pray he comes back approving of us because if he doesn't we are finished!' She continued after calming down. 'I personally find him strange but believe me, whatever he says is gospel.'

'What are you talking about? Who cares about your uncle's gospel?' The unpleasant narrowing of his eyes and the sneering curl of his upper lip said it all. 'You were actually thinking of committing suicide? Lola for once you've shocked me beyond words! I don't know which is more shocking; the fact that he told me or because you actually contemplated something so abhorrent.'

'Yes, so is *Magun*!'

'What the hell is *Magoon*? How could you believe in such hocus-pocus?'

She not only wished to withhold his cruel and frightening derisive look but also to retaliate immediately.

'Yes?' They both yelled and vented their anger at the unknown person knocking on the door.

'It's only me again.' Daddy Kahf said before showing his face. 'You two should share this after drinking the one on the table.'

Lola's shocking reaction began to fade after picking the positive hint in her uncle's voice. 'Okay sir.'

'What is it sir?' Adam decided to repay him back with his coin.

'Call it a specially combined drink.'

'Sir?' He stopped and enquired with his body language instead.

'They are written out extracts from the Quran mixed and washed with water.' His eyes thinned when he saw the way Adam dismissed the concoction but continued calmly. 'It's a cure for her affliction and we've only got one more day to go. I believe she'd told you already.'

'Kind of, but I still don't get it sir.'

'She was afflicted with *Magun* through this into her reproductive organ to conjoin with her sexual partner.' He produced a ring from his pocket and smiled weakly at him. 'She has completed her medication and been fully cured of it but I'm taking an extra mile of trying to reverse the curse back to its source instead of her sexual partner.'

'In other words me.' He continued without waiting for his reply and looked at him briefly but concentrated more on the ring. 'Why does this *Magoon* have to be reversed instead of simply curing her?'

He moved closer to him. 'This is more for you than her and to bring the culprit to justice.'

'Why sir?'

'Because whoever did it to her suspected she was sleeping with you.' He waited for it to sink in and saw him frown. 'My great niece had been cured but the condition and component of this particular *Magun* required it to be reversed. Moreover, my utmost concern is my great niece and her loved one.' He smiled for the shock on his face to dissipate.

He stepped backwards. 'What if your cure doesn't work sir?' He immediately wished he hadn't.

His face immediately hardened leaving only a shadow of a smile that once existed and his eyes suddenly went cold. 'I'm a physician that saves lives!' His words and tone deliberately controlled. 'She had received a one hundred percent more treatment than any outsiders have ever had, moreover if I can't exorcise my own family and their loved ones who would?' He calmed down before moving closer to whisper into his ears. 'Two other lives solidly depend on it and I'm not taking responsibility for my sister's death.' He stepped backwards and continued in his usual tone of voice.

'I have strictly adhered to every detailed rules, regulations and conditions revealed to me and left no stone unturned. Luckily for her there was a link which helped us expedite her recovery process and explained why she was quarantined for only five days intensive treatment.' He struck his forefinger up. 'Above all she's family.'

'Does it kill?'

'Yes, could have and much faster than AIDS. Instant, sudden death with no prior symptom or illness is another name for it.'

'Faster than AIDS?'

'Instant sudden death with no symptoms or prior illness.'

Adam's mind went blank as he sat on the edge of the bed before his knees gave way. He quickly glanced from one face to the other with his mouth agape and wondered what would have happened if they weren't interrupted earlier. If he didn't understand *Magun* its comparison to AIDS brought the harsh reality home.

'It was a good thing we caught it in time.'

'In other words she could have died?'

'Sure, if I didn't detect it when I did.'

'Did you say she is cured now?'

'Yes, absolutely.'

'Can I use your toilet please?' He asked instead.

'Yes, just beside you.' Daddy Kahf replied without taking his eyes off Lola who wouldn't stop sobbing.

She not only sensed Adam's guilt and regret but noticed cracks of vulnerability in his well-fortified personality. 'Daddy, why did you have to be so blunt?' She managed to ask amidst heavy sob.

'He has a right to know, were you going to lie?'

She shook her head.

'Then let's put our fate in Almighty The Creator, The Controller of faith and destiny's hands.'

'I'm still not going to sleep with just any man for the sake of it alone.' She grumbled rebelliously.

'You won't have to if you do it for the right reason.'

'I've told you and Mama that I'd rather die a virgin than have sex with someone I don't love. I've sacrificed too much for that.' She continued bawling.

He moved closer to her and rested one hand on her shoulder for an eye contact. 'Do you love Adam?'

'Yes sir, but …'

'But what?'

'I don't think he would be interested after all the details from you.'

'As someone always says, Love conquers all.'

'No Mama always said death conquers all.'

He shook his head harshly. 'Let's think of love and hope now, shall we?' He urged and was quickly by the door again. 'Let me get Sister for you.'

Lola began to sob immediately and howled after the door was shut crouching the pillow tighter than usual.

Thirty minutes later she was still crying with no sign of Adam, she got out of bed to check him and was surprised to find the bathroom and its surroundings vacant. Without further ado she automatically accepted he'd absconded and left her to her demise. As she crawled back into bed with more tears, she accepted her fate and not to expect much overnight. Not many love flourishes in such adversity; she admitted secretly but equally thanked her uncle for relieving her conscience and spilling the bean so bluntly. She was still wailing when sleep took over.

Adam on the other hand genuinely went to the toilet to ease himself and was returning when he heard them whispering but was eavesdropping when Isa's text message interrupted him that their plan had been foiled. He quickly called Isa to concoct another lie when his dad answered the phone and ordered him to meet them outside immediately. Adam swapped to meeting his dad briefly for Lola's desperate bawl he heard from the toilet with every intention of returning shortly. He had barely got to the car when his elegantly dressed dad ordered him to get into the jeep before asking questions.

He only concurred because he thought he would soon be excused but changed his mind when he saw his austere stare.

After driving for nearly four hours, and two previous stops including one clothes shopping Adam checked his watch and eased his breath gently. He glanced at his dad settling into his back seat after the third stop. He rubbed his back hand against his chin whilst desperately trying to cook up another excuse. 'Dad …'

'No more silly excuses, we promise you a good time.'

'We?'

'Yes, your mother and I.'

'I can find my own date thank you.' He hissed under his breath before expelling a gulp of frustrating air. 'How many dates are you introducing me to?'

'We are going to a get-together.'

'Dad I'm not dressed for such.'

'Here you go.' He stretched a transparent nylon protecting a lace material towards him. 'You'll be fine.' He assured his son after seeing his frown.

Adam reluctantly accepted defeat. 'I hope they are better looking than those two I met yesterday.'

'What about them?'

'One was fat and fake whilst the other looked like a Dalmatian dog.' He grumbled underneath his breath but loud enough for everyone around to hear.

'A what?' He for once took his eyes off the newspaper he was reading.

'A breed of dog that has a white coat covered with black or brown spots.'

Dad reeled in laughter for a while. 'So you don't like any flesh on your women?'

He was about to describe Lola as his ideal woman when he realised he was talking to his dad and not one of his peers. With a loud chuckle he placed the newspaper aside. 'I'm saving the best for the last and you tonight are going to thank us for this.'

He was already regretting not hearing her side of the story. Everything had happened so fast, the last woman he knew wasn't keen to move out of her house in Birmingham and how did she get here. Something is seriously wrong somewhere!

He looked at the rear view mirror and fully understood his dad's fears, but doubted he was going about it the right way when he saw the smirk of approval on his face. He concluded that his timing was more than perfect with his parents resolving their differences especially his dad's sincere apology to them. After their meeting at his office on his first day of arrival, they went home to meet all his family members with many old faces apologising for their bad deeds especially his two half sisters and their mum. He'd deliberately put Adam on the spot by openly reminding him the role of a first son and telling everyone he was single and ready to settle down. He also introduced his mum as his new wife and also announced that she would be setting up a beauty saloon and gym shortly.

He agitated as his thoughts wandered back to Lola and wished he'd temporarily said goodbye. He had meant to tell her a lot about himself the moment he got to her house especially about his maternal uncles and her workplace but he failed because he couldn't resist touching her and one thing led to another until her uncle spoiled it all.

'Dad what is *Magoon?*' The uncontrollable urge propelled him to ask.

'What?'

'Never mind.'

'Where did you hear that from?'

'In the plane, a man accused a woman of possessing it.' He lied.

'Poor woman, it's going to be difficult to cure her. They don't possess it; they are normally afflicted with it.

'Can men be afflicted too?'

'Yes, but more women fall victims to it than men.'

'Really? How mean, but is it curable?'

'Yes it is, but imagine how many man or woman would want to knowingly have sexual relationship with someone that had been allegedly cured of AIDS. No one really wants to have sexual intercourse with them afterwards.'

'My argument is carriers who don't tell their sexual partners should be prosecuted for manslaughter.'

'My dear son, that's the European law, *Magun* is Jungle justice.'

'In what way?'

'It is a Yoruba way of dealing with promiscuous partners. It is a swift judgement with victims and their sexual partners hardly ever living to tell the tale.'

'Why?'

'Because they hardly knew they'd been afflicted until after sexual intercourse which would have almost been too late.'

'Which means the lady would stand a better chance of surviving if she was aware of it ever before sexual intercourse, right?'

'Which is impossible.'

'I think it's possible dad.'

'Isa is it true?'

The driver giggled cautiously. 'Yes sir, very rarely, but only made possible by experienced physicians or spiritualists.'

'I would need to see that to believe it.'

'No problem dad.'

He tapped Adam gently on the shoulder so their eyes could meet. 'Is there something you are not telling me?'

He would have candidly replied if Isa hadn't interrupted.

'Here we are sir,' he jumped out to open the door for his boss and immediately did the same to Adam.

Father and son stood side by side to assess the fleets of various jeeps and other makes of expensive cars parked up. 'One can obviously imagine the calibre of the guests invited just from looking at these vehicles.' He flipped his *agbada* over his shoulder and smiled. 'Why don't you get dressed now?'

'Later,' his eyes already focused at the tall, strange building shaped like a fish where he suspected the noise was coming from.

The inside of the restaurant and hotel was breathtakingly beautiful and spacious with shimmering chandeliers of various sizes and colour, the interior decor were made of ornate carved woodwork alternated with gold colour.

'The newest and the best restaurant and hotel in town.' His dad whispered behind him. 'Come on, let me introduce you to the celebrants,' he led him to the hall where most of the guests were. Amidst the crowd was his mum, talking to another white woman dressed in a complete traditional outfit with headgear and heavily adorned with matching jewellery. Nearby was his step mum with another group of women all wearing the same outfit with matching headgears but styled differently and enough jewellery to make a few goldsmiths millionaires. She walked out of the group to snuggle his dad, which irritated Adam because he was now obliged to greet everyone that acknowledged their presence. He was still wondering how quickly his dad adjusted to his polygamous lifestyle when he saw his mum and her new friend approaching them but were intercepted by the tallest female he'd met in Lagos yet, she was stunning and dual heritage too!

'*Ahaha*!, Sinmidele meet my son, Bamidele.'

'Please call me *Sinmi*.' She added without removing her hand. 'I've heard so much about you.'

Adam returned her smile but was more embarrassed by his dad's presence and scrutiny.

He looked away from his dad back at her to see the most dangerously attractive woman, lanky and leaned face with the most appealing lips he'd ever seen; her turquoise traditional outfit almost matched the colour of her sensual eyes. Yes, she was a complete package and would be every virile man's dream.

His dad's voice interrupted his thought. 'Sinmi, I'm sure you'll look after him.' Anyone could detect the underlying pleasure in his dad's voice. 'Hello Mrs Orija.' He greeted the two women just joining them and winked at his mum before snuggling her.

'Hello you've finally met my daughter,' Mrs Orija's beaming smile brightened the room more than her complexion and outfit. 'Meet Bamidele's mum.' Sinmi going on her knees prompted him to prostrate to the two women with his mum humouring him because she'd never seen him do that before.

'Ensure our guest is well entertained.' Mrs Orija spoke in a full cockney accent.

'How are you finding Lagos?' Sinmi asked after prompting him to follow her.

'Very good so far.' Walking closely beside her made him taller despite her turquoise high-heeled transparent wedges that made all heads turned their way.

'Do you understand Yoruba?'

'Just a bit,' he cautiously replied and wondered why she wanted to know but most importantly what was coming next.

'My parents have been kind enough to give us our own space.' She pushed open a double glass door to reveal another slightly smaller hall. 'Almost everyone here is single.' The soft lullaby in the background further confirmed the ambience. 'Where would you like to sit?'

'Anywhere is fine by me.'

'You can sit next to me.' She led him to an oblique area and pointed to a seat next to a handbag matching her shoes. She sat facing him after he settled down and served him a cocktail of drink that reminded him of Lola's medicine.

Adam received it reluctantly but smiled.

'Drink it, you'll like it.' She continued after he had a sip and nodded his approval. 'Do you want to go first?'

'For what?'

'Tell me about yourself.'

'No you go first.' He teased her as he sipped his drink.

'Well you know my name; I'm twenty four and a personnel manager in the best merchant bank in Lagos.' She smiled. 'Your turn.'

'When did you leave England?'

'That's cheating, you haven't told me about yourself.'

'I am nearly twenty eight and I'm a senior partner in a legal firm.'

She suddenly seemed keener and pouted her lips before moving closer to him. 'The first dance is mine.' Her voice was as warmly caressing as her eyes.

Adam stared back into her lovely inviting eyes before nodding.

'Do you love my outfit?' She was so close that he felt her breath fanning his face.

He liked the way she teased him. 'Oh yes, absolutely.'

'I'm glad you appreciate it.'

Her closeness prevented him from thinking of an appropriate reply but focused on her sensuous lips until he was distracted by the noise in the hall because of a new arrival.

Like a prompt, she slightly jumped at a new guest's voice before clearing her throat as if she was out of a trance. 'What would you like to eat?'

If he was surprised at her tone, he recovered quickly. '*Fried rice or jollof rice with dodo please.*'

'On its way,' she replied and was gone.

He watched her move gracefully to the other side of the hall and whisper to one of the attendants before pointing in his direction. He observed how she hugged every man calling out to her and never for once stopped looking his way until he was joined by another man about his age two seats away.

'Excuse me, that seat is reserved.'

'Okay.' Adam scanned the newly arrived guest's round baby face then his long skinny neck before smiling and looking back at Sinmi's shoes to confirm it was actually her seat. He pointed in her way but was surprised she now had her back to them. 'My host chose this seat for me.' He replied before facing the crowd again.

The sweet aroma of food permeated his nostril into his stomach to remind him his only meal was nearly ten hours ago. Just as the attendant was coming his way with a tray of food, he saw one of yesterday's match made suitor coming too.

'What would you like to drink sir?' The attendant asked as she dropped a plate of *fried rice with salad, dodo and chilli marinaded fish*.

'Anything is fine.'

'Alcohol?'

'Except that.' He replied as he tucked into his food and ignored the hostile look he was receiving from the man two seats away.

'Who say make he sit there?' Jealous lover boy asked the attendant in Pidgin English.

'*Oga I no know, aunty Sinmi say make I serve am here*.' The attendant replied fretfully.

'I beg my drink please.' Adam snapped in Pidgin English to assert his control over the situation and continued with his meal. When he stared back at him, his neck seemed longer whilst his eyes was fuming with rage and jealousy

By now the D.J. was playing one of his step mum's favourite track that always alienated him whilst she danced and sang with her two girls. His parents had tried to match him with someone they perceived him to be compatible with, in terms of beauty and elegance no rivalry but he still felt restrained by something unexplainable.

He finished his meal and had just belched quietly when he saw Sinmi walk up to the D.J. and whisper into his ears before heading his way. He noticed she had changed into a sparkly peppermint green coloured evening gown with sequins at the hem. As she got closer he noticed how the accessories complimented the clinging gown that showed all the right curves at the right places.

'Let's dance.' She literarily dragged him to the dance floor before he could reply.

Luckily for him the D.J. was playing *Marvin Gaye's Sexual Healing* and almost everyone was responding positively.

In the beginning he felt a bit awkward with where to place his hands but she placed them on her hips and smiled at him when their eyes met. In a different meeting environment, he would have thrown modesty out of the window but restrained himself to avoid any negative feedback to his parents. She wrapped her arms around his shoulder to deliberately elevate her bosoms to his. 'What do you think of our parents' effort to match make us?'

'I think they meant well.' He wondered why he felt no intrinsic sensation that he'd taken for granted with some of his women especially with Lola, he shamefully admitted feeling more sensuous on his first day of walking her home than now. His mind quickly drifted to their first intimate kiss at the Chinese restaurant where she rocked his groin. He involuntarily felt a sweet tremor all over for remembering today's encounter with her and wondered what would have happened if they weren't interrupted.

'Are you into any serious relationship?' Her question brought him back to reality.

'Not really, are you?'

'No.' She giggled with her warmly caressing voice.

He stepped back to read her expression but she looked serious and unwavering. 'Okay let me rephrase my question, are you sexually involved with anyone at the moment?' Before hugging her closer, they sought each other's gaze and held it for a while.

'I said no.'

'Then I can categorically say we will not disappoint our parents.' He stated with his deep seductive voice before tightening his grip. Yesterday, he was planning his future with Lola and today it was with Sinmi who seemed to know what she wanted and that seemed okay for now. Things are happening too fast but strangely to his liking. With her last reply, Adam's hands roamed all over the curves in her body freely and sensuously as the dance got dirty.

She responded with a more seductive and horny giggle.

'Who is that man sitting on our table?'

'That's Deji. He's the D.J. friend. Let me just say he is a very good friend.' She added when he looked at her critically.

'Nothing more?'

She instead replied with a shake of her head.

'Then why his sore face?'

Instead of a reply, she hummed the sexual healing lyrics into his ear before snuggling closer. And so they danced for over an hour to more eighties soul music.

When the track *Love Zone by Billy Ocean* stopped, she broke away and requested to go to the toilet. They both left the dance floor holding hands, as all heads turned their way and applauding, he squeezed her hands as she was about to leave for the ladies. He'd met his match on the dance floor and he believed it offered them a perfect opportunity to know more about each other. As he sat down he wondered why he felt uneasy, but eventually blamed it on the renewed rage he saw on Deji's face. Sinmi's unsurpassed beauty, saying all the right things at the right time and being an excellent dancer, was all impressive but why he was not titillated despite their intimacy eluded him. Yes, they'd both danced really well and was even sure someone like Deji was deeply jealous but he felt proud not fulfilled. He wouldn't need to be so close with Lola before all his senses responded with a big yearn for more, but he instantly decided not to disappoint his parents. His mum would be especially gobsmacked that they got it right for once.

He glanced away from the dance floor only to catch Sinmi sending a text with Deji chuckling for suddenly receiving a text message. His loud chuckle distracted Adam and locked their frosty gazes for a while before he pushed his chair back and shortly disappeared from sight. He was initially surprised to equally find Sinmi out of sight but was more shocked at who was coming his way. It was the

Dalmatian girl from yesterday's match make attempt!

'Hello.' She immediately sat facing him and didn't wait for his reply before she continued. 'Why didn't you call me back as promised?'

He leaned back on his chair to try and see beyond the spotty face and neck, but in vain. He watched the disappointment and despair on her face whilst he desperately tried to remember her name. 'I said within twenty four hours.'

'I know but I thought it could be sooner.' She looked at him and her face sobered but she glanced away quickly.

Adam could tell she wanted to dance but was too shy to ask for fear of being turned down, this to him confirmed how well cultured and ladylike she was. For once, he saw where his dad was coming from and pitied her for lacking Lola's beauty, refinement and wittiness but was certain her equanimity and demeanour would someday suffice to make a good wife and mother. He had the sudden urge to tell her he knew how she felt and was sorry for contributing to it, but another half of him wanted to ask her for a dance out of pity's sake, eventually his gut instinct told him either move would complicate matters further. He didn't fancy her period! It's a close call between Lola who suddenly stopped his heart from beating when she confessed her love to him yesterday and Sinmi his parents' ideal choice for him. He decided to gladly go along with his parents' choice since they both knew what they wanted and was certain that within a short space of time, his feeling for Sinmi would be unrivaled. Her keenness and willingness would pace up their love and ease his task unlike Lola that had exhausted him financially, morally, culturally and emotionally. To avoid giving her the wrong impression, he got on his feet like a propeller and excused himself without any particular place in mind.

He shortly discovered two little staircases that led to another narrow, dark passage near his original seat and was still contemplating whether to trek it down or not when he heard a soft whisper. Adam remained still for a while until he heard an all too familiar female giggle and laughter that seemed to be coming from underneath the staircase. Desperate to confirm, he used the flashlight from his mobile phone for guidance before seeing a little door handle. Whilst waiting for courage to open the small door, he heard sensuous moans and the horny giggles again. He yanked the door open and was astonished to see Sinmi on the floor stark naked with Deji on top. First was the shock then horror on the trio's face for different reasons, but they quickly glanced away because of shame whilst Deji's neck suddenly shrank with humiliation contrary to the previous arrogance displayed. Heavily disappointed but without a word Adam left the scene and the party altogether. Shortly afterwards, he located his dad's jeep from the fleet of cars. Still fuming he banged hard on the driver's door to wake Isa who quickly jumped from his slumber to open the passenger door.

He checked the time on his wristwatch after settling beside him. 'What time do you think they'll finish in there?' He gazed at the twenty-five-year-old driver married with two kids' slumbering eyes and felt his pressure.

'I don't know, I'm only assigned to you tonight.'

'Who will be dropping the adults' home?' He challenged annoyingly.

'I think daddy said they'd be going in your mum's new car.'

In normal circumstances, he should be delighted by the news unlike now that his mind was in turmoil. 'Good, take me to Lola's house.'

'Okay sir.' He stretched before starting the engine.

He turned the music on before reclining the seat. What a complete and utter fool he'd been! He'd chosen the desire of flesh over that of his heart. Despite all Sinmi's beauty, elegance and grace he'd gullibly believed that his feeling for her would sufficiently fulfill him and his parent's desire. He could still live with that, but the blatant lie was to him unforgivable and to be so desperate to get laid on a bare floor at the age of twenty-four was either sexual addiction, insanity or both. And yet, she was not afflicted with *Magoon* for being a lying, promiscuous cow! Could one just be in and out of love within hours?

Was it lust or love? Another voice asked.

'It must be lust.' He only realised he'd said it loud when Isa glanced at him again.

Could he ever imagine being that desperate with anyone at his age or had he been when he was much younger? Yes with Lola anytime anywhere. Just thinking of her alone evoked something powerful and uncontrollable in him. Now that is love! And he would never deny her. If Sinmi loved Deji why did she deny him and if she didn't why having sex with him? The other voice added again.

'And the bond!' He whispered this time but the driver still heard it. It was the same bond and connection he was expecting from every woman he'd dated. How bizarre that Lola was the only woman that possessed it, despite her epitomising everything he hated, despised and wanted to abscond from. Obviously love has no principle, it's either you click it or not. But since he'd recognised it and the fulfillment could he ignore it? The powerful emotions nearly gave him a panic attack for suddenly becoming over anxious to get to her.

'Are you alright *Oga*?'

'Yes thank you; please don't address me as boss again.' He gently massaged his chest to ease the pressure.

'Sorry sir, I can't.'

'Are we not related?'

'Yes sir, but you are still older than me.' He defended.

'Please don't address me with Sir or call me boss again.'

'Okay uncle s-'

They both laughed simultaneously as Adam realised the futility behind it all. It's a cultural thing! With Lola, his heart ruled but his groin ruled with Sinmi, which made him wonder what would happen after satisfying his curiosity. 'It's nearly six thirty, this fifty pounds is yours if we make it to Lola's house before half seven.'

Isa smiled at the money and still had his eyes stuck on the crispy note when he accelerated.

He would have to trust her great uncle a bit more on the *Magoon* aspect and hope for the best. It is at least better to have loved and lost rather than not to love at all! He realised he'd already disappointed his parents because erasing Sinmi's action off his mind would be impossible but choosing Lola over Aileen, Karel, Paige and Leah would eventually ease their anger and disappointments. Another option was for him to think of number one and rekindle any of the old flames, but then he never felt whole as he did with Lola. To start a new relationship and entirely forget about Lagos, Nigeria and pleasing his parents is not a big deal if he was happy and fulfilled but could he ever match and beat what he had with Lola? Which would prompt a question of who he really was; a question he'd asked his mum once but without a satisfactory answer. What would become of his mum, her relationship and her sacrifices? She'd after all told him she was doing all this for him and his future in the Salvador's household. He initially had his doubt but his welcome home gathering confirmed it all. He got angry as more riddles filled his head. Hell! Sod it all!

'What do you think of Sinmi?' He finally asked the driver out of the blue.

'Who?'

'Sinmi, the celebrant of the party we left behind.'

'Oh pretty.' He whistled. 'She's very pretty but …' He instead concluded with a throaty laugh and a shrug of his shoulder.

'But what?' Adam sat up and looked straight at him.

'She's not a wife material and I'm sure that uncle Deji is just using her.'

'So everyone knew of her and Deji?'

'Not everyone sir, only their three driver's sir, one of them told me.'

He slowly leaned back on his chair and shut his eyes. If only his parents knew what they were letting him in into. To him, all they could see was a pretty face, similar physical resemblance, heritage and background but they were totally different. How absurd! He left England to bridge the gap between him and Lola and there he was jumping at the first pretty face that was thrown at him. Yet, he was blaming her for running away from him but he simply did the same when she needed him most. Did he really think he could easily fall in and out of love just like that or that whatever propelled him from England could be easily swept under the carpet? He would have fallen flat on his face if he hadn't witnessed Sinmi's sordid affair or whenever his lust for her ran out and vice versa. She must have taken him for a buffoon!

'Isa, so you know of someone that can cure *Magoon?*'

'One of my uncles said he had sex with this woman afflicted with *Magun.*'

Adam sat upright with his eyes wide open. 'Did he die?'

'No, he is still alive.'

'How did he do it?'

'He said his daddy gave him one charm to wear around his wrist.'

'How does it work?'

'He said he used the charm to massage her stomach and womb to shift the *Magun* up till he finished.'

'And the *Magoon* comes down afterwards?'

'Allegedly.' Isa shrugged his shoulders and laughed throatily.

'So there is truly a cure then.'

'Yes, for most of it and once the component of that particular *Magun* is known.'

'How many types are they?'

'Plenty o! But I'm sure nobody knows exactly.'

He saw the big satellite dish erected a few houses away from Lola's before asking his question. 'Are we nearly there?'

'Yes sir. We are there.'

Adam checked his wristwatch before speaking. 'The time is seven twenty two. Well done.' He shook his hand before giving him the fifty pounds note. 'I need you to do me a favour.'

'Yes sir?' He faced him squarely still smiling.

'Please wait for me to enter before you take off.' He stepped out of the car, waved at him before pressing the bell by the gate and eventually pushed it open when no one answered. He was unfortunately going through the same situation at the main door to the house when Daddy Kahf turned up.

'Hello welcome.' He stepped back to let him in with an impassive expression.

'Can I have a word with you in private first sir?'

'Okay,' Daddy Kahf led him to the room beside Lola's where he could hear her being consoled by Mama and resisted every urge to go straight to her room. He concentrated fully on Adam as he presented his case to him as the head of the family.

With all his questions on Magun answered, he'd been given some mixtures to drink and bath with. Daddy Kahf had not only reverted him but reminded him all the vital things about Islam. First of the five pillars was Shahadah, his testimony that there is no other Deity worthy of worship but God, The Almighty, The Creator of the Universe and that the Prophet Muhammad, Peace and blessing upon Him was his last Messenger. Then his ritual bathe and the ablution to cleanse himself of his major and minor impurities. He progressed onto his duties and responsibilities as a believing Muslim to himself, his family and his community at large. The second pillar of five daily prayers, which was as usual and ever his biggest challenge, was once again reinforced in him. He today confirmed his dad's simple explanation that it was easy if his mind was set to it and that each prayer at their designated times took only a couple of minutes by finishing Maghrib- the sunset and the fourth daily prayer under five minutes with Daddy Kahf. His biggest challenge right now was his insistence on him memorizing the Opening Chapter of the Quran: Surah Fatihah and his refusal to let him leave unless he memorized it.

'Why?' He'd angrily challenged the Scholar after thirty minutes of unsuccessful attempt. Adam was surprised at how indifferent he was to Lola's bawling noise from next room.

His poker faced look of; you *are the one who wants our daughter not me!* said it all. He then relaxed his face and smiled before he answered. 'Trust me; you'll thank me for it. Moreover, it is sufficient to say your five daily prayers with it.'

He instantly regretted asking to speak with him first, but he knew that was inevitable if he was serious about Lola. Despite Adam's intention of just pleasing the man to get what he wanted he was amazed at how quickly he learnt it afterwards.

An hour later, fulfilled, proud and confident Adam smiled with an eagerness to face his responsibility as he was escorted to the door. He knocked on the adjoining door thrice, waited for reply until he was advised to gently push the door open to surprisingly meet Mama's angry look combined with Lola's red and puffy eyes. Even in adversity, the look on her face made his heart tumble slightly and confirmed that she was worthy of it all! He only stepped inside when advised, followed by the relief across Mama's face unlike Lola's impassive and frosty look. Without a word, she pulled the pillow to her stomach and lied back down facing the wall.

Mama quickly leaned over to wipe her tears and acknowledged his polite bow before getting on her feet. 'I think I should leave you two alone.' She whispered smiling, pulled some of the side curtains around the four bed poster and left the room.

Adam in the end climbed into bed after spending minutes watching her and equally giving up hope that she would turn around or even speak to him. Lying on his back suddenly reminded him of the endless days and nights he'd spent nursing her both at the hospital in Birmingham and her house. He rubbed his forehead for calm when he remembered his efforts to counter Mr James's exploitation and how he almost punched the policeman for being boorish. He had never in his life had such an intense relationship with any woman but he honestly enjoyed it all. Some hours ago, *Magun* scared him to death but Daddy Kahf had not only reassured him but kitted him up as well. There was no going back because he would never forgive himself if he didn't try. Imagine Sinmi's situation, God knows what baggage the next woman might bring with her. He rolled over to face her back before closing the gap between them and pecking her neck.

'Daddy Kahf was telling me an interesting story about Prophet Musa being sent to gain more knowledge but was warned by his learned teacher that he'd only learn if he was patient. The prophet constantly judged and criticised his teacher's actions and decisions so much that the teacher sent him off prematurely ...' He deliberately uncompleted his sentence to get her attention. 'In a nutshell, patience, my dear, is virtue.'

'I'm surprised you came back.'

'I'm surprised too, but I had to leave or let you all see me having a row with my dad.'

'Why would he make a scene in someone else's house?'

'He would if I disobeyed him flagrantly; moreover, his effort to make up for the lost years motivated me to comply.'

'So he took you to a fragrance shop to make up for the lost years or what?'

'Far from it, I just didn't want to upset him.'

'Sorry, I still smell conflicting fragrances.'

'Face me.' He requested instead.

She turned around and faced him. He was about to kiss her beautiful lashes that were still tightly shut when he noticed the tears. 'Please stop crying.' He pulled her closer and continued patting her back whilst pecking her face. After calming her, he guarded her face with his hands and looked straight into it before confessing. 'I'm truthfully scared of this *Magoon*.'

She opened her eyes and looked straight into his but couldn't analyse his expression. 'Me too, but it is my cross.' Her voice began shaking.

'No our cross.'

His encouraging response not only dilated her eyes but made her lock his gaze and see the flood of passion and hope she took for granted in Birmingham.

'Lola I love you so much that I can't imagine living without you, even though I'm scared of *Magoon* but I'm scared of loosing you more.'

She only realised how quickly his confession melted her anger and fear away. 'I'm scared of dying but more frightened of living without you.' She admitted shamefully and amidst tear.

Looking straight into her puffy eyes he stroked her lashes.

She wriggled and he wondered why. 'It tickles.'

He smiled. 'Another sensitive button,' he kissed her tears away before pecking her forehead and finally her lips. The kiss was long, passionate and titillating for both.

He moved his hand to another angle and she vividly remembered that same hand rescuing her in her dream when her stomach caught fire. 'Do you have a ring on?'

'Yes, why?'

She was initially stunned. Then she realised he was not only her eternal love but her saviour. She tried to speak but became enthralled with emotions and pleaded with her hands to hear her out. 'Adam I love you with all my heart and soul.' She placed his hand on her chest right between her breasts as she gasped for breath. 'I swear with my heart and on my mother's grave that there is no other man for me except you.'

He knew she'd said it all and was scared of letting her down. 'What if I let you all down?'

She shrugged her shoulders. 'We can only try our best.'

'Even if I die?'

'You will not die, but God forbid it happening I will be right behind you because my life will be nothing without you.'

He'd been waiting for such a sincere admission about her feelings for a long time and now he wondered whether she was just desperate or truly in love.

'I promise you, we will survive it.' She complained of cold and slightly juddered from the relief of the burden she'd hoarded for too long.

He remained perplexed and continued watching her with his head resting on his palm, he frowned at her suddenly and wanted to ask if she loved him as much as Yusuf but rephrased it. 'Why didn't you tell me about Yusuf?'

'You never asked?'

'I did.'

'When?'

'After your first nightmare in my car on our way home from the hospital.'

'I didn't think we would have any future together and if I could remember correctly you weren't in the best of moods either.'

He raised his brows surprisingly. 'Do you honestly think I'd invest my time, money and cancel many dates for just friendship?'

She stared back at him and shrugged her shoulders. 'I honestly don't know and didn't think of it that way.'

Adam had never experienced such intense feeling nor had anyone evoked it from him and this new discovery scared him. He continued watching her as one particular question needled him and he knew he wouldn't rest until he did even if it caused him greater sadness. 'Have you ever been in love?'

'I thought I was.'

'Who with?'

'Yusuf of course.'

'And now?' He held his breath for her answer.

She looked straight into his eyes. 'You are my knight and shining armour, my heart, my soul and my everything.'

'And you promise to forsake all other men?'

She nodded.

'Even Yusuf and Akin?'

'Sure and without any contest.'

'Promise me.'

'*Wallahi* I swear to the Almighty Lord of all lords.'

He finally expelled a long and windy breath of air before shifting his attention away from her face to her top and noticed she'd changed into a button through pyjamas. He undid the four buttons, and suddenly stopped with a frown.

'What's wrong?' Embarrassed, she quickly covered herself up.

He gently pushed her hand away. 'They are beautiful.' He gently led one of her breast into his mouth and sucked it. 'I've wanted to do this since the day I set my eyes on you.'

'On these?' She indicated her breasts. 'Or on me?'

'Both especially after I bought you those bras.'

'You bought what?' She asked surprisingly.

'The bra you are wearing.'

'I thought Roxanne bought this for me.'

'Well you thought wrong.' He deliberately paused.

'Can I honestly say you've been stalking on me for a while then?'

He nodded impishly before clambering over to unhook her bra and was about to complain when he kissed to shut her up.

With the bra finally loose, his glance fully focused on her two erect breasts but resisted the urge to touch them. 'Just the perfect size for my hands.'

Her shy reaction not only confirmed his doubts about her but he immediately understood her angry reaction the first time he intimately kissed and snuggled her. 'No, don't do that.' He removed her hands from the fabric. 'They are gorgeous.' He moulded one of her breasts in his hand before kissing the other one passionately and only stopped when she shuddered. He impulsively jumped up to close the curtains of the bed. 'We are going to make love like the first and the last time.' He lifted her up to kneel on the bed with him before looking at her confused face. 'Are you ready? We'll get married after this ordeal, right?' Without waiting for her reply he began kneading one nipple and nibbling the other.

She nodded and moaned with pleasure.

After a while he placed her hand on his erect manhood 'Undress me,' he spread eagle. 'Please!' He insisted when she hesitated.

She continued watching his chest fall and rise before concentrating at his bulge that seemed about to rip his trouser any moment. 'Please be gentle.' She pleaded as she nervously undid the two buttons of his top and slowly removed it. She shut her eyes as her previous sexual attempts suddenly flashed before her eyes. 'Adam I can't do it,' she sobbed.

They sought each other's gaze and held it. 'Are you still a virgin?'

She didn't respond but hugged him closer and welcomed him as their heartbeats rhymed into one.

As he assured her with his warm smile, something clicked deep inside him, fulfillment, hope, desire or just dream but whatever it was felt powerful and overbearing but it's goodness made him realise she was a one in a million woman. Despite her epitomising everything he reviled and abhorred she'd circuitously forced him to embrace and face his darkest shadows culturally and religiously but he couldn't accept ignoring one for the other. 'I should tantalise you more.' He removed the top before undoing the only button on her pyjamas bottom and let it drop before moving his head backward to admire the mat of dark hair in her private area.

Lola looked into his eyes and saw the strength of character, body, mind and soul that warned her never to mess with him because he would not tolerate it. So she knew he would either want her to love him fully or not bother at all. As his eyes danced mischievously, he emitted the air of strength, determination and power, but above all the unsurpassed love.

He kissed her dimples before passionately progressing to her lips, then her neck and finally her already erect nipple. She moaned softly and pleaded for more as he progressed to kissing her all over. His hands travelling to her down below coincided with when he felt her body melting under his touch, he lifted his head for her approval and wasn't surprised to see her gasp with pleasure for more.

Still reeling in the newly discovered pleasure zone, she stopped to gaze into his erotically charged eyes and tried to pull his trouser down when she felt a renewed intruding excitement all over her body. She undid the zip and immediately pulled his white boxer down when her body responded to his demanding call with shudders of pleasure. Gripped by the newly discovered sensation she nibbled his shoulder to restraint herself from screaming and was glad he responded positively. This sheer pleasure was beyond what Mama or anyone had described! She'd always known him to be of a peculiar personality; sometimes domineering or patient, thoughtful or kind, loving or withdrawn, there were times he would only tease and talk but she was just discovering another side of him that could not be expressed with words but with feelings that surpassed description because she just couldn't control it!

Adam withdrew his hand to watch the satisfaction on her face and prepare her for the big adventure but had his head and all other areas of his body filled with the effect of her sensuous body rubbing on him. Silenced by the speed of passion rushing through his loin like a gush of reckless wind he gently pushed her back onto bed and slowly eased himself into her soft, inviting area without warning. He initially struggled with the pressure of penetrating just as she cried immediately he thrust into her. He quickly kissed her tears before arresting all other pains about to emerge.

His mouth moved from one nipple to the other whilst he thrust freer and deeper into her as she increased the flame of passion burning in him by continuously stroking his nape. The next thirty minutes spiralled from rising and falling within her into mutual exchange of pleasure, moans, promises and pleas until the soaring effect of his loin not only fulfilled their ultimate desire beyond their imagination, but landed them to simultaneously explode with pleasure they never knew existed …

CHAPTER 25

For over forty minutes Mama remained unnoticed in the next room listening to her granddaughter and Adam's passionate lovemaking and waiting for any mishap whilst actually hoping it didn't. She thanked God for the light wall between the rooms originally for her protection and was glad she stood her ground in insisting Lola stayed in one of her two en suite bedrooms, her argument was its easy accessibility and convenience for all. She heard another moan of pleasure and remembered her youthful days where a vanguard of parent's honour was the celebration of their daughter loosing her virginity on her wedding night.

Now in her late seventies, she recollected her nervousness on her wedding night with Bayo's dad coupled with the pressure that her mother and mother-in-law were waiting outside to spread the news to the members of both families. Her mother later told her of her anxiety and panic over whether the outcome would be positive or negative and her eventual relief that she was not "damaged goods" as it was normally described then. She smiled briefly as she remembered the countless, expensive presents and harvests her parents received and the disgrace to her best friend's parents when her husband discovered she wasn't a virgin, despite her claim that he was her first love. It was a culture that was already dying in her days mainly because of the disgrace and humiliation suffered by many parents and families especially the least unexpected ones. She was certain the culture would have been extinct long before then if many people were like her son, Bayo, who vehemently opposed her actions.

Daddy Kahf sneaked in and whispered if everything was okay. She responded with a nod and thanked God before she continued with the supplication her brother prescribed. 'Find a good time to give this to them.' He left another potion beside her and was gone within seconds.

Judging from their sensuous whispers and tone, Mama literarily crossed her fingers when she realised they were about to peak from their passionate liaison again. She breathed a sigh of relief when she heard giggles and kisses afterwards. Pleased with nothing else to worry about, she took the content to the room some minutes after hearing Adam get up to go to the toilet and asking her to come with him. She smiled when she heard Lola complain of hunger and he added he wanted another round before any meal. As their voices faded away with laughter, she sneaked in and left the medication on the dressing table before checking for the bloody spot on the white bed sheet. Apart from the relief of satisfying her curiosity, it was comforting to know that it might be used as a gift if need be. And most of all, she didn't deserve the affliction after all! She immediately left her flat for the family living room to call her mobile and inform her of their new medication.

'We'd just come back from having a shower.' She replied her grandma's question of why it took her so long to answer the phone.

Mama suspected something was wrong and quickly terminated their conversation before immediately alerting her brother.

Adam had finished drying himself and was doing the same to her.

'Who brought the concoction?' Lola suspected her grandmother knew something from her tone but couldn't see any sign of interference in the room.

'Possibly one of your uncle's assistant.'

Her attempt to probe further was sabotaged by Adam showering her with kisses and fondling.

'What would you two like to eat?' She continued with a shaky voice when his mouth nibbled her right breast and his tongue probed her already tender nipple. 'Adam!' She moaned softly as she sat on his lap as he wanted.

I'm so grateful you stood by me but I most importantly thank God that we are alive and we've survived the *Magun*. Those were the words she'd meant to utter but somehow couldn't.

'When do we get married?' He asked unexpectedly but continued with his performance and only stopped when he felt her stiffness. He tried reaching into his pocket for the engagement ring but felt restrained. 'Say something, the suspense is killing me.' He panicked but couldn't move.

She wanted to shout okay, no problems, but was overwhelmed with her senses shutting down except to have physical contact, so she hugged him instead and began to sob.

He felt her tears on his shoulder and tried to pull her off but unsuccessful. 'Help!' He struggled to shout from the top of his voice.

She also tried to break off and kiss him but felt glued to him and tried to wriggle herself out but simultaneously felt paralysed and choked. Utterly static, attached, dumb but not deaf and could smell nothing but death hovering and draining her!

She was eventually snatched out of her sticky situation by a crashing noise and Mama screaming for her brother before they were finally split up with a cold liquid over them. They both hit the bed coughing and equally gasping for breath whilst Daddy Kahf quickly rushed in between them to lie Adam on his side before rubbing a burning ointment on his face, chest and finally another one to inhale. 'When did you two drink the last mixture?' He wiped the blood gushing out of Adam's nose.

'They didn't, I had to pour it over them even though I asked her to take it immediately they came out of the bathroom.'

'Bathroom? Hope they didn't shower?'

'I'm sure they did.'

'What?' He eyed the pair as he wiped Adam's bloody nose and the blood dripping from his mouth before watching them regain their breath slowly.

Just then Bayo Anifolase walked in and stood beside his mother. 'I thought you said everything was alright?' He whispered.

'So did I.' She eyed her son for his deliberate lateness. 'They've missed out on some of the instructions,' and was prevented from further complaint by knocks from both entrances of the flat. Mama and her son left Daddy Kahf with the young couple whilst they attended to the doors.

On Mama's side was the panicky gateman. 'An angry man was banging on the gate asking for Adam Bamidele Salvador and I told him there was nobody as such here ma.'

'Don't worry, you go back and man the gate, I shall send someone down in a while.' She stepped to let one of her brother's assistant in.

'Ma'mi!'

She responded to Bayo's call to find more people in the room and was still wondering who they were when he continued. 'They are Adam's family.'

All heads turned and moved towards Adam who'd begun to convulse violently.

'What's wrong with him?' Tunji Salvador's concerned voice reverberated through the room but was more worried when Lola fainted.

'We don't know.' Mama replied and was caught winking at others.

'Mama, why did you wink if you knew nothing?' He pushed his way through to get to his son. 'Bamidele what happened?' He removed his outer garment and handed it over to his driver.

'It's important their treatment is not delayed or interfered with.' Daddy Kahf gestured his nephew to help suppress Adam from any movement. 'Repress

him in every possible way, Sister pour this over her.'
He watched them for a while before speaking again.
'They must for now remain separated and repressed.'

'Adam!' Lola shouted immediately she regained
consciousness and sat up to watch him.

'Why did you have a shower?'

'We forgot.' She cried and sobbed.

Daddy Kahf's eyes widened with disbelief before
looking back at Adam flying his limbs violently to
fight the repression and get closer to her. He
instructed one of his assistant who walked in to bring
his fragrance collection. He took the smallest bottle
and pushed it close to his nose before pouring some
over his head.

'What the hell is wrong with my son?' Sherry
asked tearfully.

'Help us repress him, I shall explain later.'

He watched Daddy Kahf mischievously before
joining in. 'Sherry is he epileptic?' He moved his
face to avoid his son's right arm hitting him.

'No. Haven't we been through this before?'

He ignored her comment and rephrased his
question. 'Any history of epilepsy or similar illnesses
in your family?'

'No what about you?'

'None whatsoever!' He surveyed everyone's
mood but only saw panic and regret. He finally
rested his gaze on Lola's tearful face and saw guilt.
He quickly got up and nodded as if he remembered
something vital. 'Is this the lady you said Adam told
you had *Magun?*' He winked at his befuddled driver.

'Yes sir,' he replied nervously with his face down and tightly gripping Adam's legs down.

'What's *Mag-oon*?' She looked poignantly around for anyone to answer but eventually moved close to Daddy Kahf who was engrossed with his prayer over her son. He distracted her by stretching his back and telling the three men to let go of Adam.

'Baba are you sure?' Tunji asked repugnantly as he eyed everyone repulsively.

'Yes, the urge to somersault or move had totally disappeared.' Relief crossed his face as Adam slightly twitched but the new development offered no respite to Lola who was still bawling terribly. He then asked his parents to lay him face up him on top of the stained bed and move back.

Having done what Daddy Kahf said, Tunji Salvador rolled his eyes at everyone except Lola and his wife before catching up with Bayo in one giant stride. For over five minutes, the men chatted and argued silently until Bayo was punched in the face. This led to the two men scuffling. 'I'm going to kill you before this prostitute kills mine.' With the two men already fighting it out, Mama and Sherry rushed to intercept and prevent further escalation.

'Let me be.' Tunji Salvador insisted with his hands up in the air. 'That whore passed *Magun* onto my son, look at the state he is in.'

Sherry looked in Lola's direction and wanted to repeat her question of what Magun was but was yet again prevented by the circumstances.

'I'm sure she was a prostitute taking advantage of my son's innocence.'

Bayo's anger kept rising but was restrained by his mother and Isa. 'Just tell him not to use those filthy words and gutter language in my house.'

'She is a whore, a prostitute, a harlot! How else would she have got *Magun?*' He winked at his upset wife to support him. 'There is no way you are walking scot-free with my son in such a vegetable state and if he survives you two are still history.' He pointed his index finger at her in an undignified manner. 'I'd die first if I have to choose this slapper over Sinmidele!' He spat on the floor.

Bayo clenched his fist to knock him out but had his mum clinging onto him and too close.

Lola's heart sank deeper into the abyss as she was abused, accused but was more importantly regretful that she was the cause and yet a victim herself. How could she forget a simple instruction of not to shower! All her life, she put other people's needs before hers, for once, someone else sacrificed his life for her and this is it! She looked at Adam's vegetative state and wondered if she should fulfil her promise now or give him more time. And even if he did pull through his dad had made it perfectly clear that his son would have absolutely nothing to do with her, which defeated her whole object of her not giving her virtue to just anyone. It definitely would be the end of their relationship if any of the parents kicked against it. With this level of noise, how would she dispel the news from the neighbours? Who would believe her innocence this time? She claimed to be a victim with Yusuf, then Akin, finally loosing her honour with Adam ended all regrets and innocence! What's going to be her next excuse?

Still crying, she took one final look at two grown men that should have been in-laws scuffling and three other adult trying to calm the situation and wondered if anyone would really miss her. She watched Daddy Kahf and wanted to ask what his chances were but he was busy with his assistant over Adam. She knew she would miss Adam's presence, voice, smell and his smile that always sent numerous shockwaves all over her body. It's definitely him who could do this to her! His thick fully curved lips now look more attractive than ever. Could she forget his slightly sharp pointed ears that complement his rectangular shaped face and the height that always made him stand out of the crowd? How could he have so much effect on her? His vegetative state made him look dangerously attractive and peaceful with his square jaw, wide forehead, quirky nose, proper bridge and the deep intense hazel eyes she remembered vividly but now tightly shut. Adam with his dangerous attraction screamed of nothing but a boyish charm that was God sent to her! Now she messed it up!

Suddenly, the sixteen feet by sixteen feet room seemed cramped with the scuffle noise, suffocated, she gave up and wanted out again. How could she miss the simple instructions and implicate an innocent man? How would she be able to live with herself afterwards? Palpitating tearfully, she edged over and kissed his face before stabbing herself in the chest with the knife she'd secretly stuffed in her pillow and away from her family.

'Sister!' Daddy Kahf's desperate call temporarily silenced the mêlée and diverted everyone's attention to him whilst he remained stretched and clambered over Adam with the booklet in his breast pocket to prevent Lola from stabbing herself deeper.

Adam's parents quickly rushed to prevent him from dropping off the four poster bed whilst Mama fainted when she saw blood dripping from the knife stuck on Lola's chest.

Bayo was torn between the two women but eventually chose his mother over daughter whilst Isa was forced to help him. The assistant guarding Lola was on standby and watching everyone's move, especially his mentor's.

Whilst holding the bloodied knife to prevent further damage, praying over Adam and watching his sister's progress, some blood accidentally dropped onto him. As he was wiping it off he felt a shock from him and knew he would regain consciousness but was also glad he prevented the knife from penetrating into Lola's internal organs. He was immediately relieved by a loud thump from Adam hitting the floor and didn't complain because he realised what had just happened.

'My arm gave way!' Sherry panicked tearfully.

'Mine too, it felt like electric shock.' Echoed her husband.

Daddy Kahf acknowledged their comment with a nod of his head and a renewed certainty that their son was not only alive but would soon regain full consciousness.

Sherry was already in tears with worry over further damage they inflicted on their helpless son whilst her husband tried to hide his worry but became more concern when he misinterpreted the look on Daddy Kahf's face.

Adam suddenly opened his eyes to meet his parents worrying eyes and quickly sat up. 'Mum, dad what are you doing here? Why are you crying?' He was interrupted by intense hugs and wet kisses from his mother.

'*Alhamdulillah!*'

'Thank God indeed.' Tunji Salvador agreed and hugged the physician for his outstanding effort.

With a respectable bow and smile Adam accordingly thanked him for his efforts and would have prostrated if he was stronger. 'Where is Lola?' He asked weakly with his unwavering gaze still at Daddy Kahf.

Lola almost crushed him when she jumped off the assistant and onto him from the other end of the bed.

'Don't crush him! He'd just cheated death and still very weak!' Tunji Salvador snapped angrily.

'No dad, we both cheated death and we are both weak.' He pulled her closer and wiped her tears away before noticing the blood on her. 'She crashed before me.'

'Which means she nearly got you killed with *Magun.*'

'I know, but she wouldn't have had Magoon if I wasn't in the picture in the first place.' Still hugging her he wanted to ask about the blood but was yet interrupted by his dad's comments.

'You mean she was cheating on her partner?'

'No dad,' he dragged the reply to express his frustration.

'You are a fool for believing anything she says.' He hissed vehemently.

'Dad give her a chance, you've only just met her.' He pleaded.

'I think I've known enough already. You'd rather spend the rest of your life with *Magun and death* looming over your head than with a healthier, prettier woman with better potentials?'

'Yes dad.' He suspected what was coming next.

'What about Sinmidele?'

'What about her?' He looked at Lola and pecked the tip of her nose.

'You'd rather turn me into a laughing stock because of her?' He waved his hand at her rudely again.

'No Sinmi already did that successfully.'

'I'd already said whilst you were unconscious that I'd be damned if I let you choose this walking dead woman over Sinmidele.'

'Right, would you have bastard grandchildren from a dog, slut, a whore and a hooker?'

'No, but I'd trust any offspring from her than this empty shell whose days are already numbered.'

'Dad I wouldn't touch that dog called Sinmi with a barge-pole. I caught her having sex with Deji underneath the staircase on the floor. I would only do that if I was really desperate or deeply in love. And if I choose the former she is a dog- a bitch and if it's the latter I understand how it feels to love so deeply.' He looked into Lola's eyes before pecking her forehead.

'Who the hell is Deji?'

'The dog should tell you.' He turned to Isa. 'He knows who he is too.'

Everyone turned towards Isa. 'Who is Deji?'

'Sir?'

'Tell dad who Deji is?'

'He is a D.J. and Sinmi's lover.' Isa replied. 'Chief Orija's second driver told me.' He added when his boss frown turned murderous.

'Haven't we met before?' Sherry surveyed Lola critically with a frown. 'You had a hat on in a post office near Merry Hill. You were asking about posting a parcel to Nigeria ...'

'Must be the day we went for your hospital appointment after the bomb blast.'

'Bomb blast?' Sherry asked surprisingly.

'Yes and could have died.'

'You see, I was right about death hovering around her and you are wrong if you think my son is coming with you. Walking corpse!'

Sherry noticed Lola was getting lethargic and decided to act swiftly. 'Let's get your wound treated and prevent further loss of blood my love.' She reached to guide her up.

'What are you calling her *love* for? ' He deliberately tried to provoke Bayo who was coming their way having successfully resuscitated his mother.

'Dad, I disvirgined her tonight on this bed.'

'If you truly did, show me the proof.' His voice was crisp with authority.

Adam was assisted up to pull the bedcover aside for him to see the red spot on the white bed sheet and waited for his response but was surprised at his silence. He moved closer to him and whispered to him. 'Sinmi assured me she was single and had no one in her life hours before I caught her in the act.'

'Did she see you?'

'Yes, they both did.'

'Are you really sure of what you are saying?'

'Yes and why?'

'Because it might lead to the two families falling out, especially if she denies it.'

Adam shrugged his shoulders, 'My hands are clean and I'm glad it turned out this way.'

His dad grumbled and swore silently.

'I need to go and check Lola out.' He was stopped by his dad.

'Are you not bothered about her *Magun* at all?'

Adam gazed at the ceiling for a while, 'Of course I was, but I'm sure we are out of the woods.' He noted his dad's concern and wondered how he would handle the news. 'This wouldn't have happened if we'd remembered not to shower. I'm going to ask her to marry me.'

His dad was immediately gobsmacked and lowered his head with disappointment. 'Are you sure you're not doing this out of guilt?'

'No, we are going to be married because I love her beyond words; she's my lifeline, my soul mate. Believe me dad I tried to love someone with less complicating background but I'm now glad that no one came close.' He clasped his palm over his wrist and smiled. 'You should be pleased for me.' He looked towards the bathroom door and tried to get on his feet. One of the assistants was quickly by his side to support him. 'I've got to check her out. You should start making plans for a quiet traditional wedding. She's a whole package.' He shouted halfway across the room before he finally disappeared.

Daddy Kahf was trying to catch up with him and take advantage of the opportunity when Lola and Sherry suddenly appeared.

'You two need to bath with the last mixture,' he glanced from one face to the other. 'Please leave it to dry out.'

'You mean we shouldn't use the towel to dry ourselves?' They asked together.

'Exactly and please don't make love until I say so.' He watched their embarrassing reaction. 'That's if you two are pro living.'

Embarrassed Adam bowed his head for getting caught. 'How many days are we talking about sir?'

'Maximum of one hour I'd say.' He saw the relief on his face and smiled weakly. 'One of my boys will bring it to the bathroom for you now.' He faced Sherry and smiled. 'Madam we need you here.'

'Why?'

'We need to resolve the stalemate between the two families especially now that your son had asked for our daughter's hands in marriage.'

'Has he now? It's his dad you need to talk to. Those two men are just too stubborn.' She spread out her hands helplessly. 'Are all Yoruba men so stubborn, even my Adam is not different?' She followed him to a seat beside her husband just as Bayo returned from getting his mother a cold drink.

'No, all men are stubborn and egoist.' Daddy Kahf interjected.

'Where is the young lady's mother?' Tunji asked to melt the tension.

'She died when she was a toddler.' Bayo replied frostily, obviously still upset that he had an upper hand over him in his own territory.

'So you remarried?'

'Of course I remarried, or you expect someone of my age not to have a wife?'

Tunji noted the anger in his voice and decided not to pry anymore.

Daddy Kahf found the mediating role daunting as the silence stretched. He finally cleared his throat. 'Before we go any further, I would like to apologise

on behalf of my family for all that happened today.'
He surveyed everyone's mood before he continued.
'It was due to misunderstood instructions from our
kids.'

Tunji quickly raised his hands up to speak and got
up. 'I should be the one to apologise and I'm sure
you'll not only understand why but also forgive me.'

Daddy Kahf bowed his head in appreciation. 'I
would not recommend us beating about the bush
over this matter but I also want the couple concerned
to be present, so we should meanwhile entertain you
as our guests the appropriate way.' He prompted his
nephew to take over whilst he excused himself with
Isa, the driver.

'I object to my daughter marrying into this
family.'

'Why?' Mama challenged authoritatively.

He rubbed his eyebrow for a while. 'He's not my
ideal son-in-law.' He stated hesitantly.

Sherry wanted to speak but was restrained by her
husband.

'He is Lola's choice and she'll be the one to live
with him.' She eyed him. 'Stop throwing pebbles in
cooked rice.' She scolded with her eyes rolling up
and down.

'I can honestly say they are truly in love and are
most importantly very compatible.' Daddy Kahf
supported his sister and measured everyone's
reaction. 'They will both prosper.' He took a little
Quran from his side pocket and raised it to the

ceiling. 'I swear by this.' He was gone by the time they finished examining his words.

'We need your attention here,' Bayo shouted after him.

'I just need to check that our young couples are fine.' He jogged towards the other room.

'Shall I come with you?' Sherry shouted after him.

'No madam,' he gestured at her to remain seated.

'Whilst waiting for our children to join us, we'd like to know what we can offer you.' Mama guessing her son's obstinacy immediately took over from where her brother stopped. 'We have rice, eba, or you want snack?' she directed her statement to Sherry but had her eyes on Tunji.

'We were just coming from a party ma ...'

'... but would like any soft drink please.' Sherry interrupted her husband.

'Can you send for someone to get us some drinks?' She asked her son.

Bayo nodded at his mum but didn't want to leave her alone with the guest for fear of saying the wrong thing to them. He continued looking around for someone until he saw one of his uncle's assistants approaching.

Two hours later, Daddy Kahf returned with Adam and Lola into the living room to find their families watching television and laughing whilst their dads played Ayo game together. 'Mums and Dads, your children would like to have your attention please.'

They all stopped their games to focus on the speaker.

Adam cleared his throat before speaking in a sitting position as advised by Daddy Kahf. 'Meeting Lola some months ago had completely changed my outlook on life and given me a newly found pride as a Yoruba man but has above all taught me the importance of parents in one's life. So we want to thank you all for your love and support over the years and especially these past hours. Please continue to pray for us as we embark on this journey of life and love. But I would most importantly like to seize this opportunity to ask for Lola's hand in marriage even though we'd placed the cart before the horse, which we want you our parents to interpret as the depth of our love.' He thanked them once again before asking if she had any addition, but she shook her head.

'You must speak,' her dad insisted.

'Even if it's just a word,' her grandma added.

Lola went on her knees to thank her relatives that stood by her in the most trying periods of her life and Adam for giving her the benefit of doubt. She started crying when she remembered the turbulent period that Adam stood by her, believed in her, guided and guarded her and above all loved her. She concluded by accepting his marriage proposal and pleaded with his parents to take her as one of their children since she was sure hers had already accepted him.

'Do any of the parents have any objection?' Daddy Kahf waited as he glanced from one face to another. 'I'm proud to say we've survived the first and the most important hurdle. In the absence of any objection from either parents or witnesses the husband must now present his wife a Dowry.' He waited for the eight people facing him to quieten down before he continued. 'Our daughter's dowry is one of the Chapters of the Quran.'

They all watched Adam hold Lola's hand as he perfectly recited Suratul Fatihah completely before sliding a big sky blue diamond ring on her finger. She was moved to tears as it's glitter reflect all over.

Daddy Kahf now implored the newly weds to kneel whilst he prayed for them. He then rounded the gathering up with another prayer for everyone present.

Lola was mostly surprised to see her step mother join Mama, Adam's mum shed tears of joy.

Tunji stepped in between the couple to hold their hands before speaking. 'Since you two have recently joined us, I'd like to apologise for my earlier outburst and action. Even though it was excessive, many loving parents would do same. My in-laws, my son and daughter, please forgive me. I'm proud of the effort and courage you've shown. According to our Prophet Muhammad, may the peace and blessing of the Almighty God be upon him, I can proudly say said say that the main requirements in a valid marriage have all been fulfilled here today. So I would like to suggest that the traditional wedding ceremony be postponed to a more convenient date.'

'Agreed, but what date do you have in mind my son?'

'That will be decided by your family Ma.'

'In that case we would hold a family meeting and get back to you.'

'Okay ma.' He bowed respectfully before returning to sit beside Sherry.

'Anything else?' Mama asked her younger brother.

'Nothing except merriment.' He replied with glee. The housemaid knelt beside Lola's step mother to whisper into her ears which was ultimately passed to her husband.

'Ladies and gentlemen let's proceed to the dining area.' Bayo led the way with Tunji as the two men started talking about one of the Nigerian Ministers that happened to be one's in law and the other's cousin.

Lola and Adam waited for everyone to go. 'It's nearly four in the morning.' He whispered into Lola's ears. 'We should be in bed.'

'I know, it's nearly over. But I love the way it's all turned out.'

'Me too, can we sneak away first?' His eyes remained focused on the cleavage on her lilac blouse.

'Why?'

'I need some privacy with my wife,' he whispered into her ear and nibbled it afterwards. 'I can't believe we held six adults up for two hours whilst we made sweet love.'

'I know.'

'Your uncle said they needed it.'

'And he was right. Can you hear them talking about one of the Ministers and the politicians?' She yawned before looking at him and felt all the emotions she had successfully suppressed for so long suddenly surge.

Adam took her hand into his and stroked the engagement ring for a while before placing it on his lip. 'I didn't think it would fit.'

'I'm surprised you got my size right.'

'I'm just elated I did.' He whispered and remained pensive for a while.

She studied his wide forehead then only to notice that the hot fire burning in his eyes was dazzling her, after a while she interrupted his wandering mind. 'I love you so much Adam Salvador.'

When the heat from his eyes met her intense gaze a happy smile spread all over his face. 'You keep saying it whilst I keep proving it to you, Mrs Salvador!' He placed her hands on his shoulder and kissed her passionately. 'Can't we lie that you are weak and I'm taking care of you.'

'I hate to interrupt you, but I'd been asked to summon you two to the dining room.'

Adam raised his emotionally filled eyes to his mother standing a few feet away. 'Let's go whilst I can still control myself.' He said lazily as he dragged Lola onto her feet. 'Are you okay?' He asked and quickly supported her when she staggered

She exhaled deeply. 'I feel dizzy.' She shut her eyes and leaned on him solidly for a while 'I need eternal weeks to catch up on my sleep.'

'And I need you to catch up on mine.' Adam added softly and saw his mum smile at his comment. 'What's going on in there mum?' He received a cold, wet handkerchief she stretched towards him with thanks before gently placing it on her forehead.

'Nothing but merriment and the desire to get to know our daughter-in-law better.'

'There is nothing to know except we are both fugitives of love.'

Sherry wanted to reply but had already stepped into the crowded room.

'Let's have a toast for Mr and Mrs Salvador Junior!' Tunji prompted everyone to get up and raise their drinking glasses to the young couple walking in. 'We wish you a happy and prosperous married life with blessed children.'

'Amen!' echoed everyone.

'And we pray that this time next year, we would have had an additional member of family.' Mama added just before she sat down.

'Amen!' Everyone cheered again.

EPILOGUE

At exactly eight months and twenty-seven days after the toast between the two families, Lola gave birth to a baby boy weighing seven pounds seven ounces after nearly six hours of labour. Adam was overwhelmed with emotions as he looked at the newborn wriggling in his arms and desperate to be fed. He glanced from the new life form back to the love of his life that did all the hard work and almost called his dad a liar for saying men don't cry! Today, he realised men do cry but differently, especially towards the end of her labour when the doctor suggested caesarean delivery. She was fortunately able to deliver naturally shortly afterwards, but it was all worth it! They've grown in love as they fought the battles together but was more relieved she wouldn't return to A.B.C. & D. despite uncle Billy's attempt to convince him.

Daddy Kahf was right when he said life would be sweet, kind and prosperous to them as a couple. It's taken him this long to distinguish between an Islamic scholar and hocus-pocus. Agreed, things between him and Lola were going smoothly but thanks to their commitment, hard work, determination and honesty. He was just glad he listened to his inner gut back then. It was nothing but his uncle's and wife's determination combined with all the incriminating evidences that got Akin and Bob prosecuted.

He finally handed the baby to Lola when his shrilling voice pierced through his thoughts whilst phoning Lagos about the news. Lola's aunt would be arriving tomorrow to support her till his mum arrives after the naming ceremony in Lagos. Should he still be scared of the pokerfaced woman? He is still as determined to avenge and punish the transgressors. A lot of water had passed underneath the bridge, but above all, he's wiser, calmer but their love is most importantly stronger.

Eight days later in Lagos, the Salvador and the Anifolase households were having a low-profile naming ceremony of the newborn according to the Islamic rites. According to Yoruba tradition, Mr Salvador senior had to name his first grandchild and he called the baby *Abdallah Enitan* Salvador.

'Dad said *Enitan* means *someone of historical moment*.' He nodded with appreciation and agreed to the most memorable moments in his life, Lola's and both families. Who could have predicted this is where doing his aunty a favour by walking her dog would lead him to?

She considered it and couldn't explain it any better. 'Yes. And you still remember what Abdallah means?'

'Yes.'

'And we shall name him *Toluwalashe*' Lola added after receiving the name list whilst breastfeeding.

'How in God's name do you expect me to say that?'

'It means God's will shall prevail.'

'I like that but it's still a mouthful.'

'And could be shortened to Tolu.'

'Now she tells me,' he placed the pepper soup she'd prepared earlier on the table beside her.

'With practice you shall be perfect.'

He smiled and pecked her. 'I'll stick to Tolu whilst you call him the other one and start speaking Yoruba to him straight away so we can both learn it.' He stroked her hair for a while before he continued. 'Did your aunt enjoy her stay?'

'I'm sure she did. We should call to check if she got home safely. '

'Will you be okay till mum arrives?'

He answered his mobile phone before her reply. 'It's the office.' He listened for a while before speaking again. 'Bob and Akin have been found guilty of fraud but would be sentenced next month.' He replaced the phone and heard it bleep and decided to read his message. "I remember when your wife used to beg me to have sex with her, but then she wasn't good enough and she still isn't. Anyway I might just consider it if she is still as willing as before." Adam remained thoughtful for some minutes before looking at his wife. 'Who the hell is this?'

'Your guess is as good as mine.'

'It's Akin?' He half asked half stated. His phone bleeped of another message. "It's not over yet, if this *Magun* didn't work another one will." He slammed the phone on the table. 'I told you I should prosecute this bastard!'

'Adam why are you falling for his trap, remember Daddy Kahf said he would reverse it.'

'He wouldn't be bothering us if he did!'

'I believe he did and just wanted to bait you out of spite.'

'Okay we'll see.'

She swallowed a spoonful of hot, chilli, watery but tasty soup. 'Initially, you were against reversing it. You said it was wicked, did you not?'

He looked at her blankly and ignored her by picking the phone again to reread the text before gazing back at her. 'Do you think it has anything to do with Mr James's disappearance?'

She was about to reply when his phone rang again

…